WARRIOR

TAM DERUDDER JACKSON

Editor: Nikki Busch Editing
Copy Editor: Rhiannon Root
Cover Design: Steamy Designs
Formatting: Damonza

Books in the Talisman Series

Talisman
Warrior

For Grady
Always

and

For my sons, Austin and Trey
I love your more.

CHAPTER ONE

Summer Solstice

IO SHERIDAN TOOK a long pull from his beer and watched the party with thinly veiled disgust. *The woman is shameless.*

A single talisman in a party full of warriors, and she flirts outrageously. He shifted his gaze to his fellow warrior. *Seamus isn't any better. He must have tried his sign on her, which obviously didn't work, yet he acts like they have plans for later. Maybe they do. After all, his sister thought nothing of stealing another talisman's warrior.* He snorted. *Probably a family trait.*

"Hey little brother. No one needs to breach your shield to know what you're thinking," Rowan remarked as he joined Rio at the edge of the reception.

Sipping his beer, Rio didn't take his eyes off Seamus dancing with Ceri. "I think you should be careful around your new wife's best friend. She doesn't appear to have any scruples about horning in on warriors who aren't hers."

"Ceri? Without her, we wouldn't be enjoying my *very* happy wedding day," Rowan said, his tone warning Rio not spoil it. "She did all the work for this reception so Alyssa could finish her master's thesis, earn her degree, and still marry me on the day we wanted." Rowan stared him down. "I owe her a ton, and I won't have you attacking her based on some half-assed idea she's a flirt."

Rio shrugged.

Rowan cocked a brow at him and smirked. "Maybe instead of judging her, you should ask her to dance."

Rio ignored Rowan's suggestion. "Speaking of your new wife, Alyssa looks lovely today. You're a lucky man." He clinked his beer to his brother's. "You found your talisman in time, married her on your birthday no less, and thumbed your nose at the goddesses so determined to keep you apart." He sipped his beer. "I wouldn't be too cocky if I were you though. The day isn't over."

Rowan shot him a side-eye. "Between Alyssa's grandmother's protections over this house and Siobhan's reinforcements, I think we're safe for the day." He glanced up at the knotwork design on the outdoor canopy. "Morgan and Maeve are probably in Scotland or Ireland licking their wounds from the sweet little comedown we gave them in LA last winter. Still, I'd rather not upset the cosmos by discussing them on my wedding day." He clapped a hand on Rio's shoulder. "Lighten up and join the party. Today's a great day, and Alyssa and I want you to celebrate—please."

"I've been doing a number on the imported beer you're serving. I'm celebrating." He laughed hollowly and moved off to join his twin Riley and Riley's wife Lynnette.

Being the last unbonded and unmarried Sheridan compounded his sour mood. That and it didn't matter where he strolled among the wedding guests, he could still hear Ceri's tinkling laugh like happy chimes on the wind.

Standing beside his twin, his attention zeroed in on one stunning Ceri Ross.

She'd twisted her hip-length, honey blond hair into some

sort of braids and curls concoction that spilled gracefully from the side of her head down over her right breast. The light green satin sheath she wore deepened her sparkling green eyes. The dress hugged her long lithe body, outlining every luscious curve, and his hands itched to smooth over the fabric clinging to her exquisite figure.

In a moment he'd later regard as damn weakness, he downed the last of his beer and strolled over to where Ceri stood in animated conversation with Alyssa's old protector, Finn Daly.

"Afternoon, Finn. You clean up good for an old warrior," Rio said, unapologetically interrupting them.

"You do too. And who are you calling old?" Finn puffed himself up. "I think I had a few moves you didn't know at Scathach's last training session." His lively gray eyes twinkled.

"Thanks for going easy on me. I'd already had quite a day before you showed up," he said with a smile.

"It's your story. Tell it any way you want, Rio." Finn winked.

"Will I put you out too much if I steal your companion for a dance?"

"Not at all. I'd much rather see you dancing than scowling by yourself over your beer."

Rio ignored the old man's barb and turned his attention to Ceri. "Shall we?"

He placed his hand on the small of her back, propelled her toward the dance floor, and took her into his arms. His hand engulfed her slender one as he held it loosely. Resting his other hand on the small of her back, he guided her around the dance floor. Though he kept his touch light, she remained tense in his arms.

Leaning in, he whispered in her ear, "Relax. It's only a dance. We're not making a commitment here."

His breath fanning her ear had the opposite effect, judging from the way she missed a step. Tightening his hold on her, he pulled her against his chest. She gasped. He willed himself to remain relaxed while every nerve ending came alive with her response and the touch of her lush curves against his body.

She felt even better than he imagined, all toned and sensuous. Like a siren, she called to him everywhere their bodies touched. Like a siren, she was dangerous, even deadly. But like the ancient mariners, he couldn't resist her. Instead of righting her when she'd stumbled, he'd pulled her closer, relishing her firm round breasts pressing against his chest, her soft hand resting easily in his palm, her lovely toned thighs occasionally brushing his.

"You did a nice job with the wedding. Rowan told me he owes you," he said blandly to break the stiff silence.

"Thank you. Alyssa and I have been best friends since we were six, and I knew she didn't have time to plan this. I wanted to keep her from eloping because I selfishly wanted to be part of her wedding day," Ceri blurted. Her face pinkened, and she looked away.

Rio tried to reconcile her gushy answer with the picture of sophistication and poise she radiated to the world. *Huh. I make her nervous.*

"Eloping doesn't sound like a half-bad idea, but I think my parents would never have let Rowan hear the end of it if he hadn't included everyone on his big day, especially with today being his birthday and all."

"Did you see I had the caterer include 'Happy Birthday Rowan' on the wedding cake?"

"No, I hadn't noticed. I just grabbed the biggest piece before Seamus could beat me to it."

"Oh." Ceri's face fell. "Well, Alyssa and Rowan seemed to like it."

The disappointment in her voice gave him heartburn. When the song ended, Ceri stepped away from him like he'd scalded her.

"Thanks for the dance. Hope you enjoy the rest of the party." She turned on her heel and headed straight for the back door of Alyssa's house.

That was smooth, dumbass. She ran away from you. He scrubbed a hand over his face. *Why do I feel so attracted to such an obvious flirt?* Glancing up, he caught Seamus's eye and scowled. *What does he have that's so appealing to the ladies while I make them nervous? 'Course, Ceri Ross probably should feel nervous considering what I've been thinking about her.*

❦

The wedding and reception were held in the former Alyssa Macaulay's backyard, complete with a temporary dance floor set under an awning elaborately painted with Celtic designs. Ceri hustled out of the reception and through the back door of the house. Making a beeline for the bathroom in the hall, she closed and locked the door and sat down hard on the edge of the tub, her emotions roiling.

All day she'd been enjoying compliments on her planning and hard work, but maybe she'd been too preoccupied with her part rather than the reason for the day in the first place. Did Rio think her full of herself? Her silly response to his blasé comment about the wedding certainly didn't improve his low opinion of her. *For someone who can usually carry a conversation, I was an idiot out there.*

Taking a deep breath, she tried to calm her swirling emotions. She checked her appearance in the mirror and thought of mundane items to disguise the distress in she saw her eyes. It was a trick Aunt Shanley made her practice repeatedly as part of her talisman training. "Never let the enemy guess what's going on inside your head," Shanley had admonished Ceri so often it had become her mantra.

When she was ready to face the party with at least the façade of her usual cheerful self, she exited the bathroom and returned to the reception. Promptly, she sought out Seamus's sister, Siobhan MacManus. During the rehearsal the evening before, she'd noticed

Rio pointedly avoided Siobhan and her husband Duncan. Perhaps if Ceri spent time talking to them, Rio wouldn't feel obligated to ask her to dance or even to speak with her again before the end of the afternoon.

As she made her way to where Siobhan and Duncan sat near the refreshment table, Seamus intercepted her.

"What happened between you and Rio that sent you into the house and him to the bar right after the two of you danced?" he asked as he twirled her over the dance floor.

Ceri glanced up at the burly blond giant, deliberately widened her eyes, and teased, "Do you need details about how I realized in the middle of that dance I needed to use the ladies room? I don't think I've taken a break from the party since I joined you to witness the wedding hours ago."

"So that was it." Seamus's speculative gaze made her uncomfortable. "Why do I have the distinct impression the two of you weren't getting along?"

Tilting her head, she asked, "Were you spying on us?"

"I noticed you from the edge of the dance floor, Ceri. I saw you blush and his face remain blank. I've known him long enough to know he's not happy about something when he looks like that."

He dipped her, and she gasped, but his ploy didn't work. "We were talking about the wedding. He isn't keen on the finer points of wedding planning and execution, and I may have let my feelings get hurt. Now I'm over it. Satisfied?"

"For the record, you're quite welcome to plan my wedding. I rather like what you did with this one. Maybe that can be your next business venture if you tire of selling real estate." His smile mollified her.

"You're a very nice man, Seamus Lochlann. Too bad I'm not your talisman. You at least appreciate my considerable party-planning skills." She batted her eyes at him.

The night they'd met, Seamus and Ceri had figured out they

weren't destined for each other after he tried his sign and discovered she wasn't his. However, she enjoyed his easy company. Unlike Rio Sheridan. Out of the corner of her eye, she caught him scowling at them from his place by the bar, and a shiver stole over her.

∽

"Alyssa, I hate to ask, but may I borrow your car? Shanley drove off without me, and I doubt you need a chaperone on your wedding night," Ceri said with a grin. The stragglers had left the reception, and the caterers had dismantled the tents, loaded up the tables and chairs into their vans, and driven away minutes earlier. Ceri assumed only she, Alyssa, and Rowan were left at the house.

Rio walked down the hall and entered the kitchen.

"Oh, hey, Rio. Could you give Ceri a ride back to town? It seems Shanley drove off without her," Alyssa said.

Ceri's heart dropped into her stomach.

"Your *aunt* left you? Don't you mean your date?" Rio frowned.

Ceri furrowed her brow. "I didn't have a date."

Wrapping his arm around Alyssa, Rowan interrupted. "Listen kids, no fighting on the way to town."

"Alys, about using your car—"

"That's silly, Ceri. Rio is headed to town too." Rowan stared down his brother. "He can be civil enough to give a pretty lady a lift, can't you little brother?"

"Come on, Ceri. I think the newlyweds want some privacy."

It wasn't the first time in the six years since Alyssa had bought her house that Ceri wished ten miles didn't separate it from town.

"Congratulations again you two. I'm so happy you found each other." First, she hugged Alyssa then Rowan.

She retrieved her ivory shawl from where she'd laid it over the back of the love seat in the great room and walked to the front door. Desperately, she filled her head with mundane items like trees, peanut butter sandwiches, and patio furniture to calm down and reveal none of her trepidation about the ride into town with a man to whom she was so attracted and who felt nothing except maybe loathing for her.

Once they were in Rio's big black pickup truck, she couldn't keep her mind on anything ordinary, which likely meant her shield wasn't strong. So she attempted distraction. "Do you work for your family's business too, like Rowan and Seamus?"

"Yeah."

"Oh." She watched the scenery on the mountain road and tried again. "Do you work out of the local office or one of the other branches?"

After several awkward moments when he didn't answer, she snapped. "I'm not planning to write an exposé. I was trying to make conversation. Usually, the polite thing to do is to ask about the other person who politely replies with *something*."

Rio slid her a side-eye before returning his attention to the twisty road. "I work with Riley in the western part of the state, but I'm filling in for Rowan while he takes Alyssa on their honeymoon. Polite enough for you?"

"Gosh, that was difficult—and enlightening." She crossed her arms and stared unseeingly out the passenger window.

"How long have you known you were a talisman?"

"That was random."

"The polite thing to do is to ask about the other person who *politely* replies with *something*."

She blinked and wondered about his hostility, but responded anyway. "Since I was tiny, since my parents died," she said quietly.

Seeming to ignore her answer, Rio asked, "How long have you known Alyssa was a talisman?"

"Almost from the moment we met when we were six."

"In nearly two decades, you didn't tell her? You didn't help her with her training?"

The accusation in his tone stunned her.

"Like your parents did, I imagine, my aunt warned me not to seek out other kids like me and not to give it away if I met or sensed other kids like me. Doing so would put us all in danger, which was enough when I was tiny." She tightened her wrap around herself. "As I grew older and more rebellious, I was determined to talk to Alyssa about it, but her grandmother forbade it, and I knew better than to cross a druid of Afton Sinclair's caliber."

"You're saying Alyssa's grandmother deliberately kept her ignorant? *Unbelievable.*"

"Ask Finn. They fought about it often, but Afton wouldn't budge. Having seen her whole family die at the hands of the Morrigan caused her to try to protect Alyssa by keeping her ignorant."

Ceri stared as Rio's knuckles turned white as he gripped the steering wheel. "Her ignorance nearly cost my brother and her their lives. Too bad her grandmother was a healer rather than a prophet. Maybe she would have done things better." Waves of his anger washed over her.

"Who are you to criticize?" She bristled. "Afton did everything she could to help Alyssa be ready when the time came, if it did, without telling her who she really was. Why do you think Alyssa is a Celtic scholar? Why do you think Alyssa's house even now is nearly an impregnable fortress against unruly gods with vicious intents?" She sat back hard against her seat. "You're too quick to judge before you have all the facts, Rio Sheridan." Folding her arms protectively over her chest, she looked resolutely out the passenger window. Conversation didn't seem important any more.

"If someone close to her"—he took his eyes from the road for a minute—"would have helped her, Seamus wouldn't have had to teach Alyssa how to shield her thoughts, and the whole family wouldn't have had to rally at the training room while Scathach gave Alyssa a crash course in talisman training that left no time for visualization, something Rowan's been teaching her over the past few months." He blew out a disgusted breath. "And she still hasn't mastered it."

His vibrating antagonism filled the cab of the truck. Ceri remained quiet. What more did he want her to say?

"Damn it, Alyssa should have been well trained when Rowan met her. You, as her 'best friend'"—he air-quoted with one hand—"should have insisted on it. Especially after her twenty-first birthday."

They rode rest of the way to town in silence. When they reached the city limits, Ceri tersely directed Rio to her condo and barely thanked him for the ride as she scrambled out of his truck. Hugging her shawl to herself, she all but ran to her front door.

Before she could slide her key into the lock, she gasped as he placed his big hand on her shoulder and turned her toward him.

"I didn't mean to piss you off, Ceri." He pushed his fingers into his hair. "But I can't understand why Alyssa's grandmother left her so woefully unprepared and you were complicit in that. I also don't understand why I can't stop myself from doing this when I know better."

Answering her unspoken question, he cupped her face in his hands and kissed her. When their lips met, her senses exploded, and the gentle kiss he promised with a barely-there caress morphed into something dark and intense in half a heartbeat. She opened for him, their tongues sliding and gliding like they'd done this dance together many times rather than once.

When he finally tore his mouth away from hers, he left her speechless. Gingerly, she touched her fingertips to her kiss-bruised lips.

"Sorry. I couldn't resist. Goodbye, Ceri." The roughness of his voice sent a shiver through her. Turning on his heel, he strode determinedly to his truck, climbed into it, and backed out of her driveway without once looking at her while she stared after him long after she could no longer hear the truck's engine humming in the still summer twilight.

CHAPTER TWO

Autumnal Equinox

"WHAT DO YOU mean by a legacy?" Ceri asked, confused.

Every year since Ceri's parents' deaths at the hands of the Morrigan, her aunt, Shanley Conlan, treated her to a lavish dinner out. Her twenty-fifth birthday was no exception until Shanley slid the deed to their family's ancestral estate in Scotland across the table to her.

"Following ancient Celtic maternal traditions, the oldest daughter in the family inherits the family home. Your mom had it for about three years before Morgan escorted her and your dad into the mists." Shanley picked up her wine, sipped, and stared pensively at the envelope on the table. "Somehow Becca must have known what Morgan planned for them because she made a will and gave me a key to a safe deposit box where I found all her papers, including guardianship for you and this deed." For a moment, she seemed far away.

"I can barely remember my parents." The sadness of that reality left her feeling hollow, and she reached across the table to squeeze her aunt's hand. "I've often thought myself lucky you lived nearby and were willing to take me in. You've been a great mom to me, so that must be a family tradition as well."

Shanley gifted her a watery smile. "There was no doubt about where you'd go. You were all I had left."

"Still, I wonder if you might have found your warrior if you hadn't been saddled with your wild five-year-old niece." Ceri's smile flipped upside down.

"Don't sing that old song again." Shanley squeezed Ceri's hand back and returned to her meal. "Like I've told you many times before, you didn't stop me from doing anything I wanted. I made myself available in the warrior community, but my warrior never found me. That happens sometimes, you know." She forked a bite of eggplant parmesan, chewed, and swallowed. "Morgan is a formidable enemy who's in it to win. She's escorted thousands of warriors across the ford over the last millennia, and she's not done yet, even with your friends' recent successes against her."

Shanley's admonition weighed on their evening as each of them thought about what she meant.

When word had circulated through the warrior community that the two strands of Findlay and Ailsa Sheridan's line had met in the marriage of Alyssa Ailsa Macaulay and Rowan Findlay Sheridan, there had been joyous celebration. Morgan had tried desperately for years to stop that particular event, attacking the families of talismans she thought might be responsible for lifting the curse she'd put on warriors when she stole Findlay Sheridan's wife Ailsa a thousand years ago. Among the consequences, Alyssa and Ceri had grown up orphans, Alyssa reared by her grandmother, Ceri by her aunt.

The theft of Ailsa Sheridan all those years ago ushered in a lean time for warriors cursed to find their talismans before their twenty-eighth birthdays or face a life on the run or become rogue warriors in Morgan's vicious army. Neither option appealed to men of honor. However, Morgan sometimes sweetened the offer by introducing desperate warriors to her alluring and lusty sister Maeve who enticed men of weak character to join the goddesses in their quest to take as many warriors as possible into the afterlife. Always, the goddesses looked for ways to thwart warriors from finding their talismans, their fated mates, though sometimes fate intervened on their behalf. Shanley was an example of fate's cruel intervention. She'd spent as much time as possible before her twenty-eighth birthday traveling to places where warriors met even after she assumed guardianship of Ceri. Shanley had never met her warrior, so she settled down to a quiet life of rearing and training her niece and trying to keep both of them safe. They owed much to Finn Daly who, following the death of his wife, watched over Alyssa and her grandmother and Shanley and Ceri as well.

Thinking about the past didn't ruin Ceri's delectable seared halibut like it would have done once. But it was time to leave the past in the past.

"What can you tell me about this house in Scotland?" she asked.

"It's a manor that's been in our family for generations. Your mom and I visited it after she inherited it." Shanley dabbed her mouth with her napkin and pushed away the remnants of her eggplant parmesan. "It's quite impressive if a bit cold and gloomy. To be honest, after your mother's death, I didn't have the heart to go back over to check on it. A caretaker has looked after it these last twenty years."

Ceri's eyes saucered. "That must have been a real drain on your finances. Why didn't you sell it?"

"It didn't belong to me. Plus, it's part of the protections that keep Conlan women safe," her aunt explained.

"Forgive my irreverence, but how did that house protect my mother?"

"If your mother had spent her allotted year there, I think

she may have avoided the fate Morgan served her. As it was, she had a baby and a husband here, and she hated being away from either of you for any time, certainly not the year she needed to spend there."

Worry edged into Ceri's consciousness. "Why would she have had to spend a year there?"

"The protections the house offers are imbued in those who live in it over time. The longer you live there, the more protection you enjoy. A powerful druid priestess somewhere back in our ancestry blessed it like Afton blessed Alyssa's home. Since then, it's been a safe haven for our family, a safety that follows us for a while after we've left the physical building."

Ceri sat back and regarded her aunt over her glass of white wine. "If this is all true, why did our family ever leave Scotland?"

"Good question. It seems somewhere several generations ago, an eldest daughter gave birth only to sons. They immigrated to America, and it wasn't until my mother that there were any daughters to inherit, so the property has been held in trust. Like Becca, our mom only spent a short time there before returning to her home here, and like Becca, Mom didn't live long after her return to the States." Shanley signaled to the waitress.

"Yes, ma'am?"

"May we see your dessert menu?"

"Of course. Would you like coffee?"

"Please," both women said together.

After the waitress left them, Ceri returned to the matter at hand. "It seems the house is more cursed than blessed. If I don't want to live there and I return to the place I've always known as home, I can expect a short life even if I have a warrior. Both Mom and Grandma were married." She stared meaningfully at Shanley. "Without a warrior, my time will probably be even shorter than theirs. Maybe I should sell the place."

"That's something you'll need to decide after you visit it."

"Even with everything that's happened in our family, you think I should go over there and spend time in that house?" Ceri asked incredulously.

"You could stay in a hotel and visit the property, look around, see what you think, what you feel. After all, real estate is your forte. It would be a shame if you never even saw your ancestral home before you put it up for sale."

"I can't figure out why you'd want me to step foot in that place knowing all you know."

"Because after your mom returned home, I spent a year there, and I've lived fifteen years past her death with nothing but my wits and occasional help from an old warrior who lost his talisman long ago. You have nothing keeping you here, so the timing of your inheritance feels like a sign."

Shanley smiled up at the waitress as she handed dessert menus to them.

Ceri ignored her menu. "What do you mean I have nothing keeping me here? My real estate business is thriving."

Shanley peered over her menu.

"And I have you." She sat back in her chair. "I've lost enough in my life. I don't want to take a chance on losing you."

A memory of a sizzling hot kiss flashed briefly in her mind before she ruthlessly dismissed it. Rio Sheridan had to have tried his sign on her and discovered she wasn't his. Like a warrior with honor, he'd walked away—another loss Ceri felt keenly for some inexplicable reason.

"You won't have trouble restarting your business when you return, and I can entertain myself for a while. After all, I'm only forty, which, contrary to you twenty-somethings' beliefs, is not one foot in the grave," she said laughing.

Ceri's face crumpled.

"You won't lose me, sweetheart. I promise."

"That's a big one, Shanley."

Her aunt reached across the table and tapped the deed.

"It seems so out of the blue that yesterday I lived in a townhouse in a university community in Montana, and today I'm the heiress of some Scottish estate. Where is Conlan Manor anyway?"

Retrieving her smartphone from her handbag, Shanley pulled up a map of Scotland on the internet. "It's tucked up here on the northern coast, kind of on its own near the village of Ullapool in Ross-shire. It's in a rugged and mountainous region, so you should feel right at home."

"You're assuming a lot." She stared dubiously at the map. "The place is a long way from anywhere, and you think I should fly over there and move in for however long by myself?"

"I'll fly over when I have time off over Thanksgiving and stay for a few days."

She held up her hands. "Wait. Whoa. Slow down. You're talking like I'm going to hop on a plane and fly over there tomorrow. I haven't even wrapped my head around the idea of any of this let alone decided what to do about it."

After placing a dessert order for both of them—a chocolate brownie with hot fudge sauce for two—Shanley calmly said, "There's nothing to decide nor any time to decide it. Once you've reached your twenty-fifth year and have been presented with the deed, you must visit the property as soon as possible or risk losing everything you have—including your life."

Ceri nearly jumped out of her chair. "What are you saying? The more you describe this place, the more it sounds as though I've inherited a curse."

Shanley smiled benignly at the nearby patrons who stopped their meals to stare them. Discreetly, she motioned for Ceri to sit back down.

"It's about protection," she said, her tone soothing. "Our line can only be maintained by our connection to Conlan Manor. You're the last hope of our family, so it's especially important you visit our ancestral home." With a grin, she dangled the carrot to which every talisman irresistibly responded. "Who knows, you may even find your warrior there."

Ceri raised her brows.

"Consider it a vacation. You love to travel, and this is another adventure."

"Sure, one with potential life-and-death consequences. Some vacation." Ceri slouched back in her chair.

"I'd go with you, but I can't leave work right now. You closed your latest deal last week, which means now is a good time for you. I'll look after your townhouse, so you can go and enjoy yourself."

Shanley tilted her head. "You know, your mother had much the same response when she received this deed. Becca felt a deep connection that scared her more than anything. I think she thought if she stayed for the required year, she'd never leave."

"What if that happens to me? What if I don't want to return?" The idea scared the hell out of her.

"What if? You won't be separated from me, and who else will you leave behind?"

"Alyssa for one. She's like a sister to me, and I can't imagine not being able to see her whenever I want."

Shanley slid her a sly grin. "You're not seeing her much since she married Rowan. He keeps her rather busy, which is why the two of us have had so much time together lately." She smacked her lips over a bite of brownie. "Stop making excuses and listen to your heart." Gesturing with her spoon, she said, "Enjoy your dessert. Then we'll go to your place and make arrangements for your trip. It might be the adventure of your life."

⌘

"You're off to Scotland?"

The summer-like day invited Ceri and Alyssa to share a patio meal, and each enjoyed a glass of white wine before returning to work in the afternoon.

"Guess so. Shanley says I have a finite amount of time after my birthday to make my inaugural trip before my protections wear off, whatever that means." She rolled her eyes.

"So much enthusiasm, Ceri." Alyssa's tone reflected her worry. "Usually, I'm the cautious one. You forge ahead and damn the consequences."

"I know. Only, there's something frightening about the situation." She blew out a breath. "I've done research, and there is absolutely no real shopping anywhere near the place. I'll have to drive all the way down to Glasgow to find any trendy stores."

"You're going to the Scottish Highlands." Alyssa stared at Ceri from beneath her brows. "How trendy do you need to be?"

"Maybe when the term ends, you and Rowan could visit me? If I'm still there, that is." She winced at how plaintive she sounded.

Alyssa's eyes lit up. "Christmas in Scotland. That's a great idea." She leaned forward, her whole body bubbling with enthusiasm. "I loved Scotland when I did my semester abroad there. I can give you the names of some excellent people who I now know are part of the warrior community. There's a druid whose special talents might be helpful to you."

"How could I forget about your semester in Scotland? That was when I ran off to Italy and tried to fall in love with a totally inappropriate civilian man." The memory made her laugh.

Alyssa grinned. "Dario did sound charming, but he still irritates me since he was the cause of you ditching me for our planned week together in London."

"You said you forgave me for that."

"I did forgive you. We were talking about Dario."

"About my invitation. You'll think about it? Run it by Rowan. Maybe he wants to see the old family stomping grounds or pay homage to Scathach in her own country?"

Alyssa leaned her forearms on the table. "There's a good thought. If nothing else, Rowan could be swayed with a trip to ingratiate himself with the Sheridan family's favorite goddess. Although that might also mean bringing along other Sheridans as well…"

"Rowan's parents are welcome to stay any time. We'll keep in touch, make a plan once I arrive," she said as she finished her wine.

"You know that's not who I meant." Alyssa raised her eyebrow in that way she had of hauling Ceri up short. "What if Rio wants to come along? Though both of you deny it, I can tell there's something going on."

"He's incredibly hot, I'll give him that, but there's nothing going on. Truly. Listen, I have some last-minute details to finish at work before I head home to pack." Ceri pulled out her wallet and placed some bills on the table. "When Shanley said I had no time to waste, she meant it. She booked me a flight out tomorrow, and I haven't even caught my breath from receiving the deed to Conlan Manor yesterday."

"Before you rush off, I have a little something for your birthday." Alyssa slid a slender package across the table.

Ceri picked up the package wrapped in eye-catching paisley paper and smiled at Alyssa while she opened the attached card:

Thanks for everything. Your impulsivity that led me to Rowan, your understanding, and your forever friendship. Love, Alyssa

Ceri blinked back tears.

"Go on. Open it."

She tore open the shiny silver paper and opened the box to find a heather-colored cashmere scarf embroidered with a meadow green Celtic forever knot. "Oh, wow. This is gorgeous, Alys. When did you have time to make it?" She wound the lovely accessory around her neck, luxuriating in the feel of the soft fabric against her skin.

"You know how I am. I need to keep my hands busy. I've had

this idea in my head since returning home from our honeymoon. It kept bugging me until I made it. On some level, I think I knew you'd need it."

She slid around the table and hugged her friend. "It's this connection I'm going to miss so much. My return date on my plane ticket is open. Shanley thinks I need to spend at least a year in Conlan Manor. If I stay that long, I'm going to miss you like crazy."

"We can always have conversations telepathically," Alyssa suggested.

"Not a good idea if we don't want to invite the nasty ladies into our enchanted homes," Ceri reminded her. Their telepathy was very useful, but it came with a price. The goddesses they tried to avoid could home in on them easily if they used their special skill too much.

Alyssa sighed. "You're right. We'll just do the best we can. There's always the phone, FaceTime, email. Besides, I'm sure I can convince Rowan to make a trip over, especially if you stay a whole year."

Alyssa looked past Ceri and caught sight of a clock. "Is that the time?" She gasped. "I teach a class in fifteen minutes. You'll let me know when you've landed safely and keep me posted on events when you arrive, right? Promise me."

"You know I will. Try to keep that husband of yours in line," Ceri said as she hugged her friend good-bye.

Chapter Three

ERI LOST HER breath when Hamish Buchanan stopped the car at the top of the hill for her first view of her ancestral home. An odd sense of foreboding flowed through her. They'd turned off the main road, traveled a short distance along a narrow, paved track, over a small hill, and down into a grassy glen from which rose three stories of golden edifice, square and solid, with a sprawling yard interrupted by terraces of flowers and trees.

"Beautiful, isnae it?" Hamish whispered.

"Wow."

She avidly drank in the scene as the druid caretaker of her home—who also happened to be her distant cousin—slowly maneuvered his car down the drive and around the house to the car park behind it.

A pallet of russet and golden flowers painted the gardens. The vibrant green of the mown lawns along the terraces popped, drawing her eye to the low bushes sculpted into Celtic knots bordering the flowerbeds. She lost her words at the beauty of the Georgian architecture rendered in golden sandstone, a stately manor fit for a queen.

She was already in love with the place, and Hamish hadn't taken her inside yet.

After parking the car at the back of the house, he said, "I usually use the servants' entrance back here because it leads directly tae the kitchen, but fer yer first time seeing the house, we'll use the front door."

He led her around to the front of the house via a flagstone path bordered with flowerbeds and a pretty trellis over the gate in the stone fence separating the kitchen gardens from the formal gardens.

"Incredible," she breathed, drinking in the gardens and the valley in which the manor sat.

After a few minutes, he said, "All right, lass, it's time fer a look around inside." He produced a key to a modern-looking lock and opened the massive, ornately carved oak front door.

At first Ceri didn't even notice the décor of the house, her practiced realtor's eye automatically taking in its bones instead. The balustraded main staircase at the far end of the entrance hall grabbed her attention, followed by the pillars rising through the middle of the house past the third floor to the ceiling. Balconies looked down on the entrance hall, and doors with doorframes of elaborate oak molding led off to various rooms.

An open door to her left snagged her attention, and she stepped over to peek into a room that at one time might have been a parlor but now served as a cozy sitting room. The furniture, upholstered in outdated fabrics with large floral prints, was modern including a recliner, a love seat and ottoman, and a rocking chair. A fireplace took up most of the wall opposite the door, and an entertainment center dominated the wall to her right. Floor-to-ceiling windows looked out on the gardens. From the looks of it, this room saw some use.

Farther down the hall, she opened a door and gasped at the size of the dining room she discovered. The long table in the middle of the room looked to seat at least forty people. Benches instead of chairs were tucked neatly under it, so maybe even fifty people could crowd around that massive table. Another fireplace took up the wall at the opposite end of the room. She walked the length of the room, drawn to the portrait hanging above the mantel. The woman in the painting had eyes the exact same shade as her own.

"What was her name?"

"Fianna. It means fighter full o' grace."

Ceri turned to Hamish with smile. "Interesting choice for a druid."

"'Tis a fitting name. Fianna was a fighter."

Inclining her head, she glided her hand along the smooth surface of the heavy oak table. "What's the reason for such a huge table?"

Hamish rested his hands on it. "Back when Fianna had the house built, she hosted meetin's o' warriors, talismans, and druids from all over the Highlands. With the Jacobin uprisin's and the last o' the Clearances happening, the Morrigan was much more active in Scotland than she is now, thank the gods, so many a meetin' commenced in this secure house."

She could almost hear some of those meetings, and she shivered at the sensation that rippled through her. "What's across the hall from here?"

"The grand salon. Shall we take a look?"

Taking up most of the front of the house, the salon looked big enough to host a grand ball. Simply roll up the beautiful Oriental rug on the floor, set up the band near the massive grand piano opposite the doors, and have a party. If the manor had been located back in the States, Ceri could see the potential for this room to host a variety of entertainments that could pay for the upkeep of the manor.

On the heels of that thought, she wondered about the

financial burden she'd inherited. "What does it cost my aunt to keep this place up?"

"Ye think Shanley pays fer this place?"

Ceri nodded.

"Nae lass. The family trust pays fer the upkeep o' the manor. A board manages it—yer aunt's a member by the way. Since ye're the lawful owner now, ye'll assume yer place and help us manage the trust, relieving Shanley of a responsibility no' her own." Hamish paused and stared meaningfully at her. "Shanley's done admirably by ye."

Her eyes widened. "It's a lot to take in all at once."

"If anyone is up tae it, it's ye, lass. Come along with ye now and let's have a look at yer bedroom. Once we lug up all yer gear"—he winked at her—"ye'll want tae leave it in yer room fer a good long time."

He'd commented plenty about the three suitcases, she'd brought. She didn't want to imagine what he would say if he'd know about the other five she'd left behind.

When she walked into her bedroom, she couldn't believe her eyes. An enormous mahogany four-poster bed dominated the room. Opposite the bed rested a matching rolltop desk and an elaborate antique dressing table with an oval mirror. A chaise lounge snuggled up to the window facing the front gardens invited daydreaming. She smiled at the massive size of the wardrobe along the wall opposite the windows. Definitely enough closet space. The oversized furniture fit with space to spare in the room the size of her entire apartment back home.

In the bathroom she discovered a deep Jacuzzi tub. The black marble tile above it gleamed as though someone shined it every day. The marble continued into the open shower stall, along the vanity, and behind to the toilet. The gold fixtures looked modern. The whole room resembled something out of a cosmopolitan design magazine.

Someone—the trust—had gone to expensive pains to entice her to stay, and Shanley had obviously been complicit in those plans. Who else could have told the renovators of this room Ceri's tastes, and who besides Shanley knew of her dream bathroom? Hamish danced from foot to foot awaiting her verdict on her room.

"Shanley told you a lot about me."

"She had tae. If ye'd grown up here as yer ancestors did, that wouldnae been necessary, but as it was…"

"I see. Well, I appreciate all the work—and the money—this room demanded. It's fantastic. I might hole up in here and never come out." She laughed, and Hamish huffed out a sigh.

"Well, then. Let's haul up that mountain o' luggage ye brought with ye and get ye settled. It's nigh on lunchtime, and I'm famished."

∽

While Ceri unpacked clothes and marveled at the grandeur of the room she would occupy for the foreseeable future, Hamish returned to the kitchen to fix their lunch.

Out of nowhere, an intercom she hadn't noticed before crackled to life, and she jumped a mile. She squeaked and hoped the system worked only one way. After answering Hamish's invitation to lunch, she left her unpacking half-finished and headed downstairs to join him.

In the kitchen, Hamish ladled generous portions of beef and vegetable stew into shallow soup bowls. Thick slices of homemade bread and tea steaming in big mugs waited beside the place settings at the rough-hewn table across from the stove. He set the bowls of savory stew on the table and pulled out her chair, an automatic gesture that earned him a big grin.

"At least chivalry isn't dead in Scotland," she said as she

sat. "Mmm, this smells delicious. I hope you made a lot 'cause I'm starved."

He grinned. "I was worried ye might be one o' those women who're always watchin' her figure when what she needs tae do is eat enough tae be useful."

She laughed then conversation stopped while each of them took care of first one and then another bowl of stew.

∽

"Ye'll have plenty o' time fer settlin' in later. Right now, we'll start the rites that keep this house and those attached tae it secure," Hamish announced after they cleaned up their lunch.

"You don't waste time, do you?" Ceri asked with a sense of trepidation. The druidic aspects of owning the manor made her nervous.

"Donnae worry lass. Yer main role in our rituals is yer presence."

"Our? Others are involved?"

"No' taeday. But on other days there will be others. *Samhain* will be an especially big day. 'Tis fortunate yer birthday fell on the autumnal equinox so we dinnae have tae wait so long tae complete the most important rituals."

He dried his hands from washing dishes and hung the towel on the rack above the sink.

"Taeday we're sprinkling herbs. We'll start at the front door. Meet me there in a few minutes, if ye please."

He disappeared down a short hallway to what she supposed were his private quarters. She wondered when she'd be invited to see those rooms. No matter that she owned the manor, she had no desire to invade another's personal space without an invitation.

A few minutes later, he joined her in the foyer.

"It's time tae start teachin' ye about yer heritage, lassie. I'll chant, and ye'll follow and repeat the chants until ye're ready tae chant them on yer own."

"What's in the basket?"

"Dried basil, cinquefoil, cowslip, elderflower, figwort, garlic, and rosemary. I grow 'em in the knot gardens out front."

"For protection spells?"

"And fer lunch." His eyes twinkled. "Several o' these herbs were also in the stew."

"Is that part of the protections?"

"Only from hunger."

Her cheeks heated.

"'Tis all right lass. Ye're a talisman. Ye're no' expected tae know all the properties o' plants. Come on then. Let's take care o' taeday's task."

Hamish began with a ritual chant at the front door, touching its four corners inside and out with sprigs of herbs tied together with leather thongs. It took her a few minutes to acclimate her ear to his soft, lilting chant before she distinguished the words. He repeated them before handing her the rowan basket and indicating she should take her turn. Following his lead, she chanted:

> *"The Sacred Three*
> *"Scathach to guard,*
> *"Brighid to bless,*
> *"Rhiannon to surround*
> *"The house,*
> *"The clan of the druid mother,*
> *"Every morning,*
> *"Every evening,*
> *"Every night,*
> *"And every day,*
> *"And every evening,*
> *"And every single night."*

She touched each corner of the door inside and out as she'd watched Hamish do, and he nodded his approval.

After they finished with the front door, they traveled in a counterclockwise circuit of the exterior of the house, brushing each edge of each window and door and the corners of the house on the ground floor with herbs, chanting as they went. When they finished outside, they returned inside and continued their journey throughout the house. In this way, she saw the entirety of every room from bottom to top except for Hamish's quarters. By the time they finished with the third floor, she was too exhausted to ask about why they didn't seal his rooms too.

Excusing herself, she went to her room for a nap before she finished unpacking. Testing the big bed, she'd expected something a little soft, a bit saggy, but the mattress was firm, and she lay back on it with a sigh.

Awakening in an utterly dark room disoriented her. Ceri reached over to the nightstand and patted around until she found the lamp and her cell phone to check the time. *It's two in the morning? How did I sleep through dinner and half the night?* Her stomach rumbled at thoughts of dinner, which sent her downstairs in search of food.

With the entire house shrouded in darkness, she felt her way down the hall to the staircase and down the stairs to the main floor. An odd noise coming from the grand salon halted her mid-step on the last stair above the foyer. Not knowing Hamish's habits, she decided to check it out anyway. When she opened the door and called softly for him, she thought she heard a sharp intake of breath, then for several seconds she heard nothing. Deciding she'd mistaken the settling noises of an old house for an intruder, she closed the door to the salon and resumed her journey to the kitchen.

A small nightlight over the stove welcomed her, giving enough light for her to find a switch for the light over the sink and illuminating the refrigerator and the cupboards. After filling a bowl with leftover stew, she microwaved it in the tiny oven beside the fridge, delighted she wouldn't have to eat her midnight snack cold.

Sitting at the kitchen table in the semidarkness, she decided the stew tasted even better warmed up. She hoped she hadn't disappointed Hamish by falling asleep like she had. Her thoughts strayed to the ritual they'd performed that afternoon. It had been interesting at first but soon became monotonous. By the time they chanted over last room, fatigue thoroughly set in. Perhaps Hamish had experienced a similar feeling and hadn't missed her at all at dinner because he'd skipped it too.

She washed her bowl and returned it to the cupboard before heading back upstairs. When she reached the main hall, once again she heard strange noises, this time coming from the vast dining room. Opening the door slowly, she stepped inside and stopped to listen. Someone was moving around in the room.

"Hamish?" she called softly.

The noise stopped abruptly, and she distinctly heard the sharp intake of breath.

"Hamish? Are you in here?"

Silence greeted her. Unease snaked up her spine.

Closing the door behind her, she hustled downstairs in search of Hamish. She hated to wake him in the middle of the night, but someone was in the house, and she had no intention of confronting an intruder alone.

Trying to knock on Hamish's door loudly enough to wake him without alerting the intruder was a challenge. Finally, after several minutes, he groggily answered.

"What can ye be wantin' in the middle o' the night lass?" The surliness of his tone did nothing for her worry.

"There's someone in the house, Hamish," she whispered urgently. "I thought I was imagining things when I thought I heard someone in the grand salon when I came down to the kitchen. But when I heard someone in the dining room a minute ago, I knew it wasn't my imagination."

"Lass, this is an old house. It makes all sorts o' noises. I locked up before I went tae bed, so I'm sure there's nae one in the house. Donnae worry yerself and go on back tae sleep."

She crossed her arms over her chest and stubbornly held her ground.

He sighed. "If it'll make ye feel better, I'll walk ye tae yer room."

"That would make me feel better, actually."

Carefully, he closed the door to his room and walked her up the stairs in silence. She strained to hear the sounds that had worried her earlier, but as they made their way up the grand staircase, the house remained eerily silent.

At her door Hamish said, "There ye are lass. All safe and sound. Next time if ye need me, press the intercom twice. That connects ye directly tae my room. All right then?"

"Thank you, Hamish. Sorry to wake you."

"Yer first night in this auld place was bound tae be a might unnervin'. Think nothin' of it. Good night."

Ceri locked her bedroom door.

Chapter Four

ERI'S FIRST TWO weeks in Scotland were interesting yet uneventful. Each day at some appointed time she could never anticipate—morning, afternoon, evening, the middle of the night—Hamish walked her around the house inside and out chanting and distributing various herbs. The chants and herbs varied, but the ritual remained the same. The chanting exhausted her, but eventually, she became more accustomed to it and only required a short nap following a session of the ritual.

Occasionally, they chanted on the roof, accessing it from a third-story balcony or through a trapdoor in an attic room. During the rituals, Ceri learned every square inch of the manor like someone who had been born there. The only rooms she never entered were Hamish's own. When she asked him about it, he insisted if she entered his rooms, it would weaken his spells since he prepared the herbs there. Privately, she thought his excuse was bull, but she let it go.

The nights she heard someone moving around in the house were another story. Hamish insisted no one could be in the house. He even brought her along with him to lock up several times. Still, Ceri knew the sounds in the various rooms on the first floor were not the natural settling of an old house. Drawers opening and closing, chairs scraping along the polished wood floors, windows rattling like someone was trying to determine if they were unlocked—those were *not* the sounds of an old house. She didn't believe in ghosts, so the only conclusion she could draw was someone had an alternate way into her home.

A someone who visited nearly every night.

Late one evening as she read old diaries in the library, she caught sight of a shadow passing outside the library door. She'd left lights on in the second floor hallway and on the stairs, places she often traveled on her way to the sitting room, kitchen, her bedroom, and the library—the rooms she used. Hamish threw his hands up at the unnecessary expense of burning all those lights, but Ceri said she'd pay for them herself if necessary. When she wouldn't budge, he'd grumbled the trust could afford some light, but she needn't be so paranoid. The place was neither haunted nor invaded.

She froze until she was certain whoever had peeked into the room had moved on. Quietly, she stood up, tiptoed to the door, and cautiously glanced down the hall, catching sight of the shadow of a man much larger than Hamish as he descended the stairs. Ceri's outrage that someone would be sneaking around in her house overwhelmed her good sense. On slippered feet, she soundlessly chased after the intruder.

Reaching the main hall, she stopped to listen for where the man could have gone. Not hearing sounds coming from any of the rooms on the ground floor, she hurried to the kitchen, flipping lights on all the way downstairs. When she reached the kitchen, she called out to Hamish and looked around the room.

"Lass, it's the middle o' the night. What are ye squallin' about?"

"There was—or is—someone in the house. I just followed him down the stairs."

At his dubious glare, she rushed on. "I was in the library reading when I saw a shadow. I got up and saw a man running down the stairs. I gave chase, but I didn't see where he went. None of the doors sounded, so I assumed he came down here."

"Lass, are ye sure?"

"Absolutely," she said, panting.

Her heart pounded and she realized how foolish her actions had been. What if she'd caught the intruder? What then?

"Let's take a look, lass."

Together, they methodically searched the house for signs someone other than the two of them had been inside. After an hour, they found nothing except a glass with milk residue in the sink, a glass neither of them had used, proof someone had been in the house. Hamish said he'd check in the village to find out if anyone else had experienced someone in their homes or had seen any odd people hanging around. Ceri decided to enlist her friends from back home when she returned to her room and locked herself in.

❧

"Isla, it's Ceri Ross. How are you?"

"Ceri!" Isla said warmly. "Are you home already? Alyssa implied you'd be in Scotland for a while."

"I'm still in Scotland, but I need some help from Security Consultants Unlimited. Is Rowan or Seamus around?"

"Rowan is in. I'll put you through. You're all right over there, aren't you?"

"If you mean 'Do I need help keeping the unpleasant gods at bay?' the answer is no. I have a druid relative who's doing a great job of that. The more suspect human element, however, is a different story, which is why I'm calling."

"Stay safe, Ceri."

She heard a click before Rowan's voice boomed over the phone. "How are you? How's Scotland?"

"I'm fine. Scotland is incredible. I've met some wonderful people in the village, and the manor is spectacular. You and Alyssa should come and see it—and maybe bring along one of your high-tech state-of-the-art security systems?"

"What's going on?"

She sucked in air and plunged in. "Someone other than the caretaker and me is spending time in my house. I need a security system, and the first person I thought of was you."

In reality, the first person she'd thought of was Rowan's brother, but she'd quickly put that thought out of her mind.

"We're in the middle of a major installation, so I can't get away. I'll check with Seamus though. He could come over and see what you need and maybe enlist a local company to help you."

"That's just it, Rowan. There are no local companies. People here live a long way from anywhere. Will you talk to Seamus? The caretaker here is a druid and a relative. He and Shanley insist I need to spend a year in this big old house, which, now that I'm here, I don't mind too much." She shifted the phone to her other ear. "Provided I'm not sharing the place with intruders. Sleeping with my bedroom door locked every night is starting to wear on my nerves."

"How long has this been going on?" Rowan sounded alarmed.

"Since my first night here. I kept hearing noises like someone walking around, but Hamish, the caretaker, insisted it was only the house I was hearing. But tonight I chased a man down the stairs after I caught him looking in at me when I was in the library. He left an unwashed glass in the kitchen, and even Hamish had to admit someone had been in the house."

"Ceri, one of us will get away in the next few days and at least see what you need over there. In the meantime, keep your bedroom door locked even when you're not in the room. From the pictures you emailed Alyssa, that looks like a lot of house you're living in, and it wouldn't take much for someone to sneak in and hide in your room while you're out."

"Thanks, Rowan. That makes me feel so much safer." No doubt her voice conveyed her eyeroll halfway across the world.

"Sorry. But do it anyway. Isla will make arrangements and let you know when to expect one of us."

At his sincerity, her sarcasm deflated out of her. "Honestly, thanks a lot, Rowan. I appreciate it."

She rang off and went in search of Hamish. Instinctively, she knew he'd protest a security system, but the gods weren't the only dangers in the world.

A thought struck her—what if the gods were using a civilian to breach the protections she and Hamish were erecting over the house? After all, they'd tried that tactic by using Alyssa's old boyfriend after Rowan discovered her to be his talisman. What if something similar was happening with her? The possibility left her nauseous.

When Rio Sheridan walked into the Anchor Bar in Ullapool, Scotland tired and irritable from his long flight and the two-hour drive from Inverness in a tiny rental car he'd stuffed with electronic gear, he couldn't contain his resentment at yet another display of Ceri Ross's flirtatiousness.

She sat at the bar sipping a glass of wine, her laughter at the men seated around her tinkling through the pub. He wanted to wrap her long honey-colored French braid around his wrist and tug. Make her give her attention to him. The heather-colored sweater she chose brought out the meadow green of her eyes that sparkled and flashed as she held court in the busy pub.

Rowan had insisted the firm couldn't spare Seamus, so it fell to

Rio to fly to Scotland. Now instead of Seamus helping Ceri with her security problem, Rio had to endure the torture of being close to her, another warrior's talisman whom he desired far too much.

His surly thoughts must have shown on his face. Either that or Ceri was no more delighted to see him than he was to be there because her face fell midlaugh when she spotted him in the doorway. An older man sitting near her glanced from Rio to Ceri and immediately rose to stand beside her and whisper in her ear. She shook her head and excused herself from the crowd of men to walk over to him, the older gentleman right on her heels.

"Rio? What are you doing here?"

"Nice to see you too, Ceri. What do you suppose I'm doing here? I came to help you with the security problem you said you have at your house. You did call Security Consultants Unlimited to request our services, didn't you?"

"Lass, ye know this man?" the old guy interrupted.

"Yes, Hamish. This is Riordan Sheridan, my best friend's brother-in-law. Rio, this is my cousin, Hamish Buchanan."

Rio extended his hand and briefly sized Hamish up before Ceri continued. "I thought Seamus was flying over to help me."

"You'd have liked that, I'm sure."

She glared at him. "Why can't you give it a rest, Rio?" You know there's nothing between us."

"'Course not."

She crossed her arms, all angry vibes, and he relented.

"Listen, I came straight through, and I'm exhausted. Any chance you can tear yourself away from your admirers and show me where this house of yours is?"

Eyeing him more closely, she said, "Fine."

He watched her relax when she turned to Hamish. "I can ride with Rio if you want to stay."

Simultaneously, both men started talking.

"If it's time fer ye tae go, lass, it's time fer me as well."

"My car is loaded with gear. I don't think you'll fit."

"I'll ride with Hamish then, and you can follow us. Let us say good night to some *friends*," she emphasized, "and we'll meet you outside."

Rio didn't move as he watched her return to the men who'd been paying court to her. Since the pub was small, he didn't have to struggle to overhear the men's curiosity about her American friend. At some point, he thought he might come back for a drink and answer their questions himself.

❧

Rio followed Ceri and the old man at a safe distance. In the slanting sun of the late afternoon, the gold and red grasses and bracken changed color on the hills around the village. Yet he couldn't appreciate the scenery. The farther from town they traveled, the more and more secluded the area became, setting him on edge. Out here, he couldn't be sure what dangers lurked and what help he could expect when it came time to face them.

They turned onto a narrow, tree-lined drive, and his concern ratcheted up from six to sixty on a scale of ten. Then they topped a hill, and he looked down on the manor and fell instantly in love.

The late afternoon sun bathed the sandstone in golden light, causing the manor to appear to glow. The Celtic knot gardens reassured him the house was a haven for warriors, the definition of the patterns soothing him. The house called to him like a fortress of light, its positive vibrations reaching out to him even from a distance. Whatever Ceri's druid had done to the place, it'd worked.

When they arrived at the manor, he watched Hamish head inside via the door in the back while Ceri waited beside the car. "Hamish says I need to escort guests through the front door to keep the protections we've already done intact. Please follow me." She sounded formal—and pissed.

She picked at the hem of her sweater, huffed out a sigh, and walked away from him around the house.

Might as well enjoy the view, Rio decided as he followed her. The sexy way she walked sent him into all sorts of fantasies he knew he'd never be able to experience. Only after they rounded the corner to the front of the house where she stopped and he nearly ran into her did he register that she'd been talking to him.

"Hello? I asked how was your flight?"

"Long and cramped. Someone is springing for an upgrade to business class for my return trip."

"I'm sure it was an oversight."

"Or Rowan trying to save money."

Frowning, she said, "But I'm paying for this, including travel. I told Rowan as much when I called."

"I'm sure you did." His tone suggested otherwise.

She glared at him before turning on her heel and nearly sprinting to the front veranda. *Damn if those tight jeans don't show off her long legs.* Then, *I'm a fool for noticing anything at all about this woman.*

Ceremoniously, she opened the door and ushered him inside. Upon entering the main hall, a sense of déjà vu warmed him. *I've come home.* He staggered and tried to pass it off as jet lag. *I need to do this job and get out. This is Ceri's home, and some other warrior is going to spend many years enjoying it—and its mistress.*

CHAPTER FIVE

N HIS PRIVATE rooms, Hamish turned toward the front of the house exactly when the warrior crossed the threshold of Conlan Manor. Ripples of energy washed through the manor, pushing against him like the incoming tide. *The prophecies about the protections the manor possesses will increase tenfold if the owner o' the manor discovers her warrior while they're inside it.* He tilted his head, listening to the house. *Always thought that warrior would be a Scot.*

He stilled. *Wonder why my Ceri and Rio Sheridan donnae get along.* He returned to his herbs and hummed contentedly to himself.

❧

Ceri showed Rio the rooms on the ground floor.

"Big place you've got here. I think I like this room best." Rio turned a slow circle, taking in the sitting room.

Ceri shot him a bemused look. "It's cozy." She turned away and headed out the door. "There's more upstairs."

His eyes wandered along the walls as he followed her up

the grand staircase to the second floor. The first room she showed him was the library with its floor-to-ceiling shelves lined with ancient and modern texts.

Here's another place I'd like to spend time in.

She only afforded him a glance into the room before she stepped out and showed him his bedroom at the far end of the hall from the library.

"Sorry for the eighties décor. The only rooms in the manor anyone's updated in years are the sitting room and my bedroom, I'm afraid."

"It's a bit dated, but that enormous king bed looks comfortable, and I like the antique dresser." He wandered over to check out the gardens from the floor-to-ceiling windows. "The view is good too."

He took a casual tour around the room, coming to the door of the en suite bathroom and stepping inside. "Bathroom looks like it works, but I'll be ducking under the showerhead." He laughed. "Nothing new there." At least the bathtub was deep though narrow in the usual British fashion. "If the place actually has hot water, I can sink in all the way to my shoulders in that tub, a real luxury if I'm called to battle during my stay."

Something flickered in Ceri's eyes before she looked away from him.

"So—where do you sleep again?"

"At the other end of the hall." She cleared her throat. "Do you need help unloading your car, or would you rather eat first? Hamish is probably putting something together in the kitchen right now."

"If there's food, I'm all over that. I'm starved."

She nodded and led the way out of the room.

Hamish was slicing bread from a fresh loaf when Ceri led Rio into the kitchen. A green salad sat in the middle of the table, and a heavenly smell of meat and potatoes permeated the room.

"Something smells delicious," Ceri said. "What's for dinner?"

"Shepherd's pie. Luckily, I made a big one since this warrior looks like he could eat half of it himself." Hamish chuckled.

"How long 'til it's ready?"

"About fifteen minutes, I expect. Why?"

"That's probably enough time to bring in your gear, Rio." she said as she headed to the back door leading out to the car park.

"Whoa, lass. How 'bout you finish slicing this bread and set the table while I help the lad haul his gear. If he packs like you, he'll need a man's strength tae help him."

Ceri glared at Hamish before she walked over to the counter to take over dinner preparations. Rio hid a smirk and headed out to his car.

Out in the car park, Rio caught Hamish surreptitiously sizing him up and knew the man had secrets of his own. Rio opened the trunk of his rental and gestured to Hamish to grab bags of gear stowed there while Rio secured the more sensitive, and therefore more important gear he'd loaded into the passenger compartment. Though several inches shorter and narrower than Rio, he noted that Hamish's size and age didn't limit his strength as he grabbed the heaviest of the gear bags with no obvious effort and headed inside the house with them. Rio followed with bags slung over his shoulders and carrying one in each hand.

"Ye want tae leave this stuff down here, lad?" Hamish asked when Rio followed him into the kitchen.

"I'd like all of it in my room if you don't mind. If someone is sneaking around in this house, I don't need him making off with my gear before I have the chance to install it." He stepped past Hamish and ascended the stairs to the main hall, ignoring the old druid's sigh.

It took the men two more trips to carry in all the equipment Rio brought. By the time they reappeared in the kitchen, Ceri had dinner waiting on the table.

As exhausted as he was, a kind of restless energy coursed through him. He ate ravenously, but he didn't miss Ceri mainly chasing her meal around on her plate. Several times he tried to breach her shield, hear her thoughts, but she was on her guard and kept him out.

Hamish broke the silent stalemate. "So yer brother and his talisman lifted the curse on warriors finding their talismans by their twenty-eighth birthdays. Did ye feel a reprieve, lad?"

"I think any warrior lacking his mate doesn't have all that much time," he replied around a bite of peas, carrots, and potatoes. "Morgan is relentless."

"Ye've been actively looking for yer talisman, have ye?"

"Since the day I turned twenty-one."

Hamish tore off a piece of bread and dipped it in his gravy. "Perhaps ye've been lookin' in the wrong places. Perhaps it was nae accident ye were summoned tae yer homeland. While ye're here, we'll take ye tae some *ceilidhs* and such where ye're sure tae meet other warriors and talismans—even a druid or twa." He glanced up from his plate. "Who knows what might happen."

The twinkle in Hamish's eye immediately put Rio on guard, not that he trusted the old man to begin with. But at the mention of meeting druids in the same conversation about finding a talisman, he set his fork down with a thump.

"Are you suggesting I should actively pursue druids as I look for my talisman?" he asked incredulously.

"Donnae see why not. Ceri's and my great-grandmother several generations removed was a druid and the founder o' this house. She married a warrior the first time. After his death, she married a druid. Thus, we have the twa lines in the family—talismans and warriors, and druids. Seems tae have worked out all right." He forked in a mouthful of shepherd's pie and chewed thoughtfully.

Rio leaned forward. "In my experience, mixing the two sides

of the community usually ends in disaster for one or both parties involved."

"It seems to work for Siobhan and Duncan," Ceri said quietly.

"Really? His talisman remains unmarried. So, how is that working for her?" Rio glared at her.

In reply, Ceri filled her mouth with a big bite of shepherd's pie.

"I take it these are friends o' yers?"

"Her brother is my brother Rowan's best friend, the one Ceri thought was coming over here to help her." He didn't bother to hide his resentment.

Seeing the old man smiling to himself didn't improve Rio's attitude.

"At any rate, ye should have a good time at the ceilidhs. We Scots know how tae throw a party, eh Ceri?" Hamish waggled his eyebrows at her.

She blushed and stared studiously at her plate. Rio scowled at her and finished off his second helping of dinner. As Hamish predicted, Rio ate half the meal by himself. Usually, he had better manners, but tonight he didn't have it in him to care.

Until Hamish brought it up. "I'm glad tae see ye still have an appetite after yer long journey. Ceri, there's some apple cobbler in the fridge if ye wouldnae mind warming some fer pudding, if ye please."

She stared daggers at the two men like she couldn't believe either of them. With a sigh, she stood and walked to the fridge to dish up dessert.

With Ceri's back turned, Hamish cocked a brow at Rio who opened his shield to the old man.

"Lad, whatever happened between the twa of ye in the past, leave it there. I have a feelin' ye're part o' the protections fer this house, and I donnae mean yer fancy gear. But I need ye tae get along with the lass. She's the key no' only tae this house but tae the continued existence of our clan."

Rio shot back. *"You haven't told her, have you? That's why she thinks she can leave any time she wants. You need to do everything in your power to keep her here. So you're tolerating the security system even though you obviously don't want it."*

Hamish arched a bushy brow. *"If ye get in the way o' what needs tae happen here, I willnae hesitate tae make yer life mighty uncomfortable, and I've lived long enough tae know how tae do it."*

Rio leaned his forearms on the table and stared down the old druid. *"I don't take well to threats, old man. You might want to keep that in mind."*

Carrying two plates of dessert in her hands, Ceri stopped short at the set of Hamish's jaw and the challenge of Rio's arms on the table.

"Where's yer share, lass?"

"I'm not in a dessert mood. I hope the two of you have worked out whatever it is about me that you don't want to share. Of course, I usually do exactly as I please. Ask Shanley. It might be good if you consulted me before you make plans or promises you can't keep."

Rio felt a flush creep up his cheeks, but Hamish looked amused.

"A lass with fire—always my favorite," the old druid joked, not even trying to deny they'd been discussing her.

"Just because I like you Hamish doesn't mean I'm always going to put up with you," she snapped before turning on her heel and marching up the stairs.

Rio grinned.

"Good night, lass."

She didn't dignify Hamish with a response.

Rio said nothing, but he thought plenty. *Her sweet ass moves in the damnedest way.* He cleared his throat. *I shouldn't be noticing that.*

"She's somethin', that one. Beautiful and smart. In the few weeks she's been here, she's learned tae recognize most o' the protection herbs in full flower and in dried forms. She's learned the most important chants, and she's spendin' her nights researchin' her family and all our various talents." Hamish sounded like a proud grandfather.

Rio bristled. "Are you trying to make her into a druid?"

"Not at all," he said breezily before he hummed around a bite of sweet apple pie. "Although she coulda been a fine one in other circumstances. As the heart o' this house, she needs tae be a part of all that goes on here, and that includes preparin' the herbs and doin' the chantin' and knowin' her history."

"That little scene in the pub when I arrived was for my benefit?"

"How could it be, lad? We were expectin' someone else entirely." Hamish spooned a bite of dessert and smacked his lips. "Nae, the local boys have takin' quite a shine tae our Ceri, as well they should with her bein' such a bonny lass. And she's game tae try anythin'." He chuckled.

Somehow Rio knew he wouldn't like what came next.

"Why, at the ceilidh the other night, she gave a go at Scots sword dancin', and she even tried the pipes. Although that was a bit of a disaster as it always is with beginners." Hamish smiled at the memory.

"You encourage her to flirt with the local men?" He slammed his spoon down on the table. "What the hell's the matter with you? Don't you know how dangerous that can be?"

He sat back in his chair, stunned. *He doesn't think it a problem for druids to marry talismans or warriors, and he's parading her like the prize at a battle feast. No wonder she acts the way she does. It's family tradition.*

"She hasnae met her warrior yet, and who's tae say he isnae a man from somewhere near her home? If she doesnae go out and meet people, how will she ever be in a position tae find him?" Hamish asked, his tone maddeningly reasonable.

That's exactly the problem. Rio kept his morose thoughts to himself. "It's been a long day, nearly twenty-four hours for me. Dinner was delicious, but if you'll excuse me, I'm headed to bed."

He picked up his place setting, carried it to the sink, and began to clean up. After he put his dishes in the drain to dry, he half turned to Hamish to wish him good night before climbing the two flights of stairs to his room.

Hamish called after him, "Donnae worry about wakin' up tae early, lad. "The house has been without twenty-first century security for four hundred years. Another day without it willnae make much difference."

"You tell Ceri that. I had the distinct impression she wanted this place secured yesterday."

This is probably a mistake, but I can't help it. When he reached the top of the stairs, he took a left toward her room. *I'm only making sure she's following Rowan's orders to lock her door,* he told himself. Trying the handle, he found it locked. *Damn.* He called softly through the door, "Just making sure you're keeping yourself safe."

"I figured out to lock my door at night even without a Sheridan bossing me. Good night Rio." The door muffled her response, but he heard the irritation in her tone loud and clear.

Can't blame her for her mood. Kinda matches mine. He stared up at the ornate molding along the walls. *Besides, what would I have done if she hadn't locked herself in? Started another argument?*

Padding silently down the hall to his appointed room, he closed the door. *Maybe I should leave my door unlocked, see if someone tries to come in.* He stared at the lock for a beat before he turned it. *Bad idea. In my whooped state, I'd probably be out cold and discover all my gear gone when I woke up in the morning.*

After undressing to his boxers, he slid between the sheets of the king-size bed. As he relaxed into the surprisingly comfortable mattress, visions of Ceri Ross intruded into his mind—Ceri in tight jeans stomping up the stairs, Ceri in a green sheath with her hair falling in curls over her shoulders, Ceri's eyes widening before he kissed her. *Oh, that did it.* Thinking about that kiss never failed to make him hard. *I certainly don't need that tonight.*

Think about the house. At last he drifted off into a deep sleep with a vision of Ceri standing in the open front door, the golden house glowing in the golden sun, haloing her in light.

∽

Ceri struggled to fall asleep. She'd been reading when Rio jiggled her door handle. When she retired to her room, she'd thought about leaving the door unlocked to see what he'd do, but the memory of the censorious look on his face when she caught sight of him in the pub smashed that idea. If he'd found the door unlocked, no doubt she'd have been on the receiving end of more of his disdain.

For the life of her she couldn't figure out why he disliked her so much. Loyalty to her friend and to her friend's grandmother had required she conceal her true self until Alyssa discovered her place in the warrior community. If Rio couldn't understand, then she couldn't explain it. At the wedding, he'd glared at her for most of the day until finally he'd danced with her, apparently feeling nothing while she sizzled in his arms. Ruthlessly, she jerked her mind from the direction it desperately wanted to go—the kiss.

That kiss taught Ceri why some talismans strayed. Did all warriors kiss like that or only Rio? For her sake, she hoped it was a warrior thing. Maybe when her warrior found her, he'd erase all the feelings Rio stirred in her.

Mid-morning, she awoke tired and crabby. On the second morning of her stay, Hamish had started awakening her over the intercom. His jovial voice announcing breakfast via the box on the wall by her door was not her favorite idea of an alarm clock. She'd tried to figure out how to disarm it with no success. Fleetingly, she wondered if Rio could rig the thing so she could turn it off at night.

Both men were seated at the table and tucking in to a full Scots breakfast when she dragged herself into the kitchen. Shuffling over to the coffee pot, she poured herself a mug of wake-up and hoped it tasted better than Hamish's usual attempts. Taking a sip, she wrinkled her nose at the bitter brew and sighed. The men burst out laughing.

"What's so funny?" she asked grumpily.

"You are." Rio laughed again.

She sucked in air as she watched laughter transform Rio's face. Even when he scowled, as he usually did around her, she thought he was gorgeous. When he laughed, his features approached sublime. A dimple creased his cheek, the midnight blue of his eyes deepened, and his straight white teeth framed by those full, sculpted lips—she almost missed what Hamish was saying.

"… and every mornin' ye come downstairs all groggy and needin' yer coffee. Ye take that first sip, hopin' I got it right, and ye wrinkle yer little nose in that endearin' way ye have before ye resign yerself tae bein' polite and drinkin' the whole cup." Hamish chortled. "If ye'd drink tea like a civilized person, ye wouldnae start yer day disappointed."

"It's growing on me, Hamish. In another month or so when I return to the States, I'll probably crave it so much I'll have to send you an airplane ticket so you can fly over to brew me some of your amazingly bad coffee." Another sip, another grimace. "Rio, are you drinking this stuff?"

"Of course not. I watched him make it and decided tea was a more palatable option. He brews tea dark enough to pass for coffee anyway." Rio gestured to her with his cup before taking a drink. "You should try some."

"Old habits are hard to break. Maybe from now on you should let me make my own coffee, Hamish."

"Och, what would be the fun in that, lass?" he asked, and Rio chuckled.

Ceri rolled her eyes at the two men and seated herself for breakfast. First, she dished up a big bowl of porridge followed by a little of everything else on the table, eggs, beans, and sausage, which she placed on a plate beside her bowl. After having mostly skipped dinner the night before, she was hungry. She looked up and caught Rio watching her with wide-eyed fascination as she tucked into a man-sized breakfast.

"What?" she asked after swallowing a bite of porridge.

He blinked and said nothing. Hamish grinned from under his bushy white eyebrows and kept his mouth shut too, for once.

Recovering himself, Rio addressed Hamish. "As I was saying, I need to see the entire house including the fuse box and all the places where electrical and phone lines come in before I can map a plan for securing this place. I brought a big system, but after the short tour last night, I'm not sure I have everything." He glanced around the room and up at the ceiling like he was already working.

"Since you've lived here a long time, would you take me on a tour of the house after breakfast please?"

"I'd show ye around, but I have an appointment in town this mornin'. Ceri's been all through the house several times already. She can show ye what ye need tae know."

She snapped to attention. "I thought we needed to make another morning round of chants today. Did I misunderstand?"

"Take yer security expert here on a tour this mornin', and we'll dae what we need tae dae later." Hamish delicately wiped his mouth with his napkin before he stood and carried his dishes to the sink.

The jovial mood of the morning abruptly degenerated into a tense knot in Ceri's stomach. Rio excused himself from the table and cleaned up after himself. Everything about this man attracted her, which meant she needed to get him out of her house as quickly as possible. With those thoughts in mind, she determined to start on the home tour immediately.

CHAPTER SIX

IT PAINED CERI to upset the old man, but she didn't feel safe in the manor. The security system was a good idea, which Hamish would see in time—she hoped. She also hoped he didn't stay in town too long. Being alone with Rio Sheridan was going to try her patience to the very last degree.

Starting with a converted storage area right off the kitchen, she showed Rio the electrical system for the manor.

"All lines—phone, internet, and electrical are housed here?" She nodded.

"That set-up might save space, but it leaves the house vulnerable. An intruder only needs to be in one place to cut off all communication," he said as he checked lines and connections. "I'll move the internet and phone lines as I wire in the security system."

He wrote something in his notes.

Hamish's rooms were another problem. "Why is this locked?" he asked.

"It's Hamish's private space. He won't let me in there—he believes I'll mess up his druidic tools."

Rio cocked an eyebrow "Really?"

She shrugged. "He stays out of my space, so I stay out of his."

"That's fine for living arrangements, but for securing this place, I need to access his room no matter what he keeps in there. If there are windows to the outside, they need to be wired into the system. Even one breach could leave the entire system vulnerable." His tone brooked no argument.

Privately, she agreed with him.

"Good luck convincing Hamish."

Rio's eyes lit up when she guided him into the enormous dining room. "I wonder what this place would have been like back in the day when the family entertained the warrior community after a hard-fought battle or during a holiday feast," he said as he ran his hand along the length of the table.

She tried not to notice the perfect symmetry of his fingers, the size of his hand—she tried not to think about it caressing her body.

Clearing her throat, she said, "I never would have taken you for a romantic, Rio Sheridan."

He shrugged. "I studied history in college. Mainly military history, but I liked all of it, European history especially. If these walls could talk, imagine the stories they could tell." He gazed at the dark oak paneling and the landscapes and family portraits spaced along the walls before he turned to her and smiled.

If she hadn't found him attractive before, this relaxed smiling Rio would have done it. As it was, she struggled to form a coherent thought.

Turning away from temptation, she walked over to the fireplace. "The woman over the mantel is Fianna Conlan, the matriarch of the clan and founder of this house. According to Hamish, she hosted all sorts of the parties you describe." Pointing to her left, she said, "Behind the fireplace is a hidden stairwell down to the kitchen so grand dinners could be served by discreet servants who seemed to appear and disappear as if by magic, or so Hamish tells me."

Get a grip, girl. You're gushing.

"Next is upstairs."

She hustled from the dining room and ascended the stairs to the second floor. They toured bedrooms along the hall until she reached hers at the end of it.

"Very nice. Modern."

"There's a trust for the upkeep of the manor. My aunt, who sits on the board, advised them of my tastes, so they renovated this room for me. The bathroom is through here," she said leading the way. "Since it has a window, you should probably look at it too."

Seeing Rio in her private space made her itch. He looked entirely too perfect there.

"Whew. This is some bathroom, lady. Jacuzzi tub and stand-alone shower big enough for two." He ran his hand over the black marble tile of the shower walls.

"Back in the day, this bathroom was a dressing room for the master suite, and the adjoining bedroom would have belonged to the mistress of the manor. Don't worry, I keep the door between the rooms locked at all times," Ceri added quickly when Rio raised an eyebrow. He'd trained that look on her often enough she knew it meant he didn't believe her.

"On to the third floor," she said, sounding fake to her own ears as she led the way out of her room.

On the third floor, they checked out more bedrooms. When she showed him the grand ballroom taking up the side of the mansion opposite the bedrooms, Rio grinned. The dreamy look on his face stole her breath. Somehow, she knew what he imagined even though she couldn't breach his shield. She'd had the same reaction the first time she'd stepped into this room weeks ago.

She'd pictured eighteenth-century dandies dancing reels with full-skirted ladies. An adjoining refreshment and card room called to mind parties lasting well into the wee hours of the morning. However, her enjoyment of the ballroom and its antechamber was tempered by the amount of chanting each had required. These rooms more than any others in the house, except perhaps for her own rooms and the dining room, had most exhausted her when she and Hamish executed the druidic securities for the manor.

Seating herself on one of the high-backed chairs lining the walls of the room, she awaited Rio's perusal of the space. The fireplace at one end didn't seem large enough to warm it, yet she knew with a room full of dancing people, that fireplace would emit more than enough heat. A dais opposite the fireplace could host a band. Electrical outlets lined the wall behind the dais, implying in modern times the ballroom had been put to its appointed use.

Cream-colored swag drapes with deep blue abstract floral patterns covered the tall windows. The drapes needed dusting. Perhaps when the men determined the house secure enough, she could address some of the more obvious cleaning that had been neglected for a while.

Rio interrupted her reverie. "This is quite a room."

"I can picture a ceilidh in here. Maybe Hamish and I will host one sometime before I leave."

"A kay-lee? He mentioned that before."

"It's a Scottish party with pipers and singers, sword dancing and haggis. Everyone drinks whisky and has a big time. 'Course, it might be too much fun for someone who would rather spend his time scowling over his beer at a party."

Her reference to his behavior at his brother's wedding changed the mood, and she regretted her words as soon as she said them.

He made a noncommittal sound. "Is this it? Hamish said something about accessing the roof."

"I almost forgot. You can go up there two ways: through a trapdoor in the attic or by using a ladder on a balcony outside that window." She pointed to one nearest the dais. "I can't imagine why outside access is necessary, but there it is," she babbled as she led him out of the ballroom to a door at the end of the hall. Fishing the master key Hamish had given her from her jeans pocket, she unlocked it. The door creaked as she pulled it open to show Rio the steep stairs leading to the attic.

As he climbed up ahead of her, she admired the view. His long legs ate up the stairs, and his firm ass in the tight-fitting Levi's he preferred gave her thoughts that would have confirmed his low opinion of her if he could hear them. Forgetting to pay attention to her footing, she stumbled, crying out as she grabbed the banister.

"You all right?"

"Yeah." She huffed out a mirthless laugh. "First day with the new feet."

She let out a breath of relief when he resumed the climb into the attic. Chalk up clumsiness to the list of poor traits Rio probably despised about her.

"Where is the roof access?" he asked from the top of the stairs.

"Right over here."

She led him around an old wardrobe to a short set of stairs located in the middle of the room.

After she unlocked the trapdoor at the top of the stairs, she turned to let him pass her to lift it since it had proved too heavy for her when she tried with Hamish. Rio, not noticing she had no intention of continuing up through the door, ran right into her.

As their bodies collided, she could swear she saw sparks fly in the dim light of the room, and he didn't look quite so indifferent to her as he had when they'd danced at Alyssa and Rowan's wedding. For a long moment, they stared at each other unmoving, and she had the uncomfortable idea he might kiss her. The thought thrilled and terrified her. But his mask dropped again.

"What are you doing? Are you trying to injure both of us?" he growled.

"N-no. The door is too heavy for me. I was trying to move out of the way so you could open it. Sorry."

She squeezed past him along the rail.

He blew out a breath and pushed the heavy door aside with more force than seemed necessary.

Once he was on the roof, he extended a hand to her and then seemed to think better of it. Instead, he stepped out of her way.

"Hamish brought you up here? Why would he bring you to such a dangerous place?"

With his hands planted on his hips, he looked around at the fans, pipes, and chimneys protruding through the roof.

"We have to chant over all of the manor, not only the inside," she said in Hamish's defense.

Rio didn't relent. "This roof is dangerous, especially with that low balustraded rail surrounding it." He stepped over to it. "It barely reaches me midthigh." He glanced over the edge. "If one were caught too close to this railing in a wind—or a battle—it wouldn't take much to plummet three stories to certain death." He glared at her. "You said there's an external way up here too?"

"It's back here accessed from a balcony outside the ballroom."

Rio walked over to the side of the roof at the back of the manor and inspected the ladder. "Did Hamish say why there's external access?"

"No, but we did climb it to come up here once. He wanted me to do it again, but I almost retched the first time. Even chanting couldn't keep my mind off the fall I would have taken if I'd lost my footing on that ladder."

She shuddered at the memory.

Rio swore viciously under his breath.

"Part of the security system will include alarms should anyone try to access the ladder from the ballroom. That thing is too dangerous for words," he said heatedly as he took one last look over the edge of the roof. Turning back to her, he asked, "Is that everything?"

"You've seen the entire manor, bottom to top."

"Except for Hamish's rooms."

There was an implied threat in his comment. He turned his attention to the notebook he carried and made some notations. Once finished, he followed her down into the attic.

"We've been touring all morning. Are you hungry? Would you like some lunch?"

"Yeah. That would be great. Thanks."

He pulled the door closed and locked it before following her out of the attic.

૭

As Ceri warmed the leftover shepherd's pie, she wondered at Rio's moods. At the start of their house tour, he came across as all professional interest in the manor. When he saw her room, he seemed to heat up, making her acutely aware of him as a man. In the dining room and ballroom, he'd seemed entranced and approachable, which she'd spoiled with her ill-timed comment. In the attic, he was by turns grumpy and something electrifying. On the roof, he seemed angry and secretive, like he knew things she couldn't possibly know but should. Rio Sheridan was an enigma—and far too attractive for her own good.

While she busied herself making lunch, he sat at the oak table and made notes and diagrams of the house. "From what I've seen, I'm seriously underprepared with equipment. I'll email Isla to ship more ASAP. But I can wire the kitchen, the pantries, and depending on what Hamish is hiding"—he shot her a look—"Hamish's rooms as well as the main floor with what I brought with me." He returned his attention to his sketches.

"It's a start. Anyway, lunch is ready."

As if on cue, Hamish walked through the back door.

"I made it in the nick o' time. Set out another place, won't ye, please, lass? I'm famished," he said jovially as he hung up his coat on a rack inside the door.

Looking over Rio's shoulder, he said, "I see ye've finished yer tour o' the manor. Dae ye reckon ye brought enough electronic gadgets tae keep out the bad guys?" His tone said he didn't take Ceri's fears seriously at all.

She glared at him.

Rio didn't rise to the bait. "Actually, I only have enough equipment for this part of the house and the main floor." Leaning back casually in his chair, he shot the druid a bland look. "I need to see your room Hamish. Ceri's master key didn't fit the lock on it."

"Nae need tae worry about my room. There's nae access tae it from the outside, so nae one can get in without a key," Hamish said amiably as he seated himself at the table.

"Is that right?"

Ceri tensed at Rio's drawl as she joined them at the table.

All of Rio's pretend calmness evaporated. "I noticed a window outside corresponding directly with your room, Hamish, so you want to try that again?"

"Did ye try tae take a peek inside, lad? Bet ye couldnae see anythin' since I boarded it up. The work I dae in there with my herbs requires a cool, dark space, and curtains still let in some light. So ye see, nae need fer security when I got my own." Dismissing Rio, he turned to Ceri. "Please dish me up some o' that pie, will ye lass? It's always better the second day."

She breathed a small sigh of relief when Rio let the matter drop. Though she too wondered what Hamish hid in his room, she didn't want the two men to come to blows over lunch.

"What were you doing in town, Hamish?" she asked.

"Buyin' groceries. This great brute of a warrior ye invited here eats like he's preparin' fer battle." Hamish grinned. "Ye can help me carry 'em in after lunch, lad."

"I'm always prepared for battle, Hamish. That's what it means to be born a warrior."

"Will ye need tae dae some trainin' while ye're here?"

"I hadn't thought so when I left home, but after seeing the size of the job, I'll probably be here for a while. So yeah, I'll need to train while I'm here. Is there a training room nearby?"

Ceri's heart leapt at the idea Rio would be spending more time at the manor. As quickly as she reacted, she furiously tamped down her emotions. Him being here for an extended stay would be torture.

"As a matter o' fact, there's a room at the base of *An Teallach*, the big Munro across the loch. I'll take ye there when ye're ready."

At Rio's questioning glance, Hamish continued, "*An Teallach* is the tall mountain ye see across Loch Broom from the village." Turning to Ceri, he added, "Perhaps ye should come along when I take Rio tae train, lass. It's good fer talismans tae see warriors train. Let's ye know more about what ye need tae dae tae help them when the time comes."

Rio's eyebrows disappeared beneath a lock of hair on his forehead. Then he schooled his features and stuffed in another mouthful of food.

"In the meantime, if ye donnae mind, I need the lass this afternoon. I'm sure ye have much tae dae with them drawin's I saw ye makin' when I came in."

"Yeah, I need to construct a grid for the system and determine the best places to move the phone and internet lines. Having everything all together—phone, internet, electrical panel—might seem efficient, but it's dangerous if the house is ever attacked."

"Hadn't thought o' that. Guess that's why the lass hired ye. Ceri, we need tae dae some harvestin' out in the gardens taeday. We'll dae the bare minimum so as not tae tire ye out before we meet our friends at the pub this evenin'."

Rio's head snapped up. Ceri squirmed and looked down at her meal.

"I don't know, Hamish. Rio and I went over every square inch of the manor this morning, and right now I think I could go for a nap. If we spend the afternoon in the gardens, I won't be able to stay awake for dinner let alone an evening at the pub."

"Och, lass, how is Rio going tae meet people here if we donnae take him out?"

Studiously avoiding eye contact with Rio, she said, "Maybe the two of you can go. You can get to know each other better."

"And disappoint the lads?" Hamish looked positively aghast. "I donnae think they'll let me in the pub if ye're not with me." Mischief danced in his eyes.

With a sigh, she sneaked a peek at Rio who scowled.

Standing, she began clearing the table. Hamish and Rio took the hint and carried their dishes to the sink.

"It's too crowded here for three of us. How 'bout the two of you bring in the groceries you said you bought, Hamish, and I'll clean up lunch."

"Great idea, lass. Come on, lad. Let's unload my car."

What was Hamish doing? Matchmaking and trying to make Rio jealous were equally bad plans. She didn't know when Rio had tried his sign on her, but at some point, he must have done so, and the fact they weren't destined for each other had to be obvious to Hamish. He was up to something. Ceri wished she could figure out what—and how to stop him.

CHAPTER SEVEN

"HAMISH, OLD FRIEND! Good tae see ye!" a guy about Rio's age called out when the three of them walked through the door of the Anchor. "Did ye bring along yer pretty relative, I hope?"

"'Course I did, not that it'll do the likes o' ye any good," Hamish said, laughing.

The guy grinned at Hamish over his beer before calling out to Ceri. "Hello lass. Ye're lookin' as beautiful as ever. Shall I order ye a pint, or are ye havin' the usual?" he said with a deliberate stare in Rio's direction.

"The usual, Davy. In this place, a girl needs to keep her wits about her," she said as she approached him.

Though Rio kept his expression bland, inwardly, he seethed. *"The usual?" So, she's made at least one conquest so far. Why am I so attracted to a confirmed flirt?* He balled his fists in his pockets. *This guy looks to be in fighting shape, and he clearly has designs on her. Dammit.*

After she accepted a bottle of mineral water and a glass of ice from the bartender, she widened her eyes at Rio who didn't budge at all.

Seemingly oblivious to Rio's little drama with Ceri, Hamish made introductions. "This is Rio Sheridan, a friend o' Ceri's from the States. He's here tae dae some work fer her at the manor. Rio, this is Davy Sutherland, a very good friend o' mine."

He turned to the man and extended his hand. "Pleasure to meet you, Davy." It wasn't. "What are you drinking?"

"Stout."

Rio signaled the bartender. "I'll have what he's having and pour the man another. Hamish, what can I get you?"

Hamish ordered a pint of stout too and nodded at Rio. An annoying grin played about the old man's mouth.

"How are you and Hamish gettin' along in that big old house of yers, Ceri?" Davy asked, gesturing at the barstool beside him, which Ceri, of course, sat on.

"Hamish is teaching me all kinds of things about the house and gardens. It's quite daunting, to be honest. But I'm enjoying the place. Hopefully, we'll take a break soon and go exploring." She directed her comments to Hamish over the top of her glass. "Hamish promised to show me the sights, but so far he hasn't delivered."

"All in good time, lass," Hamish said and blinked as though a thought had struck him. "Davy, you could take Ceri on a tour, maybe show her Loch Broom, take a ferry out tae the Summer Isles fer the day."

"It would be my pleasure. What do you think, Ceri?"

She took a sip of water before answering. "That would be great, Davy. I would love to see the loch and the Summer Isles."

Apparently thinking he'd won the second round, Davy turned to Rio. "What is it Ceri asked ye tae do at the manor, if ye donnae mind my askin'."

"Some specialized consulting." He let the innuendo hang.

"That so?" Davy turned back to Ceri. "Nothin' someone from around here could do?"

"I know Rio's family's work, so I thought of them first. No offense I hope," Ceri said with a nervous-looking smile.

He tipped his glass in Davy's direction.

Round three to me.

"None taken, lass. Just wonderin' is all. Ye've been at the manor fer nearly a month, and there's been no official welcome. When's the ceilidh, Hamish?"

"Around Samhain, I expect. Still some things tae dae tae settle Ceri properly. Donnae worry, Davy, ye'll be the first tae know." Hamish's eyes twinkled.

Rio gave serious consideration to dumping the old man on the side of the road on the drive back to the manor.

"Ye ever been tae a ceilidh, Rio?" Davy asked.

"Haven't had the pleasure—yet. Hamish tells me they're quite a party."

"They are at that." Davy went fishing. "Will ye be around until Samhain fer the one at Conlan Manor?"

Rio stood a little closer behind Ceri. "Depends on how my consulting goes. From what I can tell, it's a distinct possibility."

Round four to me too.

"Lass, ye look a might tired. Guess we should call it a night," Hamish said with an eye on Ceri.

"Hamish, ye're actin' like an old man. Ye've only had one pint," Davy protested.

"It has been a long day. I'm ready to head back too," Rio said as he downed the rest of his pint at a go.

"I hope ye're in better form taemorrow night."

Rio shot Davy a questioning look, which he ignored.

"We'll make plans soon fer that ferry trip, Ceri," he added.

"Oh yes. That'll be fun."

He knew it was wrong, but Rio couldn't help his smirk at the lack of enthusiasm he heard in her voice.

Either Davy didn't notice or pretended not to. "Tell Hamish

tae slow down. He really doesnae need tae do everythin' at once and wear out the prettiest woman in the whole county," he said as he gave Ceri's hand a squeeze that seemed to Rio to last way too long.

He glared at the action before he caught himself and nodded at Davy. *Round five to you, buddy, but I'm staying at her place for an indefinite time. Then, what the hell's the matter with me? She doesn't belong to either of us, but we're both going to be a problem for her when her warrior finds her if we pursue her.*

Oblivious to the undercurrents swirling between Rio, Ceri, and Davy, Hamish said, "Good night, Davy. Take care," as he led the way out of the pub.

"Yes, good night." Ceri sighed as she slipped off the barstool.

Before following the two out of the pub, Rio bent down and whispered in Davy's ear. "You *do* know she's a talisman, which means she belongs to a warrior, not a druid."

"That's not always the way it works, friend," Davy responded in a low tone.

"Let her be," Rio growled. "She has a duty to a warrior somewhere, and she won't need any distractions when the time comes for her to fulfill her role."

On that parting shot, he spun on his heel and exited the pub behind Ceri and Hamish.

Ignoring the tense atmosphere in the car on the ride home, Hamish regaled Ceri and Rio with tales of Davy's druidic exploits. "Davy is my most accomplished student. He's destined tae dae great work in his life, saving many warriors and talismans from Morgan's tricks along the way. O' course, it doesnae hurt he's also accomplished with a claymore and trains regularly. Perhaps ye'd like to train with him, Rio?"

"I'd enjoy training with him," he said and didn't even try to sound friendly.

When they arrived at the manor, Hamish had barely put the car in park before Ceri flew out of it, calling good night to the men over her shoulder as she raced inside. Before either man entered the kitchen, she'd already ascended the stairs above the main floor, her long legs taking the flights two stairs at a time. It appeared she couldn't distance herself from them fast enough.

Shifting his eyes from Ceri's retreating figure, Rio lit into Hamish. "I don't know what you're up to, old man, but the games you're playing have life-and-death consequences. Morgan is not the only source of danger to our community." His voice dropped like always when he was angry. "Sometimes the most dangerous situations start within relationships between warriors and druids." He stepped into the old man's space. "You should be careful."

Appearing not the least intimidated by Rio or his veiled threats, Hamish said, "I'm always careful, lad, especially with precious talismans. Ask Ceri about her aunt some time." With that enigmatic response, Hamish left him standing alone in the middle of the kitchen.

What the hell did he mean by that, and how can I get Ceri to tell me about Shanley Conlan?

◈

The routine for Rio's stay continued over the next week as Hamish left Rio and Ceri alone in the mornings and returned in the afternoons. During the mornings, Rio and Ceri worked together to wire the house, establishing a reluctant camaraderie while he tried to deny his attraction to her. In the afternoons, Hamish took her into the gardens for her lessons on the flora the manor grew and the ways Hamish used it. Rio continued to put in security features, using his time alone to add details Ceri hadn't necessarily asked for.

One of his additions included a discreet motion sensor he wired around Hamish's door and attached to a direct line to the guest room where he was staying. He planned to add a second line directly into Ceri's room for when he returned to the States unless Hamish relented and let Rio run security directly into his room. By the weekend, the line would be operational, and Rio thought he might get a handle on the weird noises he too had heard in the house late at night.

Hamish seemed oddly unconcerned about the apparent intruder in the manor, someone who hadn't stopped his activities even after Rio arrived. Rio had the uncomfortable idea Hamish knew exactly who infiltrated the manor, perhaps through Hamish's room. Rio nearly caught the man once when he tried the lock on Rio's door. When Rio chased him down the stairs and out through the French doors in the dining room, he estimated the man to be at least a head taller than Hamish, his movements indicating someone much younger and fit. He had the distinct impression the man was a warrior. Asking Hamish about it yielded nothing more than an assurance that not only was nothing in the manor amiss, but also that all of Rio's security was completely unnecessary.

In the evenings, they went to the pub. On several occasions, Ceri tried to beg off, but Hamish always insisted she come along. Usually, they met Davy and a few of Hamish's local civilian friends, but last night there had been several warriors from the next county in attendance. Rio watched them closely, seeing at least two of them try their signs on Ceri with no effect, much to his tremendous relief. He needed to finish the job and leave Ceri Ross as fast as he could, or something terrible was going to happen—he was going to lose control and take her for himself, consequences be damned.

Today, the routine changed, and his sour mood demonstrated precisely what he thought of that. At dinner the evening before, Hamish had declared that Ceri should take a break and go out on the ferry with Davy. Again, she tried to beg off, using the security system installation as an excuse, but Rio figured out too late that Hamish had cleverly circumvented her. He'd asked Rio earlier about what the plan for today would be, and he'd inadvertently given Hamish the green light to arrange Ceri's excursion. He'd be wiring boxes, work Ceri couldn't help him with.

As he drilled the holes for the main box in the wall beside Ceri's bed, the controls in the master suite where she could access them easily and where they were the most centrally located, Rio swore under his breath. He imagined all sorts of scenarios happening on that ferry, none of them flattering Davy or Ceri, all of them driving him so crazy jealous, he shook with it. Already, he'd had to redo the box on the ground floor twice, and he was on try number three with this one. Knowing he needed to get a grip on himself did nothing to improve his mood.

∽

The beauty of the Highlands stole Ceri's breath. In their vibrant fall coat, the heather glowing russet in the slanted autumnal light, the rugged mountains rose up from the loch to scrape the sky. The ferry etched the mirror of the loch as it glided over its surface. Though Davy proved a delightful companion full of stories and good humor, she couldn't help but think she would've enjoyed the trip even more if a certain dark-haired warrior with midnight blue eyes were standing beside her instead.

Several times Davy had to drag her wandering mind back to him after she'd drifted off to wonder what Rio was doing. Yet, Davy didn't give up easily. After the ferry docked, he offered to treat her to steak and wine before he returned her to the manor.

Knowing she needed to finish the day out of politeness both to Hamish and to Davy, she agreed. But all she wanted to do was return to the manor to gather her thoughts. The last days working with Rio intensified her interest in him, a dangerous situation for her heart. Even though he was usually terse with her, she couldn't help but notice his keen intelligence, the flashes of humor he sometimes let her see, and the patient way he taught her everything about what he was doing as he built her security system. After his instruction, she thought she could install a security system all by herself. Certainly, she'd be able to troubleshoot the one he was building for her.

"Penny for your thoughts?" Davy asked for the fourth or fifth time since he'd picked her up that morning.

"Sorry. I was thinking about my friend Alyssa. She'd love the tour you took me on today."

"Why would that be?" he asked with a gentle smile.

"She's a Celtic scholar, and all the stories you told today would probably send her off to a library for a month researching their origins. She would have especially liked the one about the lonely giant, Angus MacAskill. Probably, she'd be holed up on her computer directly after dinner searching university data bases for the Blue Bay or deciding that something like the estuary where Loch Broom meets the sea would be the ideal location for such a bay." She smiled at him. "It's a lovely story, you know, how the giant changes form in order to have his true love, no matter how that change affected him."

Davy clapped his hands in delight. "So ye *were* listenin'."

"Of *course* I was listening. Your stories are wonderful."

She'd been miles away for at least part of the day, so she couldn't blame him for the gentle dig.

"I have lots more where those came from. It's a druid's lot tae be a storyteller as well as a wise man and a healer, ye know."

He spent the next hour and a half regaling her with more fables and tales as they savored their dinner. She enjoyed herself immensely as he gave her no time to think about anything other than the next story until her day caught up to her, and she tried to yawn discreetly into her palm.

"Time tae go, lass," he said, his smile a little sad.

When they crested the hill leading to the manor, she couldn't help but watch for lights in Rio's room. Seeing none, she knew she should be glad she wouldn't have to face his attitude, but for some reason disappointment filled her. He'd hardly said two words to her since dinner last night, yet to her everlasting humiliation, she missed him, even his sarcasm and disapproval. At least when he censured her, she had his attention.

Davy pulled up to the back of the house like he'd done it a million times. Hoping to avoid any awkwardness, like a kiss good night, Ceri turned to him and thanked him in the adroit way she'd developed with civilian dates she didn't want to encourage, extending her hand and smiling in an overtly friendly way. He chuckled at the brush-off and wished her good night with good grace and a chivalrous brush of his lips over her knuckles.

Letting herself in quietly through the back door into the dark kitchen, she nearly jumped a foot when a deep voice from some-where behind her snarled. "How was your date with the druid? Did he have to practice his magic on you, or did you make it easy for him?"

It took her several breaths to control her heartbeat before she rounded on Rio. "You waited up for me. That's so nice of you, Dad, but I'm a big girl, so you don't have to do that anymore." Her voice dripped sweetness.

"You didn't answer my question."

"It's none of your business," she ground out before making a beeline for the stairs.

Rio was quick and stepped in front of her as she crossed in front of the scarred oak table. "I'm making it my business. A tal-isman who dates a druid is begging for trouble."

"You don't have a horse in this race, so walk away Rio and let me be."

"I'm a warrior, and I'll do whatever I can to help other warriors find their talismans, even—especially—if that means keeping a talisman away from a druid."

"Is that why you resent Siobhan so much, because she 'stole' a warrior from a talisman?" Sarcasm oozed from her lips.

Which Rio ignored. "That whole relationship is unnatural."

"Sometimes fate isn't what we anticipate, but in the end, we have no choice but to accept it. Excuse me please," she said quietly as she tried once again to step around him.

"No, fate isn't always what we anticipate it to be."

She heard Rio's thought right before he put his hands on her shoulders and inclined his head to kiss her. Stunned, she didn't resist. Instead, she relaxed into his touch. When he brushed his lips over hers, she couldn't hide her sigh. When he slipped his tongue into her mouth, she met him eagerly with her own. As if they had a mind of their own, her hands slid up the hard plane of his chest and over the bunched muscles of his shoulders to meet behind his neck. She fingered his silky chestnut curls with her right hand while she clung to his shoulders with her left hand. Her nipples pebbled beneath her sweater as his hands explored their way down and up the sides of her torso until he slipped them around her back and pulled her tightly against him.

He tasted faintly of beer and man, which intoxicated her far more than the little bit of wine she'd drunk at dinner. Tilting his head, he changed the angle of the kiss, deepening it, and she wanted to climb him like a tree, losing herself in the heat and wonder of Rio Sheridan. The heat intensified until at last, some semblance of sense must have crept into his mind, and he tore his mouth away from hers. He was panting when he touched his forehead to hers. She had to work to slow down her breathing and regain her self-control.

In that moment, his insinuations from when she'd walked in the door flooded her mind. "Well, at least the only man I kissed tonight was a warrior. That should keep me in good stead with

those who wish to maintain boundaries within the warrior community," she whispered shakily.

Instead of the anger she expected for her smart-ass comment,
he laughed hollowly and said, "Touché," before he dropped his
hands and stepped aside for her to pass.

Ceri walked unsteadily to the stairs, grabbing the handrail
to climb the two flights to her bedroom. As she started up the
second flight, she heard him swear softly to himself and thought
she understood Rio's frustration. She felt a lot of it herself.

CHAPTER EIGHT

HE NEXT MORNING, Hamish hummed as he dished up breakfast, ignoring Rio's bad mood. Uncharacteristically, he didn't comment when Ceri didn't come down to breakfast.

"Ye've been hard at it fer a couple o' weeks now. How much work dae ye have tae dae tae make this place 'secure' enough tae suit our girl—and yerself?"

At the reference to "our girl," Rio ducked farther down into his breakfast than he'd already tried to go, stuffing his mouth with sausage and eggs. Ceri's absence chafed his already-raw conscience. What was he thinking kissing her like that? Like she'd said, her date with Davy was none of his business. But he couldn't stop himself from waiting for her, baiting her, kissing her—that part most of all. What if he turned out to be as flawed as his late uncle's talisman who'd cost his uncle and her their lives? What if he denied fate the way she had? He knew the answer, which didn't make him feel any better about his behavior—or his thoughts about a certain beautiful talisman.

"As I was sayin', how much more work dae ye have?" Hamish asked again, a twinkle in his tone.

Swallowing his mouthful of food, Rio said pointedly, "The two upstairs floors—and your rooms," his surly mood finding a target.

Hamish didn't rise to Rio's bait. "Well then, ye're half-way there."

He sighed. "Yeah, but I'm about out of gear. I'm waiting on my order from the States."

"Did ye try tae find what ye need here?"

"Our equipment is made especially for our company by a group of warriors in America. Rather fitting businesses for war-riors, don't you think?"

He only revealed half the truth—even if the equipment had been readily available somewhere in Scotland, he didn't want Hamish to know exactly what he installed in the manor as another layer of protection for Ceri. He didn't entirely trust the old man with his locked room, his mysterious morning disappearances, and his insistence on putting Ceri on display in front of the local single civilians, druids, and warriors nearly every night of the week.

"Aye lad, protectin' civilians is always a noble pursuit." Hamish poured himself more tea from the pot resting on a trivet on the table. "Since ye seem tae be at a stoppin' point, ye might think about havin' some fun." He added milk and savored a sip. "We're invited tae a ceilidh taenight, and most of the local popu-lation will be there. Perhaps ye want tae attend."

From Ceri's and Hamish's descriptions, the evening sounded like something designed to tear his guts out watching her flirt with civilians, warriors, and druids. He didn't know if he could face it. A vision of his own behavior flashed in his mind, and he reprimanded himself for a being fool. The party might be an opportunity for him to find his mate since there would probably be several unattached talismans in attendance. Besides, he couldn't do any more on the security system without additional gear, which wouldn't arrive in Scotland for days.

"Sure Hamish, sounds like a plan," he agreed and wondered what he'd do until evening with Ceri avoiding him like the plague.

Seeming to read his mind, Hamish said, "What dae ye say tae takin' a boat ride with me? I'll show ye the trainin' room hidden inside o' *An Teallach*."

Knowing training would take his mind off his beautiful employer, he readily agreed to spend the day with Hamish. It took all his willpower not to stop at her room, though, to check on her before they left. But he thought he saw her curtains move when he looked up at her windows as they drove away.

⁓

Ceri discreetly watched Rio and Hamish drive away, leaving her alone and curiously bereft. She should be happy she didn't have to face Rio first thing in the morning after making a fool of herself with him.

On a sigh, her thoughts turned to the ceilidh they'd be attending in the evening, and she wondered if Hamish had extended an invitation to Rio. Perhaps his plan was to tire Rio to the point where he'd want to spend the evening alone at the manor. That way, she could be pursued in peace without him silently branding her a flirt for doing what talismans were expected to do—find a warrior and support him in his battles against Morgan's incessant wars and other assorted evil activities.

The idea of Rio spending the evening alone while everyone else enjoyed the party certainly didn't make her feel festive. On the other hand, the idea of catching him looking at her censoriously with that arched eyebrow, his arms crossed over his massive chest, took away some of her anticipation for attending another ceilidh.

The uniquely Scots party gave Ceri such pleasure. The music, the dancing, the piping in of the haggis, all of it pulled at some deep part of her psyche. From the very first one she attended, she felt a connection to these people and this place. Certainly,

Hamish had had much to do with her response—he did cook all her meals after all, and she wasn't so naïve as to believe he did so solely because he loved to cook—she thought she'd have felt the connection on her own anyway. The people's happy camaraderie and easy acceptance of others mirrored her approach to the world.

Today, she felt a vague sense of dread about the party.

To occupy herself while she had some time alone, she decided to walk around the grounds of the manor. Since the day dawned cool but sunny, she thought a wander might be the thing to clear her head. Rio's kiss—and her embarrassingly eager response to it—never strayed far from her thoughts. Banishing last night's encounter from her mind was paramount if she had any chance at all of being her best at the party.

As she dressed in skinny jeans, a cotton T-shirt, and a wool sweater, she laughed. When she left home over a month ago, she couldn't imagine herself not being the height of fashion once she arrived in Scotland. Now she discovered she was much more comfortable in hiking boots, jeans, and a sweater knitted by a local artisan than in designer skirts and blouses. Of course, she didn't need to dress professionally when she wasn't selling real estate, but her casual fashion amused her. It would have made Alyssa, with her antipathy for shopping and indifference to fashion, laugh to see *her*, Ceri-the-fashion-plate, so dressed down. No doubt Shanley would be hard-pressed to stop from saying *I told you so*.

Her mood somewhat restored, she stopped in the kitchen and warmed a bowl of leftover porridge and a mug of Hamish's famously bad coffee for breakfast. Afterward, she filled a flask with water and set out to explore.

At first, she meandered in no apparent direction, soaking up sunshine and the beauty of the surrounding hills. After a while, she unconsciously headed for the corner of the property Hamish had subtly steered her away from after her arrival. Topping a low hill, she caught sight of a tiny stone house that appeared to be inhabited.

The area around the house didn't look disturbed. In fact, there were no paths or tracks around it at all to indicate someone spent time there. Yet, if it had been abandoned, it would have been in disrepair. The chimney looked in perfect condition, straight and well-constructed. The door and shutters over the windows sported freshly painted black hinges. There were no visible chinks where stones had dislodged or mortar had rotted away. Everything about the cottage indicated either Hamish had a secret hideaway, or someone else was squatting on her property.

While she concentrated on the enigma of the stone cottage, she let her guard down. As she tried to determine whether or not to investigate further, the hairs on the back of her neck stood on end, and her heart leaped into her throat as a picture of her aunt alone on the road near the manor jumped into her mind.

Attempting to disguise her instant, intense fear, she inventoried her surroundings, working in a panoramic motion from right to left. A quick flash of light behind her caught her attention, and she turned to face the danger she instinctively knew she'd find.

A tall warrior stood not twenty feet from her. The sun glinting off his claymore had been the flash to alert her she wasn't alone. The man wore his shoulder-length auburn hair tied back in a neat pony tail. His beard and mustache, a slightly darker shade than his hair, were trimmed close to his face. Though not quite as tall as Rio, he cleared six feet. A few stray gray hairs glinted in his hair and beard, but his broad shoulders and narrow waist indicated a man in prime fighting condition.

Ceri worked to quell the rising tide of panic inside her. Only a rogue would be out here on her property alone. But unlike Shanley all those years ago, Hamish wasn't around to save her. She couldn't outrun this man, but she hoped he couldn't follow her as she visualized herself into the Anchor. As she closed her eyes to see her destination, the warrior spoke.

"Ye must be Ceri Ross."

Her eyes flew open. "H-how do you know my name?"

"Hamish told me ye were coming. I've been awaitin' the Conlan heir a long time."

"Who are you?"

She backed up a step. If she put distance between them, she might have a better chance of escaping. Using visualization required several seconds, and this man looked like he could move like lightning.

"A friend. I've been lookin' after yer home fer many years."

"N-no. Hamish looks after Conlan Manor."

She took another small step away.

"Hamish takes care o' the spiritual aspects o' the manor. I look after the physical ones, like keepin' the place sound and free o' unwanted visitors."

"Like the person who's been wandering around inside it every night since I moved in? Sorry, but I don't believe you. Before you attempt to kill me with that claymore, will you tell me how long you've been a rogue?"

She took another step backward.

The warrior's face clouded. "I'm nae rogue lass. True, I'm past the age when I should have found my talisman, but I went tae ground rather than join the Morrigan. Watchin' over yer manor has kept me safe for a long time. Hamish's protections are very powerful." He folded one hand over the other on the hilt of his sword resting on its tip as he held it in front of himself.

"What's your name?"

"Alaisdair Graham. I'm distantly related tae the Conlan clan, which is why Hamish's protections have worked for me. I live over there." With the tip of his sword, he pointed at the cottage. "But I spend a lot o' time with Hamish at the manor."

"Why haven't you introduced yourself sooner? Why didn't Hamish bring me over here when he walked me around the property? Why should I believe a word you say?" she blurted.

"Until ye arrived, we thought it might be a rumor the Morrigan started as a trap, that story about yer friends levelin' the playin' field fer warriors. So I laid low." He sheathed his sword in the scabbard behind his back. "Then yer friend, the warrior, showed up, and I thought it best tae stay away so as not tae start somethin' with him. But now ye're here, and while I would rather this happened inside the manor, I canna take a chance on never havin' another opportunity."

"What are you…?" Ceri didn't finish her question before Alaisdair Graham stood directly behind her.

She'd forgotten one of the most important weapons a warrior possessed—supernatural speed. In the time it took her to form her question, he'd leaped into the future a few seconds and had her exactly where he wanted her—less than an arm's length away.

Tensing for the blow that would end her life, and indeed Alaisdair flexed his sword arm drawing her attention to the enormous blade that would make short work of her, she closed her eyes. As suddenly as he stood behind her, he stood in front of her, sheathing his sword again in its scabbard. The look on his face was so bleak she couldn't help but feel sorry for the man though she couldn't understand why he hadn't attacked.

"All these years Hamish and I waited for ye tae grow up and come over here. We thought ye were the prophesied one, the one tae give protections tae the Conlan clan for ten generations—and also my talisman. But ye're not. At least ye're not my talisman."

Ceri blinked in confusion.

"When yer friends gave warriors back our extended time tae find our talismans, we thought 'twas a sign ye were meant tae be mine."

"You tried your sign on me?" she asked incredulously. "When?"

"Just now when I distracted ye with my sword."

"Oh."

She watched him warily.

"Lass, I'm truly not a rogue. If I were, ye would have been dead when ye stopped tae puzzle out my house. I am who I say I am. Taenight at the ceilidh, ye'll see."

"You're invited to the ceilidh?" Why she was surprised, she couldn't say.

"Aye. I thought I'd make yer acquaintance taenight and try my sign on ye at the party at the manor on Samhain tae fulfill the prophecy, but ye were shakin' with fear, and I've been waitin' so long that I gave in tae temptation and gave it a go just now." Alaisdair sighed heavily.

"I havnae been tae a ceilidh in nearly fourteen years, not since I turned twenty-eight alone." He stared into the distance. "It'll be strange tae be out with people." Training his eyes back on Ceri, he said, "But I'm six months away from turning forty-two, and if I donnae find my mate by then, I'll be lost within the year. Nae one escapes the Morrigan forever."

Two strange ideas flashed into Ceri's mind: one, she believed everything Alaisdair Graham told her, and two, her aunt needed to come to Scotland for the Samhain rituals and ceilidh Hamish planned.

"Let me walk ye back tae the manor. Ye were right tae assume I was a rogue, and yer idea tae visualize yerself tae the Anchor was inspired."

She gasped.

"We're goin' tae have tae work on yer shielding when ye're in danger. Ye dinnae even make it hard fer me tae know where ye were headed," he said ruefully. "Unfortunately, ye're not safe on yer own property outside o' the house itself. Ye shouldnae walk the land alone." Alaisdair motioned for her to walk back in the direction from which she'd come.

Ceri's troubled thoughts returned to him reading her mind when he first confronted her. "My aunt was right. I thought I'd mastered shielding when I was afraid, but she said I had a ways to go. Now what?"

"Has Hamish told ye about the trainin' room at *An Teallach*?"

"I think he took Rio there this morning."

At Alaisdair's questioning glance, she clarified. "Rio Sheridan is here at my request to put in a security system at the manor. Actually, I asked his brother, the man responsible for besting Morgan last year, to come over with his wife to put in a system for me. He had another job to finish, so he sent Rio." She blew out a breath. "Anyway, I saw Rio putting his claymore and his leather jacket into Hamish's car before they headed out this morning, so I assume they're training."

They walked back to the manor over the uneven ground, the dry golden grasses swishing softly against her jeans.

"I know it's none o' my business, but why are ye putting in a security system?"

"Because someone truly has been wandering around inside the manor at night. I don't know how he's getting in, but he's a regular visitor." She shoved her hands in her pockets and glanced up at Alaisdair. "And before you say it, the person is a man, not a ghost or the creaking of an old house at night. I've seen him. I don't feel safe in my own home, so I'm having a system put in to stop his nightly visitations."

When Alaisdair didn't comment, she added, "There's also the fact Morgan uses civilians to breach druidic protections. She tried that with my friend Alyssa, and it nearly worked. I don't want that to happen to me, especially before my warrior finds me."

Alaisdair stopped dead in his tracks. "The Morrigan did *what*?"

Ceri laughed mirthlessly. "That's exactly how Hamish responded, but you can ask Rio. Alyssa had a civilian boyfriend, a real creep, before she met Rowan. Morgan enlisted the man's assistance to break into Alyssa's home and kidnap her or steal the protections her grandmother had put on her house."

Alaisdair resumed walking, picking up the pace, and she had to lengthen her strides to keep up. "The old girl is becoming desperate these days. I donnae blame ye for trying tae add protections tae yer house."

"Exactly." She changed the subject to what really bothered her. "Alaisdair, if you don't find it an intrusion, would it be possible for you to help me with shielding? Since you're apparently connected to the manor, and since I obviously have work to do."

"Hamish hasnae introduced ye tae other warriors?" His voice rose on the question.

"No, I mean yes, but not to any I know I can trust with this," she finished lamely.

"What about yer American friend?"

"Rio?" She huffed out a sad little laugh. "He barely tolerates me. He thinks I'm a terrible flirt. I could never ask him."

"Well, then, I believe we can arrange a trainin' session or two in the near future. We cannae have ye out runnin' loose with yer shield not fully formed," he said smiling at her with affection.

They arrived at the manor in time for lunch, and Ceri invited him to join her. She fixed sandwiches with leftover bread from the day before and some ham and sharp cheese she found in the fridge. To complement the sandwiches, she tossed a salad and asked him if he preferred coffee or tea with his meal. When he indicated tea, she said, "You do the honors."

He quirked a brow.

"Hamish says my tea is weak and tasteless."

"Hamish says ye cannae make good tea? Have ye tried his coffee, lass?"

"It's the worst I've ever tasted, but it's growing on me." She laughed.

As they enjoyed their meal together, he regaled her with funny tales of his and Hamish's adventures over the years, but she could tell he didn't reveal the whole story. There had to be some harrowing times for both of them with Morgan always on the prowl for warriors who hadn't found their mates.

As they finished their lunch, Hamish strolled through the back door to the kitchen followed by a sweaty but smiling Rio—until he saw Ceri seated at the table with Alaisdair.

Hamish didn't seem surprised to see them together. He walked over to Alaisdair and clapped him on the shoulder. "So ye've met the mistress o' Conlan Manor, auld friend." The electric charge between the two men lasted only a second, but Ceri saw it all the same.

Without giving anything away, Hamish went to the cupboard, grabbed a mug, and returned to the table to help himself to tea. "I see ye talked Alaisdair intae makin' the tea." Addressing Alaisdair, he said, "Good thing for ye, friend. Ceri is a fine lass, but not much fer makin' a decent cuppa."

"Do ye even taste yer coffee before ye force it on others, Hamish?" Alaisdair asked with a chuckle.

Though she pretended otherwise, Ceri remained acutely aware of Rio's mood. When he'd walked into the manor, he seemed happy, but the sight of Alaisdair having lunch with her soured him immediately. Judging from the surreptitious glances Hamish slid his way, she had a distinct notion the situation pleased her druid cousin enormously. Why he continued baiting Rio, she couldn't understand. She was the one who had insisted on the security system. Rio was only the help.

Alaisdair interrupted her thoughts. "Ye must be Rio Sheridan. Ceri told me ye came over tae install a security system in the manor, somethin' about a change in Morgan's tactics these days. I'm Alaisdair Graham." He stood and offered his hand. "I'm sort o' the handyman around here for the physical jobs that donnae involve chantin' and such."

"Pleasure to meet you," Rio said as he shook Alaisdair's hand, each man sizing up the other. "But if you don't mind my asking, if you're the handyman, why haven't I seen you these past weeks while I worked on the house?"

He exchanged a glance with Hamish. "I dinnae want tae get in yer way."

"That so? Or is it more about you being a little over twenty-eight and needing a place to hide out?"

"The man doesnae hold back, does he, Hamish?"

"Very straightforward, this one. Ye always know where ye stand with him," Hamish replied.

Alaisdair sat back at the table. "I'm a distant relation to the Conlan clan. When I reached my twenty-eighth birthday alone, I went tae ground here at the manor. Now I understand yer family has bought all of us a little more time, and I thought it would be safe tae show myself."

Rio narrowed his eyes at her. "How long have you known about your 'handyman,' Ceri?"

She counted to five in her head before answering. "I met Alaisdair for the first time this morning as I took a stroll around the grounds."

Hamish rounded on her. "What were ye doin' on the grounds by yerself, lass? Havnae I taught ye anythin' while ye've been here?"

She sighed. It seemed she hadn't the skill to make any man in her life happy with her today. "I'm sorry Hamish. I woke up out of sorts and decided a walk would clear my head. I thought I'd be safe on my own property."

"I warned her about that when I came upon her out near the cottage, Hamish. Before I walked her back tae the manor. All is well." Alaisdair stared at her over the rim of his mug. "She willnae wander around the grounds alone anymore, will ye lass?"

Ceri couldn't help it. She stole a glance at Rio who looked as guilty as she felt.

CHAPTER NINE

HE CEILIDH TOOK place at a farm a short drive up the road from Ullapool. As they passed a campground at the edge of the village, Hamish casually described his friend, Saraid, a powerful female druid, who lived in a caravan there. Sometime soon he'd introduce Ceri to her.

When he'd taken her to previous ceilidhs, Ceri's excitement radiated off her. Tonight, she remained quiet, clearly uncomfortable, a mood echoed in the passenger riding beside Alaisdair in the cramped back seat of Hamish's car.

Sliding a glance in the rearview mirror, he communicated, *"Alaisdair, what dae ye think is going on with these twa?"*

"There's history, but I cannae figure it out. I tried my sign on Ceri almost the minute I met her. I expect Rio did the same, and we were both disappointed. But he cannae seem tae walk away."

"I feel currents o' somethin' powerful runnin' between 'em. We need tae keep both o' them in the manor through Samhain. The lad ordered equipment fer the manor from the States. Ye might need tae intercept it if it comes this week."

"Ye're a devious one, Hamish Buchanan."

Hamish caught a grin ghosting Alaisdair's mouth and inclined his head before launching into a monologue about what Rio could expect from the party.

"This evening is going tae be a real treat fer ye Rio. Lots o' lassies tae dance with and quarts o' whisky tae drink. Once the warriors in attendance realize who ye are and yer part in the battle with the Morrigan last winter, ye'll have more drams o' whisky sittin' in front o' ye than any one man should drink in a year." He glanced back at his passenger and winked.

Rio looked a little green.

⤛

The cheerful glow of lanterns lining the drive greeted them as the four arrived at the farm of the druid hosting the party. Several hundred additional lanterns ringed the barn. "I take it there's a reason for all the lanterns rather than a couple of yard lights," Ceri commented.

"Indeed, lass. We're closin' in on Samhain, the start o' the year, which itself is cause fer celebration. But the wanderers among departed souls who make themselves known on Celtic New Year start gatherin' in these lands several weeks in advance, so we think it best tae light the boundaries of our parties tae keep them in their place till their appointed night." Hamish grinned. "It also helps us see where tae park the car and where tae find the front door," he said as he maneuvered the car into a parking space.

Turning to Alaisdair, she found him grinning at her as well. She smiled to hide her confusion and caught Rio rolling his eyes.

Inside the vast barn, the ceilidh was in full swing. A live band of pipes, drums, guitar, and fiddle played an energetic reel while several people laughed and danced through the cleared space in the middle. Round tables and chairs filled with revelers lined one side of the barn and half the other, interrupted by long tables piled with delectable-looking food. Drams of whisky sat in front of people seated at a bar as they engaged in storytelling, their gales of laughter drawing admiring glances from other party-goers.

Though many dressed in traditional kilts, most of the attendees dressed in casual wear of tweeds and wool trousers and skirts. Ceri relaxed. Her simple A-line wool skirt in a brown herringbone pattern and an emerald green silk blouse accented with the scarf Alyssa had given her fit right in. The approving looks on the faces of some of the matronly women seated at nearby tables told her she'd made the right choice in her evening attire.

The good mood of the party rubbed off on her, and she almost forgot the brooding warrior standing beside her as she smiled and glanced around, her foot tapping to the music. Hamish took her by the elbow and led her off to meet more of his friends—he seemed to know everyone in three surrounding counties.

As they walked away, a tittering sound snagged Ceri's ear, and she looked over her shoulder to see a rather garishly made-up woman step over to introduce herself to Rio. Ignoring the pang of jealousy roiling through her, she returned her attention to Hamish and the man he was introducing her to.

Though she enjoyed dancing with the man whose name was Angus or Magnus, she couldn't quite remember, her eyes kept straying to Rio. She couldn't believe how well he danced a Scots reel. Never having had the chance to learn before coming to Scotland, she continued to work on picking up the steps from a string of willing partners only too happy to overlook her mistakes. Rio's skill intrigued and irked her.

She tripped, and Angus/Magnus caught her, holding her a touch too long before righting her and reminding her of the steps to come in the sequence of the dance. Taking herself firmly in hand, she reminded herself Rio didn't particularly like her, so she needed to concentrate on the tasks before her—learning to dance and having a good time.

As the evening wore on, she lost track of Rio but found herself the object of several warriors' attentions. They seemed to appear out of nowhere, and though she danced with all of them, she noticed nothing out of the ordinary. A weird sense of relief stole over her that none of their signs worked on her. Guilt wormed its way inside her when she reminded herself that finding her warrior was her paramount objective at such a gathering.

Her thoughts strayed to Rio.

Every time she caught sight of him, he never seemed to lack for attention or partners. Showing up to the party in typical American attire of jeans and a charcoal-colored long-sleeved T-shirt under a matching charcoal jacket he discarded early in the evening seemed to add to his appeal with the local ladies. Ceri continuously hauled herself up short whenever her attention wandered to him—and the possibility he'd find his talisman among his admirers.

⌘

A group of warriors, several of them older than twenty-eight, sought Rio out and dragged him over to the bar. They plied him with drams of whisky and insisted he retell the story of Morgan's recent defeat that gave all of them years more time to find their mates. Not having expected this camaraderie among the Scots warriors, he was pleasantly surprised. He'd anticipated animosity over one incredibly beautiful talisman.

Even though he hadn't seen the talisman in question in over an hour, he had no doubt she too was the center of attention somewhere in the party. He wished he could breach her shield to discover if her warrior had miraculously found his way to this shindig. Until the current group of men pulled him away, he hadn't strayed too far from the dance floor where he tortured himself with covertly watching warrior after warrior try their signs on Ceri as she danced with them. The feelings of relief he had each time she didn't respond threatened to overwhelm him. When the warriors invited him over to the bar to drink, he went willingly.

By the time the pipers piped in the haggis, he was a little drunk and in need of food. Moira, the cartoonishly made-up civilian who'd initially welcomed him to the party, came to him bearing two loaded plates, making it clear to everyone she'd staked her claim. The other warriors good-naturedly teased him about conquering the local ladies, and Rio couldn't see a graceful way out of having dinner with her. As she led him to a table, he spied Ceri already seated with a blond warrior who didn't seem too worried about the niceties of flirting with another man's talisman. If he'd been Ceri's warrior, no doubt they would have already left the party together, so she didn't belong to the man.

Trying to ignore Ceri and her lack of proper talisman behavior, he sat down with Moira and let her incessant chatter wash over him as he ate his meal.

"I'm still trying tae figure out how you know how tae dance in the Scots way. I didn't think Americans danced reels," Moira said.

Before he could answer, she kept going. "And ye're so good at them. I was watching, and I don't think there was one reel ye didn't know. Who would have guessed?"

"Thanks, I think," Rio said around a delicious bite of haggis. It surprised him that sheep's innards in a spicy sausage was a dish he could never get enough of.

"From the way ye're puttin' away yer haggis and neeps and tatties, one would think ye ate Scots fare regularly." The look on her face asked the question.

"We celebrate Robbie Burns Day every January in my hometown," he said.

"Isn't that nice. Ye dance and eat haggis at these celebrations?"

"Every year."

"That explains it then." A big smile stretched her lips.

Since Moira was a civilian, Rio didn't see the point of

explaining his parents had taught him how to dance when he was a boy. As a warrior of Scottish descent, he needed to know his cultural heritage to understand what his family fought for over the centuries. Nor did she need to know his dad regularly made traditional dinner of haggis, neeps and tatties and finished with a dessert of berry torte, Rio's favorite meal. The dinner at the ceilidh had been the only part of the evening he'd looked forward to after Hamish invited him. He smiled around a mouthful and didn't contradict her.

✦

The host of the party, Blaine Shaw, an old farmer with a shock of white hair and bushy auburn eyebrows, carried an armload of claymores to the middle of the dance floor. He laid out several sets of the swords in cross patterns and invited young ladies eager to show off their skills to step out of the crowd. The pipers began a spirited tune as the dancers light-footed their way to their places. In fascination, Ceri marveled as the women nimbly danced over and between the razor-sharp blades.

At an earlier ceilidh, Hamish explained that the women learned the sword dance by using wooden swords so as not to cut up their feet on the blades of real ones. When Ceri asked why the blades had to be so sharp, he said the swords were working swords belonging to the men in the families of the dancers. He suggested that should she find her warrior in Scotland, she might want to honor him by learning the sword dance and dancing it with her warrior's claymores, an intriguing idea that terrified her.

The blond warrior named Aiden with whom Ceri had shared supper slipped behind her as she watched the dancers. She looked over her shoulder and caught his eye. "They're magnificent, aren't they?" she said, indicating the dancers with a subtle nod of her head.

"Aye, magnificent," Aiden replied, his eyes never leaving her. She blinked and turned away.

As she returned her attention to the dancers, Rio's scowl invaded her peripheral vision. The ladies hopped agilely inside the squares created with the crossed swords. Normally, their fancy footwork riveted her, but the heat of Rio's glare on her cheek stole her concentration. The pipers sped up their notes, the women's steps matched the musicians' pace, and Ceri's heart pounded at the scorn washing over her from Rio's direction.

The sword dance neared its end in a frenzied blur of feet and spinning kilts before every dancer stopped in perfect balance between the blades on the last note the pipers blew. The women's athleticism, speed, and precision in so complicated a dance left her breathless. With enthusiastic applause, she tried to break Rio's spell over her.

As the druids cleared the dance floor of swords to resume the general dancing, Rio stepped between Aiden and her. "Excuse me"—his tone said otherwise—"I'm claiming the next dance." Glaring at her, he took her by the hand and pulled her onto the floor.

"Usually, one asks a lady if she wants to dance before dragging her onto the dance floor," she fumed.

"True, but you're no lady."

"What's that supposed to mean?"

"You know exactly what it means. Tell me, Ceri, is it necessary to flirt with absolutely every warrior in attendance, even after it's clear you belong to none of them?"

"What are you talking about? All I've done is say yes when I've been asked to dance. We are at a dance after all." She tried to pull away, but he tugged her even closer.

"So that conversation about how beautiful you think Blondie is and how beautiful he thinks you are was about dancing?" Rio snarled.

"I have no idea what you're talking about. Aiden and I were talking about the sword dancing, which you have to admit is stunning. Maybe you should pay better attention when you're eavesdropping."

He glowered down at her then spun her out and back to him—hard.

"Listen, Rio, if the only reason you dragged me out to dance was to berate me for some supposed screw-up you think I've made, then I think we're done." She tried again to disengage herself from his arms.

Pulling her close, he hissed in her ear, "We're already the talk of the party. Do you honestly want to make a scene?"

"That's rich coming from you, Mr. I-dragged-you-out-here-to-tell-you-off," she hissed back.

Smiling thinly at a couple who danced too close to them, he spun with her toward the edge of the dance floor as the band wrapped up one tune and launched immediately into another. She saw her chance and pulled away from him. He let her go, but she wasn't through with him.

"For the record, it's unbecoming for the pot to call out the kettle. I think your date"—she nodded toward the table where the garish civilian sat watching them—"is mentally designing her wedding gown." She turned on her heal and marched away.

After half an hour, he caught up with her again as she chatted with one of the sword dancers. The woman lit up as she saw Rio approach, and without thinking, Ceri turned to see who had the woman's attention. Her ready smile faded on her lips as she saw him smile back at her companion before glaring at her.

"I've been looking all over for you. Hamish and Alaisdair left a while ago, and I'm charged with driving you to the manor. Are you ready to go?" His tone made it clear that driving her home rated about as high on his to-do list as mucking out a rank stall.

"You've been drinking." She held out her hand for the keys. "I'll drive."

Though the return trip to the manor was only five miles long on the narrow winding road in the dark, it took about fifteen minutes. Rio shredded her in about three minutes on the dance floor. How would she survive fifteen minutes alone in a car with his sarcasm and judgment? If it weren't so dangerous for a talisman to be out alone, she'd rather walk home. Still, she made her way through the crowd to thank their host before she joined Rio in the parking area.

As she neared Hamish's little car, her thoughts wandered to how she'd make it through the ride home without jumping out of the moving vehicle. It was too much to hope that Rio would keep his caustic opinions to himself.

She barely put the car in gear before he started.

"You know, lady, there are consequences for behavior like yours."

"What do you mean, 'behavior like mine?'" she retorted. "I met people, had some pleasant conversations *for once*, danced, and had a good time. I didn't over-imbibe or take off my clothes or sing too loud or do anything else to embarrass my host or me." She stubbornly stared out the windshield at the road. "I think my behavior was beyond reproach."

"Of course, being a monumental flirt with every warrior in the place, including the married ones, doesn't count as poor behavior for a woman like you," he growled.

"'A woman like me?'" she asked through clenched teeth.

"A woman who actively entices a warrior not her own and encourages him to forget it's his job to find his talisman to make them a team strong enough to protect both of them from Morgan."

Ceri wanted to scream. Instead, she said in a deadly calm voice, "I wasn't *flirting*. I danced with every unattached warrior in the room because I'm supposed to do that, make myself available for them to try their signs on me. The other talismans there did the same, and you didn't go around berating them when they continued dancing throughout the evening."

"The other talismans weren't actively encouraging warriors to do more than dance."

She stared at his profile in shock. "In case it's escaped your notice, I'm going home alone, so obviously I was *not* doing what you're accusing me. I don't know what your problem is, but I feel sorry for your talisman when you find her."

A muscle ticked in his jaw. "Why?"

She returned her attention to the road. "Living with a suspicious, jealous man for the rest of her life will be no picnic no matter how strong a warrior you are."

Staring out at the space where the headlights met the night, she willed Rio to stop talking. For some blessed reason, he did.

CHAPTER TEN

HEY FINISHED THE ride home in silence. Ceri exited the car almost before she put it in park. Rio couldn't resist one last barb as they entered the house.

"The warrior who gets saddled with you is never going to have any rest."

She stopped still. "What the hell do you mean by that?"

"Between fighting Morgan and keeping you away from every warrior who crosses your path, the man will be in a perpetual state of exhaustion."

"I don't know what I ever did to give you such a low opinion of me, but I have had enough of your innuendos and smart-ass comments. Whatever you need to complete the security system installation, let Hamish know. I'm sure he can take care of it. If you have a question for me, please direct it through Hamish."

Halfway to the stairs, she turned around with one last shot. "When you're finished with the project, leave the bill with Hamish and don't let the door hit you on the ass on your way out."

She spun on her heel and stalked out of the kitchen.

The fire in her eyes shot straight to his solar plexus.

As he rubbed his hand over his chest, a thought struck him. In all the time they'd known each other, in all the time they'd spent together, he couldn't recall that he'd ever actually tried his sign on her. He reached her in two strides and touched her.

She whipped around, her eyes blazing. "Ouch! If you wanted my attention, you could say something. You don't have to poke me with a …" Her words trailed off. "What did you poke me with?"

"I didn't poke you. I touched you. Like this."

Gently, he turned Ceri away from him, formed his index, middle, and ring fingers into a triangle, and touched her left shoulder. She flinched like he'd pushed her, and he had trouble catching his breath.

When she faced him again, he knew by the look on her face she understood what had happened between them. He watched in alarm as she fought hard to hide the tears swimming in her beautiful green eyes.

After swallowing several times, she choked out, "This is the mother of all cosmic jokes. I traveled half way around the world to find that my warrior has been living near me for almost a year, and he turns out to be the one man who truly, inexplicably despises me."

She raced up the stairs away from him while he stood in the middle of the kitchen, stunned.

When he finally found her seated on a stone bench behind the yew hedge in the garden, she was shivering and looking so bleak she tore his heart. *Being my talisman distresses her this much?* Then he answered his own question. *Of course it does, dumbass, after some of things you've said to her.* He winced.

He sat down beside her, but she seemed to take no notice of him.

"Your fingers are icy," he whispered as he wrapped her hand in both of his. She tried to pull it free, but he gently, firmly, held it, warming it.

After a few moments, she spoke. "When I thought about the day my warrior would find me, I always had this notion we'd have an instant attraction." She shot him a side-eye. "And we'd want to give each other a chance." Blowing out a breath, she continued. "I envisioned the fairytale, Rio, like the one Alyssa and Rowan are living, not a cosmic farce. What are we going to do? How can we be a team when you despise me?"

He squeezed his eyes shut at the sound of her tear-roughened voice.

"I've made some terrible mistakes based on assumptions and my own failings. You have no reason to believe me, but I'm sorry. I've been an ass—"

"You think?" She lost her attempt at sarcasm in a choking noise.

He cupped her cold cheek in his palm. "But in my defense, my family history clouded my perceptions." He stood and extended his hand. "Please. Let's go inside where it's warm, and I'll tell you about it, okay?"

She forced him into an eternity of patience before at last she nodded. He helped her up and wrapped his arm around her shoulders as he walked her back inside. Though she didn't pull away from him, she walked stiffly, not leaning into his warmth.

Inside the house, he led her to the small sitting room. After seating her on the loveseat, he tucked the throw from the nearby chair around her.

"Sit tight for a few minutes. I'll be right back."

Without a word, she snuggled more deeply into the blanket he'd wrapped around her.

He sprinted down to the kitchen. As he heated water on the stove, he thought about the instant hot water faucet his mother had installed in her kitchen sink and decided he'd install one in the manor. In moments like the present, such a device would be handy. Then he laughed at himself for making plans for a house he didn't share—yet.

A tin of shortbread cookies sat on the shelf where Hamish kept the hot chocolate. After he stirred boiling water into two mugs with the chocolate mix, he tucked the tin of cookies under his arm. With the two mugs of chocolate in his hands, he hurried back to the sitting room. A tiny sigh of relief puffed from his chest at finding Ceri still swathed in her blanket when he arrived.

Handing her a mug of hot chocolate, he said, "Try this."

As he set the tin of cookies on the table in front of her, he took the chair opposite. For a few moments, they sipped their drinks in silence before he began to tell her a story.

"Besides Rowan, my dad's younger brother Conor was my favorite person in the world. He laughed easily and never worried about anything. But he was one of the fiercest warriors Scathach ever trained."

He glanced at Ceri to make sure she was listening.

"When I was ten, he started training me. Being two years older, Rowan could always best me, and I wanted to keep up. Conor never teased me. Instead, he praised every effort I made, no matter how little my progress or how awkward my attempt. I worshipped him."

Painful memories washed over him.

"Right before his twenty-eighth birthday, he met Trina, his talisman. Our whole family was so relieved and happy for him, but no one knew the black cloud hanging over their relationship." Rio took a sip of chocolate.

"Why was there a black cloud? Was his talisman cursed in some way?"

"You could say that. Trina was a monumental flirt, but she danced too close to the fire when she met a warrior named Kenny Johnston." Resting his forearms on his thighs, Rio tightened his hands around his mug. "He'd passed his twenty-eighth birthday without finding his talisman, so he was on the run when they met. Since he had nothing to lose, he took another man's talisman to bed, and Trina fell completely in love with him. Discovering she had a living warrior—Johnston had convinced her otherwise as part of his campaign to have her—tore her in two."

Rio caught the look of sadness on Ceri's face, but he plunged on.

"Conor loved her almost immediately, and they married as they were supposed to. But Trina couldn't forget Johnston. Eventually, Morgan caught up with Johnston and convinced him she'd spare him if he'd kill the Sheridan who stole his woman. When Johnston challenged my uncle, Trina, with her divided loyalties between duty to her warrior husband and love for her rogue warrior, didn't do her job. Both my uncle and Trina's lover died in that battle."

Rio didn't bother to hide his bitterness.

Ceri surprised him when she reached over and covered his hand with hers. "I'm so sorry, Rio."

"In the end, Morgan gained even more than she sought."

"What do you mean?"

"Though she was weak, Trina did have feelings for Conor. My family didn't blame her or shun her after he died. When she finally faced her part in Conor's death, she took her own life. Morgan escorted two warriors and a talisman across the ford. I was sixteen, and I never forgot what happens when a talisman is a flirt."

He stared at her hand covering his.

She pulled it away.

"Did it ever occur to you perhaps all three of them were victims of one of Brisen's tricks? Creating love triangles is one of her fortes. One need only look at the mess she made with Guenevere, Lancelot, and Elaine when she tricked Lancelot into sleeping with Elaine and conceiving Galahad."

"At least Galahad came out of that mess. Nothing good came of Conor's situation." He stared into Ceri's eyes. "Brisen may be a magician and a trickster goddess, but I've never heard of her being actively in league with Morgan." He sucked in a breath. "If I'm being honest, and I need to be now, I've never actually seen you come on to any man. Men come on to you, and you're nice to them. There's a difference. I know that."

She wrapped herself more tightly in her blanket and held her hot chocolate in front of herself like a shield. "Thank you for that, I guess."

With a sigh, he said, "All the cards on the table. I've wanted you from the first time I laid eyes on you."

The sip of hot chocolate she was on the verge of taking stopped with the cup at her lips.

"You were laughing and teasing Seamus, and your ease with him and his with you made me jealous. I wanted what he had with you. Clearly, you weren't his talisman. His sign makes it so easy for him to check, I know he tried it on you about thirty seconds after you met."

Her brows shot up.

"Still, you seemed so comfortable with each other, that I thought ..." He couldn't finish the sentence.

"You thought I was another Trina and Seamus another Johnston," she finished for him, glaring at him. "That's monumentally unfair to a woman you'd just met and to your brother's best friend."

Rio ran his hands through his hair. "I'm sorry, Ceri. You have every right to be angry with me, but I've never been able to forgive Conor's death. If his talisman had been patient instead of a flirt, he might still be alive today."

"Is that why you never tried your sign on me before tonight?" She kept her eyes steady on him.

"No."

"Then why tonight?"

"The first time we met, my emotions were in an uproar about Rowan and Alyssa. I dismissed you as a flirt even though I was so attracted to you. The next time we met was at the wedding, and you were wearing a sexy strapless dress that nullified my sign, so I couldn't try it on you. When I started working here for you, I was clinging to my prejudices about you and didn't even think about trying my sign on you." He came around the low table to kneel in front of her. "Tonight when you were reading me the riot act about your job as a talisman, it occurred to me I'd never actually done my job with you."

She pulled a face and he grinned.

"When it worked, I was busy doing the happy dance in my head while you were running away from me."

"Now what?"

He stood, gently taking her cup and placing it on the table before taking her hands and lifting her to her feet in front of him. He linked her hands behind his neck before wrapping his arms around her and pulling her close.

Against her mouth he said, "You know what. Fortunately for us, we've been attracted to each other for a long time."

Ceri gasped at his audacity, and he took advantage by molding his lips to hers. He lost himself in the sensations of her lithe body filling his arms perfectly. Her breasts melded to the solid plane of his chest while he plundered the sweetness of her mouth, igniting every nerve-ending in his body.

Desire exploded when she kissed him back. The heat of her mouth, the glide of her tongue, the way she sucked at his bottom lip fired him up. Tightening her arms around his neck, she arched into him while she kissed him to the edge of sanity.

At last, he tore his mouth away from hers and rested his forehead on hers. Swallowing hard, he worked to catch his breath.

"We're going to finish this, Ceri, but not here where anyone can see."

She squeaked, and he grinned when he lifted her high into his arms and carried her out of the sitting room and across the foyer to the grand staircase.

"Rio, you convinced me that I want to go where you're taking me. You don't need to take unnecessary risks by carrying me off to bed. I can walk."

He smirked and started climbing stairs.

"I will never use my strength against you, Ceri. You have to know that."

She gasped. "You breached my shield!"

"No, you let it down. That's good. We have to trust each other enough to let each other in," he said as he took the stairs two at a time.

After he carried her over the threshold of her bedroom, he hooked his foot behind the door and kicked it closed. Without breaking stride, he carried her to the massive four-poster bed and laid her down gently on it before turning on the bedside lamp. For a few minutes, they simply stared at each other.

The wonder of Ceri Ross being his talisman surged through him, and he smiled.

"Seriously?"

"Thank you for trusting me enough to let me in—on purpose."

"The gods knew what they were doing when they determined that warriors and talismans needed to share everything with each other—minds, bodies"—*hearts, but we aren't quite there yet.* For now, he kept that thought behind his shield and smiled at her.

When she smiled back, his breath backed up in his throat before desire had him moving to the end of the bed. He unzipped her boots and tugged them off her feet. His eyes never leaving hers, he leaned forward and slipped his hands beneath her hips. She lifted up so he could unzip her skirt and tug it down her thighs and off her body.

Lightly he trailed his hands along the outsides of her legs, over her hips, and up to the hem of her sweater, but he didn't stop. Slipping his hands inside, he savored the silk of her skin, the ripples of her response as he skimmed her belly and kept going.

As he pushed his hands into her sleeves, he gave her no choice but to raise her arms above her head while he divested her of her sweater. Her long hair fell over her shoulder, covering her breast. Clad only in a lacy pink bra and matching panties, her honey-blond hair half concealing her, Ceri was the sexiest, most perfect woman he'd ever seen.

"You mean that?"

"Oh, yeah. You're gorgeous. I'm one lucky warrior."

With swift motions, he unlaced his boots and toed them off. His smile deepened as the endless meadows of her eyes deepened to forest green while she watched him unbutton his jeans and slide them off. He dragged his T-shirt over his head, pushed his boxers down over his erection, and let her have a long look.

Rio gifted Ceri with a wicked grin as he caught her thoughts.

When she tried to slide off her panties, he stayed her with a shake of his head. "This is Christmas. And you don't get to help me unwrap my present."

Fisting the sheets on either side of her, she groaned. The tiny beads of sweat gathering on her forehead and around her navel fascinated him with the story they told of her need.

Savoring the moment, he slid her panties down her long legs, his palms and fingers skimming over her, her smooth skin firing his desire. Beginning a new onslaught on her senses, he feathered his fingertips along the outsides of her legs and kissed his way up the insides as he crawled up her body. Her sighs and whimpers goaded him in his singular mission.

"That's it, sweet woman. Let me love you," he whispered as he trailed his tongue along the inside of her thigh.

When he reached the place they both wanted him to touch, he smiled darkly at how hot and wet he'd made her. He ran his tongue over her hard nub, and she rewarded him with a moan as she arched and lifted her hips in silent entreaty for more. Cupping her ass in both hands, he held her immobile while he tongued her clit, over and over again, before he added one then two fingers to her channel and pumped until she cried out his name.

Closing his eyes, he inhaled her release, delighting in her response.

As she came down from round one, he kissed his way up her flat belly until he reached the valley between her breasts. Sliding his fingers beneath the elastic of her bra, he pushed it up over her head. Sitting back on his knees, he couldn't stop staring at the perfection of her beautiful body.

Taking her full breasts in his hands, he molded and teased her nipples with the pads of his thumbs until they peaked prettily for him before he leaned in and sucked one deep into his mouth. Ceri gasped her pleasure and dug her nails into the bunched muscles of his shoulders. He growled in satisfaction and transferred his attentions to her other breast. Rewarding him, she lifted her hips insistently against him.

Rio raised his head and gazed into the deep green depths of her eyes. The desire he saw there mirrored his own, and his mouth curved up. Then the dusky pink bud glistening in the lamplight with his recent loving caught his attention. He blew on her, and her nipple miraculously tightened even more. Beneath him, she bucked and writhed, firing him even more.

"Please, Rio."

He leaned forward and kissed her mouth while she wrapped her arms and her legs around him, rubbing her slick core against his hard shaft.

"Easy, sweetheart. This is our first time. We need to treasure it—and each other," he said before he began exploring the dark recesses of her mouth with his tongue.

For several long minutes, she gave him her mouth before she tore it away, her chest heaving. "Please, Rio, please. I need you now."

"I like it when you beg."

She growled.

His lips twitched as he reached between their bodies and guided himself to her. When he found her heat, all playfulness fled. Gritting his teeth, he slowly sank into her tight wet welcome.

Fully sheathed inside her, he stared into her eyes. "Perfect."

"Oh, yes," she breathed.

After having had her warrior, how could a woman ever want another man? Ceri wondered before Rio started moving inside her and she stopped thinking at all.

Rio, however, heard her thoughts, and her response to him reassured him as nothing else ever could that Ceri Ross was his and only his.

CHAPTER ELEVEN

I N HIS PRIVATE rooms, Hamish Buchanan smiled in satisfaction. The atmosphere in the house changed the exact moment Ceri found her warrior. Somehow the fates had intervened in a most fitting fashion for Ceri and Rio not to have discovered their relationship before they reached Scotland and Conlan Manor. Though it would have been even better if they'd waited until Samhain to come together, the fact her warrior discovered her under the roof of the manor set the wheels in motion for all the prophecies to come true. It seemed the Sheridan clan's destiny to thwart the old girl and her evil activities didn't stop with reversing the Morrigan's curse on warriors on their twenty-eighth birthdays.

Thinking about the Morrigan sobered him right up. It wouldn't be long until she discovered the Sheridans had bested her again, which meant repercussions. He would need to start preparing for those right away, which meant bringing Shanley Conlan back to Scotland. Not only for her safety, but also because her presence at the rituals on Samhain would add another layer of protection for her niece and Rio Sheridan.

"I hope I caught ye at a good time, lass."

"Hamish? Is everything all right?" Shanley's voice rose.

"'Tis and 'tis, Shanley love. Yer niece has found her warrior, and they managed it here in the manor." He couldn't stop smiling.

"When did this happen? Who is her warrior? A Scot? Give me details!"

"They found each other this evening. They're working out the particulars even now, I expect."

No doubt Shanley could hear Hamish's grin from across the ocean. "What time is it there? One o'clock in the morning?"

"Close enough."

"And?"

"Her warrior is Rio Sheridan, the lad who came over from the States tae work on the security system she insisted on havin' in the manor."

He leaned back in his chair and enjoyed the surprise.

"*Rio Sheridan*? I can't imagine how he didn't try his sign on her long before she went to Scotland."

"'Twas fated fer them tae find each other here. The first part o' the prophecy has come tae pass. Now we need tae see them through Samhain and a marriage, and we'll thwart the auld girl's vicious attacks on Conlans fer the next ten generations."

"This is incredible news. I knew I was right to insist Ceri spend a year at the manor."

"Aye, ye were right. She's daein' her part, and now it's time fer ye tae add yer part as well."

"I spent a year at the manor, remember?"

"Aye lass, I dae, but now I need ye tae come back again fer a week at least. I know it's short notice, but ye need tae be here for Samhain. Ye're her nearest living relative, so yer presence is required fer everything tae happen as it should."

"It'll be tough to get off work. Samhain isn't a regular holiday over here, you know. Americans call it Halloween, and though the kids think it should be a school holiday"—she said with a laugh—"it isn't."

"Pity. Doesnae change the fact ye're needed here. If it's a matter o' money, the trust will see tae yer transportation. Ye know that."

"That's not it. I could jeopardize my job. My boss likes some notice when I want time off, especially a full week in the middle of a semester."

"I'll take care o' yer boss. Make yer plane reservations taeday. I'll expect ye at the weekend at the latest."

Shanley made a noise before she changed the subject. "Do the Sheridans know about this turn of events?"

"Unless one o' them sensed it, I donnae think our new pair has had time tae tell anyone." Hamish chuckled as he imagined Shanley coloring red at the other end of the line.

"So that's the way of it."

"Aye, lass, 'tis. Let me know when tae expect ye. It may take Ceri some time before she rings ye with the news. When she tells ye—act surprised." He could almost see his cousin rolling her eyes on her end of the call, and he grinned again. "One more thing. If she hasnae already sensed it, it willnae be long before the Morrigan is aware o' the change in the cosmos, and she's goin' tae be spittin' mad. Stay out o' sight as much as ye can. Is there a warrior ye can stay with until ye come over?"

"You think that's necessary?"

Hamish sat up straight. "Aye. We're tae close tae risk losing ye. After the comeuppance the Sheridans gave Morgan last winter, she'll be in nae mood tae be generous with anyone connected tae them, even though ye aren't—yet."

"I'll be careful. I know a warrior who will help. He's getting up there in years, but he's a good man. Perhaps the trust could take care of his transportation to the manor as well?"

"Good idea, lass. Havin' a warrior travelin' with ye will make Morgan think twice before she attacks ye. Give me a day tae take care o' yer boss before ye ask fer the time off, but make yer travel reservations. I'll see ye the weekend."

He rang off.

His next order of business involved his trusted friend and ally, Alaisdair Graham. He'd hoped Ceri belonged to Alaisdair since the man only had six months left before he'd have to go to ground for the rest of his life—not a happy prospect. It had been bad enough when Alaisdair reached twenty-eight alone, but to have to face his terrible fate twice now that he'd been granted an extension at the last hour seemed cruel.

Hoping Alaisdair hadn't gone to bed yet, Hamish summoned him. "*Though we were wrong about ye, we were right about Ceri. She's the prophesied one. Her warrior discovered their connection a little while ago here at the manor. I need ye now.*"

"*She brought someone home with her?*"

"*He's been here all along. I had an inklin' about Rio from the moment he arrived. After our trainin' session the other day, that feelin' became stronger. He's special, and now we know why. But lad, we need tae continue this conversation in the safety o' the manor.*"

"*Be there in a few minutes.*"

Alaisdair didn't bother to knock on the door separating Hamish's quarters from the tunnel connecting the manor to the stone cottage. He'd been accessing the manor via this route for years, and the two of them were used to each other.

"How d'ye know Rio is Ceri's warrior?" he asked as he walked across the room and seated himself in his favorite easy chair.

The niceties of announcing themselves in each other's homes were bygone practices. Hamish didn't miss a beat. "When they came in through the kitchen from the car park, they was arguin', so I opened my door and listened."

Alaisdair laughed. "Ye have no shame, old man."

"No' a bit." Hamish winked and handed a mug of strong tea to his friend. "Ceri told him tae go tae hell, then she yelped about him pokin' her, then they was kinda quiet before she started fussin' about him bein' her warrior. She raced outta the kitchen and up the stairs."

"No' the way it usually goes when a warrior discovers his talisman, I understand."

Hamish smirked as he seated himself in his wide old leather chair. "I heard the lad lookin' fer her, but I knew where she was."

"Where?" Alaisdair sipped his tea.

"She has a special spot in the garden. I've found her there on a few occasions since she arrived. Eventually, so did Rio. He brought her intae the house, and last I heard, they was conversin' in the sittin' room."

"At least ye have the decency tae leave 'em alone tae bond. I donnae think Ceri would take tae ye spyin' on that." Alaisdair chuckled.

Hamish waved a hand. "No' likely. Besides, the way Rio has watched her since he arrived tells me he'll have nae trouble with that part o' his duty."

Alaisdair leaned forward in his chair. "Why is it they just now discovered their relationship tae each other, I wonder?"

"That I cannae tell ye, but nae doubt the gods had somethin' tae do with it. The prophesied one was fated tae find her warrior under the roof o' this manor."

"Why is it so important fer me tae be inside the manor now?"

"Once the Morrigan discovers she's been thwarted again, all hell's goin' tae break loose. I expect it will happen sooner than later. Ye need tae stay in the manor where Ceri and I have added several layers o' protections." Hamish sucked in a breath and let it out. "Likely, ye'll also be called upon tae fight soon, and I've a feelin' the battle is goin' tae happen right here on the grounds before Samhain. Better no' tae have ye cut off out in the cottage."

Alaisdair didn't argue. "If it's all the same tae ye—and tae Ceri of course—I think I'll take a room down here."

"Suit yerself. The rooms upstairs are much nicer though."

"I'm used tae the quiet. Somehow, I donnae think it's goin' tae be all that quiet elsewhere in the manor fer a while." His eyes twinkled mischievously.

"Ye're all right, lad. I know ye're near tae yer forty-second birthday, but ye havnae given up, I hope."

"I still have six months if we survive Morgan's comin' wrath. Even if I donnae find my talisman before then, if Ceri and Rio survive tae marry, it may be enough tae allow me tae stay on here at the manor rather than go tae ground."

"That's true," Hamish replied, cheered at his friend's attitude.

He stood and walked over to the long table where his herbs and flowers lay drying. Fingering several to determine their readiness, he asked another favor.

"Ceri has one near relative still livin', an aunt who never found her warrior. She spent a year here at the manor after her sister, Ceri's mother, inherited it. I've asked her over fer Samhain." He faced Alaisdair. "We'll need her fer the rituals. She'll be bringin' an auld warrior with her, someone who has lent her protection over the years. I'll need yer help when I fetch her later this week. By then I've nae doubt Morgan will know what's happened and will be lookin' fer opportunities tae stop the completion of the prophecy."

Alaisdair nodded. "Now there's somethin' ye should know about Ceri. Rio should be told tae, but I donnae know if she'll tell him."

Hamish waited.

"She cannae shield her thoughts when she's afraid," Alaisdair went on. "When I came upon her out by the cottage, she assumed I was a rogue and thought tae visualize herself tae the Anchor."

"That was inspired, if ye ask me."

"I agree. The problem is, I heard the entire plan as she formed it."

Hamish frowned. "That most definitely is a problem. Why d'ye think she willnae tell Rio?"

"She's got her pride, and she doesnae want tae show weakness. She asked me tae take her tae the trainin' room tae help her. That's her warrior's job, now."

"I think the twa o' ye could help her with that. Workin' with ye would also help Rio learn tae trust ye, and we're goin' tae need that." Hamish gathered their cups and placed them on a side table near the kettle. "We'll give 'em a day or twa tae bond, and then dae some serious quick trainin'. Samhain is less than two weeks away."

❦

Ceri awoke to a feeling of completeness and warmth she couldn't understand until she understood her cocoon consisted of Rio spooning her under the blankets. Slowly, her awareness told her she wasn't the only one awake. Rio's hard shaft nestled along the cleft of her ass made that clear.

"'Bout time you woke up, lady." His deep voice sent shivers down her spine.

"Have you been awake long?" she asked innocently as she wiggled against him.

"Long enough for you to need to be careful how you move."

"Why would I want to do that?"

"Because it could require you to spend a full day in bed rather than only the morning," he murmured, his fingers circling lazily over her taut nipple as he cupped her breast in his free hand.

Her breath hitched. "Why is that a problem?" Her body responded to Rio's everywhere they touched and some places where she needed him to touch her.

"For one thing, I don't think there's room service." He kissed her bare shoulder.

"At the moment, I'm not that kind of hungry," she whispered.

"What kind of hungry are you?"

He adjusted himself to push between her thighs.

"Hungry for something only a warrior can give his talisman."

She turned in his arms facing him, her hand skimming along his thigh, over his hip, and up the tight obliques of his torso before resting on the hard plane of his chest.

Rio grinned, dipped his head and kissed her with a light brush of his lips across hers before he took her mouth completely, his tongue gliding over the seam of her lips, demanding she open for him. Heat flashed over her skin as his kiss fevered her blood.

At last, he pulled back enough to smile into her eyes. "Good morning, beautiful. Sleep well?" he asked as though he hadn't ignited an inferno inside her.

Her eyes widened at his nonchalance, and she deliberately reached between them to grasp his length in her hand. "Very well, thank you. And you? Did you sleep well?" She smiled saucily at his quick intake of breath as she palmed him.

"Like a rock." His lips twitched before he rolled on top of her, sliding a thigh between her legs. "Now, where did I leave off last night? Oh, yeah, I remember. I was here."

He dipped his head to taste her navel, his touch like a lover of long experience rather than the tentative explorations of someone in a new relationship. She bucked and gasped at the sensation of his mouth on her. But Rio had only begun his sensual assault on her all-too-willing body. Her skin rippled as he mapped her with his searingly hot mouth.

When he blew on her erect nipples, she arched her back in a silent plea for more. Grinning wickedly, he bypassed her breasts and kissed the sensitive hollow at the base of her throat and up the side of her neck, sending goosebumps skittering over her skin. As he traced the shell of her ear with his tongue, she wrapped her arms and legs around him and pulled him close, rubbing her slick center along the length of his cock.

The way he'd been teasing her told her he planned to prolong their climax until she begged him for it, but she had other plans. Using her inner muscles, she squeezed him tightly, leaving him no choice but to move inside her, giving her exactly what she wanted. Together they rode the tide of desire as it washed over them, leaving them spent and sated—for the moment.

After the first storm passed, they lay quietly in each other's arms. Finally, Ceri whispered, "Shanley said I must bond with my warrior, and making love would be part of it, but I don't think anything could have prepared me for the way you make me feel, Rio."

He brushed a kiss over her forehead. "My brothers said nothing compares with making love with your talisman. Until last night, I never quite believed them. If every warrior understood what awaited him when he finds his fated mate, there'd be no party boys like Seamus, or even my brother Rowan. They'd all be on a singular mission to find their talismans."

"You certainly were," she reminded him, mischief coloring her tone.

"Out of a healthy fear of a fate worse than death if I didn't."

"That's flattering," she said with a not-so-gentle punch to his shoulder.

"Like I said, I had no idea bonding would be so amazing."

Then Rio did something to truly shock her—he gave her a genuine smile, and she blinked in astonishment.

He rolled off her and landed like a graceful cat on the floor beside the bed. Reaching down, he took her hands and pulled her up and into his arms where he held her in his warm embrace while she shivered in the cold air outside the covers.

"We forgot to turn on the heat last night." She snuggled into his chest as gooseflesh pebbled her skin.

"Really? I thought you were pretty hot last night—and this morning." A laugh rumbled through his chest.

"That's not what I meant, and you know it."

Pulling back, he stared down at her. "Oh, you meant the room? Well, there are only two remedies I can think of for that."

She quirked a brow.

"One, we return to bed, or two, we take a hot shower. Me, I'm hoping for door number two. Something about a fantasy I have." He grinned at her, and she pulled out of his embrace.

"Race you!" she called over her shoulder as she ran toward the spacious en suite bathroom.

Right before she made it to the door, he caught her around the waist and spun her in his arms.

"Rio! What do you think you're doing? You can't throw me over your shoulder like, like some spoils of war!" she squealed.

"I think that's exactly what I did. Now settle down like a good little prize and let me have my way."

"You're way too bossy. The only reason I'm letting you get away with this is that I'm curious about your fantasy. Don't think you can toss me over your shoulder any time the mood strikes you," she warned.

"Sweetheart, there is something you should know about me. I dearly love a good challenge." He gave her light slap on the ass and set her down in the middle of her massive shower.

"You have some nerve," she began, but he cut her off by turning on the shower, sending a stream of freezing water right into her face. Though the facilities had been updated, the hot water still had to be pumped up from boilers in the basement three stories below.

He burst out laughing at her sputtering response. She was pretty sure she looked like a wet cat, and like a wet cat, her claws came out. With the intent of throwing it at him, she reached for the bar of soap, but he caught her hand and pulled it up around his neck as he took her in his arms and kissed her until she forgot why she was mad at him.

The shower stall easily fit the two of them. Gently setting her from him, he took the soap and began lathering it up in his hands before he washed her slowly and carefully, worshipping her body with his hands and his eyes.

Kneeling on the tile floor in front of her, Rio glanced up from his task. "Ceri, there is nothing in the world as incredibly beautiful as you are. Your body is absolutely perfect. I love touching you."

She sighed at his words and his touch. "Keep it up, and I might melt into a delicious puddle in your hands."

Standing and stepping behind her, he worked his hands down her abdomen and back up to her breasts with methodical slowness, before he slid his hands around to wash her back and ass. As he moved to take her into his arms, she surprised him by reversing their positions. With Rio standing beneath the showerhead, Ceri grabbed the bar of soap and lathered it up in her hands. His eyes smoldered as he watched her. She made a twirling motion with her finger, and he faced the spray.

Starting with his ankles, she lathered his long, muscular legs, taking her time over his sculpted calves, knees, and thighs and reveling in his sharp inhale at her touch. When she gave her attention to his tight ass, his sleek back, and heavily muscled shoulders, it was her turn to suck in air. All this male beauty belonged to her.

Working her way over his shoulders, she couldn't resist rubbing her breasts over his back, and the way he pushed back into her told her he enjoyed the feel of her body against his. While she continued to hold herself to him, she smoothed her soapy hands down his thick arms to his hands, which she squeezed briefly in hers before she turned him to face her.

After lathering more soap into her hands, she washed his shoulders and chest and worked her way down his torso. He groaned as she tantalized him by washing all around his erect shaft. At last, she took him in her hands and carefully soaped him before she turned him again to allow the water to rinse away the suds.

"Is this your fantasy? Washing and being washed in a shower with heads built high enough to accommodate your height?" Ceri asked as she stroked him.

"Yeah, the first part."

Rio faced her.

"What's the second part?" she asked a little breathlessly.

"This."

He took her in his arms and kissed her while the water streamed over them, steam billowing toward the ceiling. Ceri rubbed her water-slicked body against Rio's, the feel of his hardness against her softness revving her up. As he kissed her boneless, he slid one hand over her ass and down the back of her thigh to her knee, lifting it and guiding her foot toward the low bench along the back wall of the shower.

With her positioned as he wanted her, he fitted himself to her and thrust deep. She moaned and tightened her arms around his neck, clinging to him as he set a delicious rhythm.

There's nothing in the world as intense or incredible as this.

"You're right, babe. Nothing compares to this."

CHAPTER TWELVE

HEN RIO AND Ceri walked hand in hand into the kitchen for brunch hours later, they found Hamish and Alaisdair seated at the table conversing over tea. Ceri blushed a pretty rose that made Rio smile. He tugged her close and kissed her temple, making sure the other men knew without a doubt his relationship with her had changed.

"Mornin'. I take it the bondin' went well." Hamish waggled his brows.

"You could say that," Rio responded with a grin.

"How d-do you know about that?"

"I heard the twa o' ye come in last night. What I'm curious about is why when ye've known each other fer a while ye dinnae know ye were each other's mates?" Hamish's tone made it apparent he thought he was owed an explanation.

"Circumstances interfered at first, old man. Then stubbornness." Rio squeezed her hand. "But eventually, Ceri got over herself and gave me a chance," he said with a straight face.

Her eyes saucered then narrowed. "*That's* how it went?" She tugged against his hold, but he didn't let her go.

Smiling at her fondly, he said, "You're so easy."

"I'll show you easy—"

He slipped his arms around her and tried to pull her in for a kiss. When she stared up at him, he saw she had no idea he was teasing.

Hamish interrupted. "It's lucky ye waited tae find each other until ye were safely under the roof o' this house. The heir's warrior findin' her here adds an especially potent layer o' protection tae the clan. Welcome tae the family." He stood and embraced Rio.

Alaisdair added his congratulations as well. "Glad tae have ye, Rio." He stood and extended his hand. Addressing Ceri, he asked, "Have ye told him about yer shield yet?"

"That was between us, Alaisdair," she said through clenched teeth.

Rio stilled.

Unperturbed, Alaisdair continued. "Aye, 'twas, but that was before ye found yer warrior. 'Tis a serious matter that needs seein' tae immediately. As the twa o' ye were bondin', did ye discover yer special gift?"

Ceri peeked up at Rio. "We didn't get that far yet."

Rio's emotions roiled.

"Ceri, lass, 'tis nothin' tae be ashamed of, but it does need addressin' right away." Hamish sat at the table and poured more tea into his mug. "No' only is it dangerous fer ye, but also fer yer warrior. Alaisdair and I were discussin' a trip tae the trainin' room later taeday, if ye'd like tae join us."

"You know?" Ceri's voice rose two octaves.

"Perhaps you'd enlighten me, Ceri, about your problem? Since I have a rather large stake here," Rio said quietly, but he heard the edge in his voice that gave away the anger and hurt he could barely hold in.

Her shoulders slumped. "We should probably sit down for this."

They seated themselves at the rough-hewn table while Hamish set two steaming mugs of tea in front of them.

Obviously, the two of them had a long way to go. Ceri took a sip before she explained something he thought maybe she should have told him already.

Addressing no one in particular, she said, "Shanley started my talisman training when I was six. Shielding was one of the first skills I mastered." She slid farther down on her seat. "Or we thought I did." Her knuckles turned white as she gripped the mug between her hands. "In my teens, we discovered I don't shield well when I'm afraid. I've worked on it continuously, but it's hard to practice without being in situations of actual danger. And we had no access to a secure training room." She glanced at him from beneath her lashes then dropped her eyes back to the table. "When I met Alaisdair the first time, we discovered I have yet to perfect the skill."

Though he kept his voice even, Rio's frustration manifested in his matching white-knuckled hold on his mug. "When were you going to tell me?"

"If you recall, since discovering what we are to each other, we haven't discussed much of anything. I hadn't even thought about it until Alaisdair brought it up." She blushed crimson and stared at the wall behind Alaisdair.

"Will you two excuse us please? It appears we have a few things to discuss in private," Rio said to the Scotsmen before he grabbed Ceri's hand and led her up the stairs to the sitting room.

"I'm sorry Rio. But when should I have brought it up? In bed last night? In the shower this morning? I wasn't keeping it from you," she started before he even closed the door.

He hung his head. "You're right." Leading her to the loveseat, he sat and pulled her onto his lap. "What skills you possess outside of pleasuring me tremendously were not foremost on my mind.

Now they are. What did Alaisdair mean when he said he was going to train you? How did he discover your weakness?"

"As you know, when I met Alaisdair, I was alone out by the cottage." She picked at the hem of her sweater. "Rogue warriors set upon my aunt when she stayed at Conlan Manor, and Hamish rescued her."

Rio started but kept his mouth shut.

"I feared a similar fate the day I met Alaisdair, but Hamish had taken you to the training room, and I was on my own. I started to visualize myself to the Anchor before Alaisdair stopped me by telling me who he was. Then he told me my idea, though inspired, wouldn't have worked because he heard me as I was formulating my escape."

Her mouth turned down, a plea in her meadow-green eyes. "Since I had no warrior, I asked him for help, and he agreed. Why he thought he had to bring it up before we even had breakfast is beyond me."

The sadness in her voice tore at his heart. With his index finger, he lifted her chin and made her look at him. "Maybe he was afraid you'd try to hide it from me until the two of you could fix it?"

The way her body stiffened in his arms confirmed his suspicion. Though the previous night and the morning forecast a promising start to their relationship, they had a history to overcome, one mostly of his creation. He sighed.

"We can't keep secrets from each other. I know you didn't mean to open your shield to me when you did last night and this morning, but I'm glad to know you'll always be faithful to me."

Her eyes widened in surprise.

"I deliberately opened my shield to you, so you'd know you please me very much. But a warrior and a talisman are so much more than lovers. We have to be a coordinated fighting unit." He took her hands in his. "That's our job, which means we have to help each other hone and perfect our combat skills. When we face Morgan, which we undoubtedly will and probably sooner than later, we have to be ready. We have to be fluid and tight."

He held her gaze.

"That's probably the reason Alaisdair didn't wait to spill the beans about your shielding weakness." He shook his head as her mouth turned down. "He's right about starting training today. I'd hoped to pursue other kinds of bonding," he gave her a naughty grin, and she ducked her head. "But if she hasn't discovered it already, it won't be long before Morgan catches wind we've found each other, and then we're going to be in trouble. We need to start preparing now."

"Rio, I didn't…" She swallowed. "I don't want to disappoint you. Please understand that." Her eyes implored him. *I need you to give me a chance and stop seeing in me another talisman who failed her warrior.*

Ceri undoubtedly thought her shield was in place, but her every word pricked his conscience.

With a nod, he stood and set her on her feet. "After my session with Hamish the other day, I bet this one is going to be a marathon. We'd better eat." She placed her hand in his, both of them recognizing their gestures for what they truly were—a chance at a fresh start with each other—a chance that might even involve trust.

⚮

When she entered the training room at *An Teallach*, Ceri's breath backed up in her throat while her heart dropped into her stomach. Built deep in the heart of the mountain, the cavernous round room seemed to swallow her whole. As she worked to settle herself down, she noticed the ornate beauty of the space. Scenes of Celtic heroes like Cùchulainn, King Arthur, Tristan, and Brian Boru engaged in battle or on the way to victory decorated the smooth stone walls. Designs of painted Celtic knot work in vibrant green, indigo, orange, and magenta swirled around the ceiling. The knot patterns in the inlaid black and white marble floor echoed the ceiling.

To the left of the archway at the end of the long dimly lit entrance hallway she spied a wooden door. "Does that door lead to another chamber, Hamish?"

"That door leads tae the washin' up room and the loo. Sometimes our trainin' sessions last awhile." He set the basket of food he'd brought under the painting of Brian Boru.

Ceri offered him a pained smile. Evidently, Rio's prediction was spot-on—her first time in a training room would be a marathon event.

As she walked around studying the various heroic scenes, Rio and Alaisdair stretched and warmed up. Like all warriors, they were athletes whose bodies were the main components of their arsenal of weapons.

Hamish unpacked the knapsack he'd brought along. On a low table, he set out several vials of liquids, a few shallow trays he filled with herbs from various pouches, a book of common spells, a series of candles, and a butane igniter before he, too, stretched and loosened up his body.

By the time she'd made her first circuit of the room, the men were ready to begin training. Via some tacit agreement, Alaisdair launched an attack on Ceri, scaring her into action. Her immediate response was to visualize herself elsewhere—this time at the manor. As she closed her eyes to visualize her escape, Rio grabbed her and held her.

"Babe, that was a good idea, but everyone in this room knew you were headed to the manor almost as soon as you decided to go," he said quietly in her ear.

When she opened her eyes and looked around, she saw the

proof of his words on Hamish's and Alaisdair's faces. She sagged against Rio in defeat.

"I always keep my shield up, Rio, always. I don't know what to do."

When Shanley had worked with her on shielding, she'd managed to master keeping her aunt out of her head. She'd kept Alyssa's Grandma Afton and their old warrior friend Finn Daly out as well. Why she couldn't keep these men out, she didn't understand.

"Ye're an open, carefree spirit who hasnae had tae deal much with the evil in the world. It's yer trustin' nature that's yer best feature and yer curse, lass. Ye also havnae had much tae dae with men in our community, I suspect. All o' that leads tae yer shield bein' a might thin," Hamish said kindly. "How did Shanley train ye tae keep yer thoughts clear?"

"She taught me to think of random, mundane objects."

"A good idea. Now the trick will be tae dae that on a conscious level while yer subconscious actually formulates yer thoughts, the ones ye donnae want tae share. We'll work on that while the warriors practice their fightin' techniques." As Hamish led her over to a pair of tall stools beside the table, he called over his shoulder, "Ye're in for a workout, Alaisdair my friend."

For the next few hours, Hamish drilled Ceri on shielding her thoughts while Rio and Alaisdair tested each other's battle prowess with their claymores. By the time Hamish called a break, everyone in the room was sweating buckets. She furrowed her brow when she caught Rio glaring at Hamish. Before she could figure out Rio's problem, an unfamiliar voice interrupted.

"Rio Sheridan, Rowan used to breach your twin's shield exactly like you are wishing to be able to breach your talisman's. You do remember the consequences, do you not?"

A vibrant woman with bright red hair and dressed in a leather vest and trousers breezed through the archway into the training room. Rio looked pained while Ceri gaped first at the incredible warrior woman and back at Rio.

"Milady, what a pleasant surprise," Hamish said, coming to his feet and bowing low.

Alaisdair, too, bowed low before the woman. "Milady."

"That didn't take long." Rio sounded grumpy.

"Of course not. Why would you think it would? One of my favorite and best warriors discovering his talisman sent a ripple through the cosmos I felt almost as soon as Ceri did, I expect," the woman replied, the side of her mouth turning up in a half grin.

Rio rolled his eyes at her.

Bewildered, Ceri asked, "You know who I am? Who are you?"

"Hamish, you are making progress with the lass, but she still needs practice," the woman said.

"Ceri, this is Scathach, goddess of warriors and my patroness," Rio said, pulling a face.

Ceri nearly choked before she bowed before the goddess.

Patting her back, Hamish chuckled. "This one trained all the great warriors represented on the walls o' this chamber."

Scathach made a slow circuit around Ceri. "You are the Conlan heir. I have paid attention to your family for generations. Most of the gods are not privy to the pairings of talismans and warriors—a very good thing in the case of my less-than-ethical sisters," the goddess added savagely. "I must admit I am extremely pleased the Conlans and the Sheridans are now joined. This is a most fortuitous pairing."

"Why?" Ceri asked then nearly bit through her tongue for questioning a goddess.

Scathach didn't seem to mind. "Because I have grown quite tired of my sister Morgan taking so many of my warriors across the ford right when they were becoming useful. Since Rio's brother Rowan and your friend Alyssa ended Morgan's curse, I have more hope my training will not be wasted as often." Her smile was positively wicked. "Since you two fulfilled another prophecy by discovering each other under the roof of the most enchanted and protected manor in Scotland, I know even more of my warriors will survive to stamp out evil in the world, making it most difficult for some of my siblings to have their way with civilians and warriors."

As though she had no idea she'd shocked Ceri to her core, Scathach turned her attention to Alaisdair. "Alaisdair here is a fine example. He is one of the best warriors I have trained, but since he went to ground—literally—thirteen years ago, I have not been able to use him much beyond small disturbances near Conlan Manor." Returning her attention to Ceri, she added, "Once we shepherd you safely through the rituals at Samhain, more of the warriors attached to the Conlan clan will be able to show themselves and help us fight evil and protect civilians from Morgan's, Maeve's, and Macha's plots."

Scathach finally stopped moving and sighed. "There is so much to do since the three of them as well as several others have been left unchecked for too long." Gathering herself, she turned briskly to Rio. "You are out of practice. Begin!" She summoned her claymore out of the air and attacked Rio who only had a split second to react.

All of Scathach's interest appeared focused on Rio. The other three in the room gaped at the graceful and deadly interplay of swords and moves goddess and warrior practiced on each other. However, Scathach was tuned in to all the players. "Hamish, I believe you and Ceri were in the middle of something important when I arrived? I suggest you continue. Alaisdair, pay attention to this series. Rio has it perfected. He is the only warrior I have trained who has figured it out so far."

She danced around Rio in a graceful staccato of steps that would have blurred a civilian's vision, her sword a flickering light in the speed with which she wielded it, yet Rio parried every blow, sidestepped every move. His skills rivaled those of the warrior goddess herself. She smiled as they practiced.

Neither Ceri nor Hamish could maintain their concentration on shielding practice for long, their attention drawn again and again to the warrior who seemed to be able to keep up with and occasionally best a goddess.

Hamish whispered in Ceri's ear. "I wondered why she put up with his surly attitude when he sassed her earlier, but now I see. She'll indulge a warrior o' such skill. It's all over in the tales of her training sessions with Cùchulainn and Brian Boru."

Alaisdair, who was standing nearby, whispered, "Ye said ye thought he was special, but he dinnae impress me in our initial bout. Now I see he was going easy on an old warrior. I've never seen anythin' like Rio Sheridan."

Trepidation seized her. How could such an amazingly skilled and courageous a warrior be mated to her? If she failed him, the community would never forgive her. Probably neither would this powerful goddess. The stress of finding out how accomplished and valuable her warrior was overwhelmed her, and she turned away. When she did, a sight more terrifying than fear of failing her incredible warrior assailed her mind.

All she could see was Rio facing an enormous warrior who used an unfair advantage of size to attack him and underhanded tactics to keep him from gaining any ground in the fight. Ceri watched Rio fall, and a scream tore through her.

❧

The hairs on the back of his neck stood up as Rio stared at his talisman.

"Ceri, lass, what is it? Why are you screaming?" Hamish placed a hand lightly on her shoulder, but it appeared she hadn't heard him.

At Ceri's lack of response, they all stared grimly at each other. She appeared to be in a trance.

"I know fer a fact no evil beings can penetrate the walls o' this trainin' room, but could someone have attacked Ceri through her thin shield?" Hamish stared at her. "I cannae penetrate her shield. Can ye?" he asked Rio and Alaisdair.

"Go to her, Rio. Talk to her," Scathach commanded.

Gently placing his hands on Ceri's shoulders, Rio tried to make her face him, but she remained rigid. He leaned into her and whispered, "Ceri, love, I'm here. Where did you go?"

A sigh of relief gusted from him as she came back to herself in a rush that would have landed her hard on the floor had he not already held her. Sucking in several deep breaths, she slowly turned around to face him, her face wet with tears.

Cupping his cheek, she said, "Rio, you're here." She gave him a watery smile. "You're here, and you're safe." Wrapping her arms around his waist, she held him like she never wanted to let him go.

"Of course, I'm here and safe. Where did you go?" he asked, his voice rough with emotion.

"I saw you. In battle," she said into his chest. "The warrior you faced was cheating, taking unfair advantage and leaving you vulnerable." She tightened her hold on him. "He-he delivered a killing blow." She pulled back and stared into his eyes. "Rio, I saw you fall." Burying her face in his shirt, she let out a sob.

"This is an interesting turn of events," Scathach observed.

"How d'ye mean, milady?" Alaisdair asked.

"It appears our prolonged training session has uncovered Ceri's special talent. She has spared Rio's life in his next battle," his patroness replied with a satisfied smile.

"Ah, a prophetess. Nae wonder she handled the rituals and enchantments with so much dexterity back at the manor. I thought her ease with 'em was strange considerin' she's so obviously a talisman," Hamish said. "I think one o' the reasons her mother never stayed the required year was because she couldnae deal with all the ritual. Ceri had nae trouble with any o' it."

"Now we know how Morgan will strike. We must prepare. But I think we have done enough for today," Scathach said as she sheathed her sword.

Rio paid scant attention to the goddess and the others. After Ceri seemed to cry herself out, she leaned back, looked up at him, and said, "I just found you, and now you're going to die anyway? How can you lose to a lumbering giant of a warrior who hasn't a thousandth of your incredible skill? And I have no way to help you."

Her lip quivered with the gathering of fresh tears when Scathach interrupted.

"You have helped your warrior tremendously. You have also now made a masterful gain in your shielding skills. None of us could see what you were seeing. We could only watch your reactions. Tomorrow, you will describe in detail everything about the vision you had. Then we will devise tactics for how to combat Morgan's latest champion and defeat him without losses of our own." Scathach emphasized the last part.

"I don't understand," Ceri said.

"Yer talisman skill is prophecy. What ye saw is a vision o' what could happen if we donnae take steps tae prevent it ahead o' time. We were so busy workin' on yer weakness we completely neglected tae try tae discover yer strength," Hamish explained.

"You are an asset to Rio, Ceri. Prophecy means he should always know when and how attacks are coming. Talismans with this talent are rare. Right now, you are in far more danger than Rio," Scathach said. "Since you have spent a good deal of time in this room today, from now on you will only access it with visualization. In fact, you will not leave from or return to the manor any other way," she commanded.

"Does that mean we're finished today, milady?" Rio asked hopefully.

"You are so transparent." Scathach grinned. "Yes, take your talisman back to the manor and enjoy some time alone. And Rio? If the only time you can be polite to me is when you want something, I will make sure you always want something."

Rio laughed. "Yes, *milady*, I'll keep that in mind."

She laughed back at him like an indulgent parent and waved him away. Rio grinned to himself at the stunned expressions on Alaisdair's and Hamish's faces.

He whispered to Ceri and cuddled her close. Then the two of them were gone, a teal-colored disturbance in the air the only sign of their departure.

~

Hamish couldn't contain himself. "Milady, Rio is a special warrior and ye think rather highly o' him, but why d'ye let him talk tae ye like that?"

"Rio never stops testing the limits, so if I set them, he pushes. It is part of what makes him such a gifted a warrior, one who has mastered every skill I have ever taught him. He will be a leader in the community one day, and I need him to know he can always speak his mind." She waved a hand dismissively. "He can be surly and saucy, but he is never disrespectful, and he always follows orders, no matter how distasteful he finds them. Ask him about the battle he fought alongside his brother that resulted in Morgan's latest defeat. The community comes first with him every time. Remember that."

"Aye, milady," Hamish replied, thoughtful.

"Close up the training room carefully. We may need it as a safe haven for our prized talisman. Have you worked out any other safe places for her should the need arise?"

"I've taken her by Ardmair Point, the caravan park north of

Ullapool where several druids live, and told her tae visualize herself there if she ever found herself in danger. Ye've given her this room. D'ye think she needs additional hidin' places?"

"We'll show her the tunnel under the manor and walk her through it tae the cottage from where we can spirit her off tae wherever ye decide will offer her protection," Alaisdair suggested.

"Excellent idea. That will be our first order o' business tomorrow," Hamish said.

"That is the second order of business. The first is a revelation of her prophecy so we can prepare for Rio's upcoming date with Morgan's champion."

"O' course, milady," Hamish said.

With her wishes clear, Scathach took her leave, disappearing in a cloud of shimmering red and gold particles. Hamish and Alaisdair followed the goddess's command and closed the training room protectively before returning to the manor the conventional way—by crossing the loch in the skiff and driving the short car-ride home.

Chapter Thirteen

RIO HELD CERI'S quaking form close when they arrived in the master suite in the manor. Remaining still, he let her gather herself. Though he tried hard to listen to her thoughts, she appeared to have been an apt pupil for Hamish. Her shield held firmly against his sneak attack, dammit.

At last she softened against him, so he pulled away enough to look at her. Even with tears staining her cheeks, she was the most beautiful woman he'd ever seen. He questioned her with a look, eliciting a wobbly smile from her, which allowed him to relax. His woman had heart—something he admired and needed in her.

"How are you?"

"Better with your arms around me." She fisted her hands in his shirt and started gushing. "Rio, the last thing I want is to let you down, but I don't know if I can face any more of those visions. I've never been more terrified in my life." Her eyes welled with fresh tears.

He set his lips on her forehead and said, "Those visions are life-saving. If you remember that, maybe it will be easier to have them."

"We'll see what you think tomorrow when Scathach makes me relive the one I had today."

Her mouth turned down.

Rio dearly loved to train and relished a battle that ended in besting whatever Morgan threw at him, but now was not the time to debrief the afternoon's training session. "You know, I wouldn't mind wrestling you out of your clothes—or letting you wrestle me out of mine," he said, waggling his brows.

"How can you have the energy to even think about that?"

"I'm holding your luscious body close to mine. What else would I be thinking about?"

"I can't believe you," she huffed.

"No? Believe this."

Leaning in, he deliberately plundered her mouth and relished the way she went from zero to climbing his ass. As he ran his hands up under her sweater and unhooked her bra, she tightened her embrace around his neck and lifted her leg high over his hip, opening herself to him. He rubbed his hard cock against her hot center, creating a beautiful friction he wanted to explore—without clothes.

He broke the kiss long enough to drag her sweater and bra over her head before his mouth was on her again, his hands roaming freely up and down the smooth lines of her back. Deep in her throat, she moaned and rubbed her body along his, begging for more. He traced his thumbs over the curves of her breasts before he slipped his fingertips beneath the waistband of her jeans.

Reluctantly, he pushed her leg back down so he could access the fly of her jeans. His mouth never leaving hers, he unfastened her jeans and slid a hand inside. Discovering her hot and slick for him, he grinned against her mouth before he kissed her harder and slipped one finger inside her. She shattered, screaming her pleasure at the touch of his fingers playing over her hard nub and plunging into her sweet pussy.

Without any finesse, Ceri grabbed two handfuls of Rio's T-shirt, ripping it up over his torso. A smile stretched over his mouth as he tried to return to manually pleasuring her, but she had other ideas. Sliding her hands between them, she undid the fly of his jeans and pushed them, along with his boxers, down over his hips enough to give her access. When she grasped his erection with both hands, she smiled mischievously into his eyes.

"What's good for the goose, and all that." She leaned forward and rained kisses over his shoulders and chest.

Rio let her enjoy herself at his pleasure until he couldn't take any more. He grabbed her wrists and pulled them up over his shoulders, drawing her into his embrace. "We're going to finish this in bed, lady," he said with a groan. He toed off his jeans before lifting and carrying her over to the big four-poster where he dropped her in the middle and fell on top of her. Her chiming laughter opened something that had been locked inside him long ago, a happiness he didn't remember until that moment. He stood up again and whipped her jeans down off her body.

"Oh, yeah?" More quickly than Rio could anticipate, she sat up, putting her at eye level with his ready shaft. She circled him with her tongue before sucking him into her mouth, and he thought he might pass out. Her unexpected and generous response made him feel more heroic than any training he'd mastered or any battle he'd won.

With one last hard suck, she let him go and sat back on the bed, her eyes glittering in challenge. "I think I'm winning the wrestling event in the bedroom Olympics."

After an exhale to master his control, Rio grinned. "Feels like a tie to me." He smoothed his hands over her body from her shoulders to her feet and loved how she shivered. Her belly rippled under his touch, and her nipples puckered sweetly, inviting his attention.

Straddling her, he dipped his head to suck first one dusky

tip and then the other, while she arched and writhed beneath him. "You're so responsive. Touching you is such a turn-on." He nudged her legs apart with his knee.

At the sight of her glistening center, his breath caught, and he murmured, "Oh, yeah, we both need this," before he plunged his cock deep inside her.

Lifting her hips, she met his thrust and cried out as she came almost instantly. In a few thrusts, he joined her. After the earthquake died down to tremors, he lay still on top of her, resting most of his weight on his forearms, but allowing his chest to flatten her breasts. Languorously, she ran her nails up and down his back. When his arms could no longer support him, Rio rolled off her and pulled her over him. She rested her head on his shoulder, one arm thrown lazily across his chest as they absorbed the afterglow of their connection.

Long minutes followed when Rio tuned into Ceri's even breathing. "Hey, babe," he whispered. "After all the working out we've done today, we should probably take a shower. I'll wash your back, and you can wash mine."

"Can't we stay here and take a nap?" she whispered back groggily.

He couldn't decide if the training or the lovemaking had left him so energized, but he needed to move. Sliding a hand down her back, he gave her ass a slap. "Wake up, sweetheart. We need a shower and supper."

Ceri growled as she pushed herself up and stared down at him. "There are subtler, more gentle and effective ways of getting what you want, you know." Her tone turned frosty as she rubbed her ass.

"Yeah, but they're not nearly as fun." He grinned and hopped off the bed. When he helped her up, he pulled her into his arms and rewarded her with a smacking kiss before he tugged her with him into the bathroom.

"We're only going to shower, lady. Don't get any other ideas," he said over his shoulder.

"Nothing like the pot calling out the kettle, warrior." She piled her hair on top of her head before stepping around him and into the spacious shower stall.

Afterward, Rio remembered he had no clean clothes in Ceri's room, and he certainly didn't want to put on his sweaty clothes from the afternoon. Scandalizing her, he exited her room wearing nothing but a towel wrapped low around his hips to walk down the hall to dress.

Two minutes later, he returned to her room carrying his duffel bag with him.

"I can't believe you did that, Rio. Anyone could have seen you."

"Like they don't know what we're doing in here?" he asked with a smirk.

"We don't have to advertise. What are you doing with that?" She pointed at his duffel bag.

"What does it look like? I'm moving in. Your shower is so much nicer than mine, and we can conserve on heat by sharing a bed. Very practical."

He winked at her.

"I'm not sure I'm ready for this, Rio."

At the look on her face, he softened his tone. "You signed on for this the minute you responded to my sign," he said quietly. "Surely, your aunt taught you this is what happens between warriors and talismans. Unless they're unlucky." The thought terrified him.

"I thought we'd take this slow, learn about each other before we made the commitment you're implying."

"What are you saying? That we might decide not to be together, find other mates and only do our duty to each other like Duncan MacManus and his talisman, Jennifer Carlin? I don't think so."

"I didn't mean that. It's ... this is all so sudden... I need to get used to it," she said quietly.

Even though he couldn't penetrate her thoughts, he determined to stop whatever crazy train she was trying to board.

"The best way I can think of to get used to our new situation is to embrace it—no excuses, no hesitations. Anyway, from what I gathered from Scathach today, the two of us can't afford to be apart, even in this house."

Rio experienced a tiny prick of conscience at his exaggerated interpretation of Scathach's meaning since he was reasonably sure Ceri didn't hear half of what Scathach said in the training room following her prophecy. But he needed her to be his completely, especially after discovering how making love with her shattered him.

He'd been wild about her from the moment he met her. Discovering that she was his talisman intensified those feelings. He wondered if the fates had decreed that circumstance as well. Still, he schooled his features into a bland mask while his emotions roiled inside him.

"I don't know what to do." Ceri sighed, her expression dejected. "I'm a hot mess."

Rio gathered her in his arms, resting his chin on her hair. "Let it work, babe. Everything will be fine in the end. You'll see."

When she relaxed, he said, "How 'bout we get dressed and see what we can find to eat. I'm starving."

She nodded.

He'd managed to win round one. Yet their history told him he had a few more skirmishes before he won her over for good. The outcome was never in question.

∽

The next morning, Rio awakened Ceri the same way he had the day before—with intense lovemaking followed by a slow shower.

Once again as she dropped down the stairs into the kitchen for breakfast, Hamish embarrassed her with his jovial interest in her night with Rio. "Are ye feelin' better then?" he asked with an innocent expression.

Alaisdair grinned as she felt her face heat.

"Those prophecies can rattle a person. 'Twas the same with yer mother."

She stopped in midstride as Hamish delivered his little bombshell, and Rio nearly collided with her as he stepped into the room behind her.

"My mother's gift was prophecy? But I thought Scathach said this gift was rare." She worried her lip. "I know exactly what happened to my mother, so you're saying nothing to bolster my confidence here."

"Aye, 'tis rare, but no' so rare among Conlan women. Had yer aunt found her warrior, I've nae doubt she too possesses this gift. It has tae do with our common ancestor, the druid who enchanted this house and family long ago. Because o' what ye are and fer whom, we must keep ye safe at all costs." Hamish directed the last bit at Rio.

"It's good your visualization skills are excellent, Ceri. If you were like your friend Alyssa, we'd be in serious trouble," Rio said, squeezing her hand as he led her to the table.

"There is that. If I could shield my thoughts like she does, we'd be much safer though."

"We'll work on that more taeday, lass. Ye better eat a hearty breakfast since Scathach intends tae join the training again, which means we likely willnae return tae the manor until late taenight," Hamish said as he dished up a steaming bowl of porridge and set it in front of her. "Alaisdair and I will gather something tae keep us goin' while the twa o' ye eat. There's eggs and bacon warmin' in the oven, Rio. Help yerself."

"Hey, Alaisdair, could you make tea? I don't think I can train on Hamish's coffee," Rio said with a mischievous grin.

Hamish scowled, but there was a twinkle in his eye. Ceri watched the men. *How long before I can so nonchalantly face the dangers our future guarantees?*

Thinking of the future reminded her she had an important phone call to make. Rio had a couple of calls to make too. "We need to let our families know about us, Rio. What time is it in Montana?"

"About supper time at the Sheridan residence. I'll call right after we eat. I'll need fortification before I talk to my mom," he said with a smirk.

"Your mom seemed very nice at Rowan and Alyssa's wedding. Why would you need fortification to talk to her?" she asked, perplexed.

"Her last son has found his talisman. It'll be all I can do to keep her from visualizing herself here on the spot. I bet you're going to have a similar problem with Shanley. Eat up."

Rio tucked into his breakfast with gusto.

Knowing she needed the sustenance, she still found it difficult to eat as she thought about Shanley's reaction to her news. Ceri knew Shanley would be relieved and happy for her, but part of her wondered how her warrior-less aunt would take the news.

After downing most of her porridge, she excused herself to make her call. Seated on the loveseat in the sitting room, she looked out at the beautiful grounds of Conlan Manor before she dialed up her aunt. Shanley surprised her when she picked up on the second ring.

"If I didn't know better, I'd think you were sitting by the phone waiting for me to call," Ceri began.

"It's so good to hear your voice. How is everything at Conlan Manor? Are you getting along all right with Hamish? How is the security system coming along?"

"Hamish is bossy but great. Rio and I have most of the basement, all of the first floor, and part of the second wired. He ran out of equipment, so we're waiting for more to arrive from home."

"You're helping Rio with the security system?"

"Yes, well, it was convenient. Now it's … well, it's more convenient."

"What does that mean?"

Ceri picked at the faded fabric on the settee. "I don't know how to say this, so I'll just say it. Turns out, Rio is my warrior. We discovered it the other night after a ceilidh Hamish took us to."

"Rio Sheridan is your warrior? Why are you only now discovering this?"

She heard the censure in her aunt's voice and cringed.

"He had some issues with a talisman who should have been his aunt, and he projected those issues onto me. It didn't occur to him to try his sign until we got into an argument the other night." She paused, gathered herself, and continued. "There's more."

"I'm listening."

"My skill is prophecy. Scathach is going to be involved in my training. In fact, we're headed to the training room in a few minutes to continue working."

"Aren't you supposed to be bonding with your warrior?"

"Bonding is apparently confined to nights now. We started training yesterday after Alaisdair spilled the beans about my lack of skill in shielding."

"Who is this Alaisdair, and how did he discover your weakness?" Shanley demanded.

"It's kind of a long story, one I'm afraid I don't have time to go into right now."

"I'm not sure I like this, Ceri."

"Listen, I know it's short notice and you don't have many days off, but would it be possible for you to come over for Samhain? Hamish is planning a ceilidh involving some sort of ritual intended to keep Conlans safe from Morgan and her nastiness. If you could be here, those protections would extend to you too."

Ceri tried to keep the worry out of her voice.

"I'll see what I can do. In the meanwhile, congratulations on finding your warrior."

She could hear Shanley's smile through the phone.

"I'm happy for you, doll. It doesn't hurt that he's hot."

"Shanley!" Ceri laughed. "Let me know your travel plans. And Aunt Shanley? I love you." She gripped the phone a little harder.

"I love you too. Never forget that."

Knowing he'd need space to pace, Rio made his phone calls from the massive salon in the front of the manor.

After breaking the news to his parents, he braced himself for his older brother's reaction. "Rowan, old man. How is married life treating you?"

"It's quite a ride. You should consider it," Rowan countered with a chuckle.

"Probably happening sooner rather than later."

He stopped wearing a trail in the Aubusson carpet as he awaited Rowan's response.

"You found your talisman!" Rowan burst out. "Some Scottish lass?"

"She descends from a powerful family in Scotland."

"Uh-huh."

"Where she inherited a manor recently."

He had to hold the phone about a foot from his head.

"*Get out!* Ceri Ross is your talisman? Why the *hell* didn't you know that before either of you went to Scotland?"

"Long story." He traced his boot along the pattern in the carpet. "Anyway, she's part of an ancient prophecy, something like you and Alyssa, so no doubt it was fated that we found each other inside Conlan Manor."

"Looks like none of us gets it easy." Rowan sighed. "Is Morgan aware of you two yet?"

Rio heard what Rowan didn't say.

"Scathach visited. We've already started training with her." He laughed hollowly. "We only discovered our relationship day before yesterday."

"Sorry, bro. The bonding is quite an experience when you're given time for it."

Rio grinned to himself. So far, bonding with Ceri had been the sweetest, hottest revelation.

Sobering, he said, "If we live through the next two weeks, we can kick everyone else out of the manor for a while and enjoy that part."

"Kick everyone else out?" Rowan questioned. "Who's with you?"

"No one yet. But Mom and Dad, and Riley and Lynnette are making plans to attend the ceilidh Hamish has planned for Samhain. He thinks that's when Morgan will likely attack."

"Hamish?"

"Hamish Buchanan is an old druid who's been caretaker of Ceri's manor for years. He has a ritual planned for Samhain, something to do with Ceri and me. He says he needs as many of our relatives who can attend to be here."

"You called the parents first. Bet Mom is over the moon."

Rio rolled his shoulders. "Actually, she was training with Riley and Lynnette, so I missed out on her screaming her excitement into my ear."

Rowan chuckled. "Don't worry, little bro. She'll uncork that explosion when she sees you. I'll have Alyssa rearrange her classes, and we'll be there by Saturday."

"What about the system you've been working on all fall?"

"The congressman is still posturing about how unnecessary home security systems are, so we'll help his campaign by cutting the workforce to Seamus."

"Thanks Rowan. With my own talisman the target of Morgan's wrath, I have a clue about what you went through last winter. Thanks for your help."

"Looking forward to it, little brother. Congratulations! This is great news," Rowan said before he hung up.

✦

Across the foyer, Ceri was on the phone with her best friend.

"He's gorgeous."

"What are you leaving out?" Alyssa asked suspiciously.

"Alyssa, my warrior is Rio Sheridan." Ceri tensed and waited.

For several seconds, the call remained silent before Alyssa whispered, "Rio Sheridan as in Riordan Sheridan my brother-in-law who professes not to like you?"

"Yeah, that Rio Sheridan. Only now I think he likes me a little," she said with a tiny grin.

"Rio never tried his sign on you any of the times you saw each other? Why?"

She stared out at the sharp blue sky over the gardens. "Timing and attitude. Why he tried it the other night when we were arguing—again—I don't know, but Hamish thinks it was fate."

Ceri explained the prophecy.

"This is eerie. First there's a prophecy concerning Rowan and me coming together. Now there's a prophecy concerning you and your warrior who happens to be a Sheridan. All of this happened for a reason."

While Alyssa listened with her customary care, Ceri explained the arrival of Scathach, her training, and the discovery of her talisman skill.

"I watched him die fighting one of Morgan's champions. I

didn't realize it was a vision until afterward, but I don't think I can view scenes like that regularly without losing my mind." Ceri stood near the window, but even the gardens in their autumnal beauty couldn't distract her from her fears. "It's a terrible gift."

"Not any worse than watching your warrior fight in real time, Ceri." The ocean between them couldn't mask Alyssa's sadness. "But it's our job. We're a team—we help our warriors fight their battles in whatever way the fates have determined is best."

Ceri sat on the loveseat, her fingers tracing patterns on the low table in front of it.

"Besides, now that you know you're seeing prophecies of what *can* happen rather than what *is* happening, you can view them more dispassionately. You can give Rio as much information as possible to prepare for what he'll face. Keep your mind on how you're helping him, and your skill will be easier to bear," Alyssa advised.

"Speaking of doing my job, Rio is standing in the doorway tapping an imaginary watch on his wrist, so I guess it's time to train. I'll talk to you again soon. Take care."

"Be safe, Ceri. Keep Rio safe too. He's truly a wonderful man once you come to know him."

CHAPTER FOURTEEN

ORRY TO CUT short your conversation, but Hamish and Alaisdair already headed to the training room. We'll visualize ourselves there—together," Rio said in a husky baritone as he walked over to Ceri and slipped his arms around her. "Ready?"

She wrapped her arms tightly around him and closed her eyes.

"Just a sec," he said.

"What?"

He lowered his mouth to hers for a scorching-hot kiss. "Something to tide us over until Scathach lets us return."

She blinked up at him, his kiss taking her mind completely off the task at hand.

"Now, visualize the training room."

Visualizing was difficult with his hot kiss lingering on her mouth. Still, they landed in the center of the room right as Hamish walked through the archway, Alaisdair trailing after him. Scathach regarded them from one side of the room, her eyes unreadable.

"No signs of my sisters last night or this morning?"

"There were nae discernable ripples around the manor

and nae strange signs along the road or out on the loch this mornin'," Hamish answered.

She paced to the middle of the room and back. "I cannot imagine they do not know something important has occurred here. Even though they have moved their home bases to America, they still feel the entire cosmos—at least I thought they did."

"Perhaps they're plannin' and donnae want tae let us know what they're up tae," Hamish said.

"That is worse. At least we have Ceri's prophecy as a start. Now then," Scathach said addressing her, "what did you see yesterday that had you screaming like a banshee, forcing all of us pay attention?"

"No warm-ups today?" Ceri asked before she remembered to whom she was speaking and ducked her head. Evidently, Scathach's abruptness was an acquired taste.

"I see your warrior is already rubbing off on you. Or he found a talisman exactly like himself," the goddess added with a wink at Rio.

Ceri gasped at Rio's audacity to wink back.

Recovering herself, she said, "I'm sorry milady. I didn't mean to be disrespectful. Only, I thought I'd have a chance to ease into it."

"The only thing we can be sure of is Morgan *will* attack. We need to prepare thoroughly and immediately. She could attack at Samhain, or she could attack at sundown tonight," Scathach said. "We do not know. But when she attacks should not matter. If we are ready, we can thwart her, and that is always the goal. What did you see?"

Ceri didn't want to disappoint the goddess, yet Scathach's power scared her to death.

She walked to the far side of the room where she'd been standing when the vision assaulted her. With her back to the others, she closed her eyes and remembered what she'd seen. She sensed

Rio behind her before he took her into his arms and pulled her against his solid chest. For a second, she could breathe.

Or so she thought.

"Describe what you're seeing. Aloud. Your shield is too strong even for me to see into your thoughts," Scathach commanded.

"It is?"

"Yes, love," Rio whispered for her ears only.

Scathach cleared her throat impatiently, giving Ceri no time to appreciate her improving skill. Instead, she dug her nails into Rio's hands encircling her waist and began. "Rio and an ancient-looking warrior tattooed in woad and wearing a kilt, a giant who towers over him, are fighting in a field. It's autumn because the grasses are golden. The giant has backed Rio to the edge of the field where it drops into a ravine strewn with sharp boulders. His strategy is to force Rio off the edge onto the boulders below."

When she stopped speaking, Rio tightened his arms around her.

"I can hear the giant's thoughts. He wants Rio to die a slow painful death from injuries he sustains in the fall."

Swallowing over the lump in her throat, she kept going.

"The giant keeps Rio's attention with his claymore while he batters Rio's free hand with a short sword. Rio's leathers are tattered, and he's bleeding profusely from that arm. As his arm weakens, the giant forces him to that side. For Rio to protect himself, he turns toward the giant who undercuts his sword with a mighty blow."

From some distance outside her, Ceri heard someone snarl. "She cheats. She always cheats."

"Knowing he cannot lose his weapon, Rio holds his sword tightly, something the giant counted on. The giant deals a second blow, forcing Rio off-balance when he sneaks in another thrust with his short sword. Rio's options are to take the short sword straight to his chest or to bend away from it. In his off-balanced state, he leans away too far and plunges over the edge onto the razor-sharp rocks." The vision of Rio's body lying inert in the ravine forced out a sob, and she sagged against him. Even knowing he held her gave her scant comfort as she recounted his death.

"He lies unmoving while blood from a piercing wound to his back flows over the pointed rock on which he landed. The giant stands at the edge of the ravine and laughs." Ceri blinked her eyes open and stared at the wall. "No, it's Morgan I hear laughing, but I can't see her. All I can see is Rio's blood flowing out of him like water."

She turned in Rio's arms, soaking the front of his T-shirt with her tears. He lifted her and carried her to a small cot Hamish had set up near the entrance archway. Her last memory before she passed out was Rio's voice.

"Do something for her!"

⮜

"She's fine. The first time a prophet recounts a vision is always like this. Lay your ear on her chest."

Rio did as Scathach suggested and sighed in relief at Ceri's steady heartbeat beneath his ear. Sitting back on his haunches while he gathered his emotions, he stared at her pale face. Smoothing the pads of his fingers over her silky skin, he reassured himself she was all right. Fear clenched his gut worse than any battle he'd ever fought as he'd listened to her tell her prophecy. The pain radiating through her as she recounted his death left him weak as he squatted beside her. More than anything, he wanted to live, to have time with this amazing woman the gods had given him. At last, he understood how much they both had at stake being fated for each other.

"Let her rest. We have work to do that does not include her for now. In fact, it will probably be easier on her if she doesn't watch." Scathach shocked Rio with her compassion. "Alaisdair, what can you do about Rio's leathers? It is his most damning weakness right now. If he does not have to protect his free arm, the giant must change his strategy."

"We can reinforce his jacket with lightweight mesh like divers use when they're swimmin' with sharks. It'll work like chain mail though it'll be a might heavy," Alaisdair said.

"He will have to be better conditioned. As will you."

Rio shrugged. Alaisdair raised an inquisitive eyebrow.

"You are a warrior still in your prime, and you will be defending Conlan Manor as usual. In the absence of your talisman and the presence of rogue warriors, you are going to need all possible protection. Reinforce your own leather as well."

"Aye, milady."

"Now, I will watch you spar. Begin." Immediately, Rio and Alaisdair engaged in a duel to hone their skills under Scathach's critical tutelage. Though the training session lasted for several hours, Rio considered it a mercy that forced his attention from Ceri's pain.

֍

Ceri awoke disoriented and groggy. She blinked at the noise pulling her from her slumber—the clamor of swords in pitched battle. As she fought to awaken fully, a picture of Hamish swam into her view, concern on his kindly face.

"Och, lass, there ye are. Ye had me goin' fer a while, but now ye're awake. Take a draught o' this. It'll restore yer energy as naethin else."

Her stomach rebelled at her first whiff of the foul-smelling broth.

Hamish grinned. "Hold yer nose and drink it all at a go. 'Tis easier that way."

Without questioning him, she pinched her nostrils and downed the contents of the cup in one long swallow. Before she had much chance to perceive the acrid taste in her mouth, Hamish handed her another mug filled with peppermint water.

"Drink all o' that as well. Not only will it rescue yer taste buds"—he grinned—"but it'll also settle yer stomach against the powerful herbs ye ingested. How are ye feelin' lass?"

Ceri stretched and smiled as she handed the mug to Hamish. "Surprisingly energized. How long have I been asleep?"

"Nearly all afternoon."

Her eyelids descended in a slow blink.

"The minute ye finished retellin' yer vision, ye passed out cold. Scathach says that's normal fer a prophet recountin' her first prophecy, but all the same, I think I'll keep some smellin' salts and my herbal broth handy from now on."

Across the room, Scathach debriefed Rio and Alaisdair about their practice. Rio glanced over and locked eyes with Ceri.

"'Scuse me, milady."

He walked away from his goddess in midsentence. Alaisdair stared after him, mouth hanging open at Rio's effrontery. Their patron merely looked amused.

Though her eyes never left Rio, Ceri heard Alaisdair's question. "Pardon me, milady, but is it wise tae allow him tae treat ye so disrespectfully?"

Her heart lurched in fear at Scathach's response. "You have fought him, and you have seen him spar with me. His skills are godlike. He is absolutely the finest warrior I have ever trained including all the great heroes enshrined on the walls of this room." Scathach nodded toward Rio with approval. "Racehorses were born to run. One may guide a racehorse, but you have to let him run."

Seeming to ignore the goddess's compliments, Rio knelt in front of her where she sat on the cot at the edge of the training room. "Ceri, are you all right? You scared the hell out of me when you fainted dead away like that." He rubbed his thumbs over the tops of her hands.

"I didn't pass out on purpose." She didn't bother to keep the snippiness from her tone.

"At least your experience didn't damage your sense of humor." His mouth quirked up in half a grin.

"Ri—ight. Watching you die twice in the last two days has been a riot." Pulling her hands from him, she crossed her arms over her chest. "Can't think why I'd want to escape those visions."

Rio laughed. "You're too easy."

She glared at him.

He waggled his eyebrows at her.

Finally, his insistent teasing cajoled a reluctant smile from her.

"We're going to be all right, sweet woman. Trust me," he communicated as he rubbed his hands up and down her arms.

Ceri smiled at him, but behind the safety of her shield she wondered. *How will I ever be able to keep watching you suffer without losing my mind?*

Scathach interrupted them. "You did well today, Ceri. Hamish can help you work on techniques so you remember you are only seeing visions, not reality. Think of them as exercises in preparedness, for that is ultimately what they are. Scenarios like those I create when I train warriors—not real battles."

"I'll work on it, milady. But it's so hard." Ceri cringed at the whine in her voice.

Scathach paid no attention. "The draught Hamish gave you will help you keep your focus next time you experience a prophecy. You will need to take some of it every day until you reach the point where you can relate the vision aloud as you are experiencing it. In the future, you may not have the luxury of time such as we have had with this first one. Rio may be facing the danger you see minutes after you see it. We must prepare for that contingency. As you have no doubt figured out, my sisters do not play fair."

Ceri tried to summon some of her usual confidence.

"You have no idea of your own strength."

A smile tugged at Ceri's mouth.

"Nor will you until it is tested."

Ceri's smile turned upside down.

"Maintain your focus on how much you love your warrior, and you will not fail him."

Having her feelings bared like that, before she'd even allowed them to form in her own mind, embarrassed Ceri like nothing she'd experienced in her life. Rio's searching look didn't improve her reaction to Scathach's words. Scathach appeared serenely unaware of the havoc she'd created in Ceri's world, but she could swear the goddess created it on purpose. She must remember never to talk back to or question her.

"We will break from training for the next couple of days," Scathach declared. "Rio and Ceri need more time to bond, Alaisdair needs time to build the armored leathers the two of you will use, and Hamish needs to enchant the grounds of the manor. That should keep each of you plenty busy." She stared meaningfully at each in turn. "I will let you know when you need to return here to *An Teallach* to train again before Samhain."

Scathach disappeared in her customary shimmering red and gold cloud, leaving her charges behind to wonder about her ultimate strategy.

CHAPTER FIFTEEN

EFT ALONE TO bond for a couple of days, Ceri and Rio had finally come downstairs to share a meal with Hamish, who had been enchanting the manor grounds, and Alaisdair, who had been reinforcing Rio's and his leathers.

"I'm headed intae Inversneckie tae pick up yer aunt. I'll be back taemorrow afternoon, lass," Hamish announced over dinner.

"She's flying in tomorrow? But Samhain isn't until Saturday," Ceri said.

"She telephoned while ye were otherwise occupied and asked if I could pick her up." Hamish grinned.

Standing from her place at the table, Ceri said, "I'll grab my purse and come with you."

Even though it had only been a month, it felt like a year since she'd seen her aunt. After everything that had happened, she needed Shanley's perspective—and maybe her shoulder to lean on.

"Lass, ye know that's no' possible. Scathach expressly ordered ye no' tae go anywhere except by visualization. Ye'll see yer aunt soon enough."

Rio slanted her a look before addressing Hamish. "Why do you call it Inversneckie?"

"It's an old Highlander name for Inverness. We also call it the Sneck, an affectionate term fer our beautiful Highland capital," Alaisdair said, his tone wistful. "Can't remember the last time I saw it."

Rio swallowed a bite of stew, wiped his mouth with his napkin, and said, "Seems a bit undignified for the capital city of the Highlands."

"Ye need tae get used tae the Scots sense o' humor lad. Nae one seems tae find fault with callin' a sea monster Nessie," Hamish said good-naturedly.

"There is that." Rio smirked.

"I know what you're all trying to do here, but it's not working. I'm not in the least distracted by all this nonsense about nicknames. What time is Shanley's plane arriving? I can visualize myself to the airport just fine," Ceri said, tapping her foot.

"None o' yer business, lass. Rio, I trust ye can keep our girl safe while I tend tae her aunt. I'm countin' on ye, lad." For once, there was no twinkle in Hamish's eyes.

"Ceri will stay right here at the manor. That's a promise, old man." Rio punctuated his vow by sliding his hand up the back of her thigh and giving her a squeeze.

She pushed his hand away. "You have nerve, Rio Sheridan. Just because you're my warrior doesn't give you the right to boss me around."

Seemingly unperturbed, Rio replaced his hand. "It does when you're deliberately planning to do something foolish and put yourself in danger because you're too impatient to wait a few hours." His voice was mild, but his eyes flashed a warning she didn't miss. "I doubt Shanley would be excited to see you if she knew the stakes for you to greet her at the airport."

Lifting her eyes to the ceiling, she gathered her patience. "I take your point, Rio. Hamish, you better not make any stops between Inverness and the manor after you pick her up."

"What if yer aunt wants tae visit an auld haunt or twa on the way? I cannae very well deny her that."

Hamish's pretend innocence as he carried his dishes to the sink exacerbated her frustration.

"You're incorrigible, you know that Hamish?"

"Ye've called me that before. I think ye mean tae insult me, but I take it as a compliment."

"Of course, you would." She glared at him. "Excuse me. I believe some books in the library need my immediate and undivided attention. You men won't mind discussing me over kitchen duty, will you?" She stood up from the table, dropped her napkin on her plate, and swept regally from the room.

As she headed up the stairs, she could hear them talking about her.

"The lady sure does know how tae make an exit," Alaisdair said, admiration in his voice.

Ceri permitted herself a small smile.

"She sure does." The humor in Rio's voice trailed her up the stairs.

Hamish laughed out loud. "Ye better see tae her then, lad. Wouldnae want her tae entertain any harebrained ideas like visualizing herself tae the airport out o' spite."

Her back went up at his insight, and she sped up the stairs.

⁓

Rio found Ceri in the library mumbling to herself about overbearing men who could use some finesse.

"Finesse is what you think we lack?" he asked good-humoredly.

Caught in the middle of her rant about the three men in the kitchen and men in general, Ceri jumped.

"Manners too. It's polite to knock to let someone know you're there before you scare the pants off them by walking into a room unannounced."

Rio looked her up and down, letting a lascivious smile play over his lips. "Scare the pants off? Though I can think of a few better ways to get your pants off, I can give scaring you a try."

"You're outrageous," she huffed before turning away from him to stare at the book in front of her.

"What are you pretending to read?" He massaged her shoulders as he looked over them at the book in front of her.

"There's no pretense. This is a family tree and history. It's part of a set I discovered before you started distracting me."

She deliberately turned a page of an enormous leather-bound book.

"Just now? Really?" He laughed.

"No, before we discovered you're my warrior."

"I love history," he said, taking a seat on an oak chair beside her at the long table in the middle of the library.

Apparently, she'd decided to forgive him. "Then, you might be interested in this." She pushed the open volume toward him. "I'm not very far into it, but there are several mentions of Rosses and Sheridans in it."

Rio's thigh brushed hers as he sat close beside her to read along with her. The fact she smelled so good, her light musky floral scent wafting over him whenever she shifted in her chair, had nothing whatever to do with why he sat so close.

Then the words on the page sucked him in. It took a bit to think in the old rhythms of the language, but the words fascinated him before they raised the hairs on the back of his neck.

"As much as Morgan hates the Sheridans, you are the prize, Ceri. I wonder if she knows."

"She didn't figure out the connection between Rowan and Alyssa or the implications for that connection for a long time. Maybe we'll be lucky?"

The hope in her eyes broke his heart.

Rio cleared his throat and returned to the book. "See where

the Conlans started marrying Sheridans?" He placed a finger on the elaborately illuminated page. "That's where the line switched from primarily female generations to male. Coincidently, that's the same time as the Highland Clearances. No wonder so many Conlans moved to the States."

"It's also the point where the Conlan, Sheridan, and Ross clans diverge." She ran her finger down the page. "There isn't a recorded marriage between a Conlan and a Ross or a Sheridan for one hundred-fifty years until my parents married."

"Now the product of a pairing of a Conlan and a Ross has found her warrior who happens to be a Sheridan." Rio slid his arm along the back of her chair. "The fact all of us are American of Scots descent shows that even geography and time can't interrupt the fates." The pretty pink color staining her cheeks told him she understood as her eyes strayed to his lips.

After a long blink, she returned to the book. "Geography and time might not be able to interrupt fate, but Morgan can. Even with your supernatural skill, you're still a man." She looked away toward the floor-to-ceiling shelves filled with leather-bound tomes. "I'm afraid of what's going to happen when Morgan decides to strike. Hamish and I were making progress with my shield that first day in the training room, but my vision interrupted us. The second day we didn't work on it at all." Her eyes returned to his. "That's a weakness Morgan is sure to discover and exploit, and then where are we going to be? I'll endanger everyone." Her mouth turned down.

"Ceri, love." Shifting in his chair, he took her hands in his and stared deep into her eyes. "When you had the vision and again when you retold it, none of us, not even Scathach, could breach your shield."

Her eyes saucered.

"I'm serious. Scathach had to ask you several times to tell us what you saw because no matter how hard we tried—and we all tried—none of us could get inside your mind."

"Really?"

"Since then, I've tried to take the occasional peek."

She narrowed her eyes, but he shrugged and said, "Hey, we're a team. We're supposed to keep our shields open to each other."

Her scowl made him smile. "Anyway, the only time I've been able to hear your thoughts is when we're making love—which I enjoy very much by the way, both your thoughts and making love." He kissed her knuckles. "Otherwise, I haven't been able to hear a thing you've been thinking unless you let me."

"Having the vision did something to my shield, you think?"

"Yeah. I think it set your shield as nothing else could. It wouldn't surprise me to discover Scathach helped you build such an impenetrable shield." He let her go. "In fact, now that I think about it, I bet she instigated that intense training session with that exact goal in mind. On some level, you were afraid for me even though you knew I trained with my goddess, which provoked a response in you."

Rio sat back in his chair, his thoughts whirling. "Scathach didn't seem at all surprised you have the gift of prophecy. She *would* know about that particular Conlan trait the same way she knows about the special fighting skills most Sheridans possess. She's sly that one." He tucked a strand of honey-blond hair behind her ear. "As soon as she sensed the change in the cosmos when I found you, she wasted no time coming to train us." His next thought sobered him. "It was only Scathach's excellent timing that saved Alyssa, so it makes sense she'd be paying attention again."

"Maybe it would be possible for me to hide in the training room until after Samhain. Maybe Morgan will go away."

Ceri's tone tore at his gut.

Rio took her face between his palms. "Hey, sweetheart, no doubting yourself or your warrior. We're going to take on Morgan and win like my brother and Alyssa did." He pulled her close and kissed her forehead. "Then we're going to take some time alone and bond properly without all these training interruptions and sharing a house with a mysterious old druid and his warrior sidekick," he said as he wrapped his arms around her.

"Not to mention all the family coming in this week," she mumbled into the front of his shirt.

"Oh, yeah, without them too," he said. "Especially without them. Sheridans tend to be loud and underfoot whenever we're together." He tested the silk of her cheek with the pads of his fingers. "I'll talk to Rowan about secure vacation spots after we get through Samhain."

She leaned back and looked up at him. "I kind of like the sound of that."

But her smile faded.

Sensing her morose thoughts, he closed the book on the table, stood up, and stretched.

"We have some time before your aunt arrives, and I have a good idea of how to spend it. Care to find out what my idea is?"

"Bet I can guess."

Still, she laughed and pushed back from the table to stand in front of him.

Taking her hand, he headed for the hallway. "Have you noticed how deep the Brits like their bathtubs? Even a guy my size can sit in one with water up to his shoulders if he wants."

"Are you sore and in need of a soak?" She stopped and tugged at his hand. "I'm your talisman, not your maid service. If you'd like someone to draw you a bath, you can look no farther than the nearest mirror."

She tried to brush past him, but he scooped her up, impeding another spectacular exit.

"I'll draw you a nice bubble bath if you let me join you in it," he whispered, his mouth on hers, tantalizing her with a soft kiss.

"You don't play fair, you know that?"

"It's a good tactic."

He traced her full soft lips with his tongue before slipping inside her mouth for a taste of hot feminine sugar. When at last he broke the kiss, he was happy she was panting. "You might regret that suggestion."

"I doubt it. You know what they say—all is fair in love and war."

"Which one are we experiencing?" she asked with a sassy smirk.

"Both. I'm a big fan of battle, but I'm coming around to an appreciation of love."

Hugging her close to his chest, he strode purposefully down the hall to the master suite.

∾

When Ceri awoke the next morning, it seemed the sun shone higher in the sky than usual. Smiling to herself, she remembered how sexy Rio looked under a blanket of bubbles. Playing with the bubbles had led to other things—like the follow-up massage in bed and an orgasm that seemed to last for hours. Just when she thought she and Rio had reached a pinnacle, he took her some place even higher.

Thoughts of the previous night heated her all over, a feeling Rio intensified by moving his big hand from its resting place over her belly down to her drawn-up knee before traveling its way back up her thigh to her hip, a teasing stop before sliding down to her mound where he gently tangled his long fingers in her curls. His leisurely exploration of her body left her wet and wanting.

"It must be late," she said softly.

"Mmm, more like early."

Ceri lifted her shoulders from the bed to see the sunlight edging the curtains. "Early?" she laughed incredulously.

"Yeah. Early afternoon." Rio sounded a little put out. "I've been waiting a while for you to wake up. In fact, I was about to wake you when I heard what you were thinking. Something after my own heart," he said as rubbed his hard shaft along the cleft of her ass.

"You're insatiable, you know that?"

She'd meant her words to be teasing, but they came out breathless as Rio's talented fingers found the hard nub between her thighs.

"No more than the other person in this bed," he pointed out, his tone infuriatingly reasonable.

She rolled over, but her retort died on her tongue when a loud commotion sounded in the hall. Hearing muffled voices and laughter moving distinctly closer to their door had Rio up and moving across the room before Ceri could even comprehend he'd left the bed.

"If I'm not mistaken, we've been invaded by the horde otherwise known as my family," he said as he locked the door.

"How can you tell it's them?"

"Trust me. When the Sheridans come to visit, it sounds like an assault."

Sighing, he headed to the bathroom. "I'm afraid we'll have to put our more pleasurable pursuits on hold, which is going to require a freezing shower for me." He gestured at the tangle of sheets and blankets in which she lay. "Just so you know, my mom will undoubtedly want the grand tour," he said over his shoulder before he disappeared into the bathroom.

Ceri bounded out of bed in a panic and started tidying the room. Their clothes were strewn in a telltale path to the bathroom, and the rumpled state of the bed left nothing to the imagination about what activities had gone on in it recently. In a desperate whirlwind to appear presentable, she had their room tidied before Rio stepped out of the shower.

Her arms loaded with a clean pair of jeans, a cotton T-shirt, and a sweater, she shouldered her way past him as he emerged from the shower. She barely registered the sexy way his towel rode low over his hips.

"Hey, it's only my family. You've met them all before. Relax." He took the clothes out of her hands and set them on the vanity before gently pulling her into his arms. Her breasts felt so good flattened to the hard wall of his chest, and his hands smoothing up and down her back kindled the fires the sounds of his family had doused. As much as they wanted each other, though, now was not the time.

Rio's lips nuzzled her hair. "I'll get dressed and greet our guests. Take your time and come down when you're ready."

"It's after one in the afternoon. What are they going to think of us not being up and around?"

He chuckled. "They're going to think they interrupted us when we were bonding."

She sagged against him in embarrassment.

"Hey, don't worry. They've all been where we are. They certainly won't think you've lured me over to the dark side." He tipped her chin up and winked. "Although now that I think about it, I wouldn't mind if you lured me over to the bed or the chaise or the shower, or—"

"*Rio Sheridan.*" The man knew exactly how to push her buttons. "Your family is outside waiting for us, you've taken a cold shower, and now you're being all suggestive again. You have no shame."

She couldn't help but laugh at the naughty expression on his face.

"Later, there will be someone luring someone somewhere—count on it, sweetheart." He slid his hand down and gave her ass a little slap. With a growl, she jumped out of his arms and headed to the shower.

CHAPTER SIXTEEN

RIO WAS STILL smiling when he exited the master suite and strode down the hall to see who all had arrived. Hearing voices in the grand salon, he loped down the stairs and opened the door wide to make his entrance. Alaisdair, standing nearest the door, greeted him first.

"Sorry about the commotion upstairs earlier. This bunch came tae the front door and marched right in when I answered it. Yer mother dinnae even stop tae look around before she headed up the stairs. I did the best I could tae keep 'em busy and give ye a little privacy."

Scanning the room, Rio saw that his parents, twin, and sister-in-law each held a mug of something in their hands as they sat together on the sofas in front of the fireplace. An urn of tea and two more mugs rested on the large coffee table in front of them. "You did fine. My family tends to overwhelm people on first meeting. Thanks for taking care of them." He clapped Alaisdair on the shoulder before he walked farther into the room.

In her typical form, Sian Sheridan stood up from the sofa near the fireplace and swept over to greet him. "Rio! I'm so glad to see you. Where is Ceri?" his mom asked as she smothered him in a warm embrace.

"In the shower. If we'd known you all were planning to come in today, I would have arranged to meet you in town and drive you out here," he said pointedly.

"What would be the fun in that, little brother?" Rowan asked, a wicked grin playing over his lips as he crossed the room from where he and Alyssa sat in a pair of chairs near the windows facing the garden.

"Rowan!" Rio clapped his brother in a bear hug.

"We heard there's going to be a big party here in a couple days and thought we shouldn't miss it."

"I'm glad you're here." Looking around at his family, Rio added, "I'm glad *all* of you are here. Scathach and Hamish think whatever Morgan has planned for Ceri and me is going to happen at Samhain, and she's going to pull out all the stops." He smirked. "Something about a drubbing the Sheridans might have given her last winter."

"Alaisdair hinted at that, son." His father smiled. "Nice to see you," Owen Sheridan added as he embraced Rio.

"We thought if we came a few days early, we might train together and figure out the lay of the land," Riley said as he stood to shake his twin's hand before pulling him into a tight hug that eventually included his wife Lynnette who joined them.

A squeal of delight interrupted the pretty little family scene playing out in the middle of the grand salon. A short, dark shape flew across the room to the doors of the room.

"Ceri!" Alyssa Sheridan yelled as she fiercely wrapped her arms around her friend.

"What are you doing here? I didn't think you could get out of teaching your classes," Ceri said as she returned her friend's embrace.

"Rowan and I decided we should be here to help."

"Ceri. It's so nice to see you again. Your ancestral home is lovely. Before the afternoon is over, I want the whole tour," Sian said.

Rio caught Ceri's eye and grinned at her.

"I took a second tour around the bedroom before I came downstairs and found a pair of my panties peeking out from under the bed where they lay over a pair of your boxers—wonder what your mom would have thought of that," she communicated to him.

"That we've been bonding and doing it well?" He smirked at her.

Deliberately, she looked away from him. "Thank you for coming. We can tour the house whenever you like," she offered.

Owen cut to the chase. "Welcome to the family, Ceri. We're sorry we didn't call ahead." His words conveyed one thing, but the playfulness in his tone said something else entirely, and Ceri blushed scarlet. He laughed and pulled her into a hug.

Rio knew his family would never let her up if she continued to respond like that.

His mom slanted his dad a look before she spoke. "Don't be embarrassed my dear. We're so thrilled Rio has found his talisman and she's someone we already know. It would have been more disconcerting to discover Rio staying down the hall than to catch the two of you in bed in the afternoon," she said matter-of-factly, but her eyes danced.

Ceri's color deepened, and both Alyssa and Lynnette flanked her, Alyssa slipping an arm around her waist, Lynnette taking her hand and giving it a squeeze. "Don't worry, Ceri. It was the same for us when we joined the Sheridans. They're always like this. It takes some getting used to, but you'll figure it out," Lynnette told her, but she was staring down the Sheridans.

Giving Ceri a squeeze, Alyssa said, "You know how private a person I am, but this bunch doesn't care. They're warriors through and through, which means they expect intense bonding. No one here is judging you, believe me."

Rio arched a brow at Ceri. *"Told you so."*

Hamish's booming voice echoed up the stairs from the kitchen. "Hello! We're back!"

"Excuse me. That's my aunt with Hamish," Ceri said before she bolted out the door and down the stairs.

"Give her a break, you guys. She's dealing with a lot here," Lynnette admonished with an arch glare at each of the Sheridans. Rio smirked to see she'd included his mom. Aside from her mother-in-law, as the talisman who'd been in the family the longest, maybe Lynnette thought it was her job to stand up for Ceri.

Rio walked over and dropped his arm over his sister-in-law's shoulders and dragged her close. "Aw, Lynnette. You know we're all teasing."

"Rio Sheridan, you know you're my favorite, but don't push it."

⁓

"Whoa, lass, slow down. She's going tae be here fer a while." Hamish laughed as Ceri leaped down the stairs and slid across the kitchen.

"You're here. You made it safely. I'm so glad to see you!" Ceri wrapped her arms tightly around Shanley. When she looked up and saw her old warrior protector, Finn Daly, she reached out an arm to include him in their embrace. "Thank you for keeping Shanley safe on the flight over."

"Hello, Ceri. I'm glad to see Rio hasn't scowled away your good humor," Finn joked.

"Judging from the color o' yer face, something amusin' must've happened," Hamish hinted.

Pulling away from Finn, Ceri rounded on Hamish. "If I didn't know better, I might believe you set us up to be caught bonding when Rio's family arrived."

"Now lass, what would be the point o' that? Ye made it clear ye already knew his family," Hamish said, his expression the very picture of innocence.

Ceri didn't buy it for a second.

"Why did you do that?" she wailed. "This has been the most embarrassing afternoon of my life, and I'm afraid the embarrassment might not be done."

"Layers, lass, layers. Ye should know that about Hamish by now," Alaisdair said as he descended the last step into the kitchen. "Hello, Hamish. Successful trip, I trust."

Something passed between the two men, but Ceri couldn't figure out what. Clearly, though, Hamish had had at least one other errand last night or this morning than merely collecting Shanley and Finn at the airport.

"Alaisdair, this is my aunt, Shanley Conlan. Alaisdair Graham is a warrior who helps Hamish look after the manor."

Alaisdair nodded.

"And this is Finn Daly, an old family friend."

Ceri frowned as Shanley stood stone still, staring gobsmacked at Alaisdair while Finn shook hands with the man.

"A pleasure," Finn said.

Alaisdair replied politely to Finn, but Ceri noticed his attention never left Shanley.

"Pleased to meet you, Alaisdair," Shanley said at last extending a hand to him.

"Likewise. The resemblance tae Ceri is remarkable," Alaisdair commented.

"The Sheridans are upstairs? We should go on up and join 'em. Have ye shown 'em the house yet?" Hamish asked.

"No," Ceri said as she watched something peculiar happen between her aunt and Alaisdair as they shook hands.

"Let's get tae it then, settle 'em intae their rooms and such," Hamish said jovially as he headed for the stairs.

❧

"Good afternoon. I'm Hamish Buchanan." He raised his voice to be heard over the laughter and conversation going on in the salon, the Sheridans making up in volume what they lacked in number. Ceri squeezed his arm and waited.

Owen introduced himself first. "Pleased to meet you. I understand from Rio you're the caretaker and resident druid at the manor. This is my wife Sian and our sons Rowan and Riley and their wives Alyssa and Lynnette."

As he named off each person, the men stepped forward to shake hands while the women inclined their heads and smiled.

"Ye're a rather handsome lot. Big too."

"Thank you, Hamish," Sian said beaming at her family.

Turning to Shanley and Finn as they followed Alaisdair into the room, Owen greeted them warmly. "Good to see you, Shanley. It appears we'll be spending much more time with the Conlans in the future."

Shanley nodded and smiled. "We've had a very fortuitous turn of events."

"Finn, old friend! I didn't know you were visiting too," Owen said as he took Finn's arm in the preferred warrior embrace, hands to elbows.

Finn glanced at Shanley. "Couldn't very well let one of my girls travel such a distance without some protection if I could provide it."

Owen's expression clouded. "From what we understand, we're going to need extra help in the coming days, and we know we can count on you."

"Ceri says ye have yet tae see the manor and settle intae yer rooms. We should remedy that before dinner." Hamish deferred to her. "Since this is yer home, lass, ye dae the honors."

Her new relationship with the Sheridans, even with her best

friend present as a buffer, felt strange and uncomfortable, but being the hostess of Conlan Manor was easy. "Right. Shall we move bottom to top or top to bottom?" Ceri asked, naturally addressing Rio.

"Bottom to top. That way I can show Dad and my brothers the security system as far as we've installed it." He glared at Hamish for a second. "And they can take notes on our mad skills," he added, grinning mischievously.

"Ha! I taught you everything you know," Rowan said.

"Except for the things I had to reteach him on the parts you made up." Riley smirked.

Rio rolled his eyes, and Sian and Owen smiled happily at the interplay between their sons. Ceri gaped at the relaxed Rio who emerged with his family. It was difficult to reconcile this guy with the intense Rio who sometimes didn't seem to trust her and the sensual Rio who shared her bed. Good thing they were starting downstairs since the height of the third-floor balconies might tip her over in the dizzy turmoil of her emotions.

Ceri led the way down to the kitchens, pantries, and Hamish's and Alaisdair's rooms. Alyssa and Lynnette chattered closely behind her while the three Sheridan brothers and their parents checked out the rooms and the security system. Hamish, Shanley, and Alaisdair, who were unusually quiet, brought up the rear.

When Ceri reached Hamish's room, she turned to him and asked, "Will any of us ever see inside this space, or is it still a sacred area off-limits to mere mortals?"

She was only half teasing.

Rio smiled. "Thatta girl, Ceri. Even my expert lock-picking skills haven't managed to open this door."

Hamish remained unperturbed. "All in good time, lass, all in good time."

"This is the only room on the lower two floors that's not wired for sound," Rio said. "Hamish assures me it isn't a problem, but he doesn't understand circuitry and the issues with exterior access to an unwired room."

"The wiring ye did outside the door here seems adequate. The way ye've set it up, lad, no civilian is going tae come through that door without alertin' the whole house. And no immortal is goin' tae come through my enchantments without upsettin' the entire cosmos, so I think between us we've met the goal o' keepin' out bad guys."

Ceri marveled at the way Hamish ignored Rio's displeasure and the rest of the Sheridans' chagrined expressions.

"Hamish, this is a serious matter. Did Ceri tell you one of the methods Morgan used to gain access to Alyssa included a civilian sent to break into her house to steal whatever protections he could find?" Rowan asked. "We could wire your rooms before dinner if you let us inside."

"She did, but it's no' time yet for ye tae go inside this room. Trust me, we'll know when that time comes. Until then, what ye're already doin' will be enough tae keep out any civilians Morgan manages tae recruit."

Obviously, he would allow access to his rooms only when he was good and ready.

"Well, that's all there is to see down here. Let's go up to the dining room, shall we?"

Ceri cringed at the fake brightness in her voice as she moved down the hallway into the kitchen.

The tour of the rest of the house took most of the afternoon. The Sheridans were suitably impressed with the manor itself, the job Hamish had done keeping it up, and the security system Rio and Ceri had installed so far. The family agreed installing as much of the rest of the system as they could in the three remaining days before the ceilidh at Samhain would be their secondary goal behind training with Scathach at *An Teallach*. The civilians

Morgan might enlist could always be bested, but her rogue warriors and zombie champions were another story.

Following the tour, the Sheridans moved into the manor in earnest. Rio put his parents in his "old room" at the end of the hall opposite the master suite since Ceri had already set up that room. Riley and Lynnette took the room next door while Rowan and Alyssa occupied the room across the hall from them. Shanley chose a room at the top of the stairs across from the library that looked out over the gardens. Finn asked for one of the small rooms on the third floor down the hall from the ballroom. Living on his own for so many years, he rather enjoyed his privacy, he said, and a room on the third floor suited him fine.

While the family settled into their rooms, Rio and Ceri joined Alaisdair and Hamish in the kitchen. Hamish had brought home an enormous roast, which he'd put in the oven to cook while the family toured the manor. Rio and Ceri found him busily preparing some sort of cabbage dish while Alaisdair carved his way through a mountain of potatoes. Rio joined Alaisdair at potato peeling, and Ceri washed the cabbages Hamish put beside the sink.

In short order, the four of them had a hearty dinner simmering on the stove, so Ceri headed upstairs to set the table in the dining room. There was no way they all would fit around the cozy table in the kitchen. While she worked, she kept turning over in her head the events of the day. Though her embarrassment at Rio's family catching them bonding rippled through her, the event that really had her going was Shanley's response to Alaisdair. If Ceri didn't know better, she'd have thought the two of them had a past. But Shanley had never mentioned Alaisdair in any of their conversations about Conlan Manor. From her aunt's descriptions, Ceri felt she already knew Hamish before she set eyes on him, yet Alaisdair had been a complete surprise.

But maybe not to Shanley.

CHAPTER SEVENTEEN

ERI RE-ENTERED THE kitchen sometime later to find Hamish, Alaisdair, and Shanley in the middle of a conversation.

"Jumped the gun, lad—again." Hamish emitted a long-suffering sigh. "Cannae be helped now. Ye best be takin' care o' business, I expect. We'll put somethin' aside fer ye fer later. Ye know where the key is."

"I know ye wanted me tae wait, but ye dinnae see her in the glow of the settin' sun. Even *you* couldnae resisted such a lovely vision," Alaisdair said.

"Shanley?" Ceri froze. "Are you and Alaisdair?" She couldn't form a complete thought as she tried to comprehend the implications of what the men were saying.

"Yes, love," Shanley said with a smile. "My warrior has finally found me. Apparently, we have some things to do now. I'll see you tomorrow."

When Ceri moved to hug her aunt, Rio put out a hand to stay her. "Not now, sweetheart. She'll talk to you later," he said so only she could hear.

Her face flamed as she realized she impeded an age-old ritual necessary for the safety of the talisman and her warrior. No one had been around when Rio found her, so she hadn't faced Shanley and Alaisdair's rather public situation.

"With Scathach insistin' on trainin' taemorrow, the twa o' ye had best make the most out o' what's left o' tonight. Ye'll know when ye're needed at *An Teallach*," Hamish said amiably as he bustled about putting the last touches on dinner.

"Give our regrets tae the rest o' yer family. I'm sure they'll understand," Alaisdair said with a grin. With a tug on Shanley's hand, he led her down the hall to Hamish's door.

Ceri followed as Rio stepped around the corner to sneak a peek into the old druid's room. Alaisdair obligingly held the door open long enough for them to have a look.

Rio stomped back to the kitchen. "There's a door leading out of your room. You said there was no way anyone could access it from the outside. What gives, old man?"

Unperturbed, Hamish pulled the roast from the oven. "The door leads tae the cottage Ceri found the day she and Alaisdair met. It's an escape route out o' the manor, and I've enchanted both the tunnel and the cottage." He grabbed a carving knife and long fork from a drawer beside the oven. "I hoped Alaisdair wouldn't have tae use it again once Ceri moved intae the manor—and he wouldn't have needed tae now if we dinnae have a houseful. Givin' his talisman some privacy when they bond was thoughtful o' the lad. Twenty years ago, I doubt it would have occurred tae him." Hamish chuckled as he lifted the heavy roast from the pan and set it on a platter to rest.

"Are you going to let us in there to wire the door at least?"

"First thing in the mornin' if ye like."

"Why couldn't you tell us when we were working down here in the first place?" Rio fairly vibrated with frustration. "It would have helped tremendously with the circuitry if we could have wired it in with the rest of the downstairs."

"At first I needed tae keep Alaisdair a secret until we knew the lay o' the land so tae speak. Then we thought it best tae keep the escape tae ourselves until we knew what tae expect from yer clan."

When she saw his fists flex, Ceri took a step toward Rio.

"Now that Shanley and Alaisdair have found each other, they're both the safer, and we've improved our odds at Samhain. With all o' ye bein' interrelated now, everyone has a stake in keepin' the manor and all o' those inside it safe. We had tae be sure."

"Thanks for the vote of trust, old man. If Ceri felt safe enough with the Sheridans to hire us to do the job here for her, and she's the heir, then you should have trusted her judgment—and us," he grumbled.

His feelings were hurt?

Hamish didn't miss a beat as he handed Ceri a bowl of salad. "Better a few ruffled feathers than a dead Conlan heir. Now, let's shake and make up before our dinner gets cold," he insisted, extending his hand to Rio who made him wait a few seconds before forgiving the old druid.

As Ceri headed to the stairs, she thought about the implications of her aunt finding her warrior so long after their twenty-eighth birthdays. If not for having to take care of her, would Shanley have returned to Scotland and met Alaisdair sooner, alleviating them of the terrible risks they'd faced daily for the past twelve or thirteen years?

"Ye're doin' mighty well with yer shield lass, but ye donnae have a poker face worth spit. What's upsettin' ye?" Hamish asked.

"If not for me, maybe Shanley and Alaisdair would have met long ago."

Rio stepped behind her and rested his hands lightly on her shoulders. Without thinking, she lifted one hand to cover his.

"No' likely. I had a hunch about Shanley, and I talked her

intae stayin' on fer more than a year. During that time, Morgan kicked up a ruckus in Eastern Europe that called away most o' the warriors includin' Alaisdair. He dinnae return until a couple o' months after Shanley went home tae the States." Hamish picked up a giant bowl of potatoes and headed up the stairs.

Rio grabbed the vegetables, and he and Ceri followed Hamish.

"He was young and carefree and full o' himself then and certainly in nae hurry tae settle down." His voice seemed to echo off the stairs. "Before we knew it, Shanley had lost her sister and inherited ye while Alaisdair searched desperately but in vain for his talisman that last year before his fateful birthday. The rest ye know."

They put the food in the middle of the long table in the dining room and headed back to the kitchen for the rest.

"Shanley could have come over with ye at any time, but she feared exposin' the twa o' ye tae Morgan by travelin' without protection, and Finn had another talisman tae look after."

Ceri frowned.

Hamish raised a bushy brow. "Yer friend Alyssa, I suspect. It was circumstance—or fate that kept them apart till now."

Hamish picked up the knife and fork and began carving the meat. "If Alaisdair had any patience at all, we could have used their mutual discovery in the rituals at Samhain tae cement the enchantments. 'Course, the same could be said fer yer warrior as well." From beneath his bushy brows, he gave Rio the side-eye. "The twa o' ye waitin' only so long and then tryin' yer sign right before the crucial time has been rather tryin' fer this old druid," he muttered.

Rio wrapped his arms around Ceri's shoulders and leaned down to whisper in her ear. "Knowing what I do now about bonding with you, if I had it to do over, I'd have discovered our relationship long before we left the States. Bet that would drive Hamish up the wall." He kissed her behind her ear and stepped away to carry more food up to the dining room, a grin playing on his lips.

CHAPTER EIGHTEEN

HANLEY AND ALAISDAIR are a pair? Guess I'm excess baggage now." Finn's mouth turned down after Rio clarified the reason for their absence from dinner.

"Finn! How can you say that? Without you, probably Ceri nor Shanley nor I would have lived long enough for our warriors to find us. We depended on your protection," Alyssa protested.

"Absolutely," Ceri agreed. "Shanley would never have made the trip over here this time if you hadn't agreed to accompany her."

Mollified, Finn said, "Well, now you point it out, maybe I have been of some use."

"Nae doubt we'll need all the warriors we can muster on Samhain. I'm mighty glad tae have ye here," Hamish said quietly, his usual teasing tone subdued.

The clattering sounds of utensils scraping plates stopped as everyone looked up from their meal to stare at the foot of the table.

"You honestly believe a major battle is going to take place on Saturday, don't you Hamish?" Rowan asked.

"I had nae doubt before Ceri's vision t'other day in the

trainin' room. Since then, I've been thinkin' about all the ways we'll need tae defend ourselves and the manor on Celtic New Year. Once Morgan realizes both Conlan talismans have found their warriors, she's goin' tae be spittin' mad." He sipped from his glass of wine as he stared down the room at the portrait of Fianna Conlan above the mantel. "I wish we had more time tae prepare, but Ceri's birthday dinnae fall until the autumnal equinox, and we had tae wait until she officially became the heir."

"You've enchanted the manor, Hamish. What about the grounds?" Sian asked.

"The gardens, Alaisdair's cottage, and the tunnel leadin' tae it. The rest o' the grounds are tae much tae enchant effectively."

Rio steepled his hands above his plate. "What exactly is going to happen at Samhain? Besides you opening up the manor to any intruder Morgan decides to send the minute the ceilidh begins." He scowled at Hamish.

"'Tis necessary, lad. Without the ceilidh and the rituals we'll disguise as ancient dances and songs, we cannae guarantee the long-term protections for the Conlan heirs as prophesied."

Hamish picked up his knife and fork and resumed eating his dinner.

Rio held himself stiffly, his jaw clenching.

"Hamish, there's something about the ceilidh that's bothering me. With all the training you're saying we'll be doing over the next three days, when will there be time to prepare food and ready the house?" Ceri asked, trying to ignore Rio's smoldering anger.

"I forgot tae mention it lass, but we're havin' the ceilidh catered by local civilians and druids who will also dress up the front hall, the stairs, and the ballroom. All will be in perfect readiness."

"Are you sure we can trust these people not to override your enchantments or sabotage my security system?" Rio asked with a scowl.

"'Course I can trust 'em. They're old friends, and some o' the druids are my students. Davy Sutherland will be one o' the helpers, and ye both know him."

Hamish kept his head down when he dropped that bombshell.

"The druid who asked Ceri out? Oh, yeah, I trust that guy." Rio glared at the top of Hamish's head.

All thoughts of dinner seemed to have disappeared as the rest of the Sheridans watched the exchange like spectators at a dodgeball tournament.

"Naethin' tae worry about. Davy's solid. Besides, Ceri will be with ye all night in order fer the enchantments tae take effect. Davy's nae threat tae ye," Hamish said with a grin.

Rio leaned back and crossed his arms over his massive chest. "I never thought he was."

Ceri caught Rowan and Riley smirking at each other.

"I don't like druids pursuing talismans. It's unnatural and could deprive a warrior of his fated mate."

The grin slid off Rowan's face. "If you're still on about Siobhan and Duncan MacManus, you can stop right now. Duncan's talisman was far less attracted to Duncan than he was to her. You have to let it go, little brother."

Red tinged Rio's cheekbones before he gave his undivided attention to his roast beef.

"Lad, I understand yer concerns, and usually the gods agree with ye. When they donnae, ye have tae accept it." A tiny grin played over his lips. "That date with Davy sure grabbed yer attention, though," he said blandly, his eyes on his plate.

It was Ceri's turn to vent her frustration. "Thanks a lot, Hamish. You have no idea the hell Rio put me through when we were wiring the house after that date."

"Just because Hamish set you up didn't mean you had to go," Rio said peevishly.

"I'm sure she didn't have any fun at all Rio, did you Ceri?" Rowan asked, grinning.

"Of course not, big brother. How could she have fun with someone who was probably nice to her when she could have been hanging out here with Mr. Personality?" Riley added, the look on his face pure mischief.

"Keep it up you two, and I'll make a special request of Scathach to train exclusively with you tomorrow," Rio said.

"Now, lad, why would you go and do that when you know how much you want to spar with me?" Finn asked, feigning innocence.

"Rio, would you help me with dessert please? Hamish's special apple cobbler is probably the right temperature to bring up and serve now." Ceri stood from the table.

"You're training her well, little brother. She's got your back no matter what battle you're fighting." Rowan leaned back and slid his arm around Alyssa, the picture of composure. "Good thing too, since you're losing this one. I can't wait to take you on tomorrow."

"Rowan, stop goading Rio. If not for him, Morgan's nasty zombie giant might have had time to set up an ambush for us last winter," Alyssa said.

"Pixie-girl, we're helping Rio lighten up, right Riley? Finn?"

"Exactly the way everyone took it," Alyssa replied dryly.

Ceri walked out of the dining room, expecting Rio to follow her, which, eventually, he did.

When they were out of earshot of the others, he said, "I don't need any help fighting battles with my family, thanks."

"You were down three to one and taking a beating. If you couldn't see that, then we're both in trouble when Morgan sends her minions after you." She stomped down the stairs in front of him.

"I noticed you didn't deny having fun with your druid on that date."

"He's not *my* druid, and I did have fun on that date." She stood in the middle of the kitchen, hands on hips. "He showed me the loch, which took my breath away, and he told me all sorts of entertaining tales about Scotland and her heroes. Not once did he take a shot at me."

She turned away to gather dessert plates, slamming cupboard doors and shoving the utensil drawer closed with her hip after retrieving forks from it.

Rio stepped in front of her before she could move toward the stairs. Taking the plates and forks from her hands, he carefully set them on the countertop beside her and gathered her into his arms. "I'm sorry. Thank you for having my back."

When she softened in his arms, a wicked grin spread over his face.

"I can tell you stories about great heroes from history anytime you want to hear them, but I'd rather do this with you," he whispered against her mouth before he brushed his lips over hers.

In two short seconds, Rio's passion stole the remnants of her anger. She wrapped her arms around his neck and held him tightly as she deepened the kiss. While he smoothed his hands up and down her back, she molded her body to his. Settling his hands on her ass, he pulled her intimately against him, leaving her no doubt that *this* meant much more than a kiss.

A noise at the top of the stairs had them backing out of the kiss.

"Hey, did you two get lost trying to find dessert?" The laughter in Rowan's voice echoed down the stairs.

"We'll be up in a sec. Have another slice of roast beef. You're going to need all the fortification you can get before you face me tomorrow," Rio called back, but there was no heat in his words.

"Guess they're ready for dessert." Ceri sighed.

"Me too, but I'll have to wait for mine." Rio waggled his eyebrows at her.

"You're incorrigible, Rio Sheridan."

"Yeah, but I bet if I slipped my hand down the front of your jeans, I'd discover you're looking forward to dessert as much as I am."

Her face warmed as he traced her cheek with his index finger.

"Uh-huh. Glad to know my woman entertains the same naughty thoughts I do, but you're going to have to save them for later. I'll make the wait worth your while, I promise," he said and slipped around her to grab the pan of warm apple cobbler.

She didn't know whether to laugh or be embarrassed, so she did both as she picked up the plates and forks and headed up the stairs.

"Hang on a sec."

She arched a brow.

"I thought I saw something outside." He set the pan of dessert down on the table and walked over to the door.

"What is it?"

He flipped on the outside light, but the bulb was so dim, she doubted he'd see anything. After he locked the door, he went over to the main security panel in the pantry and armed the entire system.

"If Alaisdair and Shanley decide to return to the manor sometime during the night—not a likely scenario"—he grinned—"but if they do, they'll come through the tunnel where the system won't affect their entry. Anyone else can stay outside."

He picked up the dessert and followed Ceri up the stairs to the dining room.

⁖

After dinner, the family adjourned to the grand salon where the women drank Ceri's tea without fussing at her a bit—something she pointed out to Hamish with relish.

"They're American and family. O' course they wouldnae say anythin' about yer weak tea," Hamish said as he offered their guests his best whisky.

After serving everyone, his attitude turned deadly serious. "Ceri's been readin' some o' the family history when she's had a spare minute, so she can tell ye the Rosses, Sheridans, and Conlans shared quite a history back several generations before the families moved tae the States. It's nae coincidence the families are comin' taegether now."

He tossed back his dram and poured another.

"The battle we face is fer the survival o' entire clans, no' only the families represented in this room. Fate brought us taegether here at this time. At the ceilidh on Samhain at precisely midnight, we'll gather in the ballroom fer what will appear tae others as a specialty reel, but it'll be the ritual fer a powerful enchantment. Each o' ye will need tae let down yer shields and follow my directions as ye dance the ritual," he said.

"What if we're engaged in battle at the precise hour?" Riley asked from where he leaned against the mantel.

"The battle will take place on another plane," Hamish said matter-of-factly, which left all the warriors in the room gaping at him. "Morgan will do everythin' she can tae stop ye, but remember, most o' what she brings is an illusion. Her warriors are dead men brought artificially tae life fer the battle at hand. At midnight civilian time, we must enact the ritual."

Rio stood up from his seat on the arm of the sofa and joined his twin in front of the fireplace. "If one of us is in danger, especially if that one happens to be a talisman, we have to rescue that one first," he insisted.

"If we donnae perform the ritual in the window o' time we have at midnight, it willnae matter if we dae or donnae rescue each other. All will be lost."

"You're saying, Hamish, we should consider ourselves in a bunker for the next few days?" Owen asked from the sofa where he sat beside Sian.

"Exactly, except tae go tae the trainin' room at *An Teallach*.

Taemorrow, ye'll have tae use civilian transportation, except fer Ceri and Rio. Scathach ordered them tae visualize themselves there. After ye see where it is, I'd advise all o' ye tae visualize yerselves there if she wants us tae train again."

"Why has Scathach ordered you to visualize yourselves to the training room?" Sian asked.

"She didn't insist I do it, but since Ceri is the real prize in all this, she has to visualize herself there. I'm not letting her out of my sight, so we go together," Rio said, his eyes finding his talisman.

"Ceri is the prize?" Rowan asked from where he stood near the grand piano in the middle of the room.

"That's the part Hamish left out, big brother. Without Ceri, the rituals won't work. No doubt she's going to be Morgan's target." He raised his brows meaningfully. "I wasn't kidding when I said now I understood what you went through with Alyssa last winter."

"Whatever happens, we can't let Ceri fall into Maeve and Morgan's hands." Alyssa slipped her hand into Rowan's. "Their tortures are excruciating. Whatever we have to do to keep her safe, we all must do it." Her voice trembled.

Rowan stepped behind his talisman and placed his hands on her shoulders. Whatever passed between them calmed Alyssa, but Rio caught the flash of fear in her eyes as she looked at Ceri.

In that moment, Ceri gasped and sat up rigidly on the sofa. Everyone watched in horrid fascination as her face contorted with pain and fear at something only she could see. Rio rushed to hold her, but he didn't try to soothe or help her. Instead, he allowed the prophecy to take its course. Watching her endure it and sensing her pain and fear was so much worse than fighting a battle. Still, he held her close and swallowed his emotions. As usual, he tried to breach her shield without success. All he could do was wait and hope she didn't suffer too much.

෨

Ceri watched her aunt's agony at the hands of Maeve and Morgan. Maeve tortured her with pictures of Alaisdair and beautiful women in the throes of passion before she handed him over to Morgan. He had eluded them for too long, and now that he'd finally attained wholeness with the discovery of his talisman, they were determined to take him, the timing too delicious to believe. Ceri cried out as she watched her aunt fade into the mists behind Alaisdair while Morgan stood across the ford smiling back at Ceri, her red eyes glowing with evil triumph.

Ceri gasped, her heart thundering in her chest as the room came back into focus. Rio held her tightly in his lap while the others hovered around them with looks of concern. As she glanced around at the familiar faces, she realized she'd experienced another vision. Morgan and Maeve hadn't stolen Alaisdair and Shanley while they bonded after all.

She struggled to rectify the vision with reality and snuggled into Rio's strong arms, incredibly grateful for the solidness of his body holding hers, her anchor in the turbulent sea of prophecy into which she'd been tossed. Losing her parents had been one thing. Losing Shanley would rip a hole in her world too big to fill. When she raised her eyes to Rio's face, her heart stuttered at the quintessential loss she couldn't face.

Hamish knelt in front of her. "Lass, I hate tae ask it o' ye, but if ye could tell us what ye saw, it would benefit us all. We're on a bit of a schedule with Samhain so close. If it's tae much, we'll wait till taemorrow at the trainin' room with Scathach," he said gently.

Ceri sucked in a breath. "It's all right, Hamish. It might be easier to share my prophecies sooner rather than later. Maybe then I won't think about them so much." Her voice cracked at her attempt at bravery. *How am I going to live the rest of my life enduring this?*

"Trust me, lass. Ye'll reach the point where ye know ye're in a vision as ye're having it, and ye can analyze it as it plays out in yer mind. If that dinnae happen, there would be nae prophets among us. They all would have gone stark ravin' mad." Hamish patted her hand and handed her a dram of whisky.

"I see I've dropped my shield again," she said wryly.

"Only when ye came out o' the vision. While ye were having it, none o' us could get in."

"I take it you all tried?" she asked as she took in the faces of those crowding around her.

"O' course, lass."

"I tried, which you know is expected of your warrior." Rio's tone brooked no argument.

"You were in such distress. I thought I could help you," Alyssa said.

"Me too. If there's some way I can help you help my son, I want to know," Sian added.

"This one wasn't about Rio. Or at least not directly. It may be related to my first vision since that one took place out by Alaisdair's cottage and this one specifically involved Alaisdair."

At Alaisdair's name, Rio tensed, and Ceri made a face at him. "And Shanley. I saw Maeve torturing Shanley with pictures of Alaisdair and other women before she gave him to Morgan to take across the ford. Shanley gave up and followed him while Morgan stared at me and laughed."

Alyssa turned white. "They're going to do it again."

Ceri shared a sympathetic look. "I know Scathach thinks I'm the key to the prophecies, but that vision makes me think it may be Shanley instead."

The thought of losing her aunt gutted her.

"We need tae think o' ways the twa o' yer visions intersect since it appears there's some relationship between 'em. Why would Rio be fightin' Morgan's champion on the end o' the property near the cottage? How might she lure him out there and when?"

"What was Ceri's other vision?" Rowan asked.

"I saw Morgan's champion force Rio over the edge of a ravine where he died on the rocks," Ceri whispered, her voice raw, the prophecy disturbing her as much in the memory of it as in the actual experience of having it.

"Alaisdair was fighting tae. Morgan took both o' them in Ceri's vision," Hamish added. "What she saw gave us insights intae how Morgan's champion will fight and how her rogue warriors will attack Rio. We've been makin' precautions tae preempt Morgan's threat."

"What sort of precautions?" Owen asked.

"Alaisdair reinforced Rio's and his own leathers with lightweight steel mesh, and I've added extra enchantments tae the manor and the cottage."

"I checked out the area where the battle might happen, and I know where I should avoid letting the zombie lure me or force me to go," Rio added.

"O' course this was before Shanley arrived and Alaisdair discovered her tae be his talisman. There may be differences now. That's the way o' it with prophecy. It's an inexact gift, but it does allow us tae plan rather than tae react."

Sian looked thoughtfully at Ceri. "I think you're the target, not Shanley. I've studied many talismans and their talents over the years, and your gift is extraordinary. To be able to see other warriors and battles beyond your own warrior is a singular ability. I've never heard of anyone having that skill before, and I'm sure Morgan would like to be sure the one who has it isn't around long to share it."

Rio's head came up at Sian's insight.

Rowan stepped forward. "Ceri's been through a lot today. All the traveling we did to arrive here has worn me out as well. It might be good to rest, think about our options, and revisit all this in daylight."

Owen stood and stretched. "Good idea, son. That plush room Ceri set up for us is calling me. Sian? You ready to call it a day?"

"We'll continue this conversation in the morning. Good night all," Sian said as she took Owen's hand and the two walked out of the salon.

"Ceri, did you say you had your family tree and history laid out in the library?" Alyssa asked.

"Alyssa, give it a rest until tomorrow. You know I sleep a whole lot better when you're sharing the bed," Rowan said, giving her puppy dog eyes.

"Oh, fine." She sighed dramatically. "I'll take a look at the family papers tomorrow. G'night, all."

She winked at Ceri before she led Rowan from the room.

The others offered their good nights and headed up the stairs. Hamish insisted on cleaning up so Rio and Ceri could retire as well.

"Thanks, Hamish. Those visions drain me," Ceri said.

"No' tae worry, lass. Ye'll need yer rest fer the day ye're likely tae face taemorrow."

"Hamish," Rio interrupted, "make sure your door is locked. I saw a shadow lurking around the back door tonight before we brought up dessert. It may be nothing, but we don't need to take any chances. I armed the system, so all is secure—except your room." The look on his face said it would be a while before he got over his mad at Hamish.

"Naethin's goin' tae breach this house through my rooms, donnae ye worry, lad. But I'll pay attention in the kitchen all the same. Thanks fer lettin' me know."

Rio nodded and turned to Ceri, swinging her high into his arms to carry her off to bed. Weak from her vision, she didn't resist. Instead, she wrapped her arms around his neck, burrowed her face into his shoulder, and enjoyed the ride.

CHAPTER NINETEEN

WHEN THEY ARRIVED in the sanctuary of their room, Rio laid Ceri carefully on the bed and slipped her shoes off. For several long seconds as he gazed down at her, she worried he thought her more a burden than an asset.

"I have to be honest, sweetheart. I'm scared."

Her heart plummeted as Rio bluntly stated her fears.

"I'm scared I won't be ready to defend you, or I'll be distracted by a ruse Morgan might set like she did when she stole Alyssa, and suddenly you'll be gone." The bed sagged as he sat beside her. "I've never been responsible for anyone else before, and it scares the hell out of me."

Having him say aloud what she'd been thinking hurt more than she wanted to admit. Without knowing how it happened, she'd fallen in love with her warrior sometime in the last month, or maybe it started with that kiss last summer—she didn't know. What she did know was she wouldn't require of him more than he could give.

"Don't beat yourself up. I've taken care of myself rather well for the last seven or eight years since I moved out of

Shanley's house, and I can keep taking care of myself. You don't have to worry about me." She rolled to the opposite side of the bed and sat up. Over her shoulder, she added, "I can stay out of your way and still share my prophecies with you no matter where you are."

She put on a brave face while her heart broke. Pushing off the bed, she headed to the bathroom before she gave into emotions she could barely contain. Before she made it two steps, Rio wrapped his arms around her and hauled her tight to him.

"You misunderstood," he whispered into her hair. "I'm scared of losing you, not of looking out for you. For the first time in my life, I'm going to be asked to fight for something bigger and more important than myself—for us—and more than anything else, I can't fail. The stakes are too high."

The rawness in his voice sounded like she mattered to him. She clung to him and let go the silent tears she could no longer dam behind false bravado. He held her and stroked her back and her hair while she cried herself out.

When she thought she could face him, she mumbled into his chest, "Sorry about your shirt. I'll wash it for you tomorrow."

"Don't worry about it. In a pinch, a shirt works as a tissue," Rio gently teased her.

She laughed weakly. "Eww. Clearly, I didn't grow up in a house full of guys."

"How 'bout we grab some shut-eye and see how things look in the morning?"

With a nod, she let Rio put her to bed.

❧

For the first time since discovering Ceri was his talisman, Rio lay beside her without making love to her. Instead, he spooned her, wrapped his arm around her, and held her until she fell asleep, which she did surprisingly quickly. He worried about the coming days and how he'd keep this precious woman safe, for he would do so, no matter the cost.

He understood now. This was what drove Rowan to such extremes for Alyssa last winter and what kept Riley so devoted to Lynnette. This all-consuming need to keep their talismans safe, not only for the women's complementary skills in battle, but also for how they climbed inside his brothers' hearts and set up house-keeping. Without even trying, Ceri had done that to him too.

As he held her, the relaxed state she'd dropped into almost immediately when he snuggled her gradually changed. Moaning, she tried to pull away from him, and he recognized a nightmare. She whimpered in fear and pain before crying out forcefully, "No! No! You can't take him! No!"

After struggling for a minute that seemed thirty times as long to Rio, Ceri slumped back into a fitful state, and he judged the nightmare had ended. He'd read somewhere it wasn't a good idea to awaken someone experiencing a bad dream, but considering Ceri's gift, he decided to wake her so she could tell him about it.

"Hey," he called softly, pulling slightly away from her, taking his heat with him.

She stirred and tried to slide back against him.

"Wake up. C'mon, sweetheart, wake up."

Rio waited while she slowly surfaced.

"What is it?" she asked groggily.

"You were dreaming. Something that scared you. I want to know what it was."

"I don't know."

Her body tensing in his arms told him she lied.

"Yeah, you do. Tell me what you saw," he insisted. "All of it."

"What time is it?"

"Late." He leaned up on his elbow and demanded her eyes.

"I feel like I haven't slept at all," she said, stalling.

"You haven't much. You barely fell asleep before the dreaming started. I know you remember. Now tell me." He paused. "Please."

Sighing at his persistence, she recounted her dream. "I saw you in battle. Maeve insisted you fight naked with only an old shield for protection." Picking at the blanket, she continued. "Morgan's bloodlust felt like waves crashing over my head, and I couldn't breathe." She closed her eyes. "Maeve kept talking about how magnificent you were and how you'd survive long enough to please her." Ceri covered her eyes with her hands. "Rio, it was terrible." Her voice constricted with unshed tears.

Gently, he tugged her hands away from her face. "Did your dream feel like your visions or like a general nightmare?"

"Like all the other nightmares I've had since our first training session with Scathach. Not so much like the visions."

"You've been having nightmares? Dammit, Ceri. Why didn't you tell me?"

Pulling the blanket to her chin, she said, "It seemed we had enough on our plates without my silly fears showing up in nightmares."

Rio cupped her cheek. "Nothing you see is silly. All of it contributes to our understanding of what those two witches are planning. From now on, promise me you'll tell me your dreams. Were you in the dream too or only watching from somewhere?"

She swallowed a couple of times and cleared her throat. "Maeve forced me to watch. I felt like I was dying too."

Ceri turned away from him, curling in on herself. He worried if he stroked her the wrong way or said the wrong thing, she'd shatter into a million pieces, but he couldn't hesitate.

Tenderly, he turned her toward him. "In case you haven't noticed, lady, I'm partial to blonds, not redheads. I also like my woman smart, selfless, and quick to laughter." His finger traced the silky strand of her hair as he tucked it behind her ear. "I like a woman who challenges me to see myself and be a better man. Seems to me that describes you, not Maeve." He cupped her cheek. "I'd never willingly go to her. She'd have to use all her supernatural skill to force me into her bed. Even then, I wouldn't pleasure her, no matter the cost."

"She's a goddess, Rio. I don't think any mortal man, no matter how strong, could resist her."

"One who loves his talisman could."

Ceri blinked up at him.

"No matter how hard she tries, she can't overcome the bond between a warrior and his talisman. It's why she tries so hard to interfere with warriors before they meet or marry their talismans. Remember the stories of Cùchulainn and Emer? Maeve often tried to steal Cùchulainn and never succeeded because she couldn't break his bond with his wife. No matter what she tries, she'll never take me from you." He stroked his thumb over the satin of her cheek.

Her smile didn't reach her eyes, which were filled with a sadness he couldn't understand. When he tried to penetrate her shield, he found, to his dismay, she had it firmly in place. Either she didn't feel any fear now, or she had at last become adept at keeping people out of her head. Both situations should have delighted him. But in a moment of pure honesty, he admitted he wanted to snoop around in her mind and discover where he'd gone wrong in the last few minutes to put so much sorrow in her beautiful meadow-green eyes.

Instead, he was forced to ask. "Why are you sad?"

"I'm all right. I'd be much better though if you made love to me."

"Are you sure? You seem tired, and I don't want to push you too hard. Tomorrow is going to be a long enough day already."

"You're saying that you'd rather not. I can understand that. Good night." She rolled over onto her side facing away from him.

"Oh no you don't. If I had my way, you'd never get out of this bed," Rio said, his voice dropping an octave as he put his hand on her shoulder and pulled her flat on her back. "I was thinking of your need to rest, but since you're the one suggesting it, I'm game for fooling around with you. It's my permanent favorite activity." He grinned her.

She reached up and stroked his face before sliding her hand around to the back of his neck and coaxing his head down to her for a lingering kiss.

Cupping her breast, he teased her nipple into an erection with his thumb while he plunged his tongue into her mouth to duel with hers. She moaned and arched into him, her hands restlessly stroking him wherever she could reach. He sensed her need in her incredible response to him.

Ceri accelerated from closed off to full arousal in the space of his kiss. Rio tore his mouth away from hers to lick and suck her nipple deep into his mouth, using his tongue and teeth to satisfy the desire flaring to life so hotly between them it nearly lit the sheets on fire. She arched up into him while she held his head to her with both hands. He growled his pleasure at her passion and smoothed his hand down her belly, relishing the creamy resilience of her skin before he slipped his hand between her legs to discover exactly how much she wanted him.

"Rio," she breathed as he dipped a finger between her slick folds and stroked her, encouraging her to open fully for him. He lifted his head from her breast and smiled at her.

Though he knew he probably shouldn't, he teased, "You wanted something?"

"Please, Rio. I can't wait any more. I need you inside me now."

Damn, he loved it when she begged.

"At your service, lady." He smiled as he settled himself between her legs.

She lifted her hips to meet him halfway, an unconscious gesture that excited him more than anything else she could have done. This incredible woman was with him every step of the way, imbuing him with a confidence far exceeding any belief his family or even Scathach ever had in him.

As Rio sank into the lush softness of her body, he lost control of his shield. *No goddess could ever transcend this.*

Ceri's lips curved into a tiny smile.

∽

Rio sensed Ceri would be embarrassed if she were caught in bed well past midmorning for the second day in a row, so he chivalrously offered to escort her to breakfast rather than go for his usual run. Maybe he could take the brunt of his brothers' and father's teasing. As they reached the main hall, they heard laughter coming from the dining room and thought they might be able to sneak by the door to the stairs leading to the kitchen and pretend they'd been up and around for longer than it appeared. However, as they tiptoed past the dining room, Rowan called out, "Hey Rio, the coffee's in here."

Exchanging a glance, they resignedly walked into the dining room.

Riley offered the first salvo. "Even as good a warrior as you are and for as good a reason as bonding with your talisman, you sure do take chances keeping Scathach waiting."

"Aw, Riley, give him a break. You know Rio had to fly halfway around the world to find what was sitting in plain sight if he'd only known how to look," Rowan teased.

"Maybe they got lost finding their way down to breakfast. This is a rather big old house. Nearly got lost myself," Owen said winking across the table at Sian. Even after thirty years together, his mom still blushed a subtle shade of rose at his dad's oblique reference.

Rio seated Ceri before taking the place beside her. "At least we made it for brunch. Can't say the same for Alaisdair and Shanley.

Anyone seen them yet?" he asked, attempting to deflect attention away from Ceri and himself.

His talisman's pink cheeks delighted him. But between her prophecies and her dreams, she'd been through enough without his family's teasing at breakfast too.

"Haven't seen nor heard from them, but I expect they know their bondin' time is limited. Knowin' Alaisdair, they'll be along before Scathach arrives at the trainin' room." Hamish blandly returned his attention to his eggs and sausage.

"What's for breakfast? I'm starved."

"Eggs, sausages, toast, porridge, and the nastiest coffee I've ever tasted." Owen stared pointedly at Hamish before returning his attention to Rio. "Worked up an appetite, did you son?"

"I always have an appetite." Rio stole a look at Ceri whose rosy blush deepened.

"Owen, I think you've had enough fun for now." Sian's tone was stern. "Ceri, dear, why don't I dish you up some porridge."

"It's all right, Ceri," Alyssa said from where she sat on Ceri's other side. "The Sheridans put all of us through this. Look at it as a rite of passage or something."

"Only you would see this in mythical terms. Me, I wish I would have called in sick and sneaked down the servants' stairs to the kitchen," Ceri whispered as she stared into her lap.

From the corner of his eye, Rio caught Alyssa surreptitiously squeezing Ceri's hand under the table. Sian interrupted with a steaming bowl of porridge embellished with cream, butter, and sugar. The rich oaty smell wafted up to Rio's nose, and his stomach rumbled in anticipation.

"Thanks very much, Sian." Ceri accepted her breakfast.

"Hey, Mom. Can I get some breakfast too?" Rio asked, looking up at her and giving her his best puppy dog eyes.

"Certainly. It's right over there on the sideboard. Help yourself," his mom replied serenely as she reseated herself at the table.

"You rate," Rio murmured in Ceri's ear before he kissed her lightly behind it and walked over to the buffet to serve himself breakfast.

The three other Sheridan men watching the exchange laughed together, and Rio grinned back at them before glancing away in feigned remorse in the face of Sian's critical glare.

"Hamish, where did you learn to make such bad coffee?" Owen asked.

"Who says I make bad coffee? A man needs somethin' strong tae get up and goin' in the mornin'. My coffee is just the ticket."

"You should stick to making tea. That at least is drinkable since you make it nearly as black as coffee," Riley said.

Rio set his full plate at his place and reached for the teapot in the middle of the table.

"I thought ye Yanks liked strong coffee."

"Coffee, yes. Tar, no." Riley laughed.

"Och, lad, dae ye need tae grow a little hair on yer chest, then?" Hamish asked, his expression the picture of innocence.

Riley scowled at the old druid while the rest of the table broke up in gales of laughter.

Rio nudged Ceri with his shoulder, and she offered him a weak smile.

"This bunch takes some getting used to, but you're up for it, babe," he said for her ears only before he tucked in to his first round of brunch.

CHAPTER TWENTY

 LAISDAIR AND SHANLEY'S entrance into the dining room temporarily impeded Ceri's uncharacteristic wallow in self-pity as the Sheridans refocused their attention on the newly arrived couple.

Owen greeted them first. "Good afternoon, you two. Decided to take a break and join us, did you?"

Ceri noticed he had no trouble ignoring his wife's outraged glare.

"Owen Sheridan, you are a ruffian!"

"Maybe, but you've been desperately in love with me for thirty years, so you must like it," he said with a smirk.

Sian batted her eyes at him while their sons laughed. Something about the manor or about two warriors finding their talismans in it or about Hamish's enchantments maybe being more than protections seemed to make the warriors wild and perhaps a bit reckless.

Shanley smiled at everyone at the table. Then her eyes landed on Ceri. *"It'll be better once you're married. Right now, it's about warriors being guys. Trust me. In a year, if the four of us want to wait and come down for lunch, not much will be said."*

"I don't know. I don't think I've ever been more embarrassed in my life," Ceri communicated.

Loud laughter redirected their attention to the special teasing to which the Sheridans subjected Alaisdair who'd had to wait longer than any of them to bond with his talisman.

"Good tae see ye, Alaisdair, Shanley." Hamish nodded at each in turn. "But it's comin' up on afternoon, so the twa o' ye should eat somethin' quick. We're lookin' at a long trainin' day at *An Teallach*, and Scathach will have some nasty reprimands tae hand if we keep her waitin'."

Hamish's warning silenced the teasing.

With a sigh, Riley said, "Every one of us has experienced Scathach's reprimands that left him bruised and sore for days afterward." He grimaced at his brothers.

"There's nothing fun about training with an angry goddess," Rowan agreed.

Ceri and Shanley exchanged a relieved glance when Hamish's admonishment doused the risqué comments like a bucket of cold water.

Shanley and Alaisdair took their meal at the fireplace end of the long dining table while the others carried their dishes down to the kitchen.

In short order, the Sheridans were ready to go. Everyone congregated in the foyer to discuss the journey to the training room.

"I'm feelin' a might uncomfortable with ye ridin' with us tae *An Teallach*, Shanley. I fear ye're as much a target fer Morgan as Ceri, but since ye havnae seen the trainin' room in such a long time, it's tae risky tae let ye try visualizin' yerself there," Hamish said.

"It's fine, Hamish. I didn't have any dreams that took place in the early afternoon. Everything I've seen happened late in the day," Shanley said.

"What are ye sayin', lass?"

The normally unflappable Hamish Buchanan looked like he might jump out of his skin at Shanley's casual revelation. Ceri took a step back and bumped into Rio.

"I've been dreaming about Alaisdair for the past two years. I thought I was seeing Ceri's warrior. Turns out, I was seeing my own," Shanley said, directing her last words to Alaisdair with a slow smile.

"Ye've been dreamin', not havin' actual visions?"

Shanley frowned. "They're not the same?"

"Apparently not. When Ceri has a vision, it's an altogether different experience than a dream. When Ceri has a vision, no one can reach her. Her prophecies come on without warning when she's wide awake. They're more about an expectation than a possibility." Owen reached out and gave Ceri's hand a squeeze. "Quite honestly, it's terrifying to watch her have one."

"You've seen Ceri have a vision?" Shanley asked, worry marring her beautiful features.

"Actually, she experienced one last night after dinner, a vision concerning the twa o' ye."

Alaisdair and Shanley gaped at Hamish.

"We should probably go tae the trainin' room now. Scathach said tae meet her there after lunch, I know, but after what ye've revealed, I'd feel much better if Ceri were safe inside the mountain," Alaisdair said.

Hamish pulled a face, and Alaisdair preempted him. "I know how many layers o' enchantments ye've added tae this house, but do ye really want tae test 'em before Samhain?"

Hamish sighed.

Rio wrapped his arms protectively around Ceri, and she

glanced up at him. The grim line of his mouth told her precisely what he thought about Hamish's enchantments.

Surprising her, Alaisdair took charge of the arrangements. "Ye arrived yesterday in twa rented cars. Taeday, we need tae leave one behind as a decoy fer any civilians Morgan may be employing tae watch the manor. We'll crowd intae Hamish's little car and one o' yer rentals fer the ride tae the loch. Unfortunately, we'll be rather conspicuous in the skiffs, but it can't be helped." He wrapped his arm around Shanley. "Shanley will ride with me o' course. It may be best tae have Owen and Sian with us while Rowan, Alyssa, Riley, Lynnette, and Hamish ride taegether in the rental."

"If it's all the same tae ye, I'll visualize myself tae. Finn can ride with Rowan while I give Rio and Ceri another layer o' protection at *An Teallach*," Hamish said.

"Good idea," Alaisdair responded. "We'll have someone familiar with the area with both sets o' Sheridans, which should increase our safety."

"I've packed up a hamper with a meal and a snack tae take with ye. If Scathach demands a longer trainin' session, we'll have tae grin and bear it," Hamish added.

Alaisdair took Shanley by the hand and led the way down the stairs toward the kitchen and the back door.

"We'll wait until you've headed up the drive before we visualize ourselves to the mountain. That way I can set the alarms on the manor," Rio said.

"See you in the training room." Owen clapped Rio on the shoulder before he followed Alaisdair and Shanley down the stairs.

"Be careful," Sian added as she joined her husband.

"You too, Mom. After all, you're the exposed ones."

Rowan grasped Rio's elbow in the way of warriors, a charged look passing between them before he ushered Alyssa ahead of him toward the door.

Riley nodded at his twin, their understanding clear without comment, as he and Lynnette trailed the others.

When they were alone in the foyer, Ceri turned to Rio and Hamish. "I'm sorry this is happening and people we all love are in such great danger because of me."

Her usual sunny attitude gave way to despair as she contemplated the stakes of the coming battle.

"You are not the cause of anything." Rio cupped her face, his eyes locking with hers. "Morgan and Maeve and their bottomless desire for blood and battle are the cause of everything we fight. As warriors, Ceri, we're obligated to take them on and win as often as we can. And we will win, have no doubt."

He pulled her into the circle of his arms, his lips skimming her temple. "Rowan and Alyssa coming together tipped the balance in favor of the warrior community. Now it's our turn to give future warriors a better chance as they take on those two old crones and their armies." Rio pressed his lips to her forehead for a long moment. "Someday our all-seeing Irish mother goddess Danu will reward her warriors for never giving up the fight against evil. Meanwhile, we have to continue to battle—all of us."

Ceri tightened her hold on him. "I don't want to lose you. I don't want to lose any of you."

"Lucky for us, we have a prophetess among us who can warn us of Morgan and Maeve's intentions and give us time to plan." Rio smiled at her. "The Sheridans have been fighting those two for generations without that kind of help. Having you on our team makes us even stronger."

In that instant, Ceri understood how much her warrior enjoyed the fight, enjoyed engaging Morgan's rogues and winning. The thought did little to soothe her fear.

She'd almost forgotten Hamish remained with them until he interrupted. "Ye had better see tae yer alarms, lad. It's time tae go."

Rio nodded and headed downstairs to the pantry to arm the

system while Hamish silently took Ceri in his arms and reassured her through his embrace.

"I donnae hold with all the bloodshed associated with warriors, but I understand being born and bred fer the role. Rio can feel nae other way than excited about taking on the Morrigan. Ye have tae trust him, lass."

It wasn't much comfort.

⤝

An Teallach was a breathtaking *ben* rising up across from the tiny village of Ullapool. Though a dock sat at the base of the mountain, it otherwise appeared wild and untouched. A thin trail carved into the mountainside by years of hikers seemed to lose itself in gorse and heather. The training room entrance was cleverly hidden in an unassuming rock cairn like so many thousands of others scattered among the mountains. No civilian would ever accidentally find it and interrupt a training session, and Morgan would have difficulty staging an attack outside it since she had no forest or other cover in which to hide her rogues and zombie champions.

A hum of conversation signaled that the Sheridans had entered the long hall leading to the training room.

Ceri, Rio, and Hamish had visualized themselves to *An Teallach* minutes before Scathach had strolled in. They'd barely exchanged pleasantries before Rio informed her of Ceri's dreams. Scathach launched into the training session already upset.

"How long have you been having these dreams, and what do you remember of them?" the goddess asked through clenched teeth.

Ceri trembled in the face of the goddess's wrath. "I … I … they started right after Rio discovered I'm his talisman."

She'd never seen anyone literally bristle up in anger before, but Scathach's hair seemed to stand straight up, and her body radiated a tangible red heat.

"What did you dream? Do not even think about pretending you cannot remember. I want to know all of it. Now."

"The dreams are mainly about Rio dying at Maeve's direction with Morgan and me watching. They refuse to dignify him with death in battle. I've also been dreaming of Maeve torturing Shanley with watching Alaisdair enjoy other women before Morgan kills him with one of her zombies."

She couldn't hide her sorrow from Rio, who laced his fingers through hers but said nothing. "The venue for Rio is a stronghold somewhere while Alaisdair always suffers on the grounds of the manor. In every dream, Morgan escorts someone across the ford while her eyes glow an unearthly red, and she cackles in delight like she's getting off on our pain."

"She *is* getting off on your pain." Scathach paced in a tight circle. "My sister goddesses have been suspiciously quiet and difficult to locate lately. Now I know why."

Rio furrowed his brow. "What do you mean, milady?"

"They are here in Scotland. They would have to be close in order to send those dreams. Somehow, they have figured out Ceri is a prophet. How they figured that out is a worry we cannot dwell on now. By sending the dreams, they hope to disrupt her abilities, making her doubt or fear what she sees to the point she cannot discern prophecy from dreaming." She slanted Ceri a look. "Which are two completely different things." She resumed pacing. "Or she cannot divide her emotions between reality and prophecy, thereby causing her to go insane."

Ceri gasped.

Scathach tapped a finger to her lips. "You are very powerful, Ceri Ross. When you have a vision, no one can penetrate your shield, not even a goddess. Which tells me your visions are close to reality. Morgan and Maeve wish to drive you insane to keep you from being able to share those visions."

Willing herself not to cry in front of the goddess, Ceri

wrapped her arms around her middle and stared at the beautiful knotwork carved into the ceiling.

"Hamish, return to the manor and work protection spells over Ceri's bed. We must keep those two out of your head when you are asleep and unable to maintain your shield."

"Can't we teach Ceri to shield her thoughts while she sleeps?" Rowan asked.

"I've tried for years to teach Ceri that skill, but she could never master it," Shanley said, walking over to rub a comforting hand up and down Ceri's arm.

"That much is obvious. Before the day is over, you will tell me everything about how you trained her," Scathach commanded, her tone sour.

Shanley's head snapped back like the goddess had slapped her.

"Have you discovered your talisman's talent, Alaisdair?" Scathach asked, her impatience discomforting everyone in the room.

"Not yet, milady. I only discovered her tae be my talisman yesterday afternoon."

Scathach huffed. "We do not have enough time before Samhain to prepare effectively for the battle we face. Your training will need acceleration. I hope you are up to it." She stopped pacing in front of Ceri and Shanley, her hands on her hips, her displeasure obvious.

Scathach's words resonated like a tolling bell through the gathering of warriors and talismans. Not for the first time since arriving in Scotland did Ceri wish she weren't the chosen one. Her long-ago ancestor could have made other arrangements, couldn't she?

Shanley shook her head at her niece. *"You are so much stronger than that, and you know it. It's no accident the gods chose you to be the talisman for the strongest warrior of our generation. Embrace your fate and do your duty."*

Ceri blinked. *"I can't stand the thought of losing any of you, especially Rio. When I thought of my warrior finding me, I didn't think past that or what finding me would mean for him. Knowing now, I can't seem to cope with my fear for him."*

"Because you love him, you'll be ready to do what needs to be done when the time comes." Shanley patted Ceri's arm and stepped away.

Ceri thought she'd concealed her feelings for Rio, but she should have known Shanley would see right through her. She smiled weakly at her aunt before sensing Scathach's angry attention on her again.

"I'm sorry milady, were you addressing me?" Her entire body heated at being caught not paying attention to their patron goddess. More than anything, she wanted to impress the Sheridans with her ability to do her job by Rio, but so far, she'd only succeeded in embarrassing herself.

"I want to hear your most recent prophecy. When you experienced it last night, I sensed the ripple in the cosmos, so you need not deny you had one."

During their last training session, Ceri had had the distinct impression Scathach was happy at the pairing of Rio with her. Today, it appeared the goddess had changed her mind.

"You kept your dreams from everyone. It is not much of a leap to think you might keep unpleasant prophecies from others as well. Out with it."

"Milady, could you ease up? Ceri didn't deliberately try to deceive anyone. She didn't want to alarm us with her dreams, which she thought were reflections of her own worries," Rio said, his hands resting on Ceri's shoulders.

"Do not interfere, Rio. I need to make it utterly transparent to your talisman that she is to hold nothing back from you or from me—ever," Scathach said before turning her attention back to Ceri. "Now, tell me your vision."

Rio squeezed Ceri's shoulders before sliding his hands down

to wrap them around her waist and pull her into his embrace, steadying her—in obvious defiance of the goddess.

Her voice trembling with fear, she revisited her vision. Scathach remained still, showing no emotion until she finished.

Then the goddess seemed to deflate.

"We are under even more pressure than I realized. You are a prophetess of uncommon ability. Once you harness your skill, you will create real problems for Morgan and Maeve. They will stop at nothing to take you or to make you lose your mind. We must keep you safe at any cost, no matter how high." Scathach scanned the assembly. "Is that understood?"

Closing her eyes, she took a deep breath, blinked her eyes open, and seemed to glow. Her energy illuminated the walls of the training room. The battle scenes came alive in the goddess's intention. "You warriors will spar. Except for you, Owen." Turning to Ceri, she said, "He trained Riley to keep a very persistent Rowan out of his head."

Riley scowled at Rowan who grinned back at him.

"So he is our best hope for helping you learn how to set your shield in your sleep."

Owen smiled at Ceri with encouragement.

Shanley, who was gazing at the wall, suddenly let out a scream and collapsed onto the cold stone floor, her eyes staring unseeing at the ceiling. Alaisdair scooped her up and cradled her in his arms.

"What is it? What's happening to her?" Ceri cried as she knelt beside him on the floor.

Rio dropped beside her. "This is what it's like when you're experiencing a prophecy."

She stared grimly at Rio as the others crowded around them, exchanging looks of horror and concern as Shanley fell into the throes of her prophecy. After several minutes, she quieted, while an ominous miasma seemed to coalesce around the warriors and talismans gathered together.

Scathach broke the tension. "I see the Conlan legacy holds true. There are two prophetesses, one in each generation leading to the time when the Conlans, the Sheridans, and Rosses come together to create a dynasty of warriors that will bring a time of great peace." Despite imparting such a profound foretelling, her tone remained dispassionate. "That might explain why Shanley couldn't train Ceri to shield properly. Alaisdair, were you able to penetrate Shanley's shield while she had her vision?"

"No, milady."

"Ceri?"

"No, milady."

"Your shields are impenetrable while you are in the throes of prophecy. Hmm. That is both helpful and harmful. We need not worry my sisters can overcome and tinker with your visions. However, none of us can see them in real time, which means we need time for you to tell them to us, time we may not have if you experience them in the heat of battle."

Ceri slumped. "You mean, we can have prophecies when our warriors are fighting? What are we going to do? We're completely at the mercy of the visions, and we have no control over when or where they happen." Tension rocked her body. "We're total liabilities to our warriors since we're unable to do anything to save ourselves when we're experiencing them." She couldn't breathe. "You say we're an asset, but outside of this training room, I don't see how we're anything but a terrible burden."

"I will train you to be both in the prophecy and outside it simultaneously. Normally, it takes years of training to be able to master the skill of compartmentalizing your mind to experience the prophecy while also remaining in the present moment, but we do not have that kind of time. At best, we have two days. At worst, we have this afternoon and evening. Either way, we need to start now," Scathach said.

Shanley groaned and opened her eyes, drawing Scathach's attention.

"I know the vision exhausted you, but we need to know what you saw, Shanley."

Shanley blinked up at Alaisdair, fear and confusion in her eyes. Tentatively, she stroked his face.

"I know 'twas a painful thing ye experienced, lassie, but we need tae know what ye saw. Please, Shanley, tell me what ye saw."

Alaisdair's soft Scots burr seemed to penetrate Shanley. After swallowing several times, she finally related her vision. When she finished, the room rang with the desperate silence of people not willing to take a breath in dread of giving the prophecy life.

"They think to bring back the *Morhaus*. Against Alaisdair no less. Morgan is furious you eluded her all these years, lad," Scathach said, pride sounding in her voice. "Well, I have a trick or two for dealing with that particular zombie champion. We will start there with our battle training."

At Scathach's pronouncement, life once again sounded in the training room. The warriors moved around, stretching and warming up. The other talismans joined their warriors. Hamish started laying out his array of herbs on the table.

"Owen, I will not need your help with Ceri after all. Shielding your dream state will have to wait," Scathach said addressing her. "I do not think Morgan and Maeve will attack until Samhain, which will give us a fraction more time. They will be vain enough to think their old champions will be enough for my warriors, but they do not know what the prophecies are, so they do not realize we know their plan of attack. We will be ready for them. All of us." She smiled triumphantly while Shanley and Ceri exchanged a look of disbelief.

How were any of them going to survive the coming battle?

CHAPTER TWENTY-ONE

IT WAS WELL after midnight when Scathach allowed the warriors to return to Conlan Manor. Though Ceri and Shanley were bone weary, Scathach insisted they visualize themselves back to the house. Rio and Alaisdair held onto their talismans for the trip through time and space to ensure their safe return while the others took the more conventional route via civilian transportation.

When they arrived back at the manor, Hamish declared Alaisdair and Shanley should sleep in the big house rather than in Alaisdair's cottage. He'd taken the extra precaution of enchanting Shanley's bed after he'd chanted the necessary spells over Ceri's. Too tired to argue, they mounted the stairs together and closed themselves behind the guest room door.

Rio had spent the day worrying about Ceri's emotional state. All day she'd been subdued and withdrawn. Whenever he'd had the chance, he'd praised her progress at dividing her prophecies from her current reality and thanked her for her willingness to continue to relive them so he could practice against Morgan's chosen champions. He could see what it cost her to practice through her fear, and he tried to let her know with compliments, casual touches, and his unshielded thoughts how much he appreciated her efforts and her growing skill.

It didn't seem to be enough. Her usual sunny nature disappeared behind clouds of unhappiness she didn't try to hide.

Instead of carrying her off to bed, which he selfishly wanted to do, Rio led Ceri to the sitting room, guided her to a chair, and put her feet up before tucking a blanket around her and instructing her to sit tight while he searched out food. They hadn't eaten since dinner, and she had to be as famished as he was.

While he rummaged in the fridge for something quick and hearty, he thought over the events of the day. The Sheridans and Alaisdair spent their training session practicing the skills they'd need against Morgan's supernatural zombie champions, men who died long ago and no longer felt anything. Part of a warrior's success against an enemy included getting in his head, but when one's enemy had no emotions nor even real thoughts, attacking psychologically didn't work at all. Rio resented Morgan's tactics, but then, he'd never known her to fight fair. Mucking about in Ceri's dreams demonstrated Morgan's unscrupulousness as well.

Rio abruptly stopped preparing their food. Though Hamish had enchanted their bed against evil goddesses breaching their shields while they slept, perhaps Rio could enter Ceri's mind and influence her dreams. As he whipped up roast beef sandwiches, he tossed the idea around in his head. What he contemplated was highly unethical, and Ceri would throw a fit if she ever discovered his subterfuge, but it was definitely worth a shot. As he carried the plate of sandwiches and the pot of tea upstairs, he stepped lightly, his mood decidedly more buoyant than it'd been when they'd returned to the manor.

In the sitting room, he found Ceri asleep. Seeing her so peaceful, he loathed waking her to eat, but he was starving, and she needed food too. While he debated what to do, his family determined his course for him. Even exhausted, a circumstance the trip across the loch and the short drive to the manor didn't help, they were still their usual loud selves as they entered the manor through the kitchen door. The distance from the back of the house to the front didn't muffle their noise as their discussions echoed up the stairs and through the foyer.

Ceri startled up from her chair. Blinking several times, she looked around in distress, her body tense.

"Shhh, it's all right. You're home. You're safe. You fell asleep while I made us a sandwich." Rio squeezed her shoulders as he eased her back into her chair.

"I thought we were under attack."

"You heard my family coming home from the training room. Subtlety isn't one of our strong suits," Rio said laughing. "Since you're awake, want to join me?"

She eyed the enormous roast beef sandwich Rio offered her. "Maybe half. Who all were you cooking for anyway?"

Rio shrugged. "It's been a long time since supper. I thought you might be hungry."

She laughed her tinkling chimes laugh, and he relaxed. "I'm not a warrior, Rio, so I doubt I need all that. Wanna share?"

Her laughter warmed him as nothing else in the world. He would have served her the full moon on a platter if he'd had it to give.

Instead he smiled. "Actually, I kinda hoped you might say that. As I walked up the stairs, I thought I might be short a sandwich."

When she grinned mischievously at him, his face heated as he realized his mistake. Hastily, he asked, "Would you like some tea? Doubt it's as stout as Hamish's, but maybe we don't need that much caffeine this time of night."

Ceri choked back a laugh. "I'd love a cup. I take mine with milk no matter how leaded it is, thanks."

Rio poured a dollop of milk into the bottom of her cup before adding hot tea and handing it to her. Their fingers brushed briefly, and a frisson of awareness sizzled up his arm before he caught her thought.

"When will I stop reacting to Rio Sheridan?"

So, she felt it too.

"Never, I hope."

"Hey, what are you doing in my head?" she asked, her voice rising.

"Making sure my talisman and I are on the same page, especially when we're so necessary to each other. Which today's training session made abundantly clear."

∽

At the mention of the training session, Ceri sobered up immediately. They cared for each other—that was their job after all. But how much did those feelings have to do with her being his talisman, and how much with chemistry—and maybe something more? The more time she spent with Rio, especially when he was attentive and sweet like the present moment, the more she had to admit her feelings had a whole lot more to do with her as a woman and him as a man than with being a talisman to her warrior.

Yet the training session today reinforced one thing that took precedence—she must do her job. Use her valuable skills to accurately and quickly prophecy what Rio could expect to happen in a battle. She must do everything in her power to aid her warrior above all else.

Though she'd had some success separating herself from the battle in her mind and the real world, she still couldn't control her emotional response to what she witnessed. Falling in love with Rio seemed a terrible liability rather than the asset Alyssa insisted it would be after Ceri confided in her best friend during a break in the day's training. Watching him battle warriors with no feelings or ethics and be wounded, sometimes mortally, took more out of her than she let on to anyone. Somehow, she needed to control her emotions or strengthen her shield, neither of which she believed she could perfect before the coming battle with Morgan. If she failed Rio, she wouldn't want to continue living. The depth of her love surprised and terrified her.

"You've been a million miles away. Did you have another vision?" Rio asked, concern playing over his handsome features.

"No."

"Then what?"

"Nothing to worry about Rio. I probably need to eat. You may need to fix another sandwich after all," she said with a chuckle, hoping to distract him.

As he studied her, his furrowed brow told her she hadn't distracted him at all, but before he could interrogate her further, Rowan stuck his head in the door of the sitting room.

"I thought I'd find Hamish in here. Didn't expect the two of you." His eyes traveled to the plates they balanced on their laps. "Sandwiches? You got any friends?" Rowan's designs on the other half of Ceri's sandwich were clear as he purposefully strolled into the room.

"Hamish is probably in his room, and you can make your own sandwich. Leftovers are in the fridge," Rio answered sourly.

"A good host would offer his starving brother a sandwich."

"A good husband would stop disturbing his brother and go make his wife a sandwich," Alyssa interjected as she walked through the door.

"Why do you need Hamish?" Rio asked.

"I noticed some footprints along the back of the house, like someone was trying windows, someone who was especially interested in Hamish's boarded-up one," Rowan replied, his expression suddenly serious.

"I warned him last night that I noticed a shadow lurking outside the back door when we came downstairs to grab dessert.

He waved me off, but it seems we need to wire Hamish's room pronto. Probably the tunnel leading to Alaisdair's cottage and the cottage itself too."

"When do you suppose we'll have time for that?" Riley asked as he and Lynnette trailed Alyssa into the sitting room.

Rio sighed. "I know. Samhain is day after tomorrow, and we haven't finished training. Suggestions?"

Ceri's sandwich turned to ashes in her mouth as she listened to the Sheridans assess their situation.

"Rowan, Riley, and I can secure Hamish's room in the morning before we train."

Owen's "suggestion" sounded more like a command as he stepped around Riley and Lynnette and into the room.

"I'll help too since I set everything to run through a box in the master suite," Rio said. Then he turned to Ceri. "Sorry, sweetheart, but it looks like there will be no sleeping in for you tomorrow."

The teasing light in his eyes didn't calm her.

"No need to wake Ceri too early. We can wire Hamish's room and the door leading to the tunnel and piggyback it to the circuitry already around the doorway to his suite," Owen said. "Once we have it in place, we can test it. That should be late morning."

"Thank you," Ceri replied quietly, exhaustion claiming her voice.

"Listen, we're all beat, but I'm famished and still wondering when my husband plans on making me a sandwich." Alyssa gave Rowan a saucy grin.

"You're rather demanding, Pixie-girl. There will, of course, be a substantial fee for my sandwich making services," Rowan said, sending a hot look to his wife.

"I'm counting on it," Alyssa responded before she turned to leave the room, an obvious cue for the rest of the family to follow her.

"She hasn't been in the family long, and she's still new to her place and understanding of our warrior community, but neither of those facts seems to slow her down when she decides to take charge, do they?" Owen asked, amusement vibrating his voice.

"Ball o' fire, that one. She needed to be to put up with this guy," Riley said as he playfully punched Rowan's shoulder before he wrapped his arm around Lynnette to escort her from the room.

"See you in the morning, son. We have all the gear, so we may start without you," Owen said before he followed the rest of the family down to the kitchen.

"I'll let Hamish know we're coming in, no matter what," Rowan said. "See you in the morning."

Rio rolled his eyes at the backs of his retreating family before he turned his attention back to Ceri. "Still have an appetite after that interruption?"

She smiled weakly. "They truly are great people, but there are a lot of you when you're all together. And yes, I still want my half a sandwich."

Ceri picked up the sandwich and started eating, hoping Rio had forgotten their interrupted conversation.

When Rio carried the remains of their midnight snack down to the kitchen, he found his family tightly seated around the scarred oak table in the kitchen, Lynnette sitting on Riley's lap to make room for Hamish. Apparently, while his brothers, sisters-in-law, and father came upstairs to bother Ceri and him, Sian had busied herself making sandwiches for the lot of them. At some point, Hamish joined them, regaling them with stories of ceilidhs in the manor in years past. From the snippet of conversation Rio caught on his way down the stairs, Hamish held a ceilidh on Samhain every year, and the locals were expecting a big one this year in honor of Ceri's homecoming. To Rio's disgust, Hamish didn't sound nearly concerned enough about the particulars of holding a huge bash in the manor with Ceri's life at stake.

Hamish took one look at him and said, "Och, now lad, donnae get yer knickers in a twist. There will be several warriors and druids in attendance, which should even the odds. Without the excuse o' the party, we couldn't amass our own army nearly as readily."

"It's not the warriors that worry me. It's the house being open to civilians Morgan can use to breach the security system and the enchantments. It nearly worked before," Rio groused as he leaned against the counter, folding his arms over his chest.

"I've been workin' on that lad. When Scathach sent me back tae enchant yer bed, I had a little extra time on my hands and added another layer o' protections tae reveal tae us any civilians Morgan might have influenced. Also, we can divest ourselves o' some o' our ethics and take peeks intae the minds of our civilian guests from time tae time—just this once though," Hamish hastily amended after the aghast looks the Sheridans leveled at him.

Sian said, "At least neither Ceri nor Shanley have had any prophecies involving battle inside the manor. Perhaps our enemies cannot circumvent your enchantments, Hamish. Let's hope that's the case anyway." She glanced at their family. "Sneaking peeks into my family's minds is one thing—mucking around in a defenseless civilian's is something else entirely. I'd rather not lower myself to Morgan's level."

"I agree, but we may no' have a choice. We shouldnae discount the option out o' hand is all I'm sayin'."

"All the same, I find the idea revolting." Sian wrinkled her nose in distaste.

"If we cancel the party, we don't have the problem," Rio growled.

"Ye forget. In order fer the rituals tae work, we have tae enact them during the ceilidh on Samhain. I'm afraid there is nae choice in this, lad."

Hamish stood and placed his hand on Rio's shoulder. "We should get what rest we can while we can. Save the washin' up till the mornin', Sian. I'll take care o' it then."

While the rest of his family returned to their appointed rooms, Rio returned to Ceri in the sitting room where she'd fallen asleep again. Gently, he gathered her up in his arms and carried her to their room, smiling to himself about how carrying her to bed seemed to have become a habit with them, one he'd like to continue for years to come.

CHAPTER TWENTY-TWO

TARANIS LOUNGED COMFORTABLY across the plush leather sofa arranged before the fireplace in the Morrigan—Morgan's—Highland retreat as she tried to pace a hole in the flagstone floor. With the season for civilian tourists ended, she was free to reassemble the "deteriorated remnant" of the tower of Castlecraig on the Black Isle to her tastes. Without the inconvenience of visitors bent on imagining romantic tales of battles and bards in the old fortification on the Cromarty Firth, she needn't stow away her belongings in a parallel time. The fact the Black Isle was anything but black in its appearance, history, or atmosphere—outside of Morgan's machinations from her stronghold there—didn't seem to faze her in her choice of location. In fact, such a beautiful area in the Highlands seemed to suit her fine. No one expected the gods' mischief to come from so lovely a place.

Taranis appreciated the way she'd decorated the great room with an inviting suite of leather sofa, settee, overstuffed chairs, and heavy dark mahogany side tables hosting gleaming brass lamps with shades depicting scenes of bloody war. The furniture rested atop a Persian rug woven in shades of deep red, colors echoed in the tapestries dressing up the stone walls and keeping out the cold winds with which he liked to batter the tower. The tapestries showed battle scenes with fallen warriors, which he knew disturbed many a warrior and civilian unfortunate enough to have seen them. Her battles left Taranis indifferent—unless she insisted he assist her with them, which she clearly intended to do soon.

The thunder god rather liked the solitude of the lone tower rising from the sheer rock face of the estuary, formidable stone cliffs guarding the building on three sides while the fourth opened to a plain from which one could see visitors for days before they arrived. The winds he unleashed across the plain warred with those he loosed over the water to create a soothing gale, calming him in the face of the goddess's rage.

"How could she decide at the last minute to stay behind? Does she not realize the magnitude of what we face here? If we don't take Ceri Ross across the ford before she marries Rio Sheridan, we will lose our advantage over three of the most powerful families in the warrior community. We simply cannot allow that to happen!" Morgan threw her arms up. "Scathach must be beside herself at the prospect of rescuing one of her pets yet again—at great price to us," Morgan fumed.

"I need clarification. Are you angry that Maeve decided to stay behind to pursue her recent interest in Seamus Lochlann or that you may be denied the ultimate orgasm of escorting the greatest warrior of the age across the ford?" Taranis drawled.

"Yes!" Morgan snapped.

"So that's the way of it. How did you need me to help?"

"I thought your supremely attractive form would be enough to entice Maeve to join me—us—but apparently, you will not be enough." She ranted on, oblivious to his arched brow. "We are on our own here, especially since that meddling druid enchanted

Ceri's bed against Maeve's lurid dreams." Morgan tapped her foot impatiently. "Hamish Buchanan is not that powerful if Maeve would apply herself." She resumed pacing. "Of course, that would mean she would have to be here—in Scotland—to be effective, but selfishly, she stays in America to try to steal Lochlann before he finds his talisman." Morgan petulantly threw herself into an overstuffed chair.

"You can be such a child sometimes, Morgan. The powerful Washer at the Ford, warrior goddess of battle and destruction, should conduct herself in a more dignified manner," Taranis said as he languidly waved his hand, intensifying the gales battering at the goddess's stronghold.

Lowering her voice, a sure sign of a change in her tactics, she purred, "One cannot help but appreciate your beauty, Taranis. The way your blue-black hair grazes the collar of your slate-gray shirt. The way your broad shoulders and deep, powerful chest fill that silk shirt to perfection." She ran her eyes along his body, stirring him. "Those long legs dwarf the length of my oversized sofa." She flicked a glance at his feet. "Thank you for slipping off your fancy loafers before you lounged on my couch. I adore your taste in civilian clothes, but I hate shoes on the furniture."

She eyed him speculatively as he lay quiet. "I must admit Maeve isn't the only goddess who desires you."

Her compliments always came with a price. He waited.

Morgan waved her hand dismissively. "Maeve loves sleeping with you whenever you allow it. The storms inside you seem to energize and satisfy her for a time after she enjoys you."

"And you?"

"I counted on that when I summoned you to Scotland. How perverse of Maeve to prefer a blond warrior to your dark perfection in physical form."

Taranis yawned.

"That is the problem with you. You do not storm in revenge or self-gain. You like to cause havoc for the hell of it." She stood and resumed pacing. "After banking the energy inside you for a time, when you feel the need to turn it loose, if humans—civilians or warriors—happen to be in the way and suffer the damages of your energies, well, those were unfortunate casualties of circumstance."

She stared down at him with her hands on her hips. "Unlike Maeve and me, you do not strike at specific civilians or warriors. Why is that?"

"I am the god of weather. Vagaries are my very nature. You know that." He brushed a nonexistent speck from his black wool trousers before gazing evenly at her. "However, I suppose I can be persuaded to unleash my storms on particular places at particular times in the interest of mollifying a goddess who will nag me unceasingly if I do not give in to her machinations occasionally."

She smiled, her eyes a banked red.

"Samhain in the Ross Highlands is going to be one of those times and places, eh Morgan?"

Usually, Taranis laid low on Samhain, preferring to let the ancestral dead make their appearances without competition. Though Morgan was well aware of his habit, she'd nagged him until he gave in this time. Which was why he lounged in her Highland stronghold. Pity. He rather enjoyed the folly of civilians when he merely blew mists and deep fog around them, allowing them to scare themselves silly on Samhain without much other provocation.

They sat in silence. At last, Taranis, wishing to unleash a little storm inside the tower as payback for Morgan insisting he come out to play on Samhain, interrupted the quiet. "'That druid' who rescued your target from Maeve's nighttime shenanigans has been thwarting you in the Highlands for centuries, in her first incarnations as a woman and now as a man. How is it you do not target him?"

"You are a devil to goad me, Taranis. If I could find a way

to escort Hamish Buchanan, long ago known as Fianna Conlan, across the ford, do you not think I would leap at the chance? Especially now when he is in league with that detestable Scathach?"

She started pacing again.

"Danu favors him as you are well aware," she said. "The only way he can be released from this earth is if a druid child comes from the union of Conlan, Ross, and Sheridan. After the debacle last winter, I cannot believe I did not see this one coming. That is why we must stop it. If we are successful, we can continue our ongoing war against the Sheridans at our leisure on our terms."

Taranis sat up. "I remind you, madam, this is not 'our' war. It is yours. The only reason I have agreed to send a storm tomorrow is that I know you will badger me without rest until I do something truly detestable rather than merely for fun, a circumstance I rather dislike." He glared at her. "Like you, I enjoy being in control. You might keep that in mind when you send your zombies, rogues, and criminal civilians against the Sheridans. I do not necessarily target any one side in battle. When I send a storm, I catch all in it."

Sighing, Morgan sat back down in the overstuffed chair across from him. "I am well aware of the great favor you are doing for me, sir. I ask that you time your storm and its intensity to give the advantage to my army rather than to the Sheridans. That is all."

"As long as we understand each other," Taranis said, rolling up off the sofa to excuse himself for the day. To create a magnificent storm, he needed to spend the remainder of the evening resting in the rather well-appointed chamber Morgan always reserved for his visits to Castlecraig. That chamber had been the only part of Morgan's summons he'd looked forward to.

∽

As Taranis strolled from the room, Morgan once again marveled at the grace of the thunder god. The loose-limbed way he moved mirrored the smoothness of the onshore gales outside the walls of her tower, the barely leashed power of his shoulders and chest a tangible manifestation of the monsoon rains and death-dealing blizzards she'd seen him explode over the land. That she could wield her power skillfully enough to cajole a mighty god to do her bidding left her giddy. Until she remembered what was at stake. If she didn't stop Rio Sheridan and Ceri Ross from marrying, they would create a warrior dynasty—one that could rival the gods themselves.

She suspected Danu to be behind the actual gathering storm of this battle. The mother goddess had been patient, willing to allow Morgan and Maeve their fun for a millennium, but now it appeared she planned to rein them in. Morgan would not succumb without a monumental fight. Her nature demanded an epic battle. Even as she appeared to do nothing but stew and half politely converse with her brother god, simultaneously, she amassed warriors to converge on the grounds of Conlan Manor on Samhain.

Though Hamish Buchanan had managed to thwart her every effort at breaching the walls of the manor, including via dreamscapes, he had yet to succeed at enchanting the entirety of its grounds. His powers, though great, remained grounded in mortality. She planned to exploit his weakness when she took not only Rio Sheridan, but also Ceri Ross, Alaisdair Graham, Shanley Conlan, and any other Sheridan who tried to save them. Stretching catlike, she licked her blood-red lips in anticipation of the orgasm she would enjoy in the coming torrent of warrior blood swirling around her thighs.

❧

The training with Scathach seemed to start in the middle, as usual. Ceri couldn't imagine she'd ever grow accustomed to it.

"We have much to do and only today in which to do it. When

we finish here, you will meet with Hamish to practice the ritual. It is paramount you protect Ceri. She is the key to the prophecies. Ceri Ross, no matter what happens, you will deny your nature to put others ahead of yourself and do whatever you must to remain safely inside Conlan Manor until the rituals are completed at midnight on Samhain. Do I make myself clear?"

She hated the idea that preserving her life could precipitate the forfeiture of any of the lives of the people she saw in the room with her. Knowing she couldn't deny the commands of the goddess, she nodded her assent and hugged her emotions more closely to herself.

Stepping behind her, Rio wrapped his arms around her, holding her tight to him. "You are stronger and braver than you know. Believe that." He kissed her lightly behind her ear, sending shivers of heat through her and distracting her from her fear.

Scathach gave her attention to Shanley and Alaisdair. "You have been dreaming Alaisdair in battles with three of Morgan's rogues. Where do these battles take place, and how does Alaisdair die in them?"

Shanley threw panicked looks first at Alaisdair then at Ceri before reciting for the goddess her dream. "He's taking on three rogue warriors. They attack him one at a time. When he starts to tire, they come at him all at once. While he's occupied with the two in front of him, one circles behind and slices his hamstrings. As he goes down, the second one stabs him in the chest while the third"—Shanley swallowed hard.

"You must finish it, lass," Alaisdair said, taking her hand in his massive one.

Shanley nodded. "The third takes a two-handed swing of his claymore and separates Alaisdair's head from his body." With her free hand, she covered her middle. "He picks up Alaisdair's head by the hair and holds it aloft in victory. Morgan watches in smug satisfaction before she stares at me in triumph with her glowing red eyes."

When she buried her tear-wet face in Alaisdair's chest, he smoothed his hands up and down her back. "Shh, lass, 'tis all right. I'm here, safe an' sound. Ye're only seein' what could happen if we aren't prepared, not what *will* happen. Remember that."

"In any of your dreams, do you see why Alaisdair is outside his cottage alone?" Scathach asked.

Shanley shook her head.

"Come, Alaisdair. Engage the three Sheridan brothers who will play the rogue warriors attacking you. We will see what tactics you can employ should this scenario come to pass." Addressing Owen, she added, "While your sons train, work with Ceri on her shield. Sian, work with Shanley. Alyssa and Lynnette, you will attempt to breach Ceri and Shanley's shields. Begin."

After an hour of intense training, everyone except the goddess dripped sweat. Warriors and talismans alike labored to draw breath, yet Scathach remained displeased.

Standing in the middle of the stone floor, her hands on her hips, she said, "Shanley's dreams are connected to Ceri's prophecies, that much is clear. We must discover how Morgan will try to lure both Rio and Alaisdair out onto the open grounds of the manor. The training has not revealed another prophecy as I had hoped. I need to think on this."

The goddess paced away from the knot of Sheridans and Conlans gathered around the cooler of bottled water Hamish supplied. Alaisdair poured a liter of frigid water over his head and chest. Rio mimicked him, and Ceri couldn't stop staring at the definition of chest and abs revealed beneath Rio's wet T-shirt. Suppressing the urge to walk over and lap at the water sliding in rivulets down his neck, she turned away to avoid drawing the ire of the goddess for her wayward thoughts.

It seemed they'd barely taken five minutes when Scathach demanded they return to training.

For the rest of the day, she ran the warriors through various scenarios. Though she admitted she couldn't conjure weather like Taranis, she did use light and sound to simulate some of Taranis's more common tactics. At some point, she said, "I anticipate thick fog will be Taranis's choice. Morgan can force Taranis to interfere with weather, but she cannot tell him what weather to call."

Ceri stared in wonder at the goddess.

"Long ago the great Irish hero, Brian Boru, won a battle because Taranis, purely to spite Morgan for badgering him, called a mist rather than the great thunderstorm Morgan had demanded." Scathach smiled at the memory. "The mist more effectively shielded Brian Boru than his opponent whom Morgan had intended to best him." She refocused, giving her attention to the assembled warriors. "It is likely Morgan remembers that particular battle as well and will not push for specific weather, leaving the choice up to Taranis and whatever mischief he will employ to encourage her to leave him alone for a while."

By dinnertime, Scathach conceded. "You have trained as much as possible to prepare for Samhain." With a sigh, she said, "Return to Conlan Manor and rest."

Ceri sagged against Rio. "I might need to return to the manor in the civilian way. I don't have the energy to visualize myself there."

"Not an option, sweetheart. Wrap your arms around me and visualize our bed," he whispered, his lips caressing her ear.

"What?" Ceri pulled back. "'Our' bed?"

Rio grinned at her. Perhaps Scathach hadn't worn him out completely.

CHAPTER TWENTY-THREE

AMISH BUSTLED AROUND the manor from the kitchen to the third story ballroom like a man half his age as he supervised the army of druids and civilians gathered to prepare the ceilidh. Civilian caterers filled the gigantic stainless-steel refrigerator in the pantry with canapés and mutton and beef dishes they could reheat before the midnight feast, plus desserts of apples and pears. Of course, they'd also delivered the haggis they'd made ahead of time so it could be cooked the following evening. Bags of turnips and potatoes lay stacked against a wall awaiting cooks to peel and boil them for neeps and tatties to accompany the haggis.

Barrels of apple cider and a keg of *uisge beatha*—the water of life—whisky—were loaded onto the oversized dumbwaiter beside the pantry and hauled up three stories to the ballroom where several burly Scots wrestled them over to the bar and set them up for thirsty revelers during the party. Hamish supplied a couple dozen bottles of his specialty mead, his recipe creating a beverage so carbonated those who shared the privilege of tasting it declared it as fine as France's best champagne. The mead would feature in the midnight salute to the ancestors whose lives they honored and whose spirits they toasted back to the next world.

Several of his druid friends, most notably Davy Sutherland, helped with the decorations for the party. They draped rowan branches and sprays of herbs around the ballroom for the ritual. Each druid chanted over his greenery in the guise of humming or singing as he worked, the civilians who helped them decorate none the wiser for what they truly did. The civilians wrapped festive bunting and long swags of tartan around the dais and along the fireplace. The tartan in the beautiful lavender, meadow-green, and heather plaid of the Conlans and the forest-green and rust of the Rosses woke up the ballroom. After a full day's work, the room looked ready to host a party.

As he decorated the front door with Hamish, Davy said, "She belongs tae the big American after all."

"Aye, my young friend, she does."

"Ye knew that, didn't ye, when ye were throwin' her at me."

It wasn't a question.

"Not entirely. I knew there was somethin' strong between 'em, somethin' that needed some nudgin' tae discover. Ye were out o' practice fer datin', so I helped ye out as well," Hamish said with a wink.

"Ye cannae help meddlin', can ye old man?" Davy chuckled good-naturedly.

"Though ye weren't the man tae entice her tae stay at the manor—" Hamish began.

"I knew ye had some ulterior motive," Davy said as he finished setting a branch.

"She needs tae stay fer the requisite year. It would be even better if she made Conlan Manor her permanent residence. Ye know that, lad." Hamish clapped him on the shoulder. "Though ye aren't her man, ye can still protect her and the legacy she is by comin' round and tellin' yer stories and chantin' with me from time tae time."

Davy nodded.

"Ye can start by makin' friends with her warrior at the ceilidh taemorrow night."

Davy pulled a face. "I do like the man. I'd have thought less o' him if he hadn't reacted the way he did tae me movin' in on an unattached talisman. But I think he's not tae keen on spendin' any time with the likes of me even if I hadn't been competin' with him." His expression darkened. "I get the feelin' he doesnae much care fer druids."

"That was true enough when he arrived here, but I think he's comin' around."

Hamish grinned conspiratorially.

Davy stopped in the middle of hanging another rowan branch. "Ye sly old devil. Been workin' on his dinner have ye? An' makin' sure tae share most o' his meals with him?" He chuckled. "I should have known ye wouldn't play fair. Ye worked me over well enough when ye were trainin' me."

Hamish curled his lips. "Hand me that bundle o' rowan branches. I need tae finish this door and head down tae the kitchens tae check on how the caterers are comin' along. Maybe ye could chime in on the chant."

Both stilled at the ripple in the cosmos when warriors and talismans visualized themselves back into the manor. Since a couple of civilians were coming down the stairs at that time, they nodded to each other and directed their attention to completing the protections over the front door. Later, after the rest of the Sheridans returned to the manor, Hamish made short work of ushering the civilian helpers on their way, assuring them their efforts for the ceilidh pleased him very much, and the family could finish any last-minute details.

He gathered the Sheridans in the kitchen to introduce them

to his protégé. "Davy, this is Owen Sheridan and his lovely wife, Sian, their sons Rowan and Riley and their wives Alyssa and Lynnette. Davy Sutherland is my most accomplished student."

Owen's eyes rounded. "You're a druid?"

Hamish grinned at what Owen really meant. Davy stood six feet. His broad shoulders and chest suggested a man who trained regularly with a claymore or who spent a good deal of time in a weight room—or both.

"We're pleased to meet you, Davy Sutherland," Sian said, extending her hand to him.

Davy laughed. "Pleased tae meet ye as well. Hamish is quite taken with the lot o' ye." Gallantly, he took Sian's outstretched hand in both of his and brushed his lips over her knuckles.

She beamed at him.

"I didn't mean any offense." Owen frowned at the exchange between Davy and his wife.

"None taken," Davy replied, his eyes dancing. "I'm often mistaken for a warrior. Here in the *auld country*, druids are still expected tae train with and in the same way as warriors. One never knows when brute force will be called for, so one has tae be prepared."

"Brute force, huh?" Rowan sounded offended, but after a raised brow from his wife, he extended his hand to Hamish's prize student.

"Donnae take me wrong. I admire yer skill and yer courage, and normally, I'm quite happy tae leave ye tae yer appointed job while I do mine, but sometimes, even a druid can't be quick enough with the exact chant or spell if some thug civilian or rogue warrior attacks a druid chantin' outside a battle zone. It's good tae have additional skills," Davy said matter-of-factly.

"Ye do remember yer history, do ye no'?" Hamish asked as he inspected the food sitting on the table. "Druids have always trained alongside warriors in addition tae honin' their skills with herbs and spells and storytellin'." He nodded in satisfaction before taking his place next to his student. "Davy took tae warrior trainin' a little more enthusiastically than most druids, I expect. Alaisdair may have had a hand in that."

"Alaisdair trained you?" Owen asked. "Why?"

Davy shrugged. "He needed the practice, and I was interested. It worked out well for both of us."

"If Alaisdair trained you, Scathach must have approved." Owen shook Davy's hand again, more enthusiastically this time.

Hamish beamed. Owen's acceptance carried weight with his family. "How did yer trainin' go taeday?" he asked.

"We're as prepared as we can be. Scathach hoped for something more, but neither Ceri nor Shanley had any more prophecies, so we worked with what we know. Honestly, I'm beat. I hope you won't need us much tonight," Owen said.

The rest of the family echoed his sentiments.

"We need tae practice an outline o' the ritual, kind o' like a weddin' rehearsal," Hamish explained.

Sian side-eyed him. "You aren't planning something sneaky here like marrying Rio and Ceri tomorrow night, are you?"

Hamish put up his hands. "We're only performin' a ritual tae marry Ceri tae her home. The fact we have a convenient stand-in fer the King Stag in the form o' her warrior is a bonus."

Sian took a step toward him. "I know about the King Stag ritual, Hamish. To all involved, it feels very much like a wedding, complete with an emphasis on privacy like a honeymoon for the joined couple following the ritual." She jammed her hands on her hips. "I will *not* be deprived of my son's wedding." With a nod to Alyssa and Lynnette, she added, "My daughters-in-law will have quite a bit to say about being left out of the preparation for Ceri's special day as well."

On cue, Alyssa and Lynnette flanked Sian, mimicking her glare.

"No' tae worry." Hamish made a conciliatory gesture. "Truly, 'tis but a ritual tae bond Ceri tae her ancestral home and tae protect her and her family. There's nothin' legal or bindin' or untoward about the ceremony and its outcome in either the warrior or the civilian communities."

"You mean like the birth of Mordred following King Arthur's participation in the King Stag ritual when he was tricked into sleeping with his sister Morgause?" Riley asked, a smile playing on his lips.

Hamish didn't rise to the bait. "Ceri and Rio were destined fer each other. Whatever comes o' this ritual will benefit those connected tae this house and their descendants. Everything about the ritual from the timin' at Celtic New Year tae the fact both Ceri and her aunt found their warriors here"—he smirked—"is thanks tae the Sheridan family."

The Sheridan men casually propped against counters or resting arms over the backs of chairs looked self-satisfied. The women remained skeptical.

"Yer coming together here is an omen o' longevity fer the participants in the ritual and their families. That whole mess with King Arthur fifteen or sixteen hundred years ago was an anomaly perpetrated by the forces o' evil. We've taken great precautions tae avoid that with this ritual." Hamish looked each person in the eye, making his convictions clear.

The ritual was serious business indeed.

"O' course, I wouldnae be adverse tae hostin' a weddin' or twa here at the manor in the near future if that's in the stars." He rubbed his hands together and grinned.

"As long as we get to plan it—or both of them—we're not averse to a wedding either. But we want to be in on the fun of planning and executing, don't we girls," Sian said, taking Alyssa and Lynnette's hands in a show of solidarity.

"After the wonderful wedding Ceri gave us, I promised I'd

help with hers. Knowing her, she'll want something elaborate," Alyssa said.

"Before we get too carried away marrying off the pairs 'resting' upstairs," Rowan said with air-quotes, "we'd better keep in mind we have to help them safely reach midnight tomorrow night. Which means we all need to be at our best. Let's grab some dinner, practice the ritual, and go to bed." He pushed away from the counter and slid Alyssa's hand in his.

"Is there anything to eat in this place that isn't marked for the party tomorrow night?" Owen asked.

"I had the caterers prepare a meal fer ye, as a matter o' fact. Davy, will ye help me set it out while these folks clean up fer dinner? I expect ye'll want tae wash off some o' the day's exertions before ye eat."

❧

"Normally, I'm looking forward to a party. But I'm exhausted, and this house feels like a hive," Ceri muttered after she and Rio visualized themselves into her bedroom at the manor.

"Yeah, I wonder how many civilians Hamish has crawling over this place and which ones are honestly helping him and which ones are trying to discover what we've done with security," Rio responded grumpily. After the day's training, his patience had worn thin.

"I'm sure Hamish knows what he's doing. After all, these are his people," Ceri said from the chaise longue as she removed her boots.

"Alyssa thought she knew that civilian boyfriend of hers too, remember." Rio whipped off his sweaty T-shirt and tossed it toward the wardrobe in the corner.

"Not the same thing at all. In the beginning, he charmed Alyssa," Ceri said, heading into the bathroom. "She let down her guard, that's all. Hamish, on the other hand, knows who he can trust. He's lived with these people all his life. You've seen him at the pub." She shot a glance over her shoulder. "You know I'm right."

"Civilians aren't strong enough to withstand *suggestions* from a god, and you know it," Rio said as he followed her. "Even talismans as talented as you and Alyssa have struggled with Maeve's attempts to influence your thoughts."

"Again, not fair." Ceri turned on the shower and began to undress. "She attacked us while we slept before we learned how to shield our dreams. Once your father taught Alyssa that skill, she was fine." She grinned at him in the mirror. "Better than fine since she told me now even Rowan can't get inside her head when she's asleep unless she's exhausted or she lets him in."

Rio frowned at her.

"We're working on my skills under Hamish's protections. You're too quick to judge, and I'm too tired to argue with you."

Her shirt hit the floor.

Rio felt guilty for goading her. He was tired and out of sorts. That's why he argued—not because he had any real point to make. Hamish had taken every precaution to keep Ceri safe, and Rio knew it would take a very sophisticated civilian with some serious skills to determine how to circumvent the surveillance and alarm system they'd installed.

As he watched Ceri peeling off clothes and dropping them wherever, he knew he was far better suited both mentally and physically to take on the dangers awaiting them, and he'd better take up his place as her protector in all ways, not only on the battlefield. A wave of tenderness washed over him as he watched her undress, the first thoughts in his mind not of seduction but of protection. Remarkable. A powerful need to care for this woman overcame him, and he acted on it.

Pushing weakly from foot to foot, she tried to discard jeans stubbornly clinging to her ankles and refusing to slide over her feet. She appeared insensible of the problem as she tried to walk and remove her jeans at the same time. Rio burst out laughing, and she scowled at him. Still grinning, he steadied her before he knelt in front of her and pulled the offending clothing off her. He slid her panties down her long legs, stood, and guided her to the shower with a firm hand at the small of her back.

Not completely convinced she'd remain standing, he didn't take his eyes from her as he stripped off the rest of his clothes, heaping them on the floor before he stepped in to join her. At first, he held her and let the twin sprays from the showerheads soothe away the soreness from tired muscles. Then he stepped back and lathered soap to wash the sweat from her body. Taking his time, he massaged her arms, legs, back, and ass before enjoying the sensations of touching her smooth taut belly and full breasts as he washed her front.

Ruthlessly denying himself the desire to push her toward activities he wasn't sure he could finish, he turned her and lathered up her long thick hair then gently guided her beneath the showerhead. While he made short work of washing himself, she closed her eyes beneath the spray, and he wasn't entirely sure she hadn't fallen asleep. When he reached around her to turn off the water, she didn't seem to notice the warm spray no longer slid over her.

Grabbing a fluffy towel from the warming rack beside the shower, he wrapped Ceri in it before vigorously drying himself off with its twin. He secured his towel around his waist before he took care drying her body and blotting her hair. After rewrapping her in the towel, he picked her up and carried her to bed.

He set her on the edge of the mattress and slipped behind her to comb out her hair. Taking his time, he patiently detangled her long locks and sucked the floral scent of the shampoo she liked deep into his lungs. The fragrance, combined with her musky, feminine scent, created a heady mix that forced him to talk himself down. Her soft sigh threatened to undo him with her absolute trust in him. This incredible woman who suffered so much for his protection trusted him to take care of her. It humbled him in a way he never expected. A bonus gift, her trust made him a stronger warrior. He'd do anything to keep her safe.

He tugged her towel from her body and guided her to lie between the sheets. When he padded back to the bathroom to hang up their towels, he shook his head at the mess they'd left in their wake on the way to the shower. When he returned to the bed, Ceri slept soundly, so he slid in behind her and spooned her close to him. He too, sorely needed a nap, but he couldn't make his mind rest. Something about the upcoming battle bothered him. He sensed he was missing something important. If only he could force out the detail hovering at the edge of his consciousness.

CHAPTER TWENTY-FOUR

Samhain—morning

AMHAIN DAWNED CLEAR and brisk. The cloudless sky almost hurt Rio's eyes as he gazed into the intense azure light of a Scots autumn morning. Though he'd only opened the curtain a couple of inches, daylight flooded the room. Ceri groaned and burrowed deeper under the covers. He smiled at her renunciation of morning before rejoining her in bed.

"It's time to wake up sleepyhead." He brushed her hair away from her neck to nuzzle her there.

"It isn't if you turn out the lights," she grumbled, but she snuggled into him, fitting her backside firmly against his front.

"Not even the gods can turn out the sun." He smiled into her neck before he kissed his way up to the sensitive spot behind her ear.

She shivered but didn't give in. "You can close the curtain, and we can pretend we have hours before daylight."

"Or we can make love in daylight, and I can have the pleasure of watching your beautiful face as you come."

"After the workout Scathach put us

through yesterday, we need more sleep," she said stubbornly, but her body betrayed her as her nipples puckered prettily when Rio rolled first one and then the other between his thumb and index finger as he palmed her breasts.

"Somehow, I don't think my closing that curtain is going to help you fall back to sleep," he said, his voice low and gravelly as he pulled her onto her back.

"That's because *someone* seems to be up in every sense of the word." Her words warred with the playful tone of her voice. "So if he's up, he thinks everyone else should be too."

She ran her hands over his chest and down his belly, stopping just shy of the place he longed for her to touch.

"That makes me sound rather selfish, and I'm not selfish at all. I plan to pleasure you thoroughly before I finish."

With a grin, he swooped down and took her nipple in his mouth, eliciting a gasp that slid into a moan. He sucked first one tight bud and then the other while she ran her fingers through his hair and arched beneath him.

"As long as I live, I don't think I'll ever get over how fast Rio arouses me."

"Mmm, I certainly hope not."

"Ugh! I thought I still had my shield up."

"Just like I want to watch your face as we make love, I want to hear your thoughts and let you hear mine. That's part of being mated to each other," Rio said. *"And in case you haven't noticed, sweetheart, you arouse me pretty fast too."*

"Oh!"

"Now, where were we? Oh, yeah, I think I was here."

Rio licked and kissed her breast, and she rewarded him with an "Oooh" of pleasure.

Kissing his way down her taut belly, he enjoyed the ripples of sensation she couldn't seem to control beneath his lips. Brushing his lips along the tops of her hips, he savored her skin before he ran his tongue along her groin. She cried out his name and opened for him.

He didn't continue his obvious trajectory to the hot place where he knew she most wanted kissing. Instead, he lightly ran his fingertips over the silky skin of her legs, planting the occasional kiss on her upper thigh, behind her knee, and beneath her ankle bone. She moaned when he gifted her with an open-mouthed kiss on the arch of her foot, writhing as he pleasured her. Her response left him deeply satisfied. He had so much to learn about pleasing her, and every time they made love, he learned something new.

Ceri sat up and pulled her feet away from him. For several seconds, they stared at each other. He could spend days in the deep green meadows of her eyes when they made love.

"Rio, your eyes darken from blue nearly to black when you're aroused. It's incredibly sexy." A slow smile spread across her face.

"Now you're getting it."

He smiled back at her, and they leaned together, their lips meeting, their tongues tangling in a kiss that left them both panting. Slipping a hand around his nape, she sank back into the pillows, pulling him down with her. Whimpering in the back of her throat, she opened her legs and urged him to finish what he'd started. Reaching between them, he positioned himself at her slick opening and thrust deeply. Still, the kiss went on, Ceri gripping Rio's shoulders while their tongues imitated the movements of their bodies.

With long full strokes, he took her slowly, building to an eventual crescendo neither of them could deny. At last he tore his mouth from hers and came up on his knees. Holding her hips steady and staring into her eyes, he increased his rhythm. She threw back her head and arched her back. Crying out his name, she shattered, her inner muscles pulsing wildly around him.

Watching Ceri slide over the edge gave Rio such an all-consuming feeling of satisfaction he couldn't hold himself back. Two hard strokes later, he joined her. For several minutes, all he could do was feel and breathe, the scents of flowers, musk, woman, and sex wrapping around him, pulling him closer to her.

At last he floated back down to earth, his body still sparking in the aftershocks of what they'd done together. He couldn't tear his eyes from hers, his love for her nakedly reflected in the meadows of her eyes. She lifted her arms to him, inviting him back into her embrace.

"Let me know if I'm too heavy, if you can't breathe," he whispered as he slipped his arms around her and held her flush to him.

She nodded into his shoulder. For a few minutes before the world barged in, they were one with the person who would be risking everything for the other.

"You're worth it, you know."

"In case there isn't time to say this later, I love you Rio."

Rio stilled and she stiffened in his arms.

He pushed off her enough to see her face. "Say that again—aloud."

Swallowing hard, Ceri whispered, "I love you, Rio."

He tightened his hold on her before he said into her ear, "I love you, Ceri. That's why you're worth the risks."

"Including the biggest risk—love itself?"

"Especially that one."

She dropped her shield again. *"I wouldn't mind if the world came to an end right now because this warrior loves me."*

"Yeah, well, I'll mind if the world comes to an end right now. I have it in my head I'd like decades of waking up with you in my bed with all sorts of possibilities for the day ahead. After I make love to you."

She laughed. "You need to lighten up. I was thinking right at this moment, I'm the happiest I've ever been in my life."

"Me too."

They lay together savoring their warm cocoon of love, enjoying the newness of sharing their feelings for each other and knowing that, for right now, they were safe. Finally, Rio rolled off her and pulled her up to rest her head on his chest. She threw an arm and a leg over him, snuggling in close. They'd started to doze off when the intercom crackled to life. Ceri almost leaped out of bed while Rio cursed.

"Hey you two. Are you staying in bed all day? Hamish and Davy have an awesome breakfast buffet set up in the dining room, but in a few minutes, there won't be any left."

Rio threw a pillow at the offending device. Rowan's laughter teased them at the other end before he switched off the intercom.

"You know what's going to be the best part of making it through Samhain?" Rio asked, irritation roughening his voice.

"Besting Morgan at her own game?"

"No." He flopped back onto the bed. "Putting my family on a plane back to the States and having you to myself in this house. One of the first items of business is going to be rigging up an intercom control we can access in bed, one we can override so we don't have to be disturbed."

"Mmm, that sounds nice."

Her stomach emitted a long, low rumble, and she laughed. "The mere suggestion of breakfast seems to have awakened another hunger." She gazed down at him. "Now that I think about it, we didn't eat when we returned from training last night, did we?"

"Nope. You could barely hold yourself up in the shower, and when I put you to bed, you were asleep before your head hit the pillow."

"Sorry."

"Don't be." He smiled at her. "I enjoyed taking care of you."

He pushed himself up and swung his legs over the side of the bed.

"As much as I hate to give in to my brother, I think we better take advantage of breakfast. Did Rowan say something about Davy helping Hamish?" Rio asked without trying to hide his attitude.

"Now don't get all huffy about Davy. It makes sense he'd be here to help out today. What with Scathach not being too sure about Shanley's and my readiness to take on whatever it is Morgan has in store, it seems we'd want every ally we can get. Including druids." Ceri stretched and walked over to the dresser for clean underwear.

"Did you know he was here?"

"Of course not!"

He immediately regretted his jealousy as he watched her good mood evaporate.

Hands on hips, she scowled at him. "I was with you all day and all night, *remember*? How would I know what Hamish was doing here at the manor and with whom?" After she pulled out some lacy things, she shoved the drawer closed with her hip. "I put two and two together and figured Hamish will use everything he has at his disposal to keep this house and its people safe from Morgan's wrath."

Rio wrapped his arms around her, preventing her from stomping away from him.

"Slow down, babe. I'm sorry. I have trouble trusting a druid who would knowingly go after an unattached talisman."

"It was one date, and at the risk of stroking your over-inflated ego, I thought about you for most of it."

"Yeah?"

"Yeah. Now can you be nice long enough for us to have breakfast?"

"Maybe if I have a little more incentive," he said with a leer.

"You're incorrigible." Then she kissed him thoroughly, making him forget everything. "Now can you behave?"

He liked how her breath stuttered.

"Probably not, but I'll feel guilty about it, I promise," he said with a grin.

"Ugh! Let me go. I'm going downstairs for breakfast."

"Teasing you is a bonus I'm going to exploit in this relationship—fair warning." He smirked and let her go.

She exaggerated an eye roll, but a smile twitched over her lips.

As he dressed, he heard her muttering in the bathroom.

"I can't believe we left such a mess."

He peeked in the doorway where he found her gathering their discarded clothing.

"You were pretty out of it. Sometimes training sessions with Scathach can be exhausting."

"You think?"

"I think you're going to need to build up your stamina 'cause she's going to demand a lot from you from now on."

"But I'm not a warrior," Ceri complained as she dumped their sweaty clothes into the hamper.

He leaned against the doorframe. "But you are my talisman, and she trains me almost that hard every time she visits." He cocked a brow. "Which is often."

"Great. I'm looking forward to all the exhaustion in my future."

He squeezed her hand. "It gets easier, I promise."

⌘

Rio greeted Shanley and Alaisdair in the hallway outside their bedroom. "I see the intercom works in your room too."

"I get the feelin' Rowan rather enjoys disturbin' people tryin' tae sleep," Alaisdair replied with a sparkle in his eye.

"You're rather forgiving of my brother's rudeness. You'll get over that."

Rio and Ceri fell into step with Alaisdair and Shanley.

"Nae, I'll just find a way tae even the score."

"The more I get to know you, the more I like you," Rio said as the four of them descended the stairs together.

"Hey, you two. Don't start something within the family, at least not before we finish what we need to finish," Shanley said.

"Wouldnae dream o' it, lass. But once we take care o' business with the Morrigan, Rowan might need tae pay attention." Alaisdair exchanged a look with Rio, and the two men grinned broadly at each other.

"Your Celtic blood flows close to the surface, doesn't it? If you're not fighting your enemies, you're fighting amongst yourselves. It's silly." Shanley shook her head.

Alaisdair threw an arm across her shoulders. "Rowan won't sustain any permanent damage."

"That depends on how often he thinks he needs to use the intercom system while he's here," Rio grumbled.

Subdued conversation filtered through the door to the dining room when they reached it.

Sensing the family's mood as the four of them entered the room, Rio asked, "Have we sustained casualties already?"

"Not yet. Hamish was telling us what he heard on the *BBC News* this morning. A bunch of out-of-work kids went on a rampage in Inverness last night. They called it a *wilding*, an excuse to overturn and torch cars and loot businesses. The police arrested several of them, but it seems the trend has caught on and is moving north," Owen explained.

"So, it begins. Morgan gathers her army of civilians tae attack us, leaving a trail o' destruction in their wake. It sounds like she's tryin' tae lure us away from the manor," Alaisdair said, his expression grim.

"That's the way I figure it." Hamish sipped his tea.

As the four seated themselves at the long dining table, Rio asked, "What's the battle plan?"

"We stay put, force her tae bring the battle here. Besides, since certain warriors dinnae let our two honored talismans out o' their rooms last night tae practice the ritual, we must practice it this mornin'," Hamish said with a slow shake of his head.

Rio helped himself to tea. "Ceri was asleep on her feet after

Scathach's training session. I doubt she could have practiced one more thing last night."

"Shanley wasn't in any better shape," Alaisdair seconded, taking the teapot from Rio.

"I trust ye're both recovered this mornin'."

There was a twinkle in Hamish's eye as he gazed at them over the rim of his cup.

Rio liked the blush that spread across Ceri's lovely face.

"As soon as I eat some of your delicious porridge and wash it down with some of your terrible coffee, I'll be ready to practice whatever you need me to practice Hamish," Ceri said.

"Davy insisted on brewin' the coffee this mornin'. The rest o' these folks say it's considerably more palatable, whatever that means," Hamish grumped.

Alaisdair scowled. "Why dinnae ye mention Davy made the coffee? I would have gone down tae the kitchens tae fetch my big mug instead o' pourin' this tiny cup o' tea."

"That good, huh?" Ceri smiled.

"Davy makes excellent coffee, and Hamish knows it. Only he hates tae admit it, dontcha, old man?"

"Be careful friend. Ye keep talkin' like that, and I might stop brewin' yer afternoon tea."

"An idle threat. Ye'd miss my company tae much, and ye know it." A grin spread over Alaisdair's face.

The newcomers stepped over to the buffet to dish up food from a succulent array of full Scots breakfast before rejoining the others at the long table. The teasing continued through breakfast, everyone knowing that when the meal was over, the battle preparations wouldn't end until they bested Morgan or died trying.

CHAPTER TWENTY-FIVE

WHY ARE YOU pacing, Morgan? I would have thought you would be dancing a jig at the destruction your little diversion caused last night," Taranis drawled from his chair near the fireplace in Morgan's Black Isle stronghold.

"It didn't draw even a ripple of attention from the Sheridans. One would have thought they'd have sent at least one warrior to see how they could help with the civilian casualties I created," she retorted testily.

"Perhaps they didn't know."

"How could they not know? Those ruffians I incited to mayhem set a substantial part of Inverness afire. A couple thousand people were involved. Highland warriors responded rather promptly to that terrorist threat I staged at the Glasgow airport a few years ago, which was a tiny fraction of trouble compared to last night's *wilding*." Morgan stared moodily out the window before turning back to him. "Someone should have shown up. They are preparing for me in a way I have not seen since ancient times when the world was so much smaller. I do not like it."

Taranis sighed. "You are going to wear out this Persian carpet—and my nerves. Stop pacing at least."

"*You* are on my nerves, lounging there like you haven't a care in the world while all my careful planning could be in jeopardy." Her red eyes glowed beneath her furrowed brow.

"You forget, Morgan. I did not ask to be involved in this battle. It is none of my concern that you have not orgasmed in your preferred fashion for a while. However, you are determined to make it my problem. Frankly, I hope the Sheridans best you again. Then maybe you'll stop badgering me for favors."

Taranis unfolded himself from his chair and strolled over to the floor-to-ceiling windows facing the sea. Taking a cleansing breath, he idly conjured a squall at the mouth of the estuary purely to show his displeasure with his sister goddess.

She stopped her pacing to stare him down in the reflection of the window. "Don't you understand, Taranis? If the Sheridans win this time, they gain even more power against what we gods can do. They aspire to be like us, maybe even defeat us completely."

"That is ridiculous. If the Sheridans best you again, they tilt the playing field to something more level. Face it, Morgan. You have had your way for far too long, taking more than your share of warriors and talismans after you set them up in unfair circumstances." Taranis crossed his arms and arched a brow. "Now Danu is allowing the fates to run their course, realigning the cosmos so warriors have an even chance. These battles with the Sheridans have been in the stars for eons. While the outcome is not assured, the fates are on their side."

Morgan narrowed her eyes. "Are you saying you are changing your mind? You will not help me?"

"Not at all." He stepped toward her and ran a finger along her alabaster cheek. "It is the time of year for thick mists and ocean squalls that ram onto shore, and I truly do enjoy conjuring a good storm." He dropped his hand. "But like the Sheridans, I do not like to be bullied. I will do as much as I feel like doing and no more." She opened her mouth, but he preempted her. "And you will be satisfied with that."

With a shrug that didn't fool him in the slightest, she changed topics. "Maeve is the most selfish goddess in the cosmos. How she can remain in America when the most important action is taking place here in Scotland is beyond my comprehension. Macha is no better, choosing to remain on Tara for the New Year."

She returned to her incessant pacing.

Taranis sauntered over to the couch and reclined into it. "Like you, those two have always been selfish. You act like you recently discovered the fact."

She exited the room abruptly. Taranis, at last relieved of her company, immediately called off the storm at sea he'd been toying with and let the sun dazzle the newly washed earth. Retiring to his lavishly appointed rooms, he rested for the havoc Morgan expected him to unleash. Havoc which hopefully would keep her off of his back for the foreseeable future.

⌘

"As ye all know, taenight at sundown when Samhain officially begins, the barrier between our world and the otherworld thins almost tae naethin', and all manner o' spirits will visit us. Mostly our ancestors, but also those the Morrigan chooses tae encourage. We must be ready, which is why Davy and I spent all o' yesterday enchantin' every door and window in this house," Hamish explained from his place on the dais in the ballroom.

Pointedly gazing at Rio, he continued. "I know ye donnae like it, but it's custom on Samhain tae leave the house open and set out extra chairs tae welcome those guests we dinnae specifically invite."

Standing in the middle of the ballroom, Rio stared at the ornately decorated ceiling but didn't interrupt.

Hamish gestured to the doors and windows, elaborately

decorated with ribbons and rowan branches. "The enchantments will keep out the unsavory spirits, and we can deal with any unruly civilians who come with a notion o' crashin' the party. Donnae worry about the integrity o' the protections o' this house."

The Sheridan and Conlan women wandered around the ballroom, admiring Hamish's handiwork, while the men stood in the middle, listening to him, except for Davy who sat on a chair beneath one of the windows and Finn who sat opposite him beside the door.

"It's your show, but keep in mind what's at stake here, old man," Rio said, almost snarling.

"We're all in this to keep Ceri and Shanley safe, son." Owen clapped Rio on the shoulder. "But as far as what will happen inside this house tonight, Hamish is the one who knows best. When the battles start on the grounds, we'll do what we've trained all our lives to do—protect ourselves, our family and friends, and our home."

"A part o' the ritual takes place before the midnight meetin' in the ballroom. That's the time I think Morgan will strike since we'll be vulnerable."

The Sheridan men crossed their arms over their chests and widened their stances.

"We walk the grounds with torches tae ward off the evil spirits wantin' tae crowd in on our festivities," Hamish explained. "'Tis an ancient custom. The civilian men will be involved while their wives will be settin' out the midnight supper."

The Sheridans exchanged glances and waited.

"The civilians will have enjoyed a quantity o' cider and whisky, so they'll be usin' battery-operated torches rather than live fire. They think this part o' the evenin' is a lark because they've strayed from the finer points o' our culture over time. However, we know spirits still walk the earth especially on Celtic New Year. We'll need tae be ready." Hamish eyed each man—and woman—in the room.

"Where will our talismans be?" Rowan asked. "I can't forget how close I came to losing Alyssa right after I found her. Not looking forward to round two of that." He turned to his brother. "Nor do I want to watch Rio's anguish if something happens to Ceri."

Rio stared incredulously at Rowan, but he merely shrugged, a ghost of a smile the only giveaway that he understood the depth of Rio's feelings for his talisman.

"All o' the women will stay inside the manor. It'll be best if they stay in my quarters. My rooms are heavily enchanted as ye've noted, and the women will be safest from Morgan's shenanigans there. It willnae be easy fer either Morgan or Maeve or Macha if Morgan's enlisted that goddess, tae penetrate my rooms tae give yer women false information tae lure them out intae danger." Hamish glanced at Davy who nodded back at him.

"If all goes tae plan," he continued, "we'll gather in the ballroom at midnight tae complete the ritual tae announce tae the warrior community the Conlan heir has found her warrior. Once we complete the ritual, we can enjoy the rest o' the party." Hamish smiled broadly. "Which likely willnae break up much before dawn, Samhain fallin' on a Saturday this year."

"What joining ritual will you use?" Sian asked.

Hamish walked over to Rio and pulled Ceri next to him. "We'll conduct a standard handfasting ritual."

He glanced back at Sian. "The civilians will see it as a joke, and the warrior community will see it as a promise of a weddin' tae come." He returned his attention to the couple. "Either way, it binds Ceri and Rio publicly."

He walked over to a chair beneath the windows and picked up a shirt. "They both will wear white shirts in compliance with the ancient wearin' o' white at Samhain. Ceri will wear her ancestral colors and a wreath o' woven wheat embellished with autumn flowers on her head." He nodded toward Davy who picked up a wreath from the chair beside him. "Rio will wear a Conlan kilt if he will consent—and a headdress made o' stag's hide."

Riley stepped up behind his twin to whisper in his ear. "Sweet."

Rio casually threw an elbow, and Riley danced away, laughing.

Sian and Hamish glared at their antics before Hamish pressed on. "After the handfastin', everyone showers the couple with Samhain herbs—dried oak bark, dried yellow cedar bark, ground acorns and hazelnuts, sage, nightshade, wormwood, and dried shavin's o' turnips. It'll make quite a mess on the floor and make it easier fer people tae slide their feet as they dance the midnight reels."

He grinned. "All the Scots in attendance look forward tae this part o' the evenin', and none o' the civilians will be the wiser there's in any special meanin' in it." He folded the shirt and replaced it on the chair.

Davy finished Hamish's explanation with a wide smile. "They'll think we decided tae mess with ye Americans tae give ye a Scots experience."

Hamish returned to the dais. "O' course, if Rio and Ceri sneak off shortly after the handfastin' and the first reel, nae one would think a thing about it," he added with a grin. Addressing Sian's glare, he said, "If there's a weddin', it'll come after Samhain. Never fear about that."

Rio's mom still had questions. "Does this ritual happen every year? You said the Scots expect it. Do you join warriors and talismans like this often?"

"It's only once in a great while we're lucky enough tae join a talisman and her warrior. Usually, we practice the ritual with civilians, which keeps us fresh fer when we need it fer real, and it's a harmless cover tae keep us from havin' tae explain it when we need tae use it fer the good of the warrior community," Davy explained.

Between all the training, his lack of rest, his worry for Ceri's safety, and now his mother's obvious misgivings about his future, Rio's patience wore thin. "Do we need to practice something, or what? If so, let's get the show on the road."

With a chuckle, Hamish said, "Can't wait tae practice, eh, son? Little wonder, Ceri bein' yer talisman and all. Let's get tae it then."

Hamish led them through the ritual. Shanley and Alaisdair flanked Rio and Ceri while the rest of the Sheridans lined up behind them in couples resembling a wedding party. Davy served Hamish like an acolyte in a religious service.

As they finished the rehearsal, Shanley and Ceri simultaneously grabbed their heads and sank to the floor in trances, wide-eyed and terrified. Alaisdair and Rio dropped down to hold their talismans. The rest of the party watched in helpless fascination as the two prophetesses experienced visions. First Ceri cried out then Shanley moaned then each of them gasped, tears streaming down their faces.

Rio exchanged a worried glance with Alaisdair. Holding their women was all they could do, while the women endured their visions. Rio stroked Ceri's silky hair and tried to remain relaxed under the strain of watching her pain without being able to do anything to alleviate it. He thought his expression probably mirrored the grim one on Alaisdair's face as he rocked Shanley close to him.

After minutes that resembled days, both women relaxed and slowly surfaced from their prophecies. Since everyone's attention centered on the Conlan women, no one noticed the red and gold shimmer in the room until Rio nodded in the direction of the fireplace. Scathach was in their presence.

"Milady," Rowan said while the others bowed their heads before the goddess.

She acknowledged them with a curt nod before descending on the pairs seated on the floor in the middle of the ballroom. "You have your prophecies now? Together? This is most strange. I know you have not processed what you have seen, but I demand you relate your entire prophecies. We have not much time to prepare."

Ceri and Shanley stared at each other. Shanley reached out to Ceri, and when the two clasped hands, it seemed as though they became one entity. A golden glow like a pulsing bubble surrounded them, and singing together, they related their vision.

"There are men—warriors and druids—walking the perimeter of the manor grounds. They carry torches. Civilians singing bawdy tavern songs accompany them, as though what they do is a game. The mists appear and thicken as the men exit the manor." Ceri's voice seemed to come from another time and place.

Shanley picked up the story. "When the group of men Hamish leads reaches the area near the cottage, a demon arises from the ground behind a large rock and breathes rank green contagion on them. The civilians pass out. The warriors prepare for battle."

"Which warriors are with Hamish?" Scathach demanded.

"Rowan, Alaisdair, and Finn," Ceri chanted.

The family exchanged worried glances as the women spoke. The quality of their voices, the aura surrounding them, and the fact neither appeared aware of the present struck fear into everyone.

Except the goddess. "Go on," Scathach said with a nod. "I thought Morgan would use this tactic."

"The demon accosts Hamish, having no interest in the others. Hamish wards it off with his torch and his chants. Morgan's champion joins the battle and draws Alaisdair away. Finn guards Hamish. Rowan aids Alaisdair. The ancient champion sent to attack Rio appears and attacks Alaisdair. Rio arrives from the other side of the cottage and calls out his opponent. The battle rages," Ceri continued.

"There is more death. The demon turns on Finn. Hamish sees an advantage, but when he moves in to torch the demon, it turns from Finn and breathes fire and putrid air on Hamish, choking him in mid-chant. The fumes swirl around him, paralyzing him. Hamish can't ward off the killing gases." Rivulets of tears raced down Shanley's cheeks.

"Finish it, lass. Ye must tell us everythin'," Alaisdair prompted gently.

"H-H-Hamish falls to the earth—dead."

On an anguished cry, Shanley dropped Ceri's hand.

The prophecy complete, Shanley turned her face into Alaisdair's chest and wept great racking sobs while Ceri silently stared straight ahead. Rio tightened his hold and rocked her in his arms.

"Describe this demon to me," Scathach commanded.

Though Rio longed to tell his patron goddess to back off, he knew better. Now was not the time to antagonize her no matter how much of Ceri's pain radiated through him.

Ceri robotically answered the goddess. "It stands twice the height of a warrior. The lower half of its body is a great black bull. Its long bull's tail twitches like an angry cat. The upper half of its body is a man, its muscles rippling as it stretches and fists its hands at its sides like it can't wait to strike a blow. Its head is an enormous black bull, the horns curving out and up into stiletto points a few feet above its head. Its huge ears stick out sideways from its head, creating an illusion of even greater size. Before it breathes its foul breath, its cave-like nostrils flare, and its black eyes glow red. It bellows out its contagion in an eerie wail momentarily paralyzing its victim, keeping him still while the rancid air envelops him."

"She plans to send the Morhaus." Scathach planted her hands on her hips and stared at the ornate ceiling. "How many times do my warriors have to defeat that beast before she decides to change her tactics?"

Blowing out a breath, she said, "We will send Rowan and Owen with Alaisdair and Hamish. Riley, you must be your brother's second. Finn will stand by with some local warriors whose help I have summoned. I had thought to scatter you, spread out the enemy, but now I think we will have more success when we are clustered together. Owen and Rowan must protect Hamish from the Morhaus."

Rio's father and brother nodded.

"Hamish and Davy, paint the faces every warrior with a salve of nightshade before they leave the manor. Paint yourselves too. It will protect you from the Morhaus's contagions. I trust you have the salve prepared."

"Of course, milady," Hamish replied.

"Put it on the warriors immediately before you leave the manor. The two of you will have to work fast. Davy, I know you had ideas about accompanying the warriors on this outing, but you must remain close to the manor. You will chant to keep Morgan's minions from entering the house. If they reach the talismans, all our work will have been for naught."

"If that's the case, why don't you leave a warrior to guard the door?" Rio demanded.

"Because the threats to your women should never reach the door to the manor," Scathach replied in a tone that said he should know better. "We need every warrior in the field doing what I've trained him to do. Do not question me on this Rio. This time, I will not indulge your insubordination. Is that clear?"

"As crystal, milady." He didn't mind the put-down—he had that coming. What rankled him was leaving Ceri vulnerable to attack. In his mind, leaving her in the care of a druid rather than a warrior left her unguarded. He needed to protect her, and that need superseded every other consideration. At the moment, he held his world on his lap, and he couldn't imagine his life without her.

Sian shook her head in warning at her son before asking the question on everyone's mind. "Milady, what does it mean that Ceri and Shanley experienced the same prophecy at the same moment?"

"I am not privy to all of Danu and the Dagda's plans. The great mother and the great father of the *Tuatha Dé Danann* do not see fit to share everything with their subjects, even the gods and goddesses in our pantheon. My guess is one or both of them has decided Morgan needs reined in, so they are giving the warrior community opportunities to even the playing field."

She stared at the Conlans for a moment. "Either that or these two are channeling their druidic great-grandmother several generations removed since they are together in this house. No matter. I am quite pleased to have their information before we engage Morgan and her army."

Davy stepped forward. "At the risk o' makin' ye angry, milady, perhaps there's another explanation."

Scathach's fists landed on her hips as she waited.

"Every year, Hamish takes great care tae invite both Taranis and the Morrigan tae the ceilidh at Samhain, as is expected with both o' them bein' such powerful deities. The Samhain rites are fer them after all."

Scathach made the universal gesture for "go on."

"But this year, Hamish decided not tae invite the Morrigan fer obvious reasons." He stopped speaking to glance at Ceri and Shanley. "Maybe she's sendin' a message conveyin' her displeasure at not receivin' her usual invitation."

"Thankfully, Morgan's powers do not extend to prophecy. That is Danu and the Dagda's exclusive realm. Still, we will keep in mind my sister may be even more vengeful since she's not invited to the festivities this year," Scathach said.

Hamish stepped between his cousins, placing a hand on each of them. "No' invitin' Morgan this year is a risk I'm willin' tae take if it means keepin' ye both safe." He looked into the eyes of each in turn. "Naethin' will happen tae me taenight, lassies. Since ye've warned us o' the danger, we'll be well prepared. Besides, ye both need me tae give ye away at yer weddin's." He winked at them.

Shanley managed a watery laugh while Ceri still seemed lost in whatever dark place her prophecies had taken her. Rio rubbed her back and arms and tried to breach her shield, which held firmly against his intrusion.

"If we're not needed here anymore, I need to speak to Ceri in private." He carefully disengaged Ceri from his lap long enough to stand up and lift her into his arms.

"You are clear on the battle plan?" Scathach asked.

"I am to stay close to the other warriors, especially my twin, wear my reinforced leathers, suffer Hamish to smear nightshade salve on my face, and pay attention to the edge of the hill when I take on my opponent. I'm to keep my mind on my battle and trust that my talisman will be awaiting me safely back here after we defeat Morgan," Rio recited almost as if by rote.

"A simple yes would have sufficed. If you did not look so grave, I would think you were mocking me, which would not have gone well for you." She let that sink in before she scanned the rest of her band of warriors. "All of you should take time to rest before your guests arrive at sundown." Her suggestion sounded more like a command.

Rio didn't await further instructions. With singular purpose, he strode down to the master suite, carrying Ceri easily in his arms. Kicking the door shut behind them, he crossed the room to the chaise lounge where he sat down with her on his lap.

"Out with it."

Almost as if surfacing from another trance, she turned to him and blinked. "Out with what?"

"Did you tell us everything, or did you leave out something you thought was too painful for the rest of us to hear?"

Her eyes widened. "No. Between us, Shanley and I told you everything unless she saw something more."

"But you didn't see anything else?" He ducked his head to stare into her eyes.

"No Rio, I swear. The vision was mainly about Hamish."

"Then what is troubling you?"

"Aren't my prophecies supposed to be confined to you? Why am I having visions of other talismans' warriors? Of a druid? It's truly terrible to have them about you, but I was starting to get the hang of having them and knowing simultaneously they were prophecies, not reality"—she blew out a breath—"which makes them marginally easier to bear."

She glanced away. "The vision I had of Alaisdair, and now this one about Hamish sent me right back to the beginning when I thought I was seeing the present, not a possibility in the future." She sagged against him, her eyes downcast. "Honestly, Rio, I don't think I can take much more of this, having prophecies about all the people I care about. It makes me think the last thing I should do is marry and have children."

His heart sank. Somehow, he had to convince his talisman everything would work out. Not marrying her scared him even more than watching her experience her visions.

"Ceri, this is all new to you. Normally, I think you would have had time to practice, get used to your skill before you were thrown into a battle where you have to use it." With his fingertips, he tilted her face up to look into her eyes. "I'm sorry Morgan has such a vendetta against the Sheridans, but you're so strong, more than you know. Why else would the gods have given you to me?" he asked with a smirk.

She pulled a face at him, and he laughed. "There's my girl. We're going to survive this. All of it. When it's over, we'll take some time away, just the two of us, and practice all kinds of ways of knowing each other, including how to control your responses to your prophecies—if we get around to that."

He leered at her, and she laughed—weakly—but she laughed.

"How 'bout if we kick off our shoes and lie down on the bed for the rest Scathach insists we need."

"Rio, I'm not up to bedroom gymnastics right now."

"Who said anything about sex? I believe the word I used was *rest*. I only mentioned taking off our shoes." He punctuated his point by reaching down to remove her flats before carrying her to their bed and laying her gently on top of the comforter. Then he shucked his boots and settled beside her.

"Let me hold you."

She turned to him and rested her head on his chest, her arm protectively across his waist while he wrapped both of his arms around her and relaxed more deeply into the mattress. "Rest, babe. I've got you," he whispered.

She drifted to sleep rather easily. When her breathing evened, Rio ventured a try at her shield, and finding it down, he took a deep breath, shut off the ethical questions inundating his conscience, and opened his mind to hers. Deliberately, he gave her a new vision: they were dancing, moving sensuously together across the floor. He enjoyed her grace and the easy way she followed him.

She smiled up into his eyes, relaxed and confident. Her response emboldened him, and he dipped his head to taste the spun sugar of her mouth while he whirled them around the dance floor. Tightening her hand where it rested at the back of his neck, she held on while she returned his kiss, her tongue dancing eagerly with his, a deep intense joining that would have sent both of them off-balance if they hadn't already been spinning around the floor.

After kissing her thoroughly breathless, he let her up for air and slowed down the speed of their dance. Her eyes darkened to a deep forest green. Through his dress shirt, he felt her taut nipples pucker even more as she pressed herself firmly against his body. He smiled at her boldness and let her feel the hard length of him against her hip.

Smoothing his hand over her satiny dress, he found his way to her ass where he cupped her in one of his hands. Her already ragged breathing caught as he caressed her through her dress, and she arched against him. Their need for each other was almost a living entity, a pulsing golden aura that wrapped around them and bound them together.

Rio joined her hands around his neck, allowing him to wrap both arms around her and hold her more intimately against him. Their dancing slowed to a gentle swaying while they stared deeply into each other's eyes. He didn't hold back, opening himself to her in every way. *"I love you Ceri Ross, you and only you, for all my life. Never doubt that."*

Rio sucked in a breath as the erotic dream he'd conjured in Ceri's mind was having some real-world consequences in his jeans. She arched against him, moaning while her hand roamed dangerously close to the part of him that had hardened considerably since they'd lain down on the bed. Knowing she needed to rest, Rio slowly faded the dream from her mind, dancing her off to somewhere private before he closed his mind to hers. He hoped he'd taken care of the monsters for the time being while letting her know he'd always want her. Then very assiduously, he focused his thoughts on freezing cold showers.

CHAPTER TWENTY-SIX

Samhain—evening

ONLAN MANOR BEGAN filling with people after sundown. When Hamish and Ceri opened the front door to welcome their first guests, all was ready for the biggest party of the year, a party even bigger and more anticipated by the inhabitants of Ullapool than *Hogmanay*, the lively Scots New Years' celebration.

Hamish seemed to know everyone in the village and surrounding countryside, and he delighted in welcoming the shire to his ceilidh, presenting a jovial come-one-come-all demeanor to all who entered the manor. Though she tried, Ceri couldn't detect a hint of nervousness or worry in his mien, even when they were greeting warriors and other druids. His calm behavior settled her.

In the ballroom, Shanley and Alaisdair greeted guests, Alaisdair, no doubt, presenting a similar air of calm. Meanwhile, the Sheridan clan, except for Rio, held court with the warriors who recognized who they were. Rio had stationed himself inside the sitting room off the front hall where he could unobtrusively observe every person who entered the house.

Hamish had insisted Rio's vigilance was unnecessary, that Morgan would probably strike the way Ceri and Shanley prophesied, but Hamish's opinion hadn't mattered to Rio. He'd made it clear that Ceri being so close to the outside where she was most vulnerable to Morgan's attack left him nervous as a cat. He'd refused to be away from her though they'd all agreed the two of them greeting guests at the door seemed like an announcement of their relationship, a circumstance Hamish insisted must wait until the handfasting ceremony at midnight.

For over an hour, Ceri and Hamish greeted a steady stream of guests, and the manor swelled with a couple hundred people. By the time Davy took over to direct the stragglers, Ceri was ready to collapse. "Hamish, give me a few minutes to rest in the sitting room," she pleaded.

"Sorry, lass. Ye're needed upstairs," he insisted.

Escorting her upstairs, with Rio trailing behind them, Hamish explained, "As the hostess, ye need tae lead the first reel tae mark the official start o' the party."

When they arrived in the ballroom, they found a jolly crowd loudly conversing and enjoying the hard cider Hamish had ordered by the barrel. When she glanced around at the festivities, Ceri's heart thrummed, reanimating her as she took in the colorful assembly of Scots, most dressed in the tartans of their families or clans. At Hamish's insistence, she and Shanley had donned ruffled white shirts, plaid sashes pinned at the hips with Celtic brooches, and full skirts in the Ross and Conlan colors respectively. Ceri loved the feeling of being right at home in the throng of people sharing her ancestry.

Glancing across the room, she spied Alyssa and Lynnette Sheridan deep in conversation. Catching Alyssa's eye, Ceri gave her a once-over and an approving smile for her friend's attire in the Sheridan tartan. For a moment, she allowed herself the fantasy of one day being able to wear that plaid as well.

Her unguarded thoughts didn't escape Rio.

"I knew you were resilient. Imagine how it's going to feel after the ritual and the special night for the King Stag."

Her eyes widened, but she didn't otherwise let on that he'd breached her shield.

"I love your outfit, by the way. Don't know if I told you that earlier. Even though it does cover you from shoulders to ankles."

She flicked him a side-eye, and he laughed.

"That stag's head brooch securing your sash tells me you're looking forward to the King Stag's night too."

"Rio! We're in public," she hissed.

"What I really can't wait for is feeling those endlessly long legs you're hiding under that skirt wrapped around me."

"Is it hot in here? I think it's pretty hot in here." She fanned a hand in front of her face.

He gifted her with a wicked smile.

"I said, did you sense anyone we should pay extra attention to?" Rowan asked.

Both Ceri and Rio jumped.

Turning from Ceri, Rio replied, "What? No, no one, though it's hard to figure out civilians until they take some sort of action."

Riley joined their conversation. "Did you see we have around thirty warriors here, several with their talismans? That can't be a happy coincidence."

"Hamish may appear the jolly host, but I've noticed he prepares well in advance and quite deliberately. Did you spot that old druid woman by the southwest corner of the room?" Rowan asked. "She took up a seat there the moment she arrived and hasn't moved since. She's some kind of sentry, I bet."

Ceri slid a glance in the direction Rowan indicated where a small, gray-haired lady rested her hands on a hawthorn cane as she sat near the fireplace.

Riley said, "Look around the room, brother. There are sentries at every window and every corner, male and female druids each carrying an oak or a hawthorn cane. Hamish is taking no chances."

"That's good. Having Ceri exposed at the front door for the first half of the evening didn't do much for my peace of mind," Rio said, his tone sour as he laced his fingers with hers.

"We have to appear strong yet unsuspecting, which gives us the element of surprise when Morgan's the one counting on it. I wonder if she's sensed how big an army Hamish has amassed here," Rowan mused.

"I hope not. If she does, she'll probably escalate the battle. After what you did to her last winter and knowing Morgan the way we do, I'd guess she's at the peak of sexual frustration, and that's a dangerous place for us."

Rio's comment chilled Ceri to the bone.

"I've always wondered about that," Riley said. "How could the Great Goddess create a war goddess who can only get off when she's wading in blood? Even when the Dagda took her and she conceived Meiche the animal killer, she was straddling a river of blood. The Dagda, the all-father for crying out loud."

Riley's complaint sounded a lot like Rio to Ceri's ears.

"She's definitely messed up. I'd like to send her away for a long while."

"Perhaps we'll get our chance tonight," Rowan said, his tone somber.

Riley blew out a breath. "I certainly hope so. Lynnette and I want to start a family, but it seems every time we have an opportunity, one or the other of you two finds your talisman and stirs the old girl up again. Honestly, it's becoming rather trying," he said with a grin.

Ceri widened her eyes and looked across the room again at Lynnette who shared a secret smile with her husband.

Rowan laughed. "You'll be fighting with extra incentive, won't you little brother?"

"Damn straight."

The bandleader interrupted them to call Ceri to lead the first reel, the signal for the ceilidh to begin. With one last squeeze, she let Rio go. Smiling at the bandleader, she walked confidently to the front of the room. After greeting the guests again, she asked Alaisdair to accompany her in the first dance. As he strode to the top of the room, she admired how he looked every inch the Highland warrior from his long, unbound hair brushing his shoulders to his unlaced kilt shirt revealing his stout neck, to the huge *sporran* holding down his kilt over his powerfully muscled legs. She noticed the bone handle of his *sgian dubh* in its sheath strapped to his calf over his kilt socks, its handle a carved stag's head. She thought the two of them together must look like characters participating in a party two hundred years in the past.

From the dais at the front of the ballroom, the band of fiddlers and pipers accompanied by a couple of men keeping rhythm on *bodhràns* launched into a lively tune. Members of prominent area families and Ullapool merchants joined Ceri and Alaisdair in the first reel, and the ceilidh began in earnest. People lined the length of the ballroom, a cavernous place except at the moment when partygoers in a festive mood filled it. The revelers clapped and cheered the dancers reeling between them. Almost instantly, Ceri forgot the cares of the last month as she lost herself in the pure joy of the party.

In the first minutes of the ceilidh, Ceri made the entire assembly her allies. As Rio gazed around the room, he noted warriors who would not hesitate to fight Morgan under any circumstances now had even more incentive. Hamish, the wily old druid, forced Rio to have even more respect for him. At this rate, he approached the esteem Rio held only for his family and Scathach, a dangerous idea for Rio to entertain about a druid.

"She's truly something, your talisman. I'm glad to see you watching her at a party without a scowl on your face," Rowan said in Rio's ear.

"Fine. I was lusting after her at your wedding, but since I thought she belonged to someone else, she pissed me off."

"And you took it out on her."

"Yeah, but I paid for it." Rio blew out a breath. "Tonight, I'm enjoying her success and hoping she can repeat it for a long time."

"That's what we all hope. Looks like the first one is over. Our turn." Rowan claimed his wife for the next reel featuring the Sheridan contingent as well as Alaisdair and Shanley.

When the Sheridans finished their reel, the crowd thunderously applauded their American guests. Ceri stole Rio's heart—again—with her radiant smile when Hamish congratulated her on the success of the party.

"The only thing missin' from yer dancin' was the kilts. Yer women, yer da and Alaisdair looked mighty fine out there in all their colors, but yer brothers and ye look American. Ye're goin' tae wear a kilt fer the King Stag ceremony at least are ye not, lad?"

Rio pulled a face. "Yeah, Hamish, I'm wearing a kilt for the ceremony. But I'd rather fight in jeans."

He realized his mistake a second too late. At the mention of fighting, he stole all the fun from Ceri's evening.

"Och, lass, donnae look so low. Yer warrior is the best fighter o' the age. The auld girl couldnae take his brothers, and she willnae take him. All will be well. Ye'll see." Hamish patted her shoulder. "They're callin' out fer another dance. Best no' disappoint yer guests."

Rio took one look at the mutiny on Ceri's face, grabbed her hand and pulled her out to her place to begin the reel. He flashed her a grin as the music began, and she had to concentrate on the steps, which he counted on when he dragged her back onto the dance floor. Before she could catch her breath from the first three reels, Davy claimed her for the fourth, daring Rio with his eyes to stop him. However, Rio needed Ceri to relax and enjoy herself rather than fret about the coming battle, so he graciously relinquished his woman to his former rival for the space of a dance.

"I hear Hamish wishes we'd all worn kilts," Riley said as Rio stepped away from the dance floor.

"Yeah. I told him I'd rather fight in jeans, *thankyouverymuch*." Rio didn't take his eyes from Ceri and Davy.

"You look handsome in a kilt, Rio. All my boys do," Sian said, joining their conversation. "Just look at your father."

"What's up with the old man wearing one anyway?" Riley asked.

Owen answered for himself as he strode up to them. "A long time ago, I took on Morgan once while wearing a kilt. It royally ticked her off when I bested her champion too. Reminded her of another time when a Sheridan took on her beasts and won." He stared meaningfully at his sons. "When I wear a kilt, I remind Morgan of Findlay Sheridan."

Rio tore his attention away from Ceri. "Are you deliberately trying to goad her, Dad? Why?" he asked, his voice breaking on his words.

"I'm reminding her that when it comes to our family, she's never going to win."

"But she defeated Findlay—she took his wife, Ailsa, across the ford and shortly afterward his son Graeme as well. And then there's your brother ... "

"You only remember part of your family history, Rio," Owen said. "Your namesake and my namesake started separate dynasties that have lasted a millennium, linking together in the marriage of Rowan to Alyssa. Morgan hasn't defeated the Sheridans, nor will she defeat us tonight. I want her to know that."

He looked to his mother for support and saw to his

astonishment she appeared serene. "How can you let him do this? Taunt a goddess as powerful as Morgan?"

"As your father said, he's not taunting her. He's sending her a message about the power of the Sheridans, a power you'll expand when you marry your lovely talisman. Speaking of which, she's an excellent hostess." Sian smiled in the direction of the dance floor. "By dancing each of the first seven reels, she shows she understands her ancestral culture. Good for her."

Returning his attention to the dance floor, he saw a brawny civilian claim Ceri from Davy. Rio recognized him as the owner of the pub in town. At some point, Hamish had informed him the man also served as mayor of Ullapool, so Ceri necessarily honored him with a dance. The mayor appeared quite possessive of his partner as he led her out for the next reel, leaning down to whisper something in her ear. Whatever he said made her laugh. The tinkling chimes sound of her mirth drew Rio to her so completely he actually took a step toward the dance floor before catching himself.

Grasping Rio's elbow, Owen steered him toward the bar. "I've sampled some of Hamish's fine whisky. You might enjoy a dram of it yourself, settle your nerves."

"Wearing a kilt and imbibing before a battle you know is coming. What's gotten into you, Dad?"

"Likely my Scots heritage," Owen said with a grin. "We take a dram of the water of life to remind us why we fight. We kiss our wives and girlfriends to remind us why we want to win. We wear our plaids to remind us who we fight for. There's a lot of history here, and fighting Morgan on our home turf should give us extra incentive."

When they reached the bar, Owen asked for two drams of Hamish's special brew, the keg of it discreetly hidden and, Owen explained, known only to the bartenders and the warriors who knew to ask for it. The bartenders poured other, less potent whisky for the civilians who were none the wiser for their host's deception. The bartenders were druids. Hamish had left nothing to chance.

Several times over the next few hours, Rio lost sight of Ceri in the crush, but right as he'd start to panic, he'd hear her laugh and knew her to be in her element, entertaining her guests. His woman was a born hostess, and he remembered with a pang the way he'd dismissed her efforts at Rowan and Alyssa's wedding. He'd have to make up for that.

Just before midnight, Ceri stepped up to the dais for an important announcement. Calling Alyssa to stand with her, she alerted the crowd to the fact that Alyssa was celebrating her birthday on this special night. During a rousing chorus of "Happy Birthday," an enormous cake borne on the shoulders of four large civilian men appeared at the ballroom doors and seemed to float above the crowd as the men made their way to the dais to present it to Alyssa.

Alyssa hugged Ceri tightly. "You're the best friend ever!" she squealed before she blew out the candles in the center of the cake.

The men carried the cake over to a buffet table where Alyssa cut the first piece and served it to Rowan who beamed his thanks at his wife's best friend.

"I hope you know how lucky you are to have such a thoughtful, selfless woman as your talisman," Rowan communicated to Rio.

"I'm figuring it out. Don't worry."

CHAPTER TWENTY-SEVEN

Samhain—midnight

S THE WITCHING hour neared, several civilian men approached Hamish about taking the annual torchlight trip around the grounds. Rio knew that for them it was an excuse to leave the women to set out the midnight supper while they indulged in something more exciting than hard cider while "protecting" the manor grounds from the "evil spirits" allowed to walk the earth on Samhain. Good-naturedly, Hamish conceded the time for the annual rite, and men gathered up their jackets and electric torches for a "walk."

Druids inserted themselves into the group of civilians. The warriors held back and let the civilians precede them while they surreptitiously gathered their leathers and their claymores. All the warriors knew the real reason behind Hamish's invitation to this particular ceilidh, and all of them appeared determined to aid the Sheridans in defense of the Conlan heir. Ceri's skill as a hostess throughout the evening seemed to have made them even more resolute to conclude the battle with a Sheridan victory.

Though she appeared calm and in

control, Rio stared intently at her from the doorway, and she let him into her head. *"I'm looking forward to that part of the King Stag ritual where I get to carry you off to bed."* Then he smiled at her and deliberately joined the stragglers exiting the ballroom in the camaraderie of other warriors.

Rio's words put a blush on Ceri's cheeks. He nodded as the druidic women in the throng distracted the civilian women by drawing them into setting up the tables, chairs, and table services in the ballroom while druids sent the food up from the kitchen via the dumbwaiter. According to the plan, the civilian women would assume the talismans were in the kitchen preparing the food under Ceri's supervision, so nothing would seem strange when so many women left the ballroom to go downstairs.

As Rio passed the grand salon on his way out the front doors of the manor, he sensed something odd in the house. He stood still in the foyer before he turned to the grand salon to investigate. A stunningly handsome man lounged indolently in one of the chairs in front of the windows as he watched the gathering mist outside. Rio realized he knew this stranger, though they'd never met.

"Taranis, how did you get into this house? Hamish has been enchanting it for weeks. While I'd rather not admit it, he's a powerful druid."

"Nice to meet you too, Rio Sheridan," Taranis drawled, the rich, lazy timbre of his voice not quite hiding his irritation at Rio's rudeness.

Not that Rio cared. "Excuse me," he said, positioning himself in a battle-ready stance, "but I'm not happy a mercurial god such as yourself is seated in Ceri's grand salon as though you own it."

"I rather like this house." Taranis cast an admiring glance at the ornate antique furnishings. "This is not the first time I have visited. Ceri's ancestor, Fianna, started inviting me here on

Samhain, and Hamish wisely has continued the invitation to his annual ceilidhs."

Rio took a step toward the god. "Hamish *invited* you?"

Just when Rio had started believing in Hamish, Taranis completely shattered his trust in the old druid.

"The people here know I cause the storms that bring food from the sea onto the shores. They often offer me ale and some of their finest fare to ensure I send a gale on this most enchanted night of the year. I would probably storm without the offerings, but it is nice to be remembered by those whose fates I hold in my hands." He held the hands in question in front of them, turning them over as though inspecting them.

Taranis's remark wasn't lost on Rio. "What offering do you want?" he asked, afraid of the answer.

"A piece of Alyssa's cake served by the lady herself. She may serve it to me in this room after all the excitement of the evening has abated."

"You ask a lot." Rio dared not give any form to his fears for Rowan's talisman in case the god determined to act on them. Deliberately, he blanked his mind.

"As does my sister Morgan. She wishes me to unleash a great storm here on the manor grounds right about now."

"What do you plan to do?"

Taranis sighed, but Rio had no idea what that meant.

"Morgan is rather trying. I conjure storms where and when they suit me. Tonight, it suits me to conjure up a squall on the North Sea, but unfortunately, that will mean only some wind and a little freezing rain here at the manor, nothing that will satisfy her. Some women refuse to be pleased."

Taranis's knowing smile made Rio uneasy.

"Freezing rain can play both ways in a battle," he observed.

"So can a thick mist, which I prefer. I rather like Hamish's gatherings, and the civilians are so easy to play with when they get lost literally in their own backyard. It keeps me entertained for most of the night." He regarded Rio with watchful eyes.

"With all due respect, I don't trust you, Taranis."

"You are wise, Rio Sheridan. You are also separated from your party now. Take care when you step outside the manor." Taranis directed his attention to the floor-to-ceiling windows looking out on the front gardens.

Rio had been dismissed. He saw Taranis had deliberately kept himself secret from the rest of the warriors, singling him out to separate him from help. Refusing to let the god see his frustration, he executed a small bow, turned on his heel, and exited the room, closing the big doors gently behind him.

He found Davy at his post on the veranda outside the front door. "Did you happen to see or feel anything different?" he asked.

"If you mean, do I know Taranis is inside the manor, yes, I know. Hamish is wise tae invite him, believe me." He stepped over to Rio to paint salve of nightshade on his face as Scathach had instructed. Davy had added some woad to his mixture, causing the warriors he protected to resemble their Celtic ancestors with their blue-painted faces as they went into battle. "Now go do what you must. All of our lives depend on your success."

Davy, too, dismissed him.

Rio ground his teeth and tried not to explode. He had to keep his emotions in check. If Ceri's prophecies were correct, the Morhaus might even now be on the manor grounds ready to take his life if he let his feelings interfere with his training. In the distance, he could make out a vague glow and decided the majority of the men who left the manor ahead of him were in the far corner of the grounds directly across from the gate at the top of the lane. As he walked toward the glow, he fixed his mind singularly on the battle he knew would start soon. Taranis had said as much, and on that score, Rio believed him.

As he made his way over the uneven ground beyond the

manicured lawns in front of the manor, a thick mist gathered around him. Taranis preferred the mist after all. Rio preferred the freezing rain. Though the battleground would be slick, at least he'd be able to see his enemy in time to brace himself. The mist afforded Morgan's champions too much cover. With his sight limited and becoming more so by the second, Rio concentrated on using his other senses, listening closely for any sounds of battle as he headed farther from the manor—and Ceri.

♻

The women awaited the coming battle in Hamish's rooms where the tension shimmered like a red mist. Though she tried desperately to see Rio, Ceri's prophetic sight had closed. Whatever he faced, she'd have to trust she'd prepared him the best she could. Shanley grabbed Ceri's hand, lacing their fingers and clinging tightly. She returned the pressure and said nothing.

"Perhaps Morgan is only toying with us, the *wilding* in the city the other night the extent of her games this time," Lynnette said, hope in her voice.

"You know better, Lynnette," Sian scolded. "Remember how she lured Rio, Rowan, and Seamus last year when she was gearing up for the battle we faced in L.A.? She worked on a smaller scale then. Have no doubt, our skills are about to be severely tested. Concentrate on feeling your warrior so when she attacks, you can see it immediately and warn him before Morgan's rogues or champions can land the first blow."

"I can't help wishing I had your gift to see the battle in real time to help my warrior as he faces his opponents. The prophecies of the last few days terrified me, and now I can't feel Alaisdair at all," Shanley said to the Sheridan talismans.

"The battle has not yet begun. When I concentrate, I can see Owen walking along with the warriors Hamish invited. They appear watchful but relaxed. Perhaps when Morgan's champions appear, you'll feel something," Sian said.

"And do what?" Desperation clouded Shanley's tone. Ceri had never seen her even-tempered aunt so agitated, and she leaned closer to reassure her.

"Open your shield to him, talk to him, but only when the time comes. Otherwise, you may give Morgan an advantage," Sian instructed.

Almost as if the druid women in the kitchens felt the undercurrent of tension among the talismans, they began chanting over the food as they prepared it, and gradually the sound made its way to Hamish's rooms where the rhythms of the chants calmed the talismans waiting there. As Ceri relaxed her grip on Shanley's hand, a prophecy formed in her mind, but she didn't disappear into it. This disturbance was a god …inside the manor.

In her vision, she saw a beautiful raven-haired man seated languidly on an antique chair in the grand salon, one leg resting lazily over the arm, the other leg stretched in front of him. He didn't bother to sit up as Alyssa entered the room to offer him a piece of birthday cake. Instead, he gazed at her with unmistakable lust smoldering in his storm-gray eyes. As though hypnotized by the sight of him, Alyssa walked forward and handed him the cake, her fingers barely grazing his as he took the plate from her. It was enough. In a flash, he stood up with her in his arms. She snuggled into his embrace, and the two of them disappeared, leaving behind a cloud of silver raindrops sparkling in the dim light of the room.

Ceri gasped, understanding the meaning of her prophecy immediately. Taranis awaited an offering in the grand salon. And he'd chosen Alyssa to present it to him. Ceri knew she must ensure he received it without sacrificing her best friend. Over the years, she'd heard stories of women from both the civilian and warrior realms who had gladly given up their lives for one night in a god's bed. No woman could resist a god who touched her.

Though she hadn't fainted during her vision as she had done every time before, she swayed on her feet, and the other women noticed.

Shanley searched her face. "What are you seeing, sweetheart? Who's been attacked?"

"It's not what you think. I don't know if it's a trap or a test, but either way, we have no choice but to meet the challenge. Taranis is in the grand salon awaiting an offering. He wishes for Alyssa to bring him birthday cake, but he wants more than that."

Alyssa's eyes widened in fear and confusion, but she said stoutly, "I will not betray my husband, not even for a god."

"He's incredibly handsome and persuasive. But we can outwit him easily, and he knows it, which is why I can't decide if this is a test or a trap." Ceri gathered her strength. "Either way, Alyssa's not going alone. We'll take along a couple of the druid women. Hamish's friend Saraid is the most powerful of the druids left here at the manor. She'll join us upstairs. Everyone else stay here in case it is a trap," Ceri said. The calm forcefulness of her tone rivaled Sian's leadership. Without realizing what she did, Ceri had taken the first step toward her role as the mistress of Conlan Manor.

"Ceri," Shanley interrupted, "Alyssa was the prize the last time the Sheridans took on Morgan, and all indications are you're the prize this time. Drawing the two of you out together and unprotected is certainly a trap. Let me accompany Alyssa."

"I had the vision, Shanley. I know what needs to be done. If this is a test, we may buy our warriors an advantage. If it's a trap, we'll have to rely on our wits and the skills of two very powerful druids in Saraid and Davy to help us escape. Either way, we have no choice. I sense Taranis is losing patience."

All the talismans in the room stopped talking as a rush of wind battered the boarded-up window of Hamish's sitting room.

"You must go to him now. Be careful," Sian warned as she hugged first Alyssa then Ceri.

When they entered the kitchens, they saw Saraid had already placed two very generous pieces of Alyssa's birthday cake on two dinner plates. She'd also poured a giant mug of Hamish's special mead and stood silently awaiting the two talismans.

"How did you know?" Ceri asked.

"Hamish always invites Taranis tae this party. In return, Taranis gifts us with a bountiful sea harvest. O' course he would choose the twa most beautiful talismans tae serve him. He may also think because the twa o' ye have had the least training, he'll have a better chance o' taking one or both o' ye. He is, after all, a god and selfish like the lot o' them," she huffed impatiently. "Take care no' tae touch him, even fleetingly," Saraid warned them.

"I saw that in my vision. Alyssa, follow my lead when we serve the cake. Saraid, you're serving him the ale?"

"Aye, milady. I will do so when his attentions are on ye. Though I'd not be a great prize, old as I am, I'd still serve his purposes I think." A small smile tugged at her lips.

The women mounted the stairs to the great hall, each carrying an offering to the god awaiting them. Two young civilian women tripping down the stairs to the kitchens thought they weren't noticed. Ceri hoped by ignoring them, they'd go on their way.

They didn't.

"Shh, Molly, look. There go the two Americans and the auld lady from the village intae the salon. Let's see what they're doin' yeah?"

"Takin' time out o' preparin' the midnight meal looks tae me like, Kadi."

"Yeah? Don't ye find it a strange thin' tae be doin' just now? Let's go take a peek."

Before Ceri could warn them off, Saraid tipped her head, and Ceri kept walking through the doors of the salon. Behind her, she could hear the girls whispering.

"I don't feel good spyin' on our hostess. She's put on a grand party fer the whole shire taenight."

"Och, Molly, where's yer sense o' adventure? It's Halloween. We're supposed tae be havin' adventures and playin' tricks, yeah? They'll think naethin' of it."

While Ceri and Alyssa introduced themselves, Saraid slid a huge mug of mead onto the side table beside the chair where a beautiful man sat.

"Hello, milord. It's an honor to have your presence—and your blessing—at our ceilidh this year. As you already know, Hamish is outside with the civilians and warriors, hoping to stop the battle Morgan insists on waging, so he couldn't be here to welcome you himself."

Ceri's breath backed up in her throat. Never before had she seen anyone quite so beautiful. It was difficult for her to keep her wits while looking at Taranis's perfectly chiseled features and broad, shirt-filling chest and shoulders.

"I do enjoy a good party, especially at Samhain when so much mischief is in the air. Is that cake for me? I imagine it's delicious. May I have a piece in honor of your birthday today, Alyssa?"

The god's intention was so obvious, in the back of Ceri's mind she almost found it laughable, but his mesmerizing stare made him so compelling, she understood he didn't need to rely on subtlety to get what he wanted.

"Of course. Also, some mead." Ceri gestured to the tankard on the table beside him. When he flicked his glance sideways, she set the plate she carried onto the table in front of him. Drawing his attention back to her, she said, "In fact, we brought you two pieces of cake. The druids made an especially fine cake with apples that I think you'll enjoy."

As Ceri kept the god's attention on her, Alyssa slid the plate she carried onto the table by the tankard of ale, and on cue, all three women took a step back away from the god.

"Beautiful and clever. I had hoped for only the former. Alas, not tonight. Tragic," Taranis drawled as he helped himself to one of the plates of cake.

"When you take on a human form, you do so completely. I hadn't expected that," Ceri commented as she watched the god shove a rather large bite of cake into his mouth.

"Shape-shifting is one of the perks of being a god. We're also quite adept at lovemaking. Care to find out?" He stretched his lips into a brilliant smile that danced its way to his eyes.

Catching everyone by surprise, Ceri couldn't suppress a laugh at his transparent attempt to take her and her friend. "You're rather straightforward in your intentions, aren't you milord?"

"And you are a rather bold and insolent woman, Ceri Ross. I find that refreshing. I would have taken my time with you had you given me a chance."

One of the civilians interrupted. "Miss Ross! Sorry tae intrude. We were on our way tae the kitchens tae see if we could be of service when we heard voices in here."

Ceri stiffened. She'd forgotten about the civilians and had no way to warn the girl off as she strode purposefully toward Taranis.

"My name is Kadi, and this is my friend Molly," Kadi said as she pulled her friend forward. Though she appeared to be introducing them to their hostess, her eyes never left Taranis who put aside his plate of cake to greet the civilians.

"Nice to meet you, Kadi and Molly. As a matter of fact, there are a few things you can help with in the kitchens. We were just going to return there, weren't we Alyssa, Saraid?" Ceri said trying to draw the young women's attention away from the dangerous god who gracefully unfolded himself to stand for an introduction.

"Who's this then? I dinnae see ye at the party."

Kadi insisted on hurtling headlong toward death, and Ceri feared she couldn't dissuade the girl.

"An old friend who likes his cake, but he has enough to keep him satisfied for now," Ceri said rather desperately. She knew she couldn't touch them, for if she did, when one of them touched the god, they'd all be lost. As she racked her brain to find a way to rescue all the women in the room, the forward girl extended her hand to Taranis to introduce herself.

"I donnae think I caught yer name, Miss Ross's old friend," she said playfully.

"Taranis," he said. He glanced at Ceri over the girls' heads. "Nice to meet you." The electrical spark that shot from his hand when he touched it to the first girl lit up the room, and the three warrior women jumped away from it while the civilians stepped toward it. "Ceri evidently expected me to have a bigger appetite than I seem to have. Would you care to share some cake with me?"

Neither civilian seemed capable of coherent speech as Taranis fed each of them a bite of cake, sealing their fates. Ceri and Alyssa stared horrified while Saraid stood stoically off to the side.

"Thank you, Ceri. I believe I will be too occupied to conjure the rainstorm you saw in your prophecy, the storm Rio thinks he would rather fight in than the mists I have sent instead. You should return to your station. The battle is about to begin."

On that parting shot, Taranis wrapped an arm around each civilian and disappeared in a silver cloud of shimmering raindrops that hung in the air for several seconds before evaporating like they'd been sucked into space.

Pressing a hand over her stomach, Ceri backed up and sat down hard on a nearby settee. Her prophecy had been partially correct. Someone had been sacrificed to Taranis's lust, and it didn't feel good that civilians rather than talismans paid the price.

"Ye knew this was comin'. Ye saw it in yer vision—a dark-haired lass sacrificed tae the god. He wanted yer friend here," Saraid pointed to Alyssa, "but he settled fer twa civilians. 'Tis a steep price tae pay fer yer warriors tae have some help in the battle, but shouldnae come as a surprise. Taranis is a trickster who's no' tae be trusted. Ye were careful." Saraid patted Ceri's shoulder. "Those twa women were some place they had nae business bein', and they'll pay the ultimate price. 'Tis no' yer fault."

"I know what you say is true, but I can't help feeling responsible. Taranis had my attention, and I forgot about those women who followed us into the room. If I had more training, maybe I'd be able to divide my concentration better. Now I have to live with the deaths of two innocents because of my lack of skill." She dropped her head into her hands.

"Is that the first time ye've seen a god?" Saraid asked.

"No. Morgan presented herself to me once last fall when she was on the hunt for Alyssa. She's terrifying, even in her mortal guise. I can't imagine what she must be like when she appears in her goddess form."

Saraid chuckled. "They're a might overwhelmin'. I've seen Taranis on several occasions, but his beauty and sheer presence always stupefy me fer the first moment or twa. It's part o' his tactics."

Saraid walked over to the small table on which the offerings to Taranis still sat, one piece of cake half-eaten. She mumbled something over them before gathering them up.

Turning back to Ceri, she said, "Ye also had the burden o' keepin' yer friend here"—Alyssa smiled wanly—"and yerself from his terrible clutches. That's a full plate fer anyone. Ye must let it go. Ye still have a job tae do taenight, and Taranis has warned ye it's goin' tae begin shortly." Saraid walked sedately toward the door. "Come, we need tae return tae the kitchens and prepare fer battle."

Ceri and Alyssa exchanged worried glances before they followed Saraid out of the salon.

⟿

When Ceri and Alyssa related the incident to the other talismans waiting in Hamish's rooms, the older, more experienced women agreed with Saraid. Their own reckless curiosity had led the civilians to be where they shouldn't have been when they shouldn't have been there. But in the back of her mind, Ceri had a strange feeling the civilians had had some help being in that room with Taranis when he summoned Ceri and Alyssa.

Alyssa and Lynnette sought out chairs, forcing Ceri's thoughts from the incident in the salon. Soon, most of the other talismans found places to sit among the overstuffed chairs and sofa as they envisioned their warriors taking on Morgan's rogues and zombie champions materializing out of the mists. By tacit agreement, Ceri and Shanley gravitated toward the door of the tunnel leading to Alaisdair's cottage. They stood apart from the others, their hands tightly clasped together as they began their long, agonizing wait.

CHAPTER TWENTY-EIGHT

EVERAL TIMES AFTER leaving the manor, Rio found himself turned around and lost. Though he knew he taunted a powerful god, he cursed Taranis and his damned mists. By the time he heard the shouts of men and the clashing of swords and fighting, he had no idea where on the manor grounds he was nor in which direction to move to join the battle. He did, however, have the uneasy feeling Morgan's champion was about to catch him alone. The mists Taranis called had turned pea green, and Rio wondered if he was seeing the Morhaus's exhalations.

The grunts and shouts of men trying to land killing blows, the clanging of steel on steel as claymores met and slid down blades to the hilts, the screams as a warrior struck vulnerable flesh was an eerie din in the mists. All this made it difficult to focus his hearing on where someone launched a new attack. As the civilians walked the perimeter of the manor grounds, the mists shielded them from hearing or seeing the battle raging beside them in a parallel time and place. Their flashlights cast a feeble light, giving Rio scant help as he listened to his fellow warriors taking on Morgan's army.

So far, he'd only encountered a rogue straggler or two, men of little honor and even less skill. He'd dispatched them easily. If Morgan thought to lull him into complacency, she must be sadly disappointed. Scathach had trained him well and tuned all his senses to the sounds and feelings of battle. Taranis's dense fog impeded his sight, but it couldn't touch his finely tuned and innate sixth sense. Something lurked nearby waiting for him to make a false move.

Following Hamish's earlier instruction, he'd spent a couple of hours in daylight walking the area where they thought the battle would commence. The uneven ground beneath his feet alerted him he'd wandered very near the edge of the hill behind the cottage, the exact area where he didn't wish to encounter the Morhaus or whatever nasty creature Morgan had unleashed. Whatever awaited him beyond his sight could come to him if it wanted a fight. For once Rio refused to succumb to his impulsive nature and wade straight into the fray.

Silently, he held his battle stance and remained alert for any movement near him. The wait was endless, and several times when he thought he detected motion, he struggled to remain patient, not seek out the source of the disturbance in the mist. At last he sensed whatever moved beyond his sight was circling him. The rogue or monster had a sense of where he was. Perhaps his opponent was trying to decide who he was.

Rio had been concentrating so much on staying patient it took him a minute to notice the mists clearing around him. He could easily see the ground beneath his feet covered in dew-slicked autumn grass, an obstacle in and of itself without the bonus of it covering several large rocks on which a man could stumble at a critical moment. For whatever reason, Taranis seemed to be backing off.

Something was up.

Then he had no time to ponder Taranis's easing of the mists

as the ancient monster Ysbaddaden loomed before him. Morgan's zombie champion bore the scar around his neck from when Cùchulainn's allies had severed his head centuries ago, a situation from which he'd miraculously recovered. Morgan had seen fit to resurrect dead champions for her evil purposes—another reason to avoid at all costs crossing the ford with her.

As in life, Ysbaddaden wielded an enormous claymore. He swung it in a long high arc as though considering the feel of it or trying to frighten Rio. Either way, Rio didn't give him a chance to finish his warm-up. When the sword reached its zenith above the giant's head, he struck, slicing his blade through the thick muscles of Ysbaddaden's abdomen. An odor of rotting flesh emanated from the wound, the stench nearly overwhelming Rio, but no blood or entrails gushed forth.

He stepped quickly away from the giant whose mighty swing seemed to change course in midair when Rio struck him. Without reacting to the blow, Ysbaddaden appeared to lose strength and some control of his weapon as his body gaped open in the middle.

The giant's eyes blazed with anger, though eerily, he made no sound as he advanced on Rio. Instead, he composed himself as he slipped into a battle stance, cocking his head to one side to discover how best to engage. The zombie lightly leaped forward, nearly landing on Rio who deftly deflected the giant's blow while ducking away from his powerful body, and their battle began in earnest.

Rio thrust and parried with the ancient Welsh giant. As their battle raged, he lost all sense of time. Though his training had put him in top shape, taking on a determined opponent nearly twice his size began to take its toll. He needed help, but it seemed the two of them fought in a vacuum, steel clanging on steel, neither one able to strike a decisive blow. Several times, the giant tried to wound Rio's sword arm and nearly succeeded once, glancing a blow that penetrated the reinforced leather of his jacket enough to draw a trickle of blood. Emboldened, the zombie redoubled his efforts.

Desperately, Rio called out to Ceri. *"Sweetheart, I know you saw the Morhaus, but that's not who Morgan sent. I need help with Ysbaddaden."*

He could hear Ceri's gasp telepathically. Then his girl did him proud when she held it together and told him her prophecy.

"You're near the edge of the cliff, the one where you slip and fall to your death on the rocks below. You'll draw the giant to you there. He'll take his shot and knock you off balance. In your weakened state, you'll not recover quickly enough. He'll engage your sword one last time, sending you over the edge to land heavily—and mortally—on the sharp rocks below."

The mists around Rio evanesced in the seconds it took Ceri to tell him her prophecy, and he saw he'd already inadvertently worked his way to the edge of the hill above the deadly rocks. Acknowledging his mistake, he began to move deliberately and slowly to the side of the giant, his goal to trade places while Ysbaddaden rained blows on him.

Rio feinted like he was going over the hill, and the giant took the bait. The maneuver gave him the chance to move to more solid ground while the ancient monster lost his balance. Ysbaddaden stumbled and fell, shaking the ground and causing Rio to stumble. The giant lay inert at the edge of the hill while Rio scrambled to keep his feet.

Once again, Ysbaddaden lumbered up into fighting stance. Rio managed to lure the giant back to solid ground when Scathach arrived, her encouragements and critiques from the perimeter of the battle renewing Rio's energy. Executing an acrobatic move the hulking giant in his zombie state could not follow, Rio slipped behind him and hamstrung him. Dancing in front of the ancient champion, Rio raised his sword above his head, exposing his abdomen. As the giant focused on attacking him there, he landed three quick thrusts in the giant's chest before lightly leaping out of his reach to land behind him.

When Ysbaddaden tried to turn to strike a blow, he buckled under his own weight, falling heavily on the rocky ground and causing a reverberation like a mini-earthquake. The earth seemed to ripple as it accepted the giant's great weight. At that moment, Rio glanced up to see Morgan standing on a hill a short distance away, the smirk on her face morphing into a blood-red rage.

Scathach shouted, "Take his head! You must take Ysbaddaden's head *right now!*"

Rio didn't hesitate. Standing over the zombie giant, he swung his claymore and delivered a blow so strong he buried his sword a foot into the earth after severing Ysbaddaden's head at the line of the scar that signaled the end of the giant's mortal life more than a millennium before. When he jerked up on his sword to free it from its temporary sheath, he lost his balance, and Morgan, seeing a second chance to claim her prize, caused him to trip on a turf-covered rock.

"I will still win this battle, Scathach," Morgan crowed, the raven flying above her echoing the sound of her voice.

"I don't think so." Scathach tossed her head, and Rio spun midfall. Instead of landing on his back on the sharp rock on which Morgan destined him to die, he landed on the gravelly scree above it and slid down to lodge against it. As he fought to remain conscious, he could hear the goddesses bickering above him.

"Danu and the Dagda are not pleased with your greed and incessant warmongering purely to assuage your lust. This is one time where you will not take what is not yours," Scathach snarled.

"You have been a thorn in my side for centuries, Scathach. I am tired of you meddling in my affairs. Look what your warriors have done to my champions," Morgan huffed.

"Ysbaddaden and the Morhaus are shells of the monsters they were in life when my warriors fought and defeated them before.

You could not take Tristan when he killed the Morhaus, so you incited Andred's lust for Isolde of Ireland and killed Tristan by stealth. That wasn't sporting of you. Cùchulainn outlived your curses and Ysbaddaden and ended his days a hero in the arms of his beloved Olwen. When will you learn that even though they are mortals, my warriors are special and not to be used as sacrifices to your terrible lust?"

Morgan laughed. "You are always so serious when this is all a game, something with which I amuse myself in the long years of eternity."

The ground shifted again, and out of nowhere, a rock tumbled down the hill. Rio blinked. Then all went black.

❧

"Once again, Morgan, my warriors are going to win this battle and regain that which you have stolen from them—and from me." Scathach smiled in triumph.

"Enough!" Morgan raged, her nonchalant façade cracking in the face of Scathach's truth. "Rio Sheridan and Ceri Ross have yet to marry, and I still have some rogue warriors in play tonight. The opening in the portal between the mortal world and the afterlife on Samhain affords me many champions from which to choose. It is not yet midnight."

With that ominous pronouncement, Morgan and her raven disappeared in a cloud of shimmering black dust.

Scathach summoned her warriors. *"Sheridans, Rio lies unconscious below the hill where the carcass of Ysbaddaden lies. Come quickly. There is no time to waste."*

At the summons of their goddess, Owen, Rowan, and Riley disengaged from the rogues they fought and visualized themselves to the edge of the hill.

"Jesus, Rio took on that giant by himself?" Riley asked

incredulously when they came upon the headless body of Ysbad-daden lying on the turf.

"See where showing off got him?" Rowan pointed to their brother lying halfway down the hill. "We'll need ropes and some sort of sling to drag him up out of there."

"I bet Alaisdair has something we can use at the cottage. I'll go after it while you guard Rio. Those rogues we were fighting will find their way here shortly, won't they, milady?" Owen said.

"No doubt Morgan is summoning them and an army of additional rogues even as we stand here planning strategy. Visualize yourself there. We have no time to waste," Scathach commanded.

⊷

"Why are you grabbing those ropes?" Ceri asked as Sian raced around Hamish's rooms. "Are the men retrieving Rio's," she swallowed and tried again. "Is Owen …?" She choked on a sob, unable to finish the question.

She'd never felt so alone. It seemed hours ago, Shanley headed down the tunnel to the cottage after Alaisdair sustained injuries defeating the Morhaus. Then Ceri had lost contact with Rio after she shared her prophecy with him. When she couldn't see him in her visions, she knew the worst had happened.

"Rio is alive but unable to help himself. Owen needs these to rescue him," Sian said as she hoisted coils of heavy rope over her shoulders.

Ceri staggered against a table in relief. Then she righted herself. Her warrior needed her. "Let me help you carry those," she said as she met Sian at the door to the tunnel leading to Alaisdair's cottage.

"I know you want to help, but you won't help anyone if you're exposed to Morgan's minions. Stay here while I take these to Owen."

Ceri shook her head.

"Please don't argue with me," Sian said. "Rio's life is at stake."

Struggling with her unwieldy and heavy burden, Sian wrenched open the door and headed down the tunnel, calling back over her shoulder, "Keep her with you Lynnette. I'll be back shortly with news."

Ceri stared at the closed door for a minute before she opened it. Instantly, Lynnette stood in front of the entrance, barring her way.

"How did you do that?" Ceri squeaked when Lynnette bent time and space like a warrior.

"It's a trick Riley taught me," Lynnette replied with a smile that didn't reach her eyes.

"Lynnette, I can't stay here and wait. I didn't have the right prophecy. I'm responsible for Rio lying helpless at the bottom of a hill. I have to go to him!" She clutched Lynnette's arm. "You'd do the same if this were Riley."

Lynnette nodded sympathetically. "Rio's my favorite brother-in-law and Riley's twin. I want him to live as much as you do. That's why I must do my best to keep you here where no one has to worry about your safety while they're concentrating on rescuing him."

"Would you wait here passively for news if Riley were the Sheridan in need of rescue?"

Lynnette seemed to deflate. "No, I wouldn't. I'd do whatever I could to reach him."

"Then you have some idea how I feel. Let me pass."

CHAPTER TWENTY-NINE

ERI HEARD SIAN speaking as she entered Alaisdair's cottage from the tunnel.

"He'll come back to you, Shanley. Don't worry. He's a warrior. No doubt he's suffered such injuries or worse while he's avoided Morgan all these years. Have faith in him."

"How do you do it Sian? How do you send Owen out the door so easily and with such confidence?"

"It's the only way I can survive being married to a warrior."

Ceri didn't bother to stop to talk to the two women who watched at the window of Alaisdair's cottage. Instead, she headed directly for the door leading out into the meadow beyond it.

"Ceri! What are you doing? You're not safe outside the manor!" Shanley cried.

"I'm waiting like you did when Rowan brought Alaisdair back here" Ceri said, her hand on the door handle.

"It's not the same, Ceri. You and Rio together are the key to the Conlan line. You must remain safe until after the ritual tonight. Lynnette, I thought I instructed you to keep her inside the manor," Sian said, turning her fear and worry on her daughter-in-law who trailed Ceri into the cottage.

Following on Lynnette's tail, Alyssa said, "She tried, Sian, but Ceri wouldn't be denied. If any of us—you included—were honest, if our warriors were in danger, we'd go to them as well."

Sian sighed. "So here we all are, defying Scathach and contributing to the dangers our men already face. Even though our warriors have defeated Morgan's zombie champions, they are not assured a victory here. Rogue warriors are every bit as dangerous since they have nothing to lose."

"Our warriors have everything to fight for. That's their strength, their advantage," Alyssa quietly reminded her mother-in-law.

"Ceri, stay inside the cottage, at least. It's enchanted, and it would be far more difficult for a rogue to snatch you from here than to kill you outright on the battlefield," Sian said. "When the men pull Rio to safety, they'll bring him straight here. Concentrate on breaching his shield, talking to him, encouraging him." She stared meaningfully into Ceri's eyes.

Ceri hung her head. "I'll wait here." She backed away from the door. "It's just so hard not to go to him."

Sian stepped into the role of general. "Shanley, alert Hamish to send Davy to the cottage."

Shanley nodded.

"Alyssa and Lynnette, envision the other side of the hill and see every danger including loose rock or rogues trying to reach Rio from the bottom of the ravine. See everything."

"Of course, Sian," Alyssa answered for both of them.

Addressing the other talismans who had followed Lynnette, Alyssa, and Ceri to the cottage and now crowded the living room, Sian said, "My friends, your warriors are all engaged with rogues. Help them create a boundary between the rogues and the rescue party."

The women nodded, and the room fell silent. Any civilian inadvertently wandering into it would have been puzzled to find so many women together and in some sort of conversation, yet there was no sound. Deep in her mind, Ceri worried so much telepathic energy would draw additional gods bent on mortal pain and destruction especially when the veil between the two worlds was its thinnest on this night of nights. However, to save the man she loved, they had no other choice.

"Rio, please let me in. Don't let the blackness take you. Don't let Morgan win. Please, love, come back to me." She chanted her words over and over as she desperately tried to reach her man.

Rio's lack of response did nothing for her nerves. She had no idea if he deliberately ignored her, if he decided he didn't want to spend the rest of his life protecting her from the myriad zombie champions which Morgan could unleash against her, if he'd fallen into so unconscious a state no one could reach him. The uncertainty left her on a knifepoint of fear and anxiety.

Outside the window, she could see warriors massed for one last titanic battle. Hamish busied himself enchanting the ground on which the warriors awaited their foes, while Scathach prowled at the edge of the battlefield.

As if by magic, Davy appeared outside the door to Hamish's cottage to fend off any rogues who thought to take an easy shot at the talismans inside. After a few moments, Finn joined him. Catching Ceri's eye through the window, he shook his head at her. Then he grinned, and she offered a weak smile of her own. After all these years, he knew she couldn't stay behind and not try to help in some way.

A vision seared her mind, and she clapped her hands to her head. Then she understood she saw something, heard something worse—real time.

As Ceri watched, Rowan and Riley slipped and slid their way down the hill to Rio, raining loose gravel on him. His lack of response to the barrage of pebbles goaded them to move faster, taking life-threatening risks. The warriors above them amassed for battle, which meant they had limited time to secure Rio and drag him to the even ground atop the hill before all-out war erupted.

Stepping on what looked to be the flat top of a boulder, Rowan shifted his weight and discovered too late that the surface was nothing more than a thin slab of loose shale. He rode the stone to a point directly above Rio, the gravel and dirt he dislodged gathering in a furrow that stopped his momentum. Rowan looked down at his brother, but Rio remained unconscious between a sharp boulder and the small windrow Riley and Rowan initially created as they made their way down the hill.

Holding tightly to the anchor rope around his waist, Rowan gingerly finished his descent to his brother.

After seeing Rowan's near disaster, Riley considerably slowed down his race to reach his twin.

Ceri's heart lodged in her throat, but she couldn't stop the images and the sounds from invading her mind.

Rowan and Riley frantically raked away the gravel and dirt along Rio's back. Right as they were positioning the blanket over the makeshift net of ropes they'd devised, shouts from above and below interrupted them.

Rolling boulders seemed a coward's way out, but with Rio's life in the balance, no one had time to reflect on the finer points of ethics. Riley looked to his right, dislodged a monster rock, and sent it down the hill at the rogues attempting to flank them.

Rowan looked away from Rio, saw the danger, and found a large stone. He aimed and hurled it down the mountain, catching the lead rogue square in the chest and sending him backward into one of his companions. A third rogue, distracted by the fates of his fellows, didn't see the boulder Riley sent rolling until it nearly reached him. By then it was too late. The boulder flattened him on its way to the bottom of the ravine.

Rowan and Riley carefully rolled Rio onto his back on the blanket. After securing him with the netting of ropes they devised, they signaled to Owen to pull them up. Rowan strained against the rope around his waist that led to safety while simultaneously holding onto the rope attached to his brother's makeshift stretcher.

"Grab his claymore, Riley," Rowan called before gritting his teeth and starting the arduous climb to the top of the hill.

"I already sheathed it with mine—if it'll stay there," Riley replied as he steadied Rio with one hand while hanging onto his own safety rope with the other.

At the top of the hill, five warriors including Alaisdair and Owen worked to pull the brothers out of the ravine. Sweat poured from the men, but none of them broke their rhythm or gave in to fatigue. Inside her mind, Ceri sighed in relief. All knew the fates of a generation of warriors depended on their success.

A surge of energy surrounded her, and Ceri blinked at the reflection of the room she saw in the window. All the talismans' faces revealed their concentration as they desperately encouraged their mates. The warriors were fully engaged in battle to defend the line Hamish had created as a barrier to buy time for Rio's rescue.

An anomaly jerked her back into her vision. A rogue sought to sever the safety ropes, sending all three Sheridan brothers to their deaths. As he raised his claymore high in the air to deliver the cutting blow, Davy appeared out of nowhere and dealt him a fatal stab to the heart, the rogue and his claymore falling backward lifelessly. Then Davy called out to Hamish to reinforce his barrier.

"Thank ye, lad. Now return tae yer post. Playin' at bein' a warrior is no' yer job."

However, his short disappearance was all the window of time Ceri needed to leave the safety of the cottage. Rio hadn't responded at all to her, and she was frantic with worry for him. Saving him, even at the cost of her life, was all that mattered. She determined to go him, to help him at any price.

Doing as he'd done for most of her life, Finn Daly stepped

in to guard her. "Ceri, return to the cottage. You can't help Rio if Morgan takes you across the ford."

She turned her tearstained face to her old protector. "He's dying. I can feel it. I can't breach his shield." She swallowed back her tears. "I must go to him, talk to him, remind him I need him. Please, Finn, don't try to stop me."

"They'll bring him straight here as soon as they can. Be patient. If you go out into that battle, you'll die, and nothin' good will come of that."

"He's right, Ceri. Stay here. Please. We cannae protect ye out there, a druid and an old warrior," Davy added as he landed back at his post outside the door.

Before she could protest further, her eyes widened in fear and surprise as five big men materialized from thin air. At first, she thought they were warriors, but their eyes glowed an otherworldly red, and she knew she'd placed herself and her friends in grave danger.

"Rogues! Behind you!" she cried.

Instantly, Davy and Finn slid into battle stance to take on the villains Morgan sent.

With Ceri's focus on the danger they faced, she didn't notice Lynnette at her side until the other woman whispered, "Come with me, Ceri. You can't visualize yourself into the cottage or you'll open a portal the rogues can follow. You must reenter in the conventional way. Come. Now."

Holding tightly to Lynnette's hand but never taking her eyes from the rogues who threatened them, Ceri inched her way back toward the cottage and vainly hoped none of the rogues would be awaiting her when she arrived at the door.

⁓

On his improvised stretcher, Rio groaned. He heard a triumphant shout ring out, but all he could think about was Ceri. Sensing her in danger, he desperately tried to swim to the surface of consciousness. When he heard the shouts of his comrades, he mistakenly took them for battle cries with his talisman as the prize.

Before he could open his eyes, he started thrashing against the confines of the ropes securing him. Owen slipped the knots holding the rope netting around him. When he was free, Rio stood up in a rush and lost his balance. Rowan caught him and held him for several seconds while he regained his equilibrium.

"Whoa! Slow down, man! You've been out cold for a while. Don't think to come up fighting after that," Rowan chided him. "At least now we know you suffered no permanent damage." His brother's laugh sounded relieved.

"Ceri," Rio said, panting, "Ceri needs me. She's in danger. Morgan is close to taking her across the ford."

The anguish in his voice sobered the warriors' celebration like a splash of ice water.

"He's right. Alyssa just alerted me that Ceri and Lynnette are outside the cottage with only Davy and Finn to protect them from five rogues who are even now bearing down on them," Rowan gritted out.

"You're in no shape to take on anything right now, son." Owen stayed him with his hand on Rio's arm. "Reassure your talisman you're alive, and let us take care of the rogues who threaten her."

Considering his thoughts, Rio had no doubt he wore a mutinous look, then he staggered and had to fight to remain upright.

"Stay with him Rowan and Riley. I'll leave behind some of the others as well. Alaisdair, I know you're in pain, but without my sons, I need you with me."

"Let's take care o' Morgan's rogues and be done with it."

"I don't think it wise to visualize yourselves anywhere with Rio in the shape he's in. He needs to walk it off. Head out along the edge of the hill. Hamish has enchanted a barrier between the rogues and you if you stay behind the warriors who fight with us."

Turning to Alaisdair and his Scots friends, Owen said, "Come, gentlemen. Morgan has moved the fight."

⁘

The ensuing battle raged on. The clanging of claymores engaging each other, the grunts and screams of men as they landed and suffered blows permeated the air. Ceri thought she'd go insane from the noise of battle. Even the usually unflappable Lynnette Sheridan stiffened in fear at the furious noise of the onslaught. Still, she inexorably led Ceri backward toward the safety of the cottage.

As the women reached the slate flagstones at the threshold of the front door, an enormous rogue standing at least six foot five stepped in front of them. Though he didn't physically bar their escape, he stopped their movement all the same.

"Morgan has promised me a night with each of you before she takes you across the ford. If you're very good, I'll see what I can do about extending that time. Of course, you'll have to give up your warriors. A small price to pay for your lives, I think," he said leering at them.

"You're disgusting. A warrior without honor. And stupid," Lynnette spat. "Morgan will never let you enjoy either of us. That would get in the way of her gloating over our deaths as she leads us across the ford in front of our warriors."

"You're wrong, little Miss Know-It-All. She wants your warriors to watch as I take you. I'm one of Morgan's favorites," the rogue boasted. "She's allowed me to live long past my twenty-eighth birthday."

"You're a fool. And you're about to be a dead fool," Lynnette said. Then she smiled.

Momentarily mesmerized by the beauty of the talismans before him, the rogue didn't notice Finn until he landed the first blow, splitting the rogue's head in two as Finn wielded his claymore like a man half his age. But he didn't have a young man's speed, and the rogue's companion who had been hiding in the shadows stepped out and struck the old warrior. At the last second, Finn spun away from the mortal wound the rogue intended, but he didn't escape entirely as the rogue sliced through his leathers and carved a deep diagonal opening in the flesh across Finn's chest.

Ceri screamed as Finn dropped to his knees. Owen and Alaisdair landed beside them, finishing the last rogue before he could strike a second blow on her old protector.

With Alyssa and Shanley in the lead, several of the talismans inside the cottage raced out to attend to Finn while Ceri stood in the protective circle of Lynnette's arms and shook with fear and grief. She'd lost Rio, and now it looked like she'd lose Finn Daly as well.

Then a shout rang out, and Lynnette struggled to restrain Ceri as she tried to break free to run to Rio who walked gingerly out of the mist between his two brothers.

CHAPTER THIRTY

WHEN THE SHERIDAN brothers crossed the line into the enchanted perimeter of Alaisdair's cottage, Scathach lifted the protective shield she'd woven around them. Seeing the knot of people in front of the cottage, each man feared the worst. It was. But not in the way they expected. Finn Daly lay on the slate walk with a gaping wound in his chest while Alyssa and Shanley worked to stanch the flow of blood. Arriving behind the Sheridans, Hamish intervened in the women's attentions to their old warrior protector.

Before she disappeared from the battlefield, Morgan called out one last time. "This is only the beginning, Scathach. Though the Sheridans are stronger, they are still mortal, still vulnerable to my will. They will be mine eventually." She quit the field before Scathach had a chance to reply, but she left behind a flock of ravens to roost on the eaves of Alaisdair's cottage and on Conlan Manor lest anyone should think she had any intention of leaving them alone for long.

The warriors didn't have the time or inclination to be relieved that, for now, the battle was over. One of their own lay on the ground, fighting for his life.

WARRIOR   299

"Och, that is a bad wound. We'll tae take Finn tae my chambers where I have the proper tools and medicines tae help him. Owen, Riley, Rowan, between the three o' ye, ye should be able tae carry him down the tunnel tae the manor. Sharp-like," Hamish said after inspecting Finn's wound. "Alyssa, lass, ye can assist me, but Ceri and Shanley, ye have yer warriors tae tend tae."

Warriors and talismans nodded at Hamish's commands.

"Donnae be long takin' care o' yer business. We still have a ceilidh tae manage and a ritual tae complete."

With those directions, Hamish led the way through the cottage and down the tunnel to the manor. Everyone but Alaisdair and Shanley followed behind him. Ceri and Rio brought up the rear in silence as Rio worked on regaining his bearings, and Ceri tried not to give in to her emotions as she eyed the gash at Rio's hairline and the blood covering his face.

So many of the local civilians were in attendance they didn't notice the absence of the Conlan family or the Sheridans. Nor did they pay attention to the Scots warriors who straggled back in with them, their wounds or soreness from the battle disguised as "accidents" attributable to too much whisky, the darkness illuminated only by electric torches, and unfamiliarity with the grounds. Since many of the civilian men bore similar wounds, no one questioned or even noticed the difference.

Ceri and Rio slipped up to their bedroom via the servants' stairs. Rio's wounds would have drawn undue attention even from tipsy civilians, a circumstance no one wanted. Once they were safe inside their bedroom, Ceri stepped away from Rio and headed to the bathroom to start the shower. Then she busied herself laying out his clean kilt shirt, kilt, socks, sporran, and sgian dubh and sheath. Nervous energy radiated off her.

"Slow down, Ceri. Come here."

She stopped in midstride on her way to check the water in the shower and spun around to face him.

"Why don't you talk to me aloud? And why do you open your shield now and not when you were on the battlefield and I was frantic with worry? You don't trust me when it matters, do you?" she said, her sadness and frustration pulsing in her tone.

"If you must know, I was testing *your* shield since you kept it firmly in place when I was trying to communicate with *you*!" he fumed.

Ceri snorted. "That's not true. I opened my shield so fully I even took a chance that Morgan or one of her minions would intercept my thoughts. I was desperate to reach you, and you shut me out!" She shook in anger, fatigue, and hurt. "When I couldn't reach you, I ran outside the cottage—"

Time stopped as she awaited Rio's anger at her betrayal.

Finally, he broke the silence. "What do you mean by you ran outside the cottage?" he asked carefully. "Scathach gave you strict instructions to stay inside the manor."

She sat hard on the chaise longue. "Finn is injured because of me. I couldn't reach you, but I knew you were hurt."

Arms across his massive chest, he waited.

"I had another prophecy. When you fought Ysbaddaden, you died on the rocks exactly like the outcome of my first prophecy with the Morhaus. Only this time, I had the vision as you engaged in battle." The fear she experienced during the prophecy shuddered through her again. "I thought I watched in real time, and I was desperate to reach you, to help you. When you didn't respond to me, I feared I'd lost you." She lifted her eyes to his. "I had to know, Rio. I had to find you." All of her pent-up emotions spilled out in silent rivers of tears streaming down her face.

Sitting beside her, Rio cupped her face in his big hands. "What were you thinking? You could have been killed out there." But his reprimand held no heat as he thumbed away her tears. "You were willing to sacrifice yourself to whatever fate Morgan decreed for a chance to save me. Jesus." He pulled her into his arms and brushed a kiss that felt like a prayer over her lips.

"We're both due for a shower. Too bad we have so many guests left in the manor. I can think of several ways you could make me feel much better. But all of them involve arriving back at the ceilidh long after midnight." His lips feathered her temple.

She pulled back enough to look him in the eyes, and the desire she saw there nearly robbed her of breath. Unable to help herself, she whispered, "Me too."

"This will have to tide us over." Rio lowered his head and kissed her more thoroughly than she'd ever been kissed in her life. Lips and tongue and teeth, giving and taking breath until he tore his mouth away, leaving her lightheaded. Which is where he left her as he peeled off his sweaty and bloodied clothes and headed to the shower.

By two minutes to midnight, Ceri and Rio and the rest of the Sheridans had joined the throng in the ballroom. Rio bore a thin gash along his hairline, and Alaisdair moved rather gingerly, but otherwise, no one could tell that any of them had engaged in a fight to the death with the forces of evil and won. When asked about his wound, Rio laughed and said something about not ducking fast enough when one of the others swung around with his flashlight. Alaisdair attributed his cracked ribs to a tipsy tumble off one of the garden terraces.

"Lads, ye should stick tae cider fer the rest o' the night. Hamish's fine whisky be wasted on the likes o' ye if ye cannae hold it better than tha'," the mayor of Ullapool joked.

"Ye just want more for yerself, Rory Stewart. Everyone knows how much ye covet yer drams o' Hamish's special whisky," Alaisdair replied with a grin.

"At least when I drink it, I donnae go fallin' down terraces or walkin' intae torches when someone is pointin' out somethin' with one," Rory said good-naturedly before giving Alaisdair a hearty slap on the back.

Alaisdair sucked a breath in through his teeth, which he bared in a grimace he tried to pass off as a smile.

"Someone always comes back from wardin' off the 'evil spirits' with some sort o' wound. Makes fer a good story over more drams o' whisky. How 'bout we head over tae the bar and commence the short tellin' o' yer stories. I doubt I'll be awake by the time ye get tae the excitin' versions," Rory teased.

"Ye go on, Rory. Seems Hamish has somethin' else even more taxin' for us tae dae right now. Likely, he's goin' tae give ye another excuse fer drinkin' his whisky," Alaisdair said amiably and pulled Shanley closer to him.

Mercifully, the mayor of Ullapool wandered off in search of a dram.

Ceri noticed Shanley flinched nearly every time Alaisdair did. Apparently, that didn't escape Hamish's keen eyes as he joined them. "Donnae ye worry about him, lass. By the time we're finished with the ritual, Alaisdair will feel much better. Yer night willnae be ruined my girl," he said with a wink that caused a deep flush to climb Shanley's cheeks.

"Does that mean Finn will be able to come out of his room for the ritual?" Ceri asked with all the hope in her heart.

Hamish sobered immediately. "Finn's wound is grave, lass. He's in a bad way." He put out a hand to stop Ceri from going to Finn's side. "Nae, lass, ye canna go tae him now. Ye're needed here fer somethin' far greater than one old warrior nearin' the end o' his life."

Ceri glared at him.

"Donnae give me that look," Hamish continued. "My druid friends are doin' everythin' they can tae help him, but his wound is serious and no' respondin' tae the various antivenins they've tried so far. Ye'll be in the way if ye go tae him. Besides, he told me he doesnae want any o' his girls seein' him as he is right now. When we finish what we need tae do here, ye can sneak off and check on him," Hamish finished, his tone kindly but solemn.

Rio slipped a hand around her waist and pulled her close to him. He brushed a kiss over her cheek and murmured into her ear, "This is not your fault."

Silently, she nodded, but knowing Finn fought for his life because of her poor choice made her heart hurt.

Hamish walked to the dais to address the assembly of warriors, druids, and civilians. "Taenight we have a special surprise. My cousin, Ceri Ross, the official owner o' Conlan Manor, along with her American friend Rio Sheridan, is goin' tae lead us in the midnight reel tae celebrate the harvest, bless the food, and ask the gods' blessin' before we sit down tae enjoy the bounty the ladies have spent all day preparin'."

The crowd applauded as Ceri and Rio acknowledged them with nods and reserved smiles.

"They'll be joined by their American friends and our own Alaisdair Graham tae round out the eight."

Davy stood beside him on the dais. Hamish ceremoniously took from him a pair of red stag antlers and a cape of red stag hide. Rio parted the crowd as he joined them on the dais. Hamish set the antlers on Rio's head and tied them beneath his chin with a leather thong to the hooting and laughter of the civilian men in attendance, many of whom made lewd comments and good-natured jokes about the prowess of the stag.

Rio smiled and laughed along with them, but the look in his eyes told Ceri this part wasn't his favorite. The civilians had lost the reason and therefore the power of the ritual. Instead, their experience devolved into an opportunity for a good laugh at the "stag's" expense like a bachelor party before a wedding.

Saraid, who'd joined Davy and Hamish on the dais, handed

him a wreath made of sheaves of barley and decorated with acorns for luck and dried fall flowers of gorse and purple asters. Ceremonially, he placed it on Ceri's head. While the women applauded this symbol of the harvest, Saraid slipped a small beribboned bag of hazelnuts around Ceri's neck and whispered, "These are fer fertility and creativity in yer upcomin' marriage."

Ceri blinked at the old woman.

Hamish gazed benignly on Saraid before calling out, "Now fer the test o' the riddle. Let's see how our American cousins do with our auld Scots tradition."

The entire party, including civilians, warriors, talismans, and druids, old and young, clamored for the riddle, delighting in the tension of this part of the ritual.

Ceri sneaked a glance at Rio who grinned at her. "After what we just went through, this is child's play, sweetheart," he said from the corner of his mouth.

Hamish cleared his throat:

"If ye chase it, ye willnae catch it.

"If ye sit still, it will come tae ye.

"If ye demand it, it will never be true.

"If ye are yerself, ye'll have it—even when ye're least deservin' o' it.

"If ye fight it, ye'll lose it eventually.

"If ye must fight fer it, ye'll cherish it all the more.

"All will die without it.

"Many will die fer it.

"What is it?"

Rio stared deep into Ceri's eyes, and her breath backed up in her throat.

"Love," he answered.

Her heart thumped in her chest at the expression on his face. The depths of emotion he let his midnight eyes reveal erased all the doubts she'd had since he first tried his sign on her.

She couldn't contain her smile, and Rio sucked in air like he'd been sucker punched in his solar plexus. A peal of pure joyful laughter erupted from her as the crowd broke into applause.

Before either of them could act on their now very public feelings, Hamish signaled the band to begin playing the reel, and the party of dancers stepped to it as they'd rehearsed. They danced the reel nontraditionally, weaving around the tables rather than dancing in a tight circle or up and down the line.

A fat candle graced the middle of each table, each glowing from a single flame a druid had carried upstairs to the ballroom from the Samhain bonfire burning in the garden, a sacred fire symbolizing the beginning of a new year. The flames flickered but didn't go out as the dancers reeled around the tables.

The white kilt shirts the men wore glowed in the candlelight as they danced their women in their colorful plaids around the room. Hamish had explained in practice the wearing of white to light the darkness of the unborn year. The spectacle delighted the civilians while the warrior community applauded them for their skill at completing the ritual dance in the complicated knot pattern symbolizing eternity.

They concluded the reel in the middle of the room to the raucous applause of the assembled guests. While they caught their breath, several young women dispersed as if by magic through the crowd, each carrying a tray laden with drams of whisky. When everyone held a glass, Hamish commanded the crowd's attention once again.

"Friends, thank ye fer attendin' our wee celebration taenight."

People laughed at his description, and Hamish let them.

He lifted a glass in Ceri's direction. "'Tis a fine thin' tae have our Ceri in residence here in her ancestral home. We hope she stays with us fer a good long visit." He nodded pointedly, and she understood his meaning even without the aid of telepathy, while several in the crowd called out their agreement.

Hamish continued. "We're also happy tae have Ceri's aunt Shanley Conlan with us as well. It has been tae long since she last visited."

Shanley nodded demurely at the crowd before raising a brow at Hamish.

Alaisdair was less subtle. Even Ceri heard his thoughts.

"Donnae meddle, auld man. I know what I'm about with the lass."

Hamish grinned. "Finally, we have most enjoyed hostin' the Sheridan family. Many o' ye taenight are aware o' some o' the great things this clan has done recently over in America." Addressing the Sheridans directly he said, "We hope ye return tae visit us often."

Rio's family smiled and nodded.

"Let's raise a toast tae our friends and family. May yer hearth fires always keep ye warm, may yer bellies be always full, may yer hearts be always filled with joy."

A chorus of "Hear, hear" followed Hamish's salute before all in attendance shot their whiskys. Afterward, the men—civilian and warrior alike—slammed their glasses down on the tables.

The midnight supper began with the piping in of the haggis, followed by the serving of turnips and potatoes—the fruits of the earth—and *cranachan*—the traditional Scots harvest dessert. The guests especially enjoyed the parfait-like dessert of toasted oats soaked in whisky layered over whipped cream, heather honey, and raspberries.

If Ceri's previous experiences were anything to go by, hours of drinking, dancing, and storytelling would follow the meal. As the night slid into the wee hours of the morning, the edges of the ballroom would fill up with sleeping children curled on and under chairs and benches and old people sitting at tables nodding and blinking to stay awake, while some of the more intrepid civilians would dance to the last note the band sounded.

However, she didn't stay long enough to witness that part.

Ceri and Rio quit the party not long after the midnight supper, the custom for the King Stag and his mate. Most of the crowd saw them to the front door of the manor since they were expected to go out into the garden, dance around the Samhain fire, and disappear. Many of the civilians had given Rio suggestions for some of the best inns to try for the remainder of the night along with some ribald advice about what they might do once they arrived. With a wink and a smile, Rio played along with them before he escorted his lady away.

The antlers of the King Stag and the wreath on the head of his mate lent an eerie silhouette to the dancing figures in the firelight. They made three circuits of the bonfire before stepping out of its light, seeming to disappear into thin air. Which of course they did as they visualized themselves into the master suite inside the manor.

The civilians, none the wiser for their "magic," trooped gaily back into the manor to continue the party, while Ceri and Rio sensed the warriors' shared relief that they'd survived the battle. More importantly, the King Stag and the Conlan heir had survived to complete the ritual and fulfill the prophecy, giving the Conlan clan generations of protections from the vagaries of the gods.

CHAPTER THIRTY-ONE

All Saints' Day

NYTHING INTERESTING IN the paper this morning?" Riley asked as he and Lynnette walked into the dining room late enough in the morning for brunch to be lunch.

"A big storm at sea sent a bit of a squall into the loch, unmooring a few boats, but not doing much damage. The locals like the storms on Samhain because they're a superstitious lot, and storms on Samhain are good omens for the coming harvests. The storms also drop kelp and other delicacies on the beaches for beachcombers to gather," Ceri summarized before she stopped, startled, her eyes rapidly scanning the page.

"What is it? Did something about the battle somehow reach the civilian papers?" Rio asked with a frown.

"No, but nearly as bad." Ceri raised sorrowful eyes to the family gathered at the long dining room table.

"What do you mean?" Riley asked.

"These girls, Molly and Kadi, were up here on holiday from university visiting their grandma. Some beachcombers found them washed up on the shores of the loch," she said. "The 'odd' thing about them, according to this article, is the beatific smiles on their faces like they died ecstatically happy."

She felt the blood drain from her face.

"Why are you so upset about these girls?" Rio asked.

"They were here last night, at the ceilidh," she whispered. "They walked in on Alyssa and me when Taranis insisted on talking to us in the grand salon."

"*What?*" Rio exploded. "Taranis wanted *what?*"

"He called us upstairs after all of you left the manor. I had a prophecy, and because of what I saw, we took great care not to go too close to him. Those girls, though, they didn't stand a chance."

Rio leaned his forearms on the table and waited.

She sucked in a breath. "He's incredibly handsome and seductive in human form. They took one look at him and couldn't wait to touch. We tried to stop them, but they wouldn't listen. They were so eager." She stared unseeing at the paper in her hands.

"When he touched them, they fell completely under his spell. He disappeared with an arm around each girl." A tear slid down her face. "I knew the risks to all of us, and I still couldn't stop them."

The lump in her throat threatened to choke her.

"That explains why the mists thinned out so much toward in the middle of the battle. Taranis had other entertainments to keep his attention," Rio said. He wrapped his arms around Ceri. "He meant to amuse himself with you. I should have known when he called me out as I left the manor."

She startled. "You saw him too?"

Rio nodded.

"Wow, I can't wrap my head around Taranis being inside this house," Riley said, sliding closer to Lynnette.

"I can't wrap my head around his audacity at trying to take talismans while their warriors fought his sister," Lynnette added with a shiver. Riley wrapped his arms around her and held her close.

"Why are you all so glum?" Owen asked as he and Sian entered the room.

"Did you know Taranis was inside this house during the ceilidh last night?" Riley asked.

Owen had been headed for the buffet but stopped midway across the room. "Taranis? Here? Didn't Hamish enchant this place to keep the gods out?"

"'Tis our tradition tae invite several o' the gods tae our ceilidh each year. The celebration has always been in their honor," Saraid said as she calmly entered the room behind the elder Sheridans.

"What were Hamish's enchantments about, then?" Rio asked, his tone wavering between perplexed and pissed off.

"Hamish enchanted the manor against any tricks the gods might use, like stealin' a talisman from her own home."

Ceri frowned. "You knew what he was up to. That's why you stood by and watched as he drew those girls to him," she accused.

"'Twas either those twa civilian lasses or Alyssa and ye. Both o' ye are tae precious tae our community tae sacrifice tae a god. He demanded a sacrifice tae spare yer warrior and Alaisdair from the Morrigan."

Ceri gasped. "Couldn't there have been another way?"

Saraid calmly poured herself a cup of tea from the pot on the buffet. "The Conlan prophetesses foresaw their warriors dying partly due tae weather conditions at the time o' the battle. Taranis needed an incentive tae thwart his sister."

Taking a seat at the end of the table, she continued. "We provided it. He wanted tae have a larger prize, but he was satisfied with what we offered instead."

Ceri shoved her unfinished porridge away from her. "Those girls weren't in the room by accident, were they?" she asked, her tone hollow.

"Nae lass, I'm afraid they weren't. I summoned them when Taranis made his desires known." Saraid's voice softened. "If it's any consolation, those girls experienced the greatest night o' their lives nae matter how long they might have lived. Doesnae seem so bad a way tae go."

"I think I need to lie down," Ceri said, and Rio rose to steady her.

"I'm sorry tae have upset ye, lass, but ye need tae know the truth. Though I would ha' waited if ye hadnae seen that article in the papers." Saraid nodded at the open newspaper in the middle of the table. "I came down because ye need tae go tae Finn. I'm afraid the gods aren't done exactin' their sacrifices in order fer the Conlan family tae enjoy relative peace."

The room erupted in a cacophony of fear and alarm.

Saraid regarded the family with a sympathetic expression. "We've done all we can tae ease him, but the rogue who wounded him dinnae play fair. He treated his blade with a mortal poison and purposefully laid open Finn's chest. I'm afraid Finn is no' long fer this earth, an' he wishes tae see ye before he goes. I'm sorry."

Rio scooped Ceri up in his powerful arms and carried her up the stairs quickly, followed by the rest of the Sheridans. When they reached Finn's room, they found Alyssa and Rowan standing near Finn's bed.

"There you are, Ceri." Finn uttered his words with a raspy wheeze.

When Rio set her on her feet, Ceri ran to Finn and knelt by his bedside, taking his limp hand in hers and rubbing her fingers over it while she looked into his dear old eyes. "Oh Finn, you can't go! What will we do without you?"

"Each of you girls has found your warriors. Your mates will offer you far more protection than a tired old man." He gave her hand a weak pat. "Don't mourn me lass. I've had quite an adventure, not the least of which was looking out for you and Alyssa," he said with difficulty before gifting her with a wan smile. Then he closed his eyes, exhaled a tiny puff of air, and passed into the next life.

Ceri and Alyssa wept openly, each turning to her mate for comfort.

"Scathach told me to stay inside the manor, but I was so afraid for you. Then I left the safety of the cottage." Ceri's guilt threatened to overwhelm her as she cried into Rio's chest. "If I'd listened, Finn would still be alive."

Rio smoothed his hands up and down her back. "You can't control fate, sweetheart. If you hadn't come out of the cottage when you did, there would have been some other danger to lure Finn to his encounter with his destiny."

Ceri clung to him and sobbed harder.

"He was a warrior. But since he didn't die on the battlefield, Morgan doesn't get to escort him across the ford into the mists. Instead, the White Lady has him," he said, kissing her hair. "He'll be remembered as a warrior who fought his last battle in defense of his friends and denied Morgan her prize. He's safe now."

"He fulfilled his destiny. His job was tae protect ye three until ye found yer warriors," Hamish said quietly from the corner of the room where he watched with Saraid. "We will honor him with a burial here on the manor grounds."

Through her tears, Alyssa overruled the old druid. "Finn once told me that when he died, he wanted to be cremated, his ashes scattered over his wife's grave. If it's all the same to you, we'll honor him that way."

"Ye knew him best. We owe Finn our gratitude fer savin' ye." Hamish walked over and placed his hands on Ceri and Rio. "He made sure ye made it tae the King Stag ceremony. The gods will often allow us our victories, but they always exact a price."

❧

Ceri sat on Rio's lap on the chaise lounge in their room and sobbed herself to exhaustion. "How could my entire world turn inside out so quickly? Finn, my parents, Alyssa's grandma, Finn. Oh Finn. Where are they now?"

Rio held her and let her emotions wash over him. He too felt a bone-deep sadness at the loss of the old warrior who in his prime Rio had no doubt had been the best of his generation. No wonder Scathach had insisted he spar with Finn on so many occasions. Ceri's sorrow seeped into Rio, and he wished he could take away her pain at the same time he knew she had to feel it to heal.

He carried his beautiful woman to their bed where he lay her down gently before lying beside her and pulling her close. He didn't try to interfere in her dreams, but he did eavesdrop on them, knowing in her grief-weakened state, she'd be susceptible to any evil influences their enemy goddesses might try to inflict. His encounter with Taranis before the battle the previous evening made him question the power of Hamish's enchantments, and he wasn't about to take any chances with Ceri's state of mind.

When at last she rested easily, her mind quieting, Rio let her be. As she slept, he replayed the past weeks in his mind, smiling often at a memory of Ceri's eyes flashing at him with indignation at some comment he'd made, her chiming laughter when he'd charmed her, her meadow-green eyes deepening almost to black with desire. Her selfless attempt to rescue him in the heat of battle.

He needed her like breathing, and he suddenly knew the exact course of action to take as soon as she awoke. Grinning to himself, he closed his eyes. If all went according to plan, he'd need a nap to sustain himself through the rest of the day.

∽

Late in the afternoon, Ceri awoke alone. Vague recollections of Rio holding her followed by a bone-deep sense of loss disoriented her. Finn was dead because she couldn't wait for word of Rio's fate from inside the safety of Hamish's enchanted rooms. Finn never tried to stop her from going to her warrior. Instead, he tried to protect her in her desperate attempt to help Rio. Finn was like that, she thought, letting her make her own choices, her own mistakes while he watched protectively over her. This time, however, the consequences were simply too much. Guilt threatened to overwhelm her, but before she could succumb to her grief, she heard a light tapping at her bedroom door.

"It's open."

Alyssa walked in, closing the door quietly behind her. "How are you?"

Ceri slid off the bed and took two steps into her best friend's embrace. "If only I'd listened. Scathach told us to stay inside Hamish's rooms in the manor, but I couldn't, not with my visions of Rio dying. Now Finn is dead."

Alyssa tightened her arms around Ceri as she sobbed. "We'll always miss Finn. If not for him, I might not have lived to find my warrior and my place in our community."

She dried Ceri's tears with her thumbs. "You can't blame yourself. Scathach instructed every talisman to stay inside the manor, and none of us did." Holding Ceri's face in her hands, she added, "The rogues were after all of us, and they didn't play fair. We each took a calculated risk, and we suffered a great loss. In all the old stories, there's a price to pay to keep evil out of our world."

"I know. But that doesn't take away the pain." Ceri hiccupped and tried to pull herself back together.

Alyssa hugged her again. "Hamish's ceremony for him will help."

"Thank you," Ceri said through a watery smile.

"You've been up here all day. Come down to the kitchen with me and let's see if we can find some leftovers."

"Do you think there'll be any?" Though Ceri didn't feel much like eating, she was grateful for her friend's suggestion.

"A fair question, considering my experience with the

Sheridans." Alyssa laughed and looped her arm through Ceri's, leading her from her suite.

As the two friends entered the kitchen, Rio walked in the back door. She thought she saw him slip something into his jacket before he stepped over to her, gathering her into his arms.

"Hello, sweetheart. Do you feel better after your nap?"

She clung to him, inhaling the scents of cold outdoors, leather, and man deep into her lungs like she could breathe him into her very being.

"You know, I could get used to this sort of homecoming. Do you need me to run any errands for you, Alyssa, something that will take me out of the manor for a few minutes so Ceri can greet me again on my return?" Rio winked.

"Go ahead, make fun of me," she grumbled into the base of his neck, but she didn't loosen her hold on him.

"Will you fix me something to eat while I go upstairs for a minute?" he asked before brushing a kiss across her cheek.

"Sure."

At last, she let him go, and he bounded up the stairs out of the kitchen.

Ceri and Alyssa perused the contents of the refrigerator where they found left-over Samhain dinner they heated in the microwave. A few minutes later, Rio hopped down the stairs to the kitchen, an air of happy mischief surrounding him.

Alyssa quirked a brow. "Why are you so cheery, Rio?"

"Good things come to those who wait," he replied enigmatically.

His light mood was infectious, and soon the three of them were chatting easily while finishing off a substantial portion of leftover haggis, neeps and tatties. Rio spent the meal regaling the women with stories of how he and Finn sparred after they met during Rowan and Alyssa's ordeal the previous year. His stories alleviated some of the sadness they each felt at the loss of their old friend.

By the end of the meal, Ceri felt significantly better than she had all day, which left her thinking about the King Stag ceremony and the hot experience following it in their bedroom.

"Glad to know that's on your mind, babe." Rio's attention seemed to be on something Alyssa had said, but his thoughts were obviously tuned into Ceri.

Her eyes widened at his comment, but otherwise, she hid her emotions.

"You have the most maddening habit of sneaking into my mind when I least expect it."

Rio laughed out loud.

.   "I take it there's more than one conversation going on here at the moment. If the two of you will excuse me, I'm going to see what Rowan is up to." Alyssa smiled and headed up the stairs.

"How 'bout if you grab a jacket and your purse while I clean up? I want to take you for a ride," Rio said.

"A ride? Where?"

"It's a surprise."

Ceri tried to read Rio's thoughts, but he kept his mind carefully blank. Pulling a face, she headed upstairs to retrieve her things.

CHAPTER THIRTY-TWO

N THE GATHERING twilight as they drove out of Ullapool, Rio still hadn't told Ceri where they were going. When they reached Inverness, he headed for the airport where a private plane awaited them.

"Exactly where are you taking me?"

"Trust me." He smiled and hustled her onto the plane.

Ceri had never flown in a private jet, and she might have found the experience exciting if the mystery of Rio's motives and destination hadn't preoccupied her.

"Relax Ceri. Enjoy the ride." He tipped his seat back and stretched out his long legs.

"I might do that if I knew where we were flying," she snapped.

"It's a short ride, a little over an hour."

"How enlightening."

He grinned and closed his eyes.

A steward offered them drinks, but Ceri opted for water. Whatever Rio was up to, she wanted to be sober enough to participate—or escape if necessary. Rio enjoyed a stout beer and didn't insist she join him. Though she quizzed the steward, he wouldn't reveal their destination. Whatever Rio was doing, he'd planned well. She nearly burst with frustrated curiosity, but obviously, he had no intention of enlightening her until he was good and ready.

When the plane touched down in Glasgow, he collected their bags. With his hand on the small of her back, he propelled her to the rental car counter where he picked up the keys to a Mercedes sedan. After consulting the GPS, he locked in a destination, and drove them to their hotel, a lovely restored Victorian affair near the train station.

Ceri marveled at the elaborate furnishings of their room from the high ceilings with their off-white moldings to the velvety apricot floral-patterned wallpaper to the thick white area rug with its beige swirl designs to the huge mahogany four-poster bed dominating the center of the room.

"Nice place. What are we doing here?"

"We're freshening up for dinner downstairs."

"We flew all the way to Glasgow for *dinner*?"

"No, we flew to Glasgow to spend the night on the way to our destination in the morning."

"And our destination is …?"

"On the agenda for tomorrow. Let's change and go to dinner already. I'm starved."

Rio reached into the duffel bag, pulled out a shirt, and headed into the bathroom.

"Hey, I didn't pack anything for an overnight stay!" Ceri called after him.

"I took care of it. Look in the duffel."

She peeked inside and found her toiletries neatly bagged in her toiletry case and also a couple of her shirts, a pair of slacks, and maybe a dress? Right when she reached deeper into the bag to investigate, Rio reemerged from the bathroom.

"Uh-uh. You're not snooping through the entire bag to figure out the plan. Grab a clean shirt and change. We have a dinner reservation in half an hour," he said, his tone playful.

Obediently, she pulled a lightweight sweater from the bag and carried it and her toiletries to the bathroom. Ten minutes later, she presented herself to him at the door to their suite.

He treated her to an elaborate steak dinner, reminding her that the American tradition of eating black Angus beef began with the export of the breed from Scotland. He kept a steady stream of conversation flowing throughout the meal, and by the end, she felt more relaxed than she had for days.

Taking her hand, Rio led her out of the hotel and down the street to the train station where they enjoyed the bustle of the commuters rushing through the station and marveled at the ingenious Victorian engineering of the building with its open grid of ironworks holding up several tons of beveled glass. The effect of the architecture gave the station a feeling at once of airiness and solidity. He bought her a bouquet of flowers from the proprietor of a tiny kiosk near the ticket booth, and hand in hand, they returned to their hotel room.

Back in their room, Ceri felt like they were together for the first time. Rio wordlessly took her into his arms and kissed her thoroughly, his tongue dancing naturally with hers, his hands roaming her back, tangling in her hair, and sliding down her back to cup her ass and pull her close.

Feeling Rio's hard length against her belly set her on fire.

He focused on pleasuring her, slowly sliding her sweater over her body that sparked with desire, taking his time removing her bra before kissing his way down the column of her throat to her chest to the tops of her breasts. He sucked first one tight bud then the other, and her knees buckled. With one arm around her back, he held her upright and kissed coherent thought out of her before he knelt on the carpet in front of her.

With his eyes on her face, he undid the button of her slacks and slid the zipper down before slipping his hands inside the waistband and pushing them down, catching her panties on the way. When she stood completely naked before him, he looked his fill before leaning forward and flicking his tongue over her clit. He pulled her hard nub into his mouth where he licked and nipped and sucked. His attentions included a tour of her channel with his lips and tongue before he returned to her clit, and she went off like Fourth of July fireworks. Standing, he smiled at her and slowly removed his shirt, jeans, and boxers, his full erection leaving her no doubt what he planned to do next.

When he guided her down to the bed, his eyes darkened almost to black with desire, intense, serious. He stretched her out and kissed her, hot openmouthed kisses that left her skin tingling everywhere he touched and raised goose bumps everywhere she wanted his touch.

He kissed her again between her thighs, and she forgot everything about the last few days—the training, the prophecies, the battle, the ritual, the death, the mystery of their journey—all of it vanished the moment he claimed her. Arching her back and lifting her hips to give him easier access, she cried out her release.

As she floated like a feather back down from heaven, Rio rose up and covered her, entering her in one long hard thrust. She pulsed around his rigid length as she wrapped her arms and legs around him, holding him deep inside her, and he let her have her moment before he started to move.

Slowly he increased his rhythms, building the sweet tension, and she moved with him, showing him with her body that she loved him, longed to be one with him. She arched again, and with a groan, he gave her what they both craved. Tiny shimmering shards of light burst behind her closed eyelids. With a shout, he exploded after her before they came back together in a hot slick embrace.

When their breathing at last approximated normal, Rio tried

to lift himself off her, but she wouldn't allow it. "Over the past weeks, you've made love to me often, and always you shattered me, took me to places I didn't know I could go. This time, though, I took you with me, and I want to hold onto the moment. Hold onto you."

"Ceri, love, I'm too heavy to lay on you like this. I don't want to flatten you," Rio said, his voice rough.

"I'm fine. Let me hold you for a few minutes."

Her mind drifted back to a time only weeks ago when Rio seemed to detest her.

"This is the beginning, not the end, love. I promise."

She tightened around him before at last relaxing her hold. He rolled off her and pulled her up onto his chest in one smooth motion. "You comfortable?"

"Mmm."

He grabbed the comforter he'd tossed aside earlier and settled it over them. Almost instantly, she fell into a quiet, dreamless sleep.

∽

Ceri awoke to cheerful whistling coming from the shower. Her body felt luxuriously heavy as she let her mind wander back to the previous night. Their lovemaking exploded everything she thought it could be. There was something so intense about Rio last night, and while it scared her a little, it thrilled her as well.

The object of her reverie emerged from the bathroom fully clothed in khaki slacks, a blue plaid dress shirt, and a midnight blue blazer. Like something out of *GQ,* he stole her breath.

"Hey sleepyhead. About time you woke up. We're on a bit of a schedule, so if you want breakfast, you better hustle through the shower."

"If *someone* would let me in on the plan, I might be able to move as fast as he wants me to," she grumbled.

TAM DeRUDDER JACKSON

"Come on, beautiful, get ready," he said, a smile dancing in his eyes.

Ceri dragged herself out of bed and padded into the bathroom. "Do I get to find out where we're going today?" she called from the shower.

"Only if we're not late."

She dressed quickly in the clothes he'd left folded neatly on the vanity for her. Why he chose the green cocktail dress she brought to Scotland she couldn't figure out. The plunging neckline and flared skirt seemed a bit much for a drive. After drying her hair enough to be presentable, she brushed on a bit of eyeliner, mascara, and lip gloss, and hoped she appeared acceptable for whatever Rio planned.

They walked a short distance to a small café where they enjoyed a full Scots breakfast of tea and toast, thick ham and eggs, sausages, beans, and broiled tomatoes. After making love all the previous night, they both were ravenous and ate everything the server set in front of them.

After breakfast, Rio loaded their scant luggage into the Mercedes, reprogrammed the GPS, and drove south out of town. The winding roads charmed Ceri, as did the rolling hills of the Borders. The low-lying shrubs were attired in their fiery autumn regalia, but the grass of the hills remained verdant and occasionally dotted with fluffy white sheep. Low walls of stacked stones delineated farms. Stone cottages appeared around bends in the road and up on hillsides, plumes of smoke curling up from their chimneys into the azure sky.

At last they drove into a rather large village. Though Ceri missed the road sign identifying the town, she figured it out rather quickly when she saw a small wedding chapel on the side of the road.

"You've brought me to Gretna Green?" she asked, dumbfounded.

"In a minute," Rio said as he studied the road and the directions the GPS gave him. Finally, he stopped the car in front of an ancient-looking blacksmith shop.

"This is it," he said.

He ignored her quizzical frown and exited the car. Walking around the front of it, he opened her door and escorted her to the old building.

"Aren't we a bit overdressed for a tour of a blacksmith shop?"

"Maybe."

Inside, Ceri discovered they weren't visiting a blacksmith shop at all. The whitewashed room might have been a blacksmith shop at one time, but the stone floors were swept clean, the enormous fireplace free of ashes, the bellows beside it silent. A radiator under a window to the right of the door now heated the room.

Garlands of holly and ivy—yin and yang, male and female—decorated the walls high up near the open beam ceiling, and several chairs sat in rows between the door and massive anvil located near the old fireplace and bellows. Two men stood beside the anvil—one she didn't recognize.

The other was Hamish Buchanan.

Ceri turned to Rio. "What, exactly, is going on here?"

"It appears, sweetheart, that I've kidnapped you with the intention of marrying you," Rio replied as he knelt in front of her and produced a velvet box from the pocket of his jacket. "If you'll have me."

For the first time since she met him, Ceri detected nerves in her warrior, a hint of fear in his eyes. Now she understood what last night meant.

"We're eloping."

"If you agree to marry me."

For a long minute, she let him worry before she placed her hand on his cheek, leaned down, and brushed a kiss across his mouth.

"I can't think of anything else I'd rather do today," she whispered against his lips.

Rio smiled, stood, and laced his fingers through hers. He led her to the anvil where hundreds of Scots, English, and Welsh couples had stood over the years to be joined together in marriage. The man standing beside Hamish introduced himself to Ceri as the local vicar. Hamish informed them he had a few things to say as part of their marriage rite—to make sure there were no questions in the warrior community. Also, he was there to stand as witness and sign the papers, which he produced from a pocket in his tweed jacket.

Rio grinned, and the ceremony began.

When the minister asked for the rings, Rio produced a beautiful golden band etched with Celtic knots and inlaid with diamonds and emeralds. When the time came for Ceri to give Rio a ring, Hamish handed her a thick gold band to place on Rio's finger.

After the vicar pronounced them married, Rio handed Hamish the beribboned bag of hazelnuts Saraid had given Ceri on Samhain, which Hamish now slipped over Ceri's head.

"When Saraid gave this to ye, she gave ye a promise. Now I give ye the reality o' yer eternal union with this warrior. May ye live long and happily taegether."

Rio wrapped Ceri in his arms and kissed her deeply, each losing themselves in the other—a promise that never again would they doubt each other.

CHAPTER THIRTY-THREE

 KNEW YOU WERE plotting my son's marriage without me, you old schemer!" Sian huffed at Hamish when Ceri and Rio returned to the manor two days later.

"They really couldnae wait tae marry. At least Rio couldnae, and who can blame him wantin' tae tie such a bonny lass tae him," Hamish said with a wink.

"He's right, Mom," Rio said laughing.

"But I thought you wanted a big wedding. When we were kids, you always talked about the beautiful wedding you'd have with all the bridesmaids and flowers and elegantly appointed reception. I honestly thought the gorgeous affair you planned and executed for Rowan and me was the dress rehearsal for your own incredible day," Alyssa said as her mouth turned down.

"I'm sorry Alyssa, but when Rio went to so much trouble to plan our elopement and mini-honeymoon, I couldn't very well say no," she explained.

At the hot look Rio and Ceri shared at the mention of the honeymoon, Owen laughed out loud.

"Well done, son. Well done." He embraced Rio in a bear hug.

"Unless Alaisdair and Shanley have similar

plans, we can all pitch in and help them with their wedding," Ceri said as Rio reclaimed her in his arms.

Hamish, who had busied himself at the bar on the side of the salon said, "Och, there shouldnae be any sad faces taeday. These twa wonderful young people are happily wed, the Conlan heir mated tae her warrior. 'Tis a great day fer all o' us." He walked among the Sheridans with a tray nearly overflowing with drams of whisky. "I saved some o' my special whisky fer this occasion, so if ye'll join me, I propose a toast." Addressing the newlyweds, he said, "Tae Ceri and Rio Sheridan. May they live long and fill this house with love and laughter all their days."

Everyone lifted a glass as Rio wrapped Ceri in his arms and kissed her like she was his whole world.

⁕

Later that evening after they entertained the well wishes of their family, Davy, Saraid, and a few of their new friends in the parish at an impromptu supper party Hamish organized, Ceri and Rio finally retired to their suite. Rio locked the door behind them as Ceri turned to him and smiled.

"I've been waiting all day for this part," she purred as she snuggled into his embrace.

"Ceri, do you feel like you missed something by not having the big wedding with all the trappings? Because if you want it, we can arrange it," he said, his expression solemn.

"Until we discovered you were my warrior, I fantasized about the huge affair I'd have when I married. But this whole experience with battles and death has taught me we need to live in the moment." She grinned up at him. "Besides, I have to admit to being very flattered you couldn't wait as long as it would take to plan a formal wedding before you married me."

Though he smiled at her, it didn't quite reach his eyes.

"There's also the romantic way you planned the whole

elopement and surprised me with it. Any woman who wouldn't love that experience doesn't deserve the man who gave it to her."

She nibbled her way up the column of his throat to his jaw. "Joining the mile-high club is everything it's cracked up to be. I think I liked that part most of all."

She kissed her way to the corner of his mouth. In a few minutes, she'd completely convinced him that she absolutely did like being stolen away and married without all the fanfare of a big wedding. Before the night was over, she'd convinced him of her feelings for their marriage—and for him.

⁂

The day after Ceri and Rio's return to Conlan Manor dawned cold and clear. Hamish presided over a memorial ceremony for Finn Daly in the gardens of the manor. Ceri, Alyssa, and Shanley prayed the old warrior knew how important he would always be to them. They also said a prayer for the two civilian women lost to the gods in the storm on Samhain. Rowan reverently carried the urn with Finn's ashes back to the house where he and Alyssa carefully packed it to fly Finn home with them. As he'd requested, they would scatter his ashes over his wife's grave, reuniting the two of them for eternity.

Alaisdair arranged to fly with Shanley back to Montana so she could finish her teaching assignment at least through the end of the term. The Sheridans also made plans for opening a branch of their firm in Scotland, one that Rio would run. Then there was nothing to do but to return to their lives during this reprieve before the vicious goddesses kicked up a ruckus again.

What started as an unsettling requirement for Ceri on her twenty-fifth birthday led to the beginning of the most fulfilling adventure of her life—sharing herself and her love with the man who was her destiny. When Rio held her in his arms as they watched their family drive away up the lane, she knew wherever life took them, she would always be with him—her husband, her one true love, her warrior.

Thank you for reading *Warrior*.
Turn the page for an excerpt from *Prophetess*, a Talisman
Series novella.
Coming in May 2020

CHAPTER ONE

Eighteen years ago, Ullapool, Scotland

HANLEY CONLAN KNEW better.

Hamish had warned her time and time again that walking alone near dusk invited trouble. Yet so far, her stay in the tiny fishing village of Ullapool had been idyllic. Until today.

Walking home when Hamish didn't answer her call for a ride hadn't seemed like a big deal. In her not-so-distant university days, she'd often walked farther than the four miles separating her from her bookshop job in Ullapool and her temporary home at Conlan Manor. The setting sun painted the hillsides along the road with a broad gold brush, calming her. The setting imbued her with a peacefulness she'd had no idea she'd needed when she decided to spend a gap year at her ancestral home after graduating university. Everything about her stay in the Scottish Highlands told her she belonged there, the land and its people seeping into the marrow of her bones.

No wonder she'd let her guard down when she stopped to sniff the bright yellow gorse on the roadside.

The backfire of the car slowing down alerted her. Someone needed to work on an engine.

A long-haired guy ogled her from the passenger window, and she remembered she was on the wrong side of the road. After watching the car drive out of sight around a bend, she crossed over to the right side. With a rueful shake of her head, she reminded herself to do a better job of paying attention to the traffic and driving rules practiced in the UK.

As she neared the curve in the road, an eerie quiet settled over her. Tall birch trees lined the narrow two-lane track, and she quickened her step. Before she could clear the long gentle bend, three men stepped from the trees in front of her. Recognizing one of them as the blond who'd hung out the window of the passing car, Shanley stopped.

It seemed even the natural world held its breath to see what would happen next. The breeze high in the trees died away. Birdsong halted mid-note. No furry creatures scurried amid the tall grasses and bushes interspersed through the trees.

Two dark-haired men flanked the blond, giving Shanley the idea he was their leader. The three of them together with their massive shoulders and ready stances filled up the entire road in front of her. None of them took his eyes from hers. None of them spoke. None of them looked friendly.

Trying not to panic, she took a step back.

The men stepped with her.

She knew she'd been caught out at the midway point between the village and the manor, too far in either direction to run. The trees' long shadows dropped the temperature, or maybe fear gave her the cold shivers. If only she'd mastered visualizing so she could do it without closing her eyes. Then she'd disappear, leaving these men wondering if they'd stopped to accost a woodland faerie or something.

But she hadn't mastered visualization, and she didn't dare

close her eyes for the minute it would take her to see her destination inside Conlan Manor.

As each man's eyes glowed red, evil smiles stretching their lips as they revealed their true selves, her blood nearly froze in her veins.

Rogue warriors.

"Out fer an evenin' stroll, are ye lass? Does yer warrior know ye're out on yer own?" the blond asked, his tone casual, his expression menacing.

How had they found her? How did they know what she was? Shanley said nothing.

"Cat got yer tongue?" the dark-haired rogue to his left asked as he took another step toward her.

The third rogue remained silent, but she didn't miss the way he flexed his hands at his sides like he couldn't wait to put them on her.

"I can't believe Morgan has any interest in me. Even if she did, she can't take me across the ford. Unless she takes me during a battle in which my warrior is engaged. I doubt she'll be happy with the lot of you if you harm me here." She crossed her arms over her chest in a show of bravado she hoped masked the way her entire body shook.

"Yer warrior has nae idea ye're out here on yer own," the blond guessed.

"Or maybe her warrior hasnae found her yet," said the second rogue.

"Even better. After we enjoy her, maybe we can turn her so she'll help us whenever the auld witch takes it intae her head tae end our lives."

Shanley stared in horrified fascination as the blond licked his thick lips in anticipation of that idea.

Once, she'd heard that when looking imminent death in its ugly eyes, your life flashes before you in a blink. Shanley's focus

telescoped down to the present moment. The birches were especially fragrant, wafting their earthy green summer scent over her.
The intense clarity of the azure sky cut into her peripheral vision.
The uniform unevenness of the gravel used in the asphalt beneath
her feet reminded her how thin the soles of her Chucks were.

*Dear Brighid, patron goddess of stories, if you're listening, could
you kindly change mine?* she silently pleaded as she took another
involuntary step back.

"Ye know it's nae use tae try tae outrun us. Nae matter which
direction ye choose, one of us will be waitin' fer ye before ye get
there," the blond rogue said, humor shimmering in his voice.

They toyed with her? Three tomcats pawing at one little mouse?
She shouldn't be surprised.

"H-how did you know I'm a talisman?" she asked, stalling.

The dark-haired quiet one spoke up. "When Morgan caught
up with us after we didn't find our talismans in time, she gave us
a special gift. You noticed how our eyes glow red?"

"Like the evil goddess herself, or so I've been told."

"She has fire, this one," the dark-haired talkative one said.

Shanley didn't consider that a compliment.

"Get on with it," dark-and-quiet growled.

"When we come upon a woman, we can see her aura—if she
has one. A talisman glows like an apricot sunset. It's even prettier
in yer case with all that hair of yers. Can't wait to wrap it around
my wrist as I take ye." The talkative one took another step in
her direction.

"Remember who saw her first and who gets the first turn,"
blondie said, his tone turning feral as he placed a restraining hand
on the other's arm.

Shanley saw her chance. "Huh. Well, as you've pointed out
so clearly, I have nowhere to run where you won't be waiting for
me. However, maybe I'd like a say in my fate. I find I rather like
the tall silent type. That is if you're not going to strangle me first."

Quirking a brow at the third rogue's still flexing hands, she waited.

The man didn't change expression, but his hands relaxed.

Shanley didn't.

"You don't get a say in this, woman. I saw you first, so I get the first turn," blondie insisted.

"Not if it's not what the lady wants."

Not talking much seemed to afford the third rogue some authority with the other two. Or they weren't used to him gainsaying them. Either way, at last the rogues were no longer looking at her as they stared each other down.

Shanley took a long step back, intending to gain enough distance from the men to close her eyes and visualize herself somewhere else.

Her breath backed up in her throat as a body impeded her progress.

"Ye should have waited fer me, lass," a familiar voice whispered.

She nearly dropped to the ground in relief, and probably would have if Hamish hadn't wrapped his arm around her waist to steady her.

"Now isnae the time tae lose yer head. Ye're no' safe yet," Hamish said. "Step behind me."

Shanley moved.

"What are ye about, auld man? This is not yer affair. Take yerself off before ye get hurt," the quiet rogue rumbled.

Hamish replied in Gaelic, a chant Shanley couldn't understand, but from the way the rogues' eyes widened, they had an idea.

"She's protected by a druid? He cannae dae much. Let's take him," the loud dark-haired one said as he summoned his claymore to his hand.

At the sight of the rogue's sword, she sucked in a scream.

Hamish continued to chant as the other two rogues summoned their claymores out of thin air and advanced on them. An unstoppable scream tore from Shanley's throat when she considered their imminent death at the hands of rogue warriors.

Without interrupting his chant, Hamish squeezed her hand and didn't let go.

A sudden calm overcame her, corking her screams in her throat. A golden glow enveloped first Hamish before emanating out to wrap around her. Still, the rogues advanced on them until the loud one raised his claymore to cleave Hamish in two. His blade contacted the glow with a clang, emitting a blinding spark, like static electricity run amok. He yelped in surprise and tried again while his friends surrounded them.

With gentle pressure on Shanley's arm, Hamish guided her backward. All the while, he maintained the steady rhythms of his chant. No matter how hard they tried, the rogue warriors couldn't breach the protected aura Hamish wove around Shanley and himself. She didn't question it. Instead, she moved slowly backward until they rounded the bend in the road where Hamish's car awaited them.

Instinctively, she entered the car via the driver's door. Hamish followed her inside, the aura of the chant now encompassing the car. He continued speaking as he started his battered ride and put it in gear. The rogues howled in frustration and pain as their claymores repeatedly bounced off their intended targets in showers of sparks. Hamish gunned his little four-seater through the rogues and up the road, never once stinting in the chant that kept them safe. In fact, he chanted for the entire drive home and didn't stop until the two of them were safely inside the Conlan family seat.

❧

Shanley collapsed onto the hard bench at the scarred wooden table in the kitchen. Sucking in air, she worked to slow her runaway heart. Hamish busied himself putting the kettle on and arranging cookies on a plate, which he set on the table beside her. A few minutes later, he set out mugs and milk and sugar. With a vague sense of unreality, she watched him as he poured boiling water over the tea in the bottom of the pot and set it on the trivet in the middle of the table to steep.

Seating himself across from her, he said nothing.

After several minutes of an uncomfortable silence Shanley had no idea how to break, Hamish said, "Would you like tae pour, or shall I?"

"My hands haven't stopped shaking enough not to make a mess."

"That certainly was a scare, lass." He splashed milk into the bottom of a mug, poured tea, and handed it to her. "One I'd rather no' repeat if ye donnae mind."

His jovial tone jerked Shanley's eyes from the teaspoon of sugar she was adding to her tea.

As she brushed the spilled sugar into a tiny pile beside her mug, he continued in the same conversational way. "What I'd like tae know is why ye couldnae wait fer me tae fetch ye."

"I'm sorry, Hamish." Using the pretense of stirring sugar into her tea, she gathered her thoughts. "The day was so beautiful. The sun shined warm for once, the sky so blue, I could swim in it. I wanted to be out in it, you know?"

"This part o' the Highlands close tae the trainin' room at *An Teallach* draws all sorts o' warriors, no' all o' 'em good guys. I warned ye about that." He grabbed a cookie, broke it in half, and dunked it in his tea.

She sighed. "It's not the same at home. I guess when one lives years of her life in relative safety, it's easy to forget how the war goddesses operate."

"I'm curious." Hamish glanced up at her from beneath his bushy white brows. "Why dinnae ye visualize yerself out o' danger when the first rogue revealed himself tae ye?"

Feeling her face heat, she looked down at the table and tightened her two-handed grip on her mug.

"I haven't mastered it yet."

"*What?*"

She put up a hand. "I can do it if I can close my eyes for a minute. But if I have to compartmentalize, keeping my eyes open to whatever danger I face and seeing in my head where I want to go, I lose focus."

Hamish thoughtfully sipped his tea. "Well, lass, since ye're so fond o' walking, I think it's time we hike tae *An Teallach* tae work on yer skills."

ACKNOWLEDGEMENTS

When I wrote *Talisman*, the first book in this series, I thought I'd written a stand-alone novel. But early readers asked for more of the story, and the next thing I knew, the characters had taken over my thoughts every chance they got. I'm so grateful for those readers and their encouragement to take the story farther.

I have no doubt *Warrior* would not exist without the cheerleading of one of those early readers, Dodo Rosling. We corresponded via snail mail and sadly, never met in person before she passed away. However, her enthusiasm for these characters is a big part of the reason I wrote *Warrior*. As a librarian, she spent her life reading books, so her opinion mattered. Dodo will always hold a warm place in my affection.

My lifelong best friend, Coleene Torgerson, your friendship is the mortar in the bedrock of my life. Your enthusiasm for my writing dream means more than I can ever tell you. The fact that you loved the earliest version of this story is why I kept working on it. Thank you for everything—and don't worry. Seamus's story is coming.

Sue Ellen Turnbull and Angie Randak, each of you has given

me so much—friendship, ideas, encouragement, and laughter. You always have excellent suggestions for my stories. As fellow writers walking this path to publication with me, your feedback means so much. Thank you for reading and commenting on early versions of this book. You make me better.

Angela Forister and Alison Packard, your generosity is the reason I have had any writing success at all. Your honest input, willingness to share your considerable knowledge of the self-publishing industry, and your own publishing successes have lighted my way from the moment we met. Thank you.

Bri Brasher, I adore you. Thank you for always making time for me and for giving the early manuscripts honest reads. You're the best.

My editor, Nikki Busch, you have helped me grow and improve as a writer every time you work with me on a manuscript. I value your opinion and your expertise. From the bottom of my heart, thank you.

Maria at Steamy Designs, thank you for another kickass cover. People do judge books by their covers, and your designs ensure my words always make a great first impression. Thank you for your patience and your willingness to play along with all of my crazy promotional schemes.

This book is dedicated to you, Austin and Trey. In the early days when I started writing the first drafts of this series, you were both still in high school. Whenever I'd talk about my dreams, the two of you would respond as though the existence of my books was already a reality. Both of you believed in me from the start, and that means more than I can ever express. When you were little, you were my sunshine—and my entertainment. You've since grown up to be my heroes, my beautiful boys. I love you.

Grady, your endless patience with me and support for whatever goofy idea I want to pursue gives me the freedom to be me and to grow and change and become the best I can be. Without you, I wouldn't be me. I love you so much.

Finally, readers, thank you! Thank you for taking a chance on me by reading this book. Ultimately, every word I write is for you. Reviews help writers to continue to reach more readers. If you enjoyed this one and would kindly leave a review on whichever review site you favor, I will be forever grateful.

You can catch up with me on my website at www.tamderudder-jackson.com and on Instagram @tamstales32. If you're interested in some ideas on how to increase your luck—or you want to share some ideas on how I can increase mine—please have a look at my blog: "Try Thirty New Things" on Word Press. Let's grow together.

About the Author

In her previous career, Tam DeRudder Jackson was an award-winning high school English teacher. Today, she's living her dream of writing novels. When she's not writing, she's reading all the books or carving turns on the ski runs in the mountains near her home in northwest Wyoming or traveling to places on her ever-expanding bucket list. Her two grown sons are the joys of her life, and she likes supporting her husband's old car habit. If you ever see her holding a map, do her a favor and point her in the right direction. Navigation has never been her strong suit.

Warrior is her second book.

CPSIA information can be obtained
at www.ICGtesting.com
Printed in the USA
LVHW030355160721
692784LV00002B/94

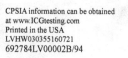